Dedicated to my husband,
Dr John Curthoys, BDS.

The Dollmaker's Daughters

Chapter One

Whitechapel, London, 1898

The wax effigy of the Christ Child flew past Ruby, narrowly missing her head, hitting the brick wall of the railway arch and landing on the concrete floor of the workshop with a squishing thud. Rescuing it from the dust, Ruby cradled the tiny figure in her arms as if it were a flesh and blood baby. Choking back tears, she wiped away the dirt and grit. Just moments ago the angelic face had been a work of art and devotion lovingly created by her father, Aldo Capretti, the best dollmaker in the East End, if not the whole of London. At least that was Ruby's opinion, and she guessed that there must be hundreds of little rich girls, proud owners of a Capretti doll, who would agree with her. Poppa didn't usually make religious icons, but this order had been an exception, a favour for Father Brennan, the fierce Catholic priest who had frightened the life out of her as a child. Even though she was almost twenty, he still had the power to put the fear of God into her. Ruby shuddered at the thought of Father Brennan's reaction when he was told that the crib at St Augustine's Catholic Church would be empty at Christmas, just days away.

Aldo, who was normally so kind and gentle, let out an angry roar followed by a stream of invective: a strange mixture of Italian and English swear words that were even more shocking to Ruby than the distorted wax face of the baby Jesus. Dancing up and down on the spot, Aldo shook his fist at her, his face purple with rage, knotted veins standing out in his throat like coiled ropes. 'You bleedin' stupid, clumsy little bitch.'

'Poppa, no. It weren't my fault.' Ruby clutched baby Jesus to her bosom. She had spent so many painstaking hours pricking each individual hair into the tiny scalp that to see such devastation was heartbreaking. What was even worse, the hair was real; she had plucked each raven-black, shimmering strand from her own head.

'Don't talk back to me. You got no respect for your poppa, that's your trouble.'

A shadow fell across the entrance to the arches. 'Hey, what's all the shouting about, old man? I bet they can hear you clear down to Wapping.'

Ruby spun round, bristling with indignation at the intrusion. 'Mind your own business, Billy Noakes.'

'Get out, you no good chancer!' Aldo made a move towards Billy, fisting his hands.

'Calm down, guv,' Billy said, grinning. 'If you don't want me to take them dollies to the wholesalers, it's no skin off my nose.'

'No, wait,' Ruby called out as he turned to go. 'Poppa didn't mean it. He ain't hisself today.' She laid baby Jesus gently on the railway sleeper that served as a workbench and, scurrying to the dark recess at the back of the arch, Ruby hefted a tea chest packed with finished dolls, complete with frilled dresses made by her mother and tiny straw hats fashioned by her grandmother. She staggered beneath the weight and Billy leapt forward, taking it from her hands.

'Steady on, girl. You should let the bad-tempered old bugger over there do the heavy work.'

Aldo lunged at him but Billy held him off with the tea chest. 'Just joking, Poppa. Can't you Eyeties take a joke?'

Aldo opened his mouth as if to say something, staggered backwards and would have crumpled to the ground if Ruby had not rushed forward to support him. She turned on Billy in a fury. 'Ain't you got no more sense than to tease a sick man?'

His cocky grin replaced by a frown, Billy nodded. 'You're right. He don't look too clever at that. Let me get this chest on me cart and I'll give you a hand to get him home.'

'Ta, but you done enough harm upsetting him like that. I can manage.'

'Suit yourself,' Billy said, with a casual shrug of his shoulders.

Struggling beneath her father's weight, Ruby regretted being so hasty as she watched Billy carrying the tea chest out to his cart, where a sorry-looking, sway-backed nag waited, placidly munching the contents of its nosebag despite the sleety rain falling from a pewter sky. Ruby hooked Aldo's arm around her shoulders in an attempt to get him onto his stool, but he seemed to have lost control of his legs and they both skittered crabwise across the concrete floor. Swallowing her pride, she called out to Billy and he came striding back into the workshop.

'Best leave the old feller to me, Ruby.' Taking Aldo by the arm, Billy hefted him over his shoulder in a fireman's lift. 'I'll drop you both back home. I got to go past Tobacco Court; it's on me way.'

Ruby hesitated, covering her head with her shawl and shivering as the icy spikes of sleet pierced the thin cloth. She didn't want to take any favours from Billy Noakes, who had a bad reputation with women and whose business dealings were on the grey side of shady, but on the other hand, there was no way she could get Poppa home on her own. She watched silently as Billy set her father down on the driver's seat, covering him with a tattered piece of sacking that smelt strongly of the stables.

'You coming or staying?' Billy leapt up beside Aldo and picked up the reins. 'I ain't got all day.'

A bitter east wind, straight off the Essex marshes, caught Ruby like an icy slap in the face, making up her mind for her. 'Just a sec,' she said, slamming the wooden gate and turning the key in the lock. Normally she wouldn't have been seen dead riding on Billy's cart, and Mum would have forty fits if she found out, but today was the exception and she clambered up beside her father just as Billy urged the horse into a shambling walk.

Cable Street was packed with the everyday chaotic mix of horse-drawn drays, carts and wagons loaded with cargo for the docks at Wapping and Shadwell. The air was punctuated with puffs of steam from the engines that rumbled along the railway tracks into Fenchurch Street station. Clouds of sweat from the flesh of overworked horses mingled with smoke from clay pipes clenched between the drivers' teeth in rictus grins. The smell of hot cinders, horse dung and chemicals from the manufactories added to the harsh stench of raw sewage floating in the coffee-coloured waters of the Thames. Huddled in her shawl, Ruby's teeth chattered so that she couldn't speak even if she had had anything to say to Billy. She clutched Aldo's hand as he slumped against her, his breathing ragged and his face beaded with sweat even though his fingers felt cold as a dead chicken's claw.

As the cart entered Spivey Street, the sleet

turned into hailstones, frosting the rotting vegetable matter and excrement that littered the cobblestones, creating a fleeting illusion of beauty until it melted into a stinking morass. Barefoot and blue with cold, street urchins huddled in doorways begging, or lingered in the shadows ready to dip the pocket of an unwary passer-by. Billy urged his old nag to go a bit faster holding his whip poised, ready for trouble, as they passed the dark slits between the buildings, little slices of hell, where prostitutes, pimps and hustlers hung out in a permanent twilight underworld. As they neared Tobacco Court, Ruby saw Billy's grip on the whip handle relax and she heaved a sigh of relief. She had been born and bred here and was streetwise, but only a fool would let their guard down in the slum area of Spivey Street. Despite the soot-blackened brickwork, the peeling paint and a general air of dilapidation, Tobacco Court was a respectable cul-de-sac lined with two-up, two-down working men's cottages. The residents were mostly artisans and manual workers, who just managed to keep their families above the breadline unless overtaken by the disaster of unemployment or chronic sickness. Ruby, who knew and was known by every family living in the Court, was thankful that the bitter weather had kept the neighbours indoors. The street was empty of the usual cluster of women standing in doorways passing the time of day, and the rough and tumble of the Court kids who were too young to work or attend the school in Kinder Street. Ruby was thankful that no one would see her or Billy as they half lifted, half dragged Poppa from the cart outside number sixteen.

'Ta,' she said, with her hand on the latch. 'I can manage now.'

Billy pushed the door open with the toe of his boot. 'Don't be daft.' Ignoring Ruby's protests, he carried Aldo into the living room and set him down on a bentwood chair. Granny Mole, who had been dozing by the fireside, opened her eyes and Sarah Capretti leapt to her feet, pale with alarm.

'Aldo!' Sarah threw her arms around him, giving him a shake as his head lolled against her shoulder. 'Aldo, can you hear me?'

'Poppa had one of his funny turns,' Ruby said hurriedly, knowing that Mum had a very poor opinion of Billy. 'And Billy give us a lift home on his cart.'

Sarah turned her head to glare at Billy. 'A gentleman takes his cap off in the presence of ladies and, anyway, you're not welcome here, Billy Noakes.'

'Ta, Billy,' Ruby said, embarrassed by her mother's rudeness. 'You was good to help out.'

'I only done what anyone else would have done,' Billy said, tugging his cap off his head. 'He don't look too clever to me, though.'

'He looks half dead to me,' Granny Mole said, huffing on her specs and polishing them on a corner of her skirt. 'But he's been acting odd for weeks. Gone a bit barmy he has. That's what comes of marrying an Eyetie. I always told you it would end in grief, Sal.'

'Shut up, Mum,' Sarah said, chafing Aldo's hand. 'Aldo, love, it's me, Sarah.'

Aldo's eyelids fluttered and opened. His mouth worked but no sound came from his pale lips.

'You've had one of your turns, ducks,' Sarah said gently. 'You sit there quiet-like and I'll make you a nice cup of tea.'

Billy backed towards the front door. 'I'd best be going then.'

Sarah snapped to attention. 'Don't think I ain't grateful but I'd be obliged if you didn't come here again. We got our reputation to think of.'

'Mum!' Ruby felt the blood rush to her cheeks; everyone knew that Billy was an undesirable who ducked and dived and only kept one step ahead of the coppers, but he had done them a good turn. 'That ain't fair.'

'Don't you cheek me, my girl,' Sarah said, bristling.

'It's all right, Mrs Capretti, I'm going.' Billy put his cap back on his head and was about to open the door when a girl, almost identical in appearance to Ruby, rushed into the room bringing with her a gust of cold, smoke-laden air.

'Well now,' Billy said, eyeing her appreciatively. 'If it ain't the other half of the pair.'

'Shut the door, Rosetta.' Sarah picked up the brown teapot from the trivet by the fire, pointing the spout at Billy. 'He's just going.'

'Hello, Billy.' Rosetta shot him a sidelong glance beneath long, black lashes, her full red lips curved in a provocative smile. 'And goodbye. Pity you can't stay.'

Knowing that Rosetta had a soft spot for Billy and that Mum didn't approve one bit, Ruby caught her twin by the arm and dragged her into the room. 'G'bye, Billy. You was a great help.'

'Glad to have been of service, ladies!' Angling his head towards Rosetta, Billy flashed her a wink and a smile. 'See you later, Miss Rosetta.'

'What did he say?' demanded Granny. 'I hates people what mumble.'

Sarah glared at Rosetta over Aldo's head as she held a cup of tea to his lips. 'He'd better not have said nothing. I don't want either of you two mixing with the likes of Noakes. He's bad news and we're respectable folk in Tobacco Court.'

'Not like them in Spivey Street,' Rosetta said, with a suggestive wiggle of her hips.

'Don't be crude, Rose. Your father is a craftsman, a master dollmaker. We're not like them in Spivey Street. We may not be rich but we got standards and don't you girls forget it.'

'Chance would be a fine thing!' Rosetta threw off her wet shawl and tossed her bonnet onto the table. 'Any tea left in the pot, Mum? I'm bloody freezing.'

Aldo raised his head, scowling. 'Wash your mouth out. I'll not have no child of mine using foul language.'

Rosetta's bottom lip trembled. 'Sorry, Poppa. I love you, Poppa.'

Aldo smiled weakly. 'You're a minx, my little Rosa.'

'You're better, Poppa.' Ruby flung herself down on her knees by his chair. 'You had us worried sick.'

Aldo patted her hand. 'It's nothing. Just a bit of colic.' He pushed his tea away. 'Can't drink no more, Momma. Tastes a bit funny.'

Sarah bridled. 'There's nothing wrong with my tea. It's you, old man. If you ate proper then you wouldn't go falling down faint and scaring us all to death.'

Aldo's expression darkened and he struggled to his feet. 'I don't have to listen to you nagging me. I'm fine now. I go back to the arches.'

Sarah pushed him back onto the chair, holding him down with her considerable weight. 'You're going nowhere, Aldo Capretti, except up to bed.'

Aldo cast an agonised glance at Ruby. 'Father Brennan!'

'He's out of his head with fever,' said Granny, wagging her finger. 'Thinks he needs a priest to give him the last rites.'

Ruby knew instantly what was worrying her father. Poor little baby Jesus with the squashed face was not going to go down well with Father Brennan. She chewed the inside of her lip, wondering if she could fix the damage on her own. Although it wasn't her choice, she had become quite competent at some of the aspects of doll-making. Poppa fashioned the bodies from linen stuffed with sawdust, the heads and limbs from papier mâché, but he kept to himself the secrets of mixing the wax with red and white lead in order to achieve perfect skin pigmentation. Ruby had learned a little about how to mould the wax but she was by no means an expert. Mainly she did the finishing off, tinting the lips and cheeks, as well as pricking in the eyelashes and the hair.

'Priest indeed!' Sarah folded her arms across her ample bosom. 'I dunno how a good Church of England girl like me got herself hitched to a blooming papist.' When no one ventured an explanation, she threw her hands up, rolling her eyes to heaven. 'What has Father Brennan got to do with the price of fish, anyway?'

Giving Aldo's clammy hand a squeeze, Ruby said nothing; it was almost impossible to pull the wool over her mother's eyes but she knew there would be big trouble if Mum found out what had happened at the arches. They were relying on the money from Father Brennan; without it, there would be no food on the table or coal for the fire.

'Well?' Sarah said, arms akimbo. 'I'm waiting. What have you two been up to?'

When Aldo did not offer an explanation, Ruby was forced to reply. 'Nothing, Mum. Honest! It's just that Father Brennan's coming to collect baby Jesus.'

'And?'

'And he won't be best pleased if he finds the door locked and no one there. I'd better get back to the arches.'

'No, I got to go myself.' Aldo got to his feet but doubled up, holding his belly. His face twisted with pain and beads of sweat broke out on his brow. 'Maybe I go later.'

'Maybe you go bed,' Sarah said, and hitching his arm over her shoulder she guided him towards the staircase. Pausing to catch her breath, she turned on Rosetta who was sitting at the table sipping a cup of tea. 'Ain't you going back to Bronski's?'

'No,' Rosetta said, with a defiant lift of her chin. 'I ain't never going back to that place, not for nothing. I done me last seam and snipped me last thread.'

Her knees bending beneath Aldo's weight, Sarah took a deep breath, her face flushing to the colour of a boiled beetroot and her blue eyes popping from their sockets. 'That's what you think! I'll have a few words to say to you, my girl, once I've got your dad to his bed.'

'I can manage on me own,' Aldo protested.

'Save your breath, old man, you're weak as a baby.' Half lifting Aldo and half dragging him, Sarah stomped up the stairs, which creaked and groaned beneath their combined weight.

Rosetta grinned at Ruby. 'I'm in for it now.'

'Oh, Rose! What you been and gone and done?'

'You know I hate this place,' Rosetta said, twisting a strand of her glossy black hair around her finger. 'I always told you I'd get out one day and now I got a chance and I'm taking it.'

Glancing anxiously at Granny Mole, who had nodded off now that the excitement was over, Ruby lowered her voice. 'What are you talking about?'

'Got me a job in the chorus at the Falstaff Music Hall in Old Street. Don't tell Mum.'

'You never!'

'I blooming well did. I weren't never going to meet a rich bloke stuck in that filthy basement, choking on cotton fluff all day and ruining me eyes.'

'Mum will kill you when she finds out.'

'Well, she won't, will she? Not unless you tells her. I got Aunt Lottie on my side. She's the one what suggested I have a go.'

'Shhh!' Ruby put her finger to her lips. 'You know what Mum and Granny think of Aunt Lottie.'

'I don't care. Lottie started in the chorus and she had rich admirers begging for her favours. Even the Prince of Wales, so she said.'

'She drinks and she's gambled all her money away. Joe told me so.'

'Our big brother likes a flutter too, but I bet he never told you that. He thinks Lottie's a good sport and so do I. Anyway, she says I got talent.' Rosetta jumped to her feet, picking up her shawl and pulling a face. 'Soaking! Lend us yours, Ruby, there's a love.'

'You're going back to work?'

'Not on your life! I'm not hanging around here just to get it in the neck. I'm going to Shoreditch to stay with Lottie. It's nearer the theatre and she won't give me earache going on and on all the time. Give us your shawl, please.'

'No, sorry,' Ruby said, snatching her shawl from the stool by the fire. 'I got to go back to the arches, right now.'

Rosetta pulled her mouth down at the corners, pouting. 'Aw, go on, Ruby. You'll be there in two ticks. I got to walk all the way to Shoreditch and you wouldn't want me to catch me death, now would you?'

Ruby hesitated; Rosetta had always been the one to fall sick with chest complaints ever since they were nippers and it was a long walk from Whitechapel to Shoreditch, especially on a bitter cold and wet day like today. Reluctantly, she swapped her almost dry grey shawl for Rosetta's scarlet shawl that was damp and studded with melting hailstones. 'What'll I tell Mum?'

'You'll think of something. You was always the clever one.' Wrapping the shawl around her head, Rosetta did a triumphant little dance, lifting her skirts to show a shapely leg even if it was clad in a thick and much-darned woollen stocking.

'I ain't going to lie,' Ruby said, trying not to laugh at Rosetta's antics.

Her smile fading, Rosetta clutched Ruby's hand. 'You will look after Poppa, won't you? You'll let me know if he gets any worse?'

'Course I will, silly billy. And you won't do nothing stupid, will you, Rose?'

'As if I would!' Rosetta's irrepressible sense of fun bubbled into a wicked grin, banishing her fleeting look of concern. 'You know me, Ruby.'

'Only too well.' Flinging her arms around Rosetta, Ruby hugged her. 'Take care of yourself, Rose.'

The thump of the bedroom door closing and the heavy thud of Sarah's feet on the stairs put a stop to their conversation and Rosetta was first out of the door, with Ruby hard on her heels. The sleet had turned into feathery flakes of snow, swirling down from the sky as if a giant feather pillow had burst above their heads. Rosetta was out of sight almost before Ruby had closed the door behind her. Putting her head down, she hurried back towards the arches, her feet slipping and sliding on the slushy cobblestones.

As she left the relative security of Tobacco Court for Spivey Street, a gust of warm air, laced with the stench of stale beer and tobacco smoke, oozed in a steamy cloud from the open door of the Nag's Head. A man lurched out of the pub, staggered and slid on the snow, colliding with a lamp post and clinging to it for dear life as his feet shot from under him like a puppet with its strings cut. He looked so comical that Ruby had to cover her face with her shawl so that he wouldn't see her laughing but, all the same, she hoped he hadn't hurt himself too badly. She crossed the street to avoid walking past the disreputable row of boarded-up, four-storey houses that hadn't seen a lick of paint since the day they were built some seventy years ago. Ragged, barefoot children hurled snowballs at each other, their thin faces wizened and pinched making them look like small gnomes, their screams and shrieks sounding more like feral animal snarls than human laughter. Ruby knew better than to interfere when they fell upon each other, snapping and snarling like wolf cubs. She quickened her pace, pulling her shawl down over her brow to shield her eyes from the snow. The east wind brought with it the stomach-churning stink of boiling bones from the glue factory, cancelling out the aroma of freshly baked bread from the bakehouse on the corner of Spivey Street. Ruby quickened her step and made her way down Cable Street to the arches. She half expected to find Father Brennan standing outside, dusted with snow and fuming with righteous anger having found the workshop closed, but mercifully there was no one waiting. Inside was barely warmer than outside and Ruby's fingers were numbed and stiff with cold. The fire had gone out in the small brazier where Poppa melted the wax and kept it malleable enough to mould. She poked the cinders, hoping to resurrect enough heat to work with, but it was no use. Her hands were cold, the wax was even colder, and, examining the damage to the once perfect face, Ruby realised that it was beyond repair.

Sifting through a wooden crate of dolls' heads, Ruby came across one that had been made for a baby doll but had been discarded by Poppa when it failed to meet his rigid standards. Father Brennan would be here at any moment and Ruby was desperate. Gritting her teeth, she prayed forgiveness for desecrating a holy object as she cut off the original head and stuck on the new one, securing it with a thin collar of wax that she had softened by slipping it down the front of her blouse. The daylight was fading fast and Ruby lit a stub of a candle. She could hear the unmistakeable brisk tread of Father Brennan's leather-soled boots slapping down on the pavement outside. The gate screamed on its rusty hinges and he stood in the doorway, his black outline absorbing the sliver of remaining light.

'Well now, Ruby, my child. Have you something for me?'

Ruby's hands were clammy with cold sweat; she swallowed hard and held the tiny figure out towards the priest. 'Yes, Father.'

'You know that this should have been ready a week ago. It's really not good enough.'

'No, Father.'

'And where is Aldo?'

'He's sick, Father.'

'You don't mean he been on the drink, do you, my child?'

'Oh no, Father. Poppa doesn't take a drop. He couldn't afford it even if he wanted to.'

Father Brennan tucked baby Jesus under his arm and reached beneath his robe, pulling out a leather purse. 'You'll want payment, although I daresay you would take it badly if I were to deduct money for late delivery.'

'Yes, Father. I mean, no, Father. I'm sorry, Father.'

As he tugged at the purse strings with fat,

mottled fingers that reminded Ruby of raw beef sausages, the purse flew from his grasp. With surprising agility, he swooped and caught it, but the sudden movement dislodged the improvised head of baby Jesus and sent it flying across the workshop floor. There was a moment of complete silence; even the rumbling of cartwheels and the clip-clop of horses' hooves in the street outside seemed to stop, as Ruby and Father Brennan watched the severed head rolling in the dust.

Father Brennan recovered first with an almighty roar. 'Sacrilege!'

Ruby scuttled across the floor to retrieve the head. 'It was an accident, Father.'

Snatching it from her hand, Father Brennan held the head up to the light. 'You wicked girl! This is a doll's head. A shameful waxen travesty of a human infant!'

'Please, Father, let me explain.'

Father Brennan strode towards the doorway. 'I'll be having words with your father.'

Ruby ran into the street after him. 'No, please don't. Poppa is very poorly. It was all my fault.'

Turning on her in a fury, Father Brennan seized her hand, folding her icy fingers around the doll's head. 'Dwell on your sins, Ruby, and when you have had time to contemplate your wicked deeds, you will come to confession.'

'But, Father!'

'And don't expect to receive payment!' Father Brennan strode off, disappearing into a flurry of snow.

Ruby stared after him with a sick feeling in the pit of her stomach that had nothing to do with the fact that she had forgotten to eat her slice of bread and dripping at dinnertime. She was not afraid of the penance that Father Brennan would hand out in the confessional, but she was afraid of telling Mum that one of Poppa's strange outbursts of temper had been the cause of them losing money. Ruby shivered as the snowflakes settling on her thin cotton blouse began to melt, sending cold trickles down her neck. She hurried back inside the workshop, blew out the candle and wrapped Rosetta's wet shawl around her head and shoulders, barely aware of the chill striking through her bones. She would have to think of some way to break the news so that it didn't sound quite so bad; at least there was the money due from the wholesalers for the dolls. After all, they must sell well, it being so close to Christmas. There must still be plenty of well-off folks prepared to spend good money on their little daughters' presents.

Ruby locked the gates and started for home. Hopefully her concern for Poppa would mellow Mum's attitude to the unfortunate accident; after all, she wasn't going to be upset that Father Brennan was put out. Mum had little or no time for popery in general and Father Brennan in particular, and neither had Granny Mole, who never passed up an opportunity to have a go at Catholics, Eyeties, Russians and Jews and in fact anybody whom she considered was a foreigner. Ruby sighed and wrapped her shawl more tightly around her head. Not only was she going to have to tell Mum that they weren't going to be paid for the Christ Child, but also she would have to break the news that Rosetta had gone to stay with Aunt Lottie. Perhaps the bit about dancing in the chorus at the Falstaff could wait a while.

It was dark by the time Ruby reached Spivey Street, passing the lamplighter as he lit the last lamp, filling the dark canyon with oily pools of yellow light reflecting off the snow. Halfway down the road, a large snowball caught Ruby smack between her shoulder blades and another hit her square in the face, half blinding her. Surrounded by a crowd of jeering boys, no more than six or seven years of age, Ruby blinked the snow out of her eyes, holding her arm in front of her face as she was bombarded by a further hail of snowballs. One of the urchins tugged at her shawl, tweaking it from her shoulders, and was about to make off with it when someone lifted him clear off his feet, holding him by the scruff of his neck and shaking him so that his skinny legs swung, kicking in mid-air.

'No you don't, sonny!'

Blurrily, Ruby saw her tormentors scatter in all directions as Billy dropped the culprit onto a pile of slush.

'Let's get you home afore you catches your death of cold,' Billy said, retrieving her shawl from the wet ground. He handed it to her, staring hard. 'Red shawl. I was hoping I might bump into Rosetta, but it's Ruby, ain't it?'

'Same difference,' Ruby said, wiping the snow from her face and drawing herself up to her full height. 'Anyway, it's okay, ta. I can get meself home. They caught me unawares but they won't get away with it a second time.'

'You're the stubborn one, you are, Ruby,' Billy said, clicking his tongue to bring his old horse ambling forward with the cart and, without a by your leave, he hoisted Ruby onto the driver's seat. 'Wrap that around you.' Billy tossed her a hessian sack from beneath a pile of tea chests.

It smelt awful but at least it was dry and Ruby huddled beneath it as Billy led the horse down Spivey Street towards Tobacco Court. Normally she would have leapt back down again, thanked him politely and gone on her way, but Ruby was wet, cold and too worried about what she was going to say to Mum to act proud and independent. Thankfully, Billy didn't seem to want to chat or ask questions and, when they neared

Tobacco Court, she called out to him to stop. 'I can walk the rest, ta.'

Billy grinned at her beneath his peaked cap. 'Afraid the neighbours might talk, ducks?'

'No, I was just saving you the trouble, that's all.'

'Don't worry. They all know as how you wouldn't give the likes of me the time of day. Now your sister Rosetta, well, she's different.'

'And what do you mean by that?'

'She's a bobby-dazzler. Nothing wrong with that, is there?'

'You keep your eyes off me sister. You keep away from her.'

'Whoa, there,' Billy said, pulling gently on the reins until the horse clopped to a halt outside number sixteen. 'Strikes me that your sister has a mind of her own.'

'Rosetta is a good girl. You got a bad reputation, Billy. Leave her alone.'

'That's right,' Billy said, grinning. 'I'm a bad lot.'

Ruby jumped off the cart. 'I ain't joking. You steer clear of Rosetta.'

'Maybe I will and maybe I won't.' Billy leapt down from the driver's seat and patted the horse's neck. 'You done well, old boy. We'll be home soon.' He went to the back of the cart and hoisted a familiar-looking tea chest onto his shoulder, dumping it on the pavement.

'Couldn't sell your dolls, ducks. Hope you wasn't relying on the bees and honey.'

Ruby's heart sank into her high-button boots but she held her head proudly erect; she wasn't going to give Billy the satisfaction of knowing just how much it mattered. 'How do I know you took them to the wholesalers?'

'I don't cheat on friends, Ruby. I took them all right, but they didn't want 'em. Said it was too late, the shops had bought their Christmas stock and didn't want no more. Hard luck, girl.'

'Hard luck?' Ruby stared at him aghast. 'You don't understand.'

'Eh?' Pushing his cap to the back of his head, Billy stared at her. 'What's up?'

'Take them away, please, Billy. I can't explain now, but just keep them for us until I can think of a way out of this mess.'

Chapter Two

By the time she reached Aunt Lottie's house in Shoreditch, Rosetta was soaked to the skin and she couldn't feel her fingers or toes. She had no clear idea of the distance between Tobacco Court and Raven Street, but it must be three miles or maybe four, if her aching legs were anything to go by. Stopping on the corner for a moment to catch her breath, Rosetta rubbed her hands together and stamped her feet in an effort to bring them back to life. Raven Street, she thought, was a step up from the rookeries in Whitechapel but it had definitely seen better days. The terrace of red-brick, five-storey town houses had been built at the beginning of the century to house wealthy merchants, lawyers and City bankers and their servants. Now, almost a hundred years on, the rich families were long gone and their large homes had been turned into cheap boarding houses, illicit gaming hells and brothels. Aunt Lottie's house was slap bang in the middle and its crumbling exterior was equal to anything in the Gothic horror stories that Rosetta loved to read. Hugging Ruby's sodden shawl a bit tighter around her shoulders she walked on, slipping on the slushy pavements and making a grab for the rusting iron railings outside the house as she climbed the stone steps up to the front door.

Lifting her hand to rap on the knocker, she took a step backwards as the door opened and a man pushed past her, his shoulders hunched beneath his green-tinged black suit and his face hidden by a battered top hat pulled down over his ears.

Throwing herself against the heavy oak door, Rosetta managed to stop it slamming in her face. 'Hello,' she called, stepping into the cavernous entrance hall. Her voice echoed eerily down the dark passageways, bouncing back off the high ceilings. 'Aunt Lottie, are you there?'

'Who calls?'

Looking upwards to the first floor landing, Rosetta saw a pale face, framed in mad grey hair, hovering above the banisters. 'It's me, Rosetta.'

'Don't loiter, girl. Come on up.' The head disappeared and Rosetta navigated the stairs, taking care not to catch her feet in the gaping holes that pockmarked the carpet as she followed Lottie into her sitting room. Directly opposite the door, a four-poster bed draped in faded silk curtains took up most of one wall. A heavily carved wardrobe was crammed against a washstand. Next to it stood a side table littered with framed photographs of Lottie in her heyday and a jumble of bric-a-brac.

At the far end of the room, two chintz-covered armchairs flanked a blazing fire and Lottie lowered herself into one of them. 'So, run away from home, have you?'

Rosetta edged towards the fire. 'Not exactly.'

'Look at the state of you. Take those wet things off before you catch your death of cold.'

Rosetta peeled off her bonnet and shawl, dropping them onto a piano stool abandoned in the middle of the room, although there was no piano in sight.

'Don't drip on me carpet, girl.'

'Sorry, Auntie.'

'And don't call me Auntie. You know I hate it.' Picking up a stone bottle from a table by her chair, Lottie half filled a tumbler with clear liquid and took a mouthful, swallowing it with a satisfied sigh.

Wrinkling her nose at the unmistakeable whiff of gin fumes, Rosetta moved closer to the fireplace. They never had fires like this at home, but then Mum always said that Lottie was an extravagant cow and that was why she had ended up like she had.

'Sit down, Rosetta. You making the place untidy.'

'I give up me job at Bronski's.' Rosetta pulled up a footstool and sat down. 'I got a job in the chorus at the Falstaff theatre, starting tomorrow, and I thought as how you might let me stay here.'

Lottie's face cracked into a crazy paving of lines as she threw back her head and laughed. 'Good for you. You done right, cara; you was wasting your life working in that sweatshop. You got looks, Rosetta, and good legs. You can go a long way with a shapely leg and a pretty pair of titties. I'd love to have seen your momma's face when you told her.'

Rosetta felt the blood rush to her cheeks and it wasn't just due to the heat of the fire. 'I never told Mum about the theatre. She don't approve of . . .' Rosetta broke off, biting her lip, stopping herself just in time from saying that Mum didn't approve of the theatre, nor did she approve of her sister-in-law, for that matter, not in any way, shape or form.

'You don't have to tell me. I know what your momma thinks of me, but you going to be the new dark sheep of the family now, Rosetta.' Chuckling, Lottie swigged her drink.

'You mean black sheep, I think.'

'You going to be famous like me,' Lottie said, raising a bony hand and patting her hair, which must once have been her crowning glory, a mass of tumbling Titian curls, although now it flew about her head in a wild tangle of pepper-and-salt frizz. 'I was the queen of the music halls.'

'You think I could be like that?' Wrapping her

arms around her knees, Rosetta searched Lottie's face for an answer. 'I want to better meself. I want nice clothes and a half-decent life. I don't want to end up old before me time.'

'You took the first step. Now you got to be tough.'

'No one at home understands how I feel, not even Ruby.'

Lottie cocked her head on one side, watching Rosetta like a blackbird eyeing a juicy worm. A slow smile curved her lips. 'I see myself in you, Rosetta, twenty, maybe thirty years ago. I had gentlemen fighting over me, showering me with gifts.'

'You had lovers?'

Lottie poured herself another generous slug of gin. 'More than I can remember. All of them crazy in love with me. Even the Prince of Wales himself.'

'So it is true?'

'It's true. I was beautiful then and my lovers give me expensive presents: diamonds, gold, a racehorse or two.'

'But,' Rosetta said, frowning as she glanced around at the shabby room, 'where did it all go? Surely you couldn't have lost it all gambling like Mum says?'

Lottie pulled a face. 'My one little weakness, cara. I couldn't resist the gaming tables or a little flutter at the racetracks. All I have now is what you see here, this house and my little mementoes. All the rest, sadly, gone to pay my debts, but I don't regret one bit of it. I lived my life, cara Rosetta. You got to live yours too, the way you want to.'

'And I can stay here for a bit?'

'You can stay here as long as you like. I don't know if we have a room free; I leave all that to your Uncle Sly. He's my man of business now. He looks after the paying guests.'

'I was nearly knocked down on the steps by one of them. A queer-looking geezer, all in black, like a crow.'

'That would be our Mr Wilby, the professional mourner. I only take in professional gents. This is a respectable lodging house, contrary to what your momma thinks.' Lottie lay back in her chair, closing her eyes. 'I'm tired. Go and find Sly. He'll sort you out a room and some food.'

'Yes, Auntie. I mean, Lottie.'

Lottie opened one eye. 'And get out of those wet things. Take what you need from my wardrobe. I don't suppose you brought nothing with you.' Waving her hand in the direction of the wardrobe, she closed her eyes and turned her head away. 'You so like me, Rosetta, so like me.'

Going over to the wardrobe, Rosetta opened the door and gasped as the pungent smell of mothballs took her breath away. The garments were terribly old-fashioned, but she managed to find a silk blouse, a black satin Spanish shawl, embroidered with scarlet roses, and a plain black bombazine skirt, which might have fitted Lottie ten or fifteen years ago, but certainly would not fit her now.

Leaving Lottie snoozing by the fire, Rosetta went in search of Uncle Silas. She found him in the steam heat of the basement kitchen where he stood by the range, stirring the contents of a large saucepan. The appetising aroma of vegetable soup made Rosetta's mouth water, reminding her that she had eaten nothing since a slice of bread at breakfast.

'Hello, ducks.' Sly's face split in a toothless grin, wobbling the fag end hanging from the corner of his mouth. 'Didn't expect a visit from you in this bleeding awful weather.'

Dropping the clothes on a chair, Rosetta went to give him a dutiful peck on the cheek. Sly smelt of tobacco, onions and sweat and she pulled away, wrinkling her nose. 'I come to stay if you'll have me, Uncle Sly. Lottie says you might be able to find me somewhere to sleep.'

Sly took the cigarette from the corner of his mouth and tossed it into the fire. 'As it happens I got a room in the attic going spare, but we ain't running a charity, I expect you to pay your way.'

'Yes, of course,' Rosetta said hastily. 'I got a job and I'll pay you at the end of the week if it's all right with you.'

'Just so long as we understand each other, Rose. I'll sort you out some bedding when you've had a bite to eat.'

'Ta, Uncle Sly.'

Taking a greasy ladle from a hook over the fire, Sly plunged it into the soup. 'Grub's extra, by the way.'

The attic room wasn't very clean and Rosetta looked round in distaste at the bare floorboards, crusty with mouse droppings, and the festoons of cobwebs hanging like dirty lace handkerchiefs from the rafters. Furnished sparsely with a single iron bedstead standing on a frayed oblong of drugget, and a three-drawer chest with a candlestick and a willow pattern washbowl on its top, the room was cold and unwelcoming. Used to Mum's strict standard of cleanliness, Rosetta felt a lump constricting her throat. She had always shared a room with Ruby and Granny Mole and this would be the first time in her life she had slept on her own; she would miss Ruby, was already missing her. Squaring her shoulders, Rosetta fought down the wave of homesickness; she simply mustn't give in now. Wandering over to the window, she wiped a clean patch in the middle of one of the small panes, peering out at the rooftops opposite and the street far below. Outside everything looked grey, fogged by swirling snowflakes. Rosetta went to pull the curtains but they disintegrated into tatters in her hands. Turning away from the window, she opened a cupboard and the smell of stale beer hit her as a jumble of empty bottles tumbled out onto her feet.

This was not how it was meant to be, she thought, kicking the bottles back into the cupboard and slamming the door. A wave of homesickness washed over her but she braced her shoulders; she mustn't give in. This was just the beginning and she would make things change for the better. Shivering as the icy temperature in the room gnawed at her bones, Rosetta knew that she had to get out of her wet things or freeze to death. She had just started undressing when a loud rapping on the door made her turn with a start.

Before she had a chance to call out, the door opened and Uncle Sly poked his head into the room. 'Are you decent, ducks?'

Without waiting for an answer, he sidled into the room. Opening her mouth to protest, Rosetta shut it again when she saw that he carried not only a pile of blankets and a pair of tatty-looking sheets, but also a bucket smoking with glowing coals.

'There you are, ducks. That'll warm the room a treat when it gets going. I'll send the girl up with another bucketful later. Fire's extra, by the way.' He dropped the blankets onto the bed and went over to the fireplace, where he tipped the coal into the grate. Taking a roll-up from behind his ear, he picked up a glowing ember with the tongs and lit the cigarette, dragging the smoke into his lungs with a cough and a grin. 'I'd lock your door tonight if I was you,' he said, as he shambled from the room.

The fire didn't make much difference at first, but its feeble glow made things look a bit more cheerful. Once she had the dry clothes on and flames began to lick up the fireback making glow-fairies in the soot, Rosetta began to feel more positive. A new pair of curtains at the window would make the room seem brighter and perhaps she could persuade the servant girl to give everything a bit of a clean. Tomorrow she would start rehearsals at the theatre and then she would be earning her own money. She would spend every spare penny of it on new clothes.

It took Rosetta a long time to fall asleep in the strange room, lying on the lumpy mattress, without the comfort of Ruby's warm body at her side. It seemed as though she had only just dozed off when a loud crash and the sound of raised voices made her snap upright in bed. The room was dark, the fire having gone out hours ago, and she could only just make out the pale rectangle of the window. For a moment she couldn't remember where she was and she pulled the blankets up to her chin as the cold struck her to the marrow. The voices grew louder and she could hear heavy footsteps lumbering up the uncarpeted staircase. Slurred speech, singing and swearing were all familiar sounds; she had heard them often enough coming from the Nag's Head on the corner of Spivey Street after closing time. Someone rattled the handle of her door and it shook as if a shoulder had barged against it. Rosetta stifled a scream by stuffing the sheet into her mouth and held her breath, her heart hammering so loudly against her ribcage that she was sure they could hear it through the partition wall. Someone uttered a string of oaths and the rattling stopped; the footsteps moved on. More sounds of laughter and slamming doors and then everything went quiet. Rosetta curled up in a ball and hid her head beneath the bedclothes.

When she questioned Uncle Sly next morning, he shrugged his shoulders, moved the fag end from one corner of his mouth to the other, and repeated his advice to keep her door locked at night. He dumped a pile of dirty plates in the stone sink, splashing greasy water all over the small girl who had to stand on an upturned bucket in order to wash the dishes. She shot him a resentful look but said nothing.

'There's tea in the pot,' Sly said, jerking his head in the direction of the range. 'The gents has eaten all the bread but I'll send Elsie down the baker's when she's done.'

Rosetta glanced at Elsie's thin shoulders hunched over the pile of washing up; she couldn't have been more than eleven or twelve and her shoulder blades stuck out beneath her thin cotton blouse like buds of angel's wings. Rosetta felt a twinge of pity for the scrawny little girl who obviously had quite enough to do without being sent to the bakery. 'It's all right,' she said, hoping that Sly couldn't hear her stomach rumbling. 'I ain't hungry, Uncle.'

'That's just as well then. You got to be quick in this drum or you don't get nothing to eat,' Sly said, slumping down in a chair by the range. 'Greedy beggars don't leave nothing on their plates. Bloody gannets, that's what they are.'

Rosetta poured herself a cup of tea and sipped it, wrinkling her nose. It was stewed, bitter and thick as tar. 'What sort of gents lodges here, Uncle Sly?'

'All sorts. Best not ask. What you don't know won't hurt you.' Sly winked and tapped his nose. 'As long as they pays their rent I don't ask no questions.'

'They was all well sozzled last night,' Elsie observed, more to herself than to anyone in particular. 'Come crashing through the kitchen, scaring the life out of me.'

'Button your lip, girl,' Sly said, scowling. 'It

were just high spirits, Rose. Don't take no notice of Elsie, she's a bit touched.' He leaned towards Rosetta, lowering his voice. 'Got beat up regular by her old man. It done something to her brains like.'

It was hard to imagine a father that could do that to his kid. Rosetta felt a lump rising in her throat as she thought of Poppa. A fleeting vision of his loving smile and the way he tugged at her curls when he was teasing her made her feel suddenly guilty. Why did Poppa have to get sick just as she decided to leave home? 'It's not fair,' she said out loud.

'Don't waste your pity on the likes of her,' Sly said, apparently misunderstanding her meaning. 'She's well fed and got a bed by the fire every night. She don't get beat, even when she's done something bad. Not that she don't need a cuff round the lughole every so often, just to remind her to keep her place.'

It wasn't what she had meant at all, but Rosetta was not going to admit that to Sly. Even so, she felt an almost overwhelming surge of pity for Elsie. No one at home had ever lifted a finger to her or Ruby, and if her brother Joe had ever had a good hiding from Mum, then it was because Joe chanced his arm something horrible. Before he'd got himself apprenticed to a printer in Fleet Street, he'd been in and out of trouble, nicking things, dipping and mixing with the Spivey

Street boys. Granny Mole always said he'd inherited the Capretti bad streak.

Sly got up from his seat, picked up the teapot and strode over to Elsie, lifting her bodily off the bucket. 'You can finish that later. Time you took Madam's breakfast up to her room.' He emptied the contents of the teapot into the sink and made a fresh brew.

Elsie darted him a look beneath her long white eyelashes and scuttled into the larder, coming out with a tray set with a plate of thinly cut bread and butter, a pot of jam and some sliced meat.

Sly put the teapot onto the tray and the weight made Elsie's knees buckle, but she staggered out of the kitchen carrying it, with her bony elbows stuck out at right angles.

'You'd best be off to the Falstaff, then,' Sly said, sitting down again and putting his feet up on the brass rail of the range. 'We'll sort out your bed and board when you get your wages.'

Rosetta bit her lip, she was hungry, and seeing the breakfast set out for Aunt Lottie had made her own stomach rumble like rainwater pouring down a drain. 'I need me duds from home, Uncle. Can I send Elsie round for them?'

Sly reached in his pocket for a packet of Woodbines, taking out the last one and lighting it with a spill from the fire. 'She can go if you gives her the price of a packet of Woods. Can't get through the day without me fags.'

Rosetta caught Elsie as she came stumbling down the staircase, rubbing her ear that looked suspiciously red. She blinked like a scared rabbit when given instructions to go to Tobacco Court. She was to ask the lady who came to the door to seek out a bag of Rosetta's clothes that she had hidden under Granny Mole's bed. Rosetta was not certain that Elsie had fully understood, and she repeated it all over again, pressing two pennies into Elsie's work-roughened hand. 'That's for ten Will's Woodbines for Mr Silas, d'you understand?'

Elsie stared dumbly at the coins.

Glancing at the long-case clock in the hall, Rosetta realised that she would be late for the theatre if she didn't leave for Old Street right away. She seized her shawl, still a bit damp, and her bonnet, still a bit limp, from the rickety hallstand and put them on. Feeling in her pocket she found a farthing and pressed it into Elsie's hand. 'That's for going. Buy yourself some sweets, Elsie.'

Elsie stared at her blankly for a moment, and then two large tears welled up in the corners of eyes that were so pale blue that they seemed almost colourless, like sheep's eyes. 'For us?'

Rosetta closed her fingers over the coins. 'The pennies is for Woods for Mr Silas and the farthing is for you. You bring me duds back here like I told you and I'll give you another farthing.'

Rosetta arrived at the theatre ten minutes late, her shoes and the hem of her skirt soaked by the piles of slush on the pavements. A pale yellow sun had fought its way through a blanket of grey clouds and a spiteful east wind had chilled her to the bone. In the rehearsal room, the rest of the chorus were limbering up at the barre under the eagle eye of a small, dark-haired woman dressed in black. She turned on Rosetta, her dark eyebrows meeting over the bridge of her aquiline nose. 'You're late.'

The other girls sniggered and Rosetta felt hot colour flood to her cheeks. She stood awkwardly, knotting her hands behind her back, knowing that all eyes were upon her and well aware that she must look a sight with her old, much-darned clothes clinging damply to her legs.

'What's your name, girl?'

'Rosetta Capretti, Miss.'

'You call me Madame. I am Madame Smithsova and you do like I say. I will not have girls in my troupe who do not give one hundred per cent of themselves to their art.'

'Yes, Madame.' Rosetta glanced at the girls who were openly grinning at her, obviously enjoying seeing someone else get the rough end of Madame's tongue for a change. They were all wearing short dresses with net skirts, pink cotton tights and ballet shoes; Rosetta felt overdressed and as conspicuous as a bluebottle on an iced bun.

'Take your clothes off,' Madame said, striking the floor with her ebony cane. 'Don't waste time, girl. You are holding up the rehearsal.'

Feeling her face glow with embarrassment, there was nothing Rosetta could do but obey and she peeled off her outer clothes until she stood barefoot and shivering in her shift and bloomers. Whispers and giggling from the girls stopped abruptly as Madame rapped her cane on the floor. 'Silence. I will not have this bad behaviour in my class. Rosetta, go to the end of the barre and follow what the others do.'

Rosetta went to stand behind a pretty girl with flaming red hair and freckles.

'Just watch me, love,' she said, with a sympathetic smile. 'Me name's Tilly, by the way.'

Madame rapped her cane on the floor. 'The four positions, girls, followed by rond de jambe à terre and pliés. And one, and two and three and four. Keep your back straight, Rosetta. Watch Tilly. And one, and two . . .'

By the end of the morning Rosetta was aching all over and almost dropping with exhaustion.

'That was terrible. You are clumsy elephants, all of you.' Madame emphasised her words by poking those nearest her with her cane. 'You are not fit for the circus, let alone the chorus at the

41

Falstaff. You may have a ten minute break and then we will practise your dance routines.' She sailed out of the room, slamming the door behind her.

Everyone began to talk at once, slumping down on the floor, massaging their aching leg muscles and rubbing their sore feet.

'Anyone would think we was in the corps de bleeding ballet,' grumbled Tilly.

'I never thought we'd have to go through all this,' Rosetta whispered. 'Is it like this every day?'

Tilly nodded. 'Today she's in a good mood. Watch out for her when she's in a bad 'un.'

'Wish I'd got a pair of bloomers like yours.' A bold-looking girl with suspiciously brassy blonde hair sauntered over to them, looking down her nose at Rosetta. 'What's your talent then? Selling ice cream from a barrow?'

'Aw, leave her be, Aggie,' said Tilly.

'Pardon me for breathing,' Aggie said, tossing her head. 'Best lend your little Eyetie friend a pair of tights, Tilly, afore we all kills ourselves laughing.'

Rosetta jumped to her feet. 'I ain't ashamed of being half Italian but I'm a Londoner born and bred. You keep your smart remarks to yourself, or I'll fetch you a smack on the kisser.'

Aggie's brown eyes flashed. 'Just try it.'

'Stop, stop,' cried Tilly, scrambling up and placing herself between them. 'Ain't it bad enough us being shouted at by Madame without you two carrying on something chronic?'

'She started it,' Aggie said, backing away.

'No I never.' Rosetta couldn't let that pass and for a moment it looked as though Aggie was about to retaliate.

'Scrap,' someone shouted and the girls crowded round, seeming to have forgotten their aching limbs, their faces alight with anticipation of a fight. Aggie squared up to Rosetta, who stood her ground, and it might have ended in a hair-pulling, face-scratching match had not the door opened at that moment.

'Hey, Rosetta!' Billy Noakes stood in the doorway, his thumbs tucked in his wide leather belt, and his hazel eyes gleaming with undisguised admiration as he glanced at the scantily clad girls. 'Morning, ladies.' He doffed his cap with a flourish, bowing from the waist, which drew a giggling response and a general flutter of excitement.

Rosetta felt her cheeks burning with embarrassment at being caught in her underwear, and she crossed her arms over the expanse of breast not covered by her shift. No man, not even Poppa or Joe, had seen her in her undergarments. She wished the ground would open up and swallow her as Billy eyed her up and down, with an appreciative grin and a twinkle in his eyes that made her heart thump even faster.

'Well, hello,' said Aggie, sidling over to Billy. 'What's your moniker, dearie?'

'Billy Noakes, costermonger and man of business. I'd give you me card but I'm waiting for a fresh supply from me printers.'

'Come and see the show tonight, Billy Noakes,' Aggie said, fluttering her eyelashes. 'Aggie Brown is always open to offers of a pie and mash supper with a good-looking fella, and afterwards I could show you a good time, like.'

Forgetting her embarrassment, Rosetta darted forward, her hands itching to slap Aggie's brazen face, but she stopped short as Madame Smithsova marched into the room, bristling like a hedgehog. 'What is the meaning of this?' She poked Billy in the ribs with her cane. 'No gentlemen are allowed in my rehearsal rooms. Is this your doing, Miss Capretti?'

'Don't blame her, missis,' Billy said, flashing her a smile that would melt bricks. 'Begging your pardon for interrupting, but I comes with a message from her poor, sick father and I can see that you're a lady what understands the importance of family life.'

Madame's eyebrows knotted together like two snakes mating, but her thin lips quivered into something like a smile. 'It's against the rules, but . . .'

Billy grabbed her round her plump waist and kissed her rouged cheek. 'I knew you for a good 'un, missis. I won't keep Miss Capretti more than a couple of ticks.' He grabbed Rosetta by the arm and dragged her out into the corridor.

'Wh-what d'you mean by coming here, Billy? How did you find me?' Rosetta's teeth chattered with cold, so that she could barely speak.

Billy took off his jacket and wrapped it around her shoulders. 'You'll catch your death, prancing round half naked.'

The jacket was warm from his body and the scent of him lingered in the cloth: the sooty smell of the London peculiar, Macassar oil and leather; a tangy mix that was his alone. Rosetta dragged her mind back to the present. 'What d'you want, Billy?'

'I brung that daft girl back to Raven Street on me cart. Found her bawling her eyes out on the pavement outside your place. I just managed to get her name out of her and where she lived.'

'I sent her to collect me things from home. I ain't got nothing decent to wear.'

Billy grinned. 'You look good to me just as you are, girl.'

'Don't be coarse,' Rosetta said, hugging the jacket round her and trying to look mortified, even though worms of excitement wriggled in her stomach at the warmth in his tone and the hot look in his eyes. 'Did she fetch me duds or didn't she? And how come you was at ours anyway?'

'I got to thinking about them dollies that your

old man couldn't sell to the wholesalers. What with Christmas coming up and then that business with Father Brennan, I guessed things might be a bit tight and I know Ruby was worried sick about the whole thing.'

'Rosetta.' Tilly stuck her head round the door of the rehearsal room. 'Madame says come back this instant or you'll be out of a job.'

'Coming,' Rosetta said, handing Billy his jacket. 'I'd say it was none of your business and what d'you care anyway?'

Billy shrugged on his jacket. 'Suit yourself.'

He turned to go but Rosetta caught him by the sleeve. 'Don't mess me about, Billy. Did Elsie get my stuff or not?'

'You're a prize one, you are. Don't you never think of no one but yourself?'

'Hurry up, do,' Tilly said, beckoning furiously.

'If you come just to have a laugh at my expense, you can sling your hook.' Rosetta tossed her head, turning away. 'Ruby will sort it out for me.'

'No need to go off in a sulk,' Billy said. 'What time d'you finish here?'

'Five o'clock,' Tilly said, dragging Rosetta into the rehearsal room. 'Sooner if you don't make yourself scarce.'

If Rosetta had found the practice session hard, then the rehearsals that went on all afternoon were even more gruelling. The rest of the troupe knew the steps but Madame made them go over and over each routine like a drill sergeant, until they were perfectly in time. In the brief rest periods, Rosetta was laced into whalebone stays that threatened to stop her breathing altogether, and fitted out with several different costumes by the wardrobe mistress.

'Back here by six sharp,' Tilly said as they struggled into their own clothes at the end of the afternoon. 'Don't be late for Gawd's sake and don't eat nothing heavy or you'll throw up all over the front row.'

Rosetta giggled in spite of the pain in her cramped muscles and the blisters on her sore feet. 'I'm fagged out. I don't think I'll make it back to me digs, let alone give a performance tonight.'

'You'll get used to it,' Tilly said, wrapping a woollen shawl around her head and shoulders. 'I just hope it ain't snowing. Me chilblains is playing up something chronic.'

Outside it was raining steadily, a drenching downpour that hit the pavements and bounced straight up again in tiny dancing fountains. Rosetta paused in the doorway bracing herself for the inevitable cold shower, putting off the moment, wondering whether it might be best to hang around the theatre for an hour rather than get soaked to the skin. She barely looked up as the rumble of cartwheels approached, slowed

47

down and stopped in front of her and she was about to turn back into the theatre when she heard Billy calling her name. She hesitated for a moment and then, picking up her skirts, she ran across the pavement, splashing through deep puddles. Billy held out his hand and pulled her up onto the seat beside him, giving her an umbrella to hold. He flicked the reins and his old horse plodded obediently forward.

'I never thought you'd come,' Rosetta said, huddling down in the shelter of the umbrella.

'Said I would, didn't I?' Billy said, not looking at her as he concentrated on driving through the crowd of carts, hackney carriages and hansom cabs that thronged Old Street.

'Don't get the wrong idea, Billy, just because I let you drive me home. I'm dead set on making me way in the theatre and I ain't got time for spooning.'

'Don't flatter yourself.'

'So why are you putting yourself out for me and my family? What's in it for you?'

'Maybe nothing.'

'I don't believe you. There's always something in it for Billy Noakes.'

Billy turned his head and grinned at her. 'It's nearly Christmas, ain't that good enough reason?'

Rosetta stared at him, but he had turned his attention back to the road, the driving made more difficult by people pouring out of shops, threading their way in and out between moving vehicles, and dazzling reflections of naphtha flares from market stalls with ragged puddles of gas light fraying out on the wet cobbles. Rosetta couldn't quite get the measure of Billy Noakes. He was a chancer and no doubt mixed up in all sorts of funny business; it was probably best not to think too hard about the way he made his money. Flashing him a covert glance from beneath the umbrella, Rosetta studied his profile as he concentrated on the road ahead. He was good-looking, in a flashy sort of way, and she sensed that beneath the charm and soft soap there lurked a will as strong her own.

'Now then,' Billy said, flicking the reins so that the horse drew to a halt at the corner of Spivey Street and Tobacco Court. 'D'you want to go in and see your folks?'

'No, just get me things for me, there's a sport, Billy.'

'Don't you even want to see your dad?'

'Are you going in there or not?'

Billy stared at her, his eyebrows raised, and then he laughed. 'I never met no one as selfish as you, Rosetta. Me own self excepted, that is.'

'Takes one to know one,' Rosetta said stiffly. 'Now are you going to get me things for me, or do I have to go in there and upset everyone all over again?'

Chapter Three

Early on the morning of Christmas Eve, Ruby arrived at Bronski's sweatshop in Henchard Alley, off Whitechapel Road. The wholesalers' refusal to take the dolls had been a bitter blow, and, in typical fashion, Rosetta had forfeited her wages by walking out of her job. Reluctantly, Ruby had come to the conclusion that there was only one way out of a desperate situation. Wearing Rosetta's red shawl and with her hair bunched up on top, tied with a scrap of red ribbon, Ruby knew she could pass for her sister as long as she kept her mouth shut. They might be identical in looks, but their voices were as dissimilar as those of a lark and a dove. Rosetta had the Italian love of music in her soul and the singing voice to go with it; even in ordinary conversation, her voice rose and fell in fluid arpeggios. Ruby was painfully aware that her own voice, although soft and low, had none of those magical qualities, and would give her away as soon as she uttered a word.

She stood in line with the other workers waiting to be let into the single-storey brick building that had once been a smithy but now housed Bronski's clothing empire. Women and girls of all ages queued in the bitter cold pre-dawn, blinking sleep from their eyes, yawning and shuffling their feet. Ruby knew them all by name as Rosetta, who was a born mimic, had made everyone at home fall about laughing with her spirited impersonations. First there was Jacob Bronski, the exiled Russian Jew, who made his living by extorting the last ounce of effort from his workers with a mixture of bullying and pleading. Then there were the women who sat, hour on hour, working the treadle machines: fat Nan, dotty Dora, little Winnie and Mad Mabel. Ruby knew she would be able to recognise the supervisor, Vinegar Lil, by her needle-sharp features and her thin, dun-coloured hair scraped back into a bun. Then there were the cutters, who worked the band-saw machine, slicing through great wodges of cloth and occasionally losing a finger or two in the process. The youngest girls, some as young as seven or eight, picked up the threads, swept the floors and did the fetching and carrying. The woman mountain standing beside Ruby had to be Big Biddy, who slaved away in the steam heat using the gas-jet iron; she was easily identifiable not only by her size, but by her muscular forearms, knotted and scarred like rope with old and fresh burns.

Biddy nudged Ruby in the ribs. 'Oy, you might

have told us you was taking time off. We've had to say you was took sick.'

Ruby smiled, pointing to her throat and speaking in a hoarse whisper. 'Lost me voice.'

'It's a wonder any of us can speak, let alone breathe proper.' The woman in front of Ruby, who couldn't be anybody other than fat Nan, hawked and spat on the pavement. 'Me lungs is so full of fluff that I could cough up a woolly hat.'

A tiny woman, with the figure of a child and the face of a wizened monkey, slipped her hand into Ruby's, giving it a squeeze. 'What'll we do without Rose to give us a giggle?'

Ruby smiled down at her; this must be little Winnie. She was beginning to put faces to names.

'Get on inside and stop gassing.' Vinegar Lil marched up from behind them to unlock the workshop door. 'Get a move on or you'll make up the wasted time at the end of the day.'

'Day,' muttered fat Nan, 'it's bloody night-time when we finish.'

'I heard that,' Lil said, glaring at Nan as she waddled into the dark interior of the workshop. As Ruby hurried past, Lil prodded her in the shoulder. 'Nice of you to turn up for work, my lady. What's up with you then, Rose? Cat got your tongue today?'

'More like a frog in the throat,' Biddy said, grinning and barging past Lil, who jumped clear.

Ruby was quick to notice that Lil didn't take

Biddy on, but that was hardly surprising as Biddy was head and shoulders taller than any of the other women and beefy as an all-in wrestler; more like a man in a woman's frock. Ruby hesitated in the doorway, peering into the gloom. The smell of the forge still lingered in the smoke-blackened brick and timber, mixing with the rancid odour of damp wool and sweat. The air was thick with dust and lint, making Ruby want to retch, although the others seemed not to notice and hurried to their workstations. There was only one place left and that was at a treadle machine in the corner of the room. Ruby went to it and sat down. No wonder Rosetta walked out of here, she thought, watching the others carefully and copying their actions as best she could. The light was poor, even when Lil lit the gas lamp that hung in the centre of the room; Ruby's corner was in such deep shadow that she couldn't see how to thread the machine.

'Here,' said Winnie, leaning over the table. 'You still feeling poorly, Rose?'

Ruby nodded.

'Let me.' Winnie moved across and had the machine threaded before Vinegar Lil had realised that the two machines in the corner were not whirring away with the rest.

'Ta,' whispered Ruby, watching Winnie set to work with a sinking feeling in the pit of her stomach. Everyone was busy. The youngest girls scuttled to and fro like small, spider crabs, in response to Lil's rapid-fire orders. The older women had their heads down, their hands guiding the material and their feet working the treadles like an army marching at the double. Concentrating hard, Ruby tried to copy them but was pounced upon by Vinegar Lil. Her work was held up and ridiculed and Lil clipped her round the ear for good measure. Humiliated, and with her ear stinging painfully, Ruby studied Winnie's expert handling of the sewing machine and made an effort to copy her deft movements. By the end of the morning Ruby had almost mastered the temperamental treadle. Her back ached, her eyes were sore and her fingers blistered and bleeding from catching them on the pins, but she was determined to persevere. How long she would be able to stand working in this living hell, she didn't know, but if she could just keep going until Poppa recovered then she could go back to helping him in the arches. Making dolls was not something she had ever wanted to do, but someone had to help Poppa. With Joe apprenticed to a respectable trade, and Rosetta being too flighty, there had been no choice. Ruby had gone into it willingly enough, setting aside her dream of studying nursing at the London Hospital, but ambition still burned deep within her like an unquenchable fire. She knew that it was almost impossible for a girl of her class to become a qualified nurse, but that did not stop her devouring the second-hand medical books that she bought for a penny or twopence in Spitalfields market.

Vinegar Lil whacked Ruby hard across the knuckles with the stick that she kept for poking slow workers. 'Stop daydreaming and get on with your work, Capretti. I'll not give you another warning.'

Bending her head over her machine, Ruby steered the thick material beneath the flying needle. One day, she thought, treadling furiously, one day I'll prove that I'm as clever as any of them well-off, middle-class girls and I'll make the London Hospital take me on as a student.

Vinegar Lil blew a whistle and everyone stopped. 'Ten minutes for your dinner break and not a minute longer.'

There was a rush for the privy in the back yard and then almost complete silence while the women munched their slices of bread and scrape, dripping or jam, washed down with a cup of weak tea.

'Hope your voice comes back soon, Rose,' Winnie said, wiping her mouth on her sleeve. 'It's your sing-songs and jokes what keeps us going.'

'Drives us nuts, you mean,' Biddy said, with a deep, rumbling chuckle.

Dotty Dora jumped up on her chair, holding

her skirts up above her knees and jigging up and down. 'I can dance if you hums a tune, Rose.'

Looking around at the expectant faces, Ruby was struggling to think of an excuse when Vinegar Lil blew two long blasts on her whistle.

'Get back to work.'

Wheezing and puffing after the exertion of hurrying in from the yard, Nan let herself down onto her seat. 'Aw, come on, Lil. It's Christmas Eve. Ain't you going to let us off a bit early?'

Vinegar Lil stood, arms akimbo, glaring at Nan. 'Oh yes, and you'd think yourselves hard done by if Mr Bronski was to dock your wages by half a day. Get back to work, all of you.'

'He won't be having boiled bullock's head and cabbage for his Christmas dinner.' Winnie slithered into her seat, winking at Ruby. 'I'd like to see him feed six nippers on what he pays us.'

Ruby nodded sympathetically; it was hard to imagine child-like Winnie having given birth to one baby, let alone six.

Vinegar Lil brought her stick down on Winnie's table with a thud, making them all jump. 'Less chatter, more work. Mr Bronski will be here any minute, so get on with it.'

Mad Mabel began to sing in a deep gravelly voice that was as musical as a cinder scraping under a door, but the song had a rhythm to it that soon had the women working their treadles to its beat.

The afternoon seemed even longer than the morning, with a five-minute break at three-thirty for a cup of tea made by one of the youngest girls. The tea leaves, Ruby thought, wrinkling her nose, must have been used and reused time and time again, making a brew that looked and smelt like water straight from the Thames.

Mr Bronski put in an appearance at six o'clock, bringing in with him a swirl of pea-green fog and bone-chilling night air. Enveloped in a black cashmere coat with an astrakhan collar, Jacob Bronski looked well fed, prosperous and out of place in the dingy surroundings of his workshop. He went straight to Lil, dumping a leather pouch on the table in front of her. 'Have we met our target for today?'

Lil shot a dark look at Ruby, shaking her head. 'Not everyone, Mr Bronski. Best dock two days' pay off Capretti instead of just one.'

'If she don't improve, sack her.' Bronski glowered at Ruby. 'I'm good to my workers, I pay a fair rate, and what do I get in return?'

'I know what he should get,' Biddy said, in a low voice.

The ripple of laughter that greeted this remark was cut short by a loud roar from Bronski. 'I deduct an hour's pay off each one of you bitches for that.' He glared round the room as if daring anyone to comment. No one did. 'You don't deserve it, but come and get your money and think yourselves lucky to have a generous employer like me.'

Before anyone could move, a mighty thud that sounded like a booted foot kicking the outside door was followed by several more and the door burst open, hitting the wall with a splintering crash. Five men armed with cudgels, knives and broken bottles rushed into the workshop. The women screamed, leaping to their feet, only to be herded into a corner like cattle, all except Ruby, who made herself as small as possible in the deep shadow beneath her workbench.

'Sit down and no one will be hurt,' snarled the man who appeared to be the leader. He caught Bronski by the throat, bending him backwards over the table. 'We come to collect, Rusky.'

Bronski's sallow skin paled to green. 'Please, I paid last week.'

'Hear that, boys? The Rusky Jew-boy paid last week.'

Vinegar Lil had picked up the pouch and was sneaking out of the back door when one of the men spotted her, caught her by the bun at the back of her head and dragged her back into the room. Snatching the pouch from her hands, he tossed it to the gang leader.

'Please,' Bronski cried, falling to his knees. 'That's all I got to pay me workers. It's Christmas

Eve. You wouldn't rob them poor women of their wages?'

'Me heart's breaking,' snarled the leader, grabbing Bronski by the throat. 'Now give us the rest or do we have to get rough?'

'Please, I'm a poor man.'

'You'll be even poorer if we smashes up your machines.'

With cudgels raised above their heads, the men waited for the signal to destroy the machines with an eagerness that made Ruby's blood run cold. They had got what they came for but now they obviously wanted to wreck things just for the pleasure that violence gave them. Vinegar Lil had crumpled to the ground sobbing, and the rest of the women and girls cowered in the corner; even Big Biddy was silent. All eyes were on the man who held Bronski by the throat. One squeeze of those big hands would snuff out Bronski's life like an altar boy putting out the candles after mass. Crouching behind her sewing machine, Ruby held her breath, her eyes drawn to a man who stood back from the rest, as if unwilling to take part in this cruel game. He carried a stick but he was holding it limply at his side. His cap was pulled low over his brow and Ruby couldn't see his face, but her heart gave an uncomfortable leap inside her chest; there was something disturbingly familiar about him. Before she could gather her thoughts it seemed

59

that all hell broke loose. The ringleader smashed his fist into Bronski's face, sending him crashing to the floor. The women screamed and the men began breaking up the chairs and tables, using their cudgels or picking up the furniture and smashing it into matchwood against the brick walls.

'That's enough.' The leader held his hand up, halting the destruction. 'We've let your machines alone, Rusky, for now. We'll be back next week.'

'I'm ruined,' sobbed Bronski, grovelling on the floor. 'I don't got no more for you to take.'

'Then better make some more, old man. If we don't protect you then the Odessans and Bessarabians will move in. Now they're real nasty buggers. Ain't they, boys?' Aiming a savage kick at Bronski's ribs, the gang leader swaggered out of the workshop, followed by his men laughing and jeering at Bronski's distress.

'You bleeding bastards!' roared Big Biddy, breaking free from the knot of women clinging to each other in the shadows. Picking up a chair leg, she brought it down with a crash on the head of the last man. He staggered and crumpled to the ground with Big Biddy throwing herself on top of him. 'Call a copper,' she screamed. 'Don't just stand there like a long drink of water, Lil. Run outside and find a copper.'

Lil ran out into the street with the others trailing after her, some sobbing, others cursing and swearing. Ruby went to Bronski who had staggered to his feet and was holding his hands to his face in a vain attempt to staunch the blood flowing freely from his nose. Snatching a scrap of cloth, Ruby guided him to the only stool that remained unbroken and, gently prising his fingers off his face, she held the rag to his nose. He gazed at her with unfocused eyes, dumbly shaking his head.

'Just hold it there,' Ruby said. 'I think your nose is broke. Sit quiet for a bit.' Hearing a screech from Biddy, Ruby turned to see her sitting on the fallen man and pinning him to the floor.

'You bastards is all alike,' Biddy roared, beating her fists on her captive's chest. 'You took the money from us what slaved away to get it. How am I to feed me kids and me old man what's sick? Answer me that, you miserable bastard.'

Afraid that Biddy was going to kill the man, who had really taken no part in the violence, Ruby hurried over to Biddy, tugging at her arm in an attempt to drag her off him. 'Get up off him, Biddy.' Ruby had to shout in order to make her voice heard above the noise coming from the street. 'You'll kill him.'

Biddy looked up. 'You got your voice back all of a sudden.'

'Shock. It's the shock!' Ruby's hand flew to her

throat and she made a gruff coughing sound. 'Don't kill him or the coppers will be arresting you and then what'll your nippers do?'

'Hanging's too good for the likes of him.' Biddy got to her feet, but not before she had given him one last punch. 'I never took you for the soft sort, Rose.' She stamped out of the work-shop, leaving the door swinging on its hinges.

'Leave him,' Bronski whined. 'Fetch me a doctor.'

Ruby had almost forgotten him in her need to stop Biddy taking her revenge on the semi-conscious man. 'I will,' she said, dropping down on her knees by the prostrate figure. 'When I've seen to this one.' Resting her hand on his chest, she could feel his ribcage rising and falling; at least Biddy hadn't crushed the life of out him. With a shaking hand, Ruby lifted his cap from his face.

'Joe!'

He opened his eyes and recognition flared. 'Ruby!'

'Joe, I can't believe you're mixed up with the gangs.'

'It's not what it looks like.' Joe struggled to sit up. 'Aw, Ruby, I can explain.'

Realising that Bronski was straining his ears to hear, Ruby lowered her voice to a whisper. 'Keep your voice down. I'm supposed to be Rose.'

'You can't fool your own brother,' Joe said,

attempting a smile and wincing as his split lip began to bleed. 'Help me up. I got to get out of here quick.'

'What's going on over there?' demanded Bronski. 'I need a doctor.'

Ruby helped Joe to his feet.

'Who is that?' Bronski called, squinting at them over the top of the bloodstained rag. 'Is that one of the gang? Hold him there until the police come.'

'I'm taking him outside, Mr Bronski,' Ruby called over her shoulder, 'to be picked up by the coppers.'

Outside the noise of shouting and screaming carried on unabated and, in the distance, Ruby could hear the shrill blasts of a police whistle. Joe leaned against the wall, his face ashen in the flickering gaslight.

'I don't understand all this,' Ruby said, wiping the blood from his mouth with the corner of her shawl. 'How did you get mixed up with them ruffians?'

'It ain't how it looks. I ain't a criminal, Ruby, you got to believe me.'

The sound of police whistles was getting closer and the hysterical cries of the women echoed up and down the alleyway. Ghostly fingers of fog curled in through the open door.

'I do believe you, but the police are coming; you've got to get away from here.' Taking Joe by the shoulders, Ruby shook him. 'Do you hear me, Joe? You've got to run for it.'

'Don't think bad of me, Ruby.' Dazed and disorientated, Joe backed towards the oncoming sound of running feet and police whistles.

'Not that way.' Diving after him, Ruby pointed Joe in the right direction and he stumbled off, vanishing into the pea-souper.

'You let him go.' Bronski glared up at Ruby as she went back into the workshop. 'You let one of the gang go free, you silly cow.'

Taking a deep breath, Ruby struggled to compose herself. She must keep calm; she must not let anyone suspect that she knew the identity of one of the gang. Whatever Joe had done, there had to be a reasonable explanation. She went over to Bronski and knelt down by his side. 'The cops will get him, Mr Bronski. Let's clean you up a bit before they arrive and then we'll see about getting you to hospital.'

'No!' Bronski's dark eyes stood out of his head like two full stops. 'No hospital and you don't tell the police nothing, not unless you want your pretty throat slit. You don't mess around with the gangs. Get out of here now, Rosetta. Go home and don't say nothing.'

With her shawl wrapped round her head and mouth to keep out the choking fog, Ruby hurried home as fast as she was able, feeling her way along walls and railings. It seemed to her that the London peculiar had silenced the whole city with a thick, stinking blanket. Battling her way through this silent, pea-green world, all she could think about was Joe. How could he have got himself mixed up with the gangs that terrorised the East End? Joe might have been a bit wild in his youth, but he was never violent, and he had a solid career ahead of him. Why would he throw all that away and break Mum's heart into the bargain? It was bad enough that Rosetta had gone off to try her luck on the stage; Ruby had had to do some quick thinking to explain her sudden departure to their mother. In the end, she had told a half-truth and said that Rosetta, hating her work at Bronski's, had gone to stay with Lottie in Raven Street and intended to seek respectable employment in a shop up West. Ma had been shocked and disappointed to think that Rose had gone off without telling her, but Ruby hated to think what her reaction would be if she learned of Rosetta's real intentions.

Now there was this awful thing with Joe; hesitating outside the front door of number sixteen, Ruby's hand trembled as she put the key in the lock. Mum and Granny Mole would want to know how it had gone at Bronski's and she would have to explain why she had not brought home any money. She prayed that Joe had not run home; he had always been a poor liar and

Mum could see through him like a sheet of glass. It would be bad enough seeing the expression on Poppa's face when she had to tell them that she had worked twelve hours for nothing, without having to admit that Joe had done such a dreadful wrong. Bracing her shoulders, Ruby went inside and was hit by a gust of warm air and the unmistakeable aroma of hot meat pie.

'Shut the door,' Granny Mole called out from her chair by a roaring fire. 'You're letting the cold air in.'

'Sit down, love,' Sarah said, bustling in from the scullery, placing a steaming pie on the table with a triumphant smile. 'We've waited for you special, though Granny wanted hers as soon as I brung it in from the pie shop, but I said we'd not cut into it until you come home.'

Ruby looked at Poppa, who sat in his chair, wrapped in a blanket. He managed a smile but he looked pale and unwell. Ruby went to him, kneeling down and taking his cold hand in hers. 'How are you, Poppa?'

'Not so good, cara. Not so good today.'

'Well if you won't eat you'll never get better,' Sarah said, cutting into the pie and putting a small slice on a plate. 'I want to see this plate clean, Aldo. Eat it while it's hot.'

Aldo shook his head. 'Maybe later.'

Frowning, Sarah wafted the plate under his nose. 'It's good. Try a bit.'

Aldo clutched his stomach, beads of sweat standing out on his brow.

'Don't, Mum,' Ruby said, pushing the plate away. 'Can't you see that Poppa's sick? He should be in the hospital.'

'Don't talk daft. We ain't got that kind of money. I couldn't have paid for the doctor to visit if Billy Noakes hadn't turned up earlier with the money for the dolls.'

'Money for the dolls? But he said . . .' Ruby stopped short, biting her lip.

'He said that the wholesalers was begging for them,' Sarah said with a pleased smile, 'and, credit where credit's due, Billy come right round with the money. He said the wholesalers was always pleased to get their hands on a Capretti doll.'

'That's what he said, Ruby.' Aldo smiled proudly, patting Ruby's hand. 'They love Capretti dolls. Maybe I misjudged Billy. He ain't such a bad bloke at heart.'

'I'll eat his pie if he don't want it, Sal,' Granny Mole said, eyeing the plate. 'Can't waste good grub.'

Sarah waved the plate under Aldo's nose. 'Just a mouthful, to please me.'

'I'm sorry, Sal.' Aldo seemed to shrink into the blanket, drawing his head in like a tired old tortoise.

'Oh, well! Suit yourself, you stubborn old

bugger,' Sarah said, scraping the piece of pie onto Granny's plate. 'Leave him be. He'll eat when he's a mind to.'

Quick to recognise the note of anxiety in her mother's voice, Ruby got to her feet, dropping a kiss on her father's forehead. 'I'll make you some bread and milk later, Poppa.'

Sarah lowered herself onto her chair at the table. 'Come and get your tea while it's still hot, Ruby.'

'What did the doctor say, Mum?' Ruby asked in a low voice as she took her seat.

'He said he reckoned that your dad's poisoned hisself with all that lead what he mixes with the wax,' Sarah whispered. 'The doctor said he'd seen it often enough with painters and the like.'

Ruby stared at the food, her appetite gone. 'Poisoned?'

Sarah shot an anxious glance at Aldo. 'Shhhh! Don't say nothing to your pa. He's got to be kept quiet. The doctor told me to give him a dose of laudanum if the pain got too much for him.'

'But there must be something else that he could do for him?'

'The doctor said that nature must take its course. Anyway, Ruby, your dad's a tough old bugger; after a few days' rest I'm sure he'll be right as rain. Now eat your tea or you'll be the next one took sick.'

Ruby took a mouthful of pie and forced herself

to swallow it. Normally this would have been a real treat but tonight the food stuck in her throat. Doctors were clever, well-educated men who had studied for years; she couldn't believe that there was nothing they could do for Poppa and, even if Mum didn't realise it, Ruby knew that lead poisoning was often fatal.

'Is that last piece of pie going begging?' Granny Mole rattled her fork on her empty plate. 'D'you want to see me fade away for want of food?'

'Billy Noakes's horse eats less than you do, Ma,' Sarah said, with a flash of her old humour, winking at Ruby as she cut the last slice of the pie in half. 'Pass that to your gran and mind she don't bite your finger off an' all.'

'Yes, and you'd take me down the knacker's yard as soon as look at me,' grumbled Granny, grabbing the plate. 'You wait till you're old and feeble, Sal. Let's hope your girls treats you like what you deserve.'

Sarah shot Ruby one of her rare smiles. 'I dunno about Rosetta, she's a flighty piece and her head's stuffed full of nonsense. I just hope she finds a decent job and that she'll get fed up staying with Lottie and come home.'

'That Carlottie's a tart,' observed Granny Mole through a mouthful of pie.

'Lottie's too old for that sort of nonsense now, Ma.' Shrugging her shoulders, Sarah turned to

Ruby, smiling. 'At least I know I can rely on my Ruby. How many girls would take their sister's place in that stinking sweatshop just to help their family? How did your day go, love?'

Ruby pushed her plate away. 'Mum, I got something to tell you.'

The news that Ruby had not been paid paled into nothing compared to the shocking knowledge that one of the street gangs was working so close to home. Granny Mole insisted that Sarah stuck a chair under the door handle, just in case the lock was not strong enough to keep intruders out. Aldo sat with tears running down his sunken cheeks, bemoaning the fact that he was too weak to protect his family; only Sarah remained calm, demanding to hear every last detail of the attack. However, Ruby was quick to notice that, after Granny Mole and Aldo had been put to bed, Mum wedged a chair under the door handle.

'I'm only doing it to keep your gran happy,' she said, meeting Ruby's eyes with a careless shrug.

'Yes, Mum.' Ruby was about to make the fire safe for the night, but Sarah pushed her out of the way.

'You get yourself to bed, ducks. You've had a time of it today.'

Any form of sympathy from her mother was so rare that Ruby was touched almost to the point of tears. She had grown up knowing that Rosetta with her rebellious, high-spirited ways was her mother's favourite, and Joe was Mum's pride and joy in spite of his weaknesses. Between them, Ruby thought, swallowing a lump in her throat, Joe and Rosetta would break Mum's heart. It would be bad enough when Mum discovered that Rosetta was about to join the chorus, but she must never find out what had really happened tonight in Bronski's sweatshop.

Having banked the fire with damp cinders, Sarah scrambled to her feet. 'At least we'll have a good blaze to see us through Christmas Day. I never thought as how I'd say it, but thank God for Billy Noakes. He may be a bit of a villain but he come through with enough money to keep us going until you get paid again, Ruby.'

'Mum, I can't go back to Bronski's,' Rosetta said, staring at her in horror. 'They'll find out I ain't Rosetta and I'll get moved from the machines because I'm not skilled at it like she was. If I can't work the machines I won't earn hardly nothing.'

'Well, something is better than nothing at all. You only got to do it until Aldo gets well again, then you can go back to the arches. We're all relying on you, Ruby.' Sarah took a saucepan off the trivet and lowered it into a haybox by the side of the fireplace, giving the porridge a final stir before clamping on the lid. 'There, that'll be ready for breakfast and, with a bit of luck, Joe will be here to share it with us. He's bound to come and visit his family on Christmas Day. My Joe never lets me down.'

Upstairs, in the tiny back bedroom, Granny Mole lay on her back in her narrow iron bed, her chin sagging onto her flat chest and her mouth open wide. Through blackened stumps of teeth, like a row of tumbledown cottages, Granny Mole's snoring rattled and wheezed, echoing off the whitewashed walls. Ruby huddled beneath a blanket on the mattress that she had always shared with Rosetta. In the flickering light of a candle stub, she slid her hand between the mattress and the bare floorboards and pulled out two medical books. Straining her eyes to read and missing the familiar warmth of Rosetta's body, Ruby absorbed everything she could find on the symptoms and treatment of lead poisoning. After a while, the words began to wriggle around in front of her eyes like dozens of tiny tadpoles and her eyelids were too heavy to keep them open. She blew out the candle and curled up in a ball, falling asleep to the rhythm of Granny Mole's pig-squealing snores.

Next morning, Ruby came downstairs to find Mum and Granny Mole seated at the table with steaming bowls of porridge in front of them. The room was warm and, after smouldering all night, the fire had been coaxed back to life, sending blue-tipped, orange flames licking up the chimney. Helping herself to some porridge, Ruby went to sit at the table.

Granny Mole scraped her plate clean and licked her spoon. 'That were a breakfast fit for a queen, Sal. I could manage a bit more.'

'What about Poppa?' Ruby demanded, glancing anxiously at Sarah.

'Your dad's sleeping so sound I didn't want to wake him,' Sarah said, heaving herself off her chair and picking up Granny's empty plate. 'I'll make him some bread and milk when he wakes.'

Ruby reached for the sugar bowl but Granny Mole grabbed it first and clung to it, glaring at her.

'Ma, let Ruby have the sugar,' Sarah said, holding the bowl of porridge just out of Granny's reach.

'She don't need it. I'm a feeble old woman; I needs me nourishment.'

A loud banging on the front door startled them all into silence. The handle rattled and the chair moved an inch or two but held firm.

'It's the gang,' muttered Granny, snatching the plate of porridge from Sarah.

'Mum, let me in.'

'Joe!' Sarah ran to the door, pulled the chair away and turned the key in the lock.

Joe burst into the room and flung his arms

around his mother, lifting her clean off her feet. 'Merry Christmas.'

Ruby leapt to her feet. 'Joe!'

Setting Sarah down with a smacking kiss on her cheek, Joe strode past Granny, dropping a kiss on the top of her grizzled head and wrapped his arms around Ruby in a bear hug. 'Merry Christmas, Ruby.' He brushed her cheek with his lips, whispering in her ear, 'You ain't said nothing?'

'No, of course I didn't,' Ruby hissed. 'What d'you take me for?'

'It's rude to whisper,' Sarah said, taking the plate of porridge from Granny before she had time to start eating and pressing it into Joe's hands. 'Sit down, son. Have some breakfast and I'll make a fresh brew of tea.'

'Here,' cried Granny, glaring at Joe. 'That's mine, you cheeky young bugger.'

Joe gave it back to her. 'Don't worry, Gran. I ain't hungry.'

'I'll make the tea, Mum,' Ruby said, picking up the teapot. 'You sit down and take it easy. Joe can give us a hand.'

Sarah sat down, smiling happily. 'Well, now I know it's Christmas.'

Dragging Joe into the scullery, Ruby shut the door. 'Don't you go upsetting Mum.'

'You worry too much, Ruby,' Joe said, giving her hair a playful tug. 'It's Christmas and I've brought presents.' Shoving his hand deep in his coat pocket, he brought out several packages wrapped in brown paper and handed one to Ruby. 'Ta, for what you done last night. You saved me bacon.'

Staring down at the small parcel lying in the palm of her hand, Ruby shook her head. 'I don't want nothing bought with stolen money.'

'It ain't what you think.'

'You was with the gang. You stole that money.'

'No, I swear I didn't get none of it.' Joe seized her hand, closing her fingers over the present. 'You got to believe me. I was there, yes, but I had no choice.'

'Of course you had a choice.'

'You don't understand.' Joe's voice broke in a hoarse whisper. 'I got into bad company, Ruby. I lost money at the gaming tables.'

Ruby stared at him aghast. 'Gambling! Joe, you never.'

'Once you get started on that route you can't stop. You wins a bit and then you loses and you think you can win it back easy. Just one more time and you'll stop – but it don't work like that. Afore I knew it I was in too deep to get out. Aunt Lottie lent me a stake . . .'

'Aunt Lottie! Oh, Joe! You should have knowed better. Gambling's done for her good and proper.'

'She tried to straighten me out. But I'd lost a

pile of money in Jonas Crowe's place. I couldn't honour me debt and it was only then I found out he was running a street gang. He said I'd have to do a job with them or get me legs busted.'

Before Ruby could answer, Sarah opened the scullery door. 'What's going on? What are you two nattering about?'

'Just catching up, Mum,' Ruby said, filling the kettle from the tap. 'Won't be a tick.'

'Oh, you two!' Sarah said, smiling. 'You was always thick as thieves. We just need Rosetta to turn up and it'll make my day. Give us the kettle and I'll stick it on the hob.' Taking the kettle, she bustled back into the living room.

'How could you be so blooming stupid, Joe?' Ruby demanded through clenched teeth. 'Have you any idea what you've got yourself into?'

'Don't fuss, sis. I can sort it. I ain't a kid.'

'No, you're an idiot. I'm furious with you, Joe, for being so – so pathetic.'

Slipping his arm round her shoulders, Joe gave Ruby a hug. 'Come on, it's Christmas. Don't be mad at me, Ruby.'

Dashing angry tears from her eyes with the back of her hand, Ruby shook her head. 'The women at Bronski's lost their wages in that robbery, Joe. There's families that won't have anything to eat because of it.'

'I really am sorry for them and I know I was a mug, but I swear I'll make it right somehow.

Can't we forget it for just one day, Ruby? After all, it is Christmas.'

Unable to resist his winning smile, Ruby nodded. 'All right, but you haven't heard the last of this, Joe Capretti.'

Hugging her, Joe kissed her on the tip of her nose. 'Open your present. It's just a bead necklace but I bought it with me wages. I never had a penny of that stolen money, you got to believe me, and next time I'll let them break me legs. Will that make you happy?'

Ruby sniffed and gave him a watery smile. 'What am I going to do with you, Joe?'

'Just say you forgive me, Ruby.'

'I do, of course I do. Just promise me you'll steer clear of the gangs and the gaming tables.'

'I promise. Cross me heart and hope to die.'

Opening the package, Ruby held up the string of brightly coloured, glass beads. 'It's really lovely. Ta.'

At the sound of Sarah's voice demanding the teapot, Ruby and Joe hurried into the living room. Granny Mole had nodded off and Sarah set about making the tea, chattering happily about everything turning out for the best. Ruby sat down by the fire, praying that it was true.

Sarah handed Joe a mug of tea. 'You take this up to your dad, Joe. The sight of you will do him more good than any medicine.'

'It's not like him to sleep on, but I'll be the first

to wish him Merry Christmas,' Joe said, taking the stairs two at a time.

Granny Mole woke up with a start, spotted the present that Joe had placed on her lap while she slept, and ripped the paper off with an exultant cry. 'Fry's Chocolate Crème!' A thin dribble of saliva ran down her chin.

'Oh my!' Sarah's eyes opened wide as she held up a string of pearl beads. 'That boy! He'll never be rich, spending all his money on us. I'll tell him off good and proper when he comes down. What's yours, Ruby? You're keeping very quiet.'

Ruby was about to show them her necklace but froze, hearing an anguished cry from above. Clattering down the stairs and jumping the last three steps, Joe skittered to a halt, white-faced and trembling, with tears pouring down his cheeks. 'It's Poppa! I can't wake him. I think he's dead.'

Chapter Four

A bone-chilling east wind that must have come straight from Siberia rampaged around the cemetery, tugging at the black veils of the mourners and toppling hats onto the mud. Clutching one of Aunt Lottie's fur-lined cloaks around her, Rosetta was grateful for its warmth, even if it smelt strongly of mothballs and was at least twenty years out of fashion. Father Brennan had said the last few words at the graveside and now everyone stood around, awkward and shivering, waiting for someone to make a move but unwilling to be the first. Staring down at the earth-strewn lid of the oak coffin Rosetta found it hard to imagine Poppa lying down there all alone in the dark. In fact, it was almost impossible to believe that he was gone forever; that she would never again be able to take her problems to him, listen to his stories about the old country, or have him call her his 'little Rosa' and tell her she was pretty. When Joe had come to the house in Raven Street on Christmas Day, bearing the sad news, it had seemed like a bad dream. She had cried herself to sleep night after night and now, to her surprise, she had no more tears to shed. Mum and Ruby had wept openly during the funeral service but Granny Mole had remained dry-eyed, giving Father Brennan the occasional black look and scowling at Lottie.

Feeling strangely detached, as though she was merely part of the audience, watching a play or a show at the Falstaff, Rosetta looked round at the black-clad mourners. Aunt Lottie was leaning on Sly, who wore an ancient mourning suit that was green-tinged and probably on loan from Mr Wilby, the professional mourner. Sly was clutching a packet of Woodbines in one hand, patting Lottie's shoulder with the other, and had the haunted look of a man dying for a smoke. Mum stood on the far side of the grave, supported by Joe and Ruby. Granny had gone to sit on the nearest flat tombstone, setting herself apart and glowering like a grumpy gnome. The cousins from Wapping, who only turned up for weddings and funerals and then, so Mum always said, just for the food and drink, hovered in the background. Rosetta was pleased and touched to see that Big Biddy and Winnie had come to pay their respects, although they had never known Aldo; still, that was the East End for you: when times were bad, folks rallied round.

Father Brennan, having said a few words to Sarah, was coming her way and Rosetta would have liked to make a run for it, but it would hardly be fitting on such a serious occasion.

'You haven't been to Mass for a long time, Rosetta.' Father Brennan's pale eyes seemed to bore straight into her guilty soul. 'Nor to confession.'

'No, Father. I'm sorry.' Rosetta could feel the colour rising to her cheeks at the thought of confessing that she danced on the stage, half-naked by Father Brennan's standards, in front of men and for money.

'Your father was a good man, Rosetta. I hope you know your duty as a good Catholic and a good daughter.'

Snakes of guilt and shame writhed in Rosetta's stomach and she nodded. 'Yes, Father.'

'I will expect to see you at Mass on Sunday.'

As she watched Father Brennan heading towards Lottie, his stern expression melting into a smile, Rosetta couldn't help wondering just how much money Aunt Lottie had put into the poor box to salve her India-rubber conscience. Never one to miss a theatrical cue, Lottie wept into her handkerchief and leaned heavily on Sly so that his skinny knees bowed beneath her weight. Father Brennan passed on quickly and went back into the church.

With the sudden feeling that someone was looking at her, Rosetta turned her head, and met the unwavering stare of a man standing by the church door. Powerfully built, although not much above average in height, he looked like a man used to command, and his expensive clothes contrasted sharply with the shabby garb of the other mourners. His steely blue eyes held Rosetta's gaze as if she were under some hypnotic spell, but she returned his challenging stare with a raised chin, and a slight feeling of unease. Who was he, this man with the sleek but dangerous allure of a black panther? And what possible interest could he have in the funeral of a humble dollmaker?

'You all right, Rose?'

Startled out of her trance-like state, Rosetta turned her head to see Billy standing by her side. She hadn't noticed him in church and she hadn't expected him to come. 'I never thought to see you here, Billy.'

'He were a good bloke,' Billy said, clearing his throat. 'I just come to pay me respects.'

Aware that the stranger was watching them, Rosetta nodded and moved away a little. Billy had made the effort to dress up in his Sunday best, but the eye-stabbing mustard and black check of his suit looked garish and out of place amongst the stark black of the mourning party. 'Good of you to come,' she murmured.

'You all right, Rose?' Billy repeated, shuffling his feet.

'I'm fine. Don't let me keep you from your business.'

'I'll be off then.' Disappointment written all over his face, Billy jammed his brown curly-brimmed bowler on his head.

'You ain't leaving, are you, Billy?' Sarah called across the yawning chasm of the grave. 'You're welcome to come back to number sixteen for a cup of tea and a biscuit.'

Lottie snapped upright, pushing Sly away. 'Never mind the tea. We got sherry-wine and fruit cake in our house. In Italy we know how to do things proper.'

'And we don't?' Sarah's angry voice rose above the wind that ripped through the grave-yard.

'Now you come to mention it, no!' Lottie said, tossing her head. 'You English got no heart, you got no soul and you got no style.'

For a wild moment, Rosetta thought that her mother was going to leap across the grave to grab Lottie by the throat, but Ruby and Joe had her by the arms and they were hanging on for dear life.

'Calm down, Mum,' Joe said, clamping his arm around her shoulders. 'Aunt Lottie is upset. We're all upset.'

'Joe's right,' Ruby added, 'this ain't the time nor the place, Mum.'

'Sock her one, Sal,' shouted Granny Mole from her perch on the tombstone. 'Don't let the Eyetie tart get away with it.'

'Who are you calling a tart, you old witch?' Lottie screamed, shaking her fist at Granny Mole.

Rosetta caught her by the arm. 'Aunt Lottie, no, please. Think of Poppa.'

Sarah broke free from Joe and Ruby and came wading through the grass round the foot of the grave to stand in front of Lottie, arms akimbo. 'Don't you call Ma names. But if it's name calling you want, Carlotta, then I got a few choice ones for you.'

'Ladies, please.' Sly tugged ineffectually at Lottie's coat sleeve.

Joe and Ruby had come hurrying after Sarah but she shot her arms out sideways, holding them back with the agonised expression of a crucified martyr. 'No, I'll have me say here and now with Aldo as me witness. I never wanted none of this papist rubbish. All I wanted was a quiet little sermon to say goodbye to my dead hubby, but no! You had to stick your beak in and have all this vulgar show.' Sarah waved her hand towards the glass-sided hearse and the four black horses pawing the ground as they waited.

'You call me vulgar?' Lottie strained against Sly's grasp, her hands clawing as though she wanted to pull out Sarah's hair strand by strand. 'No Capretti ever been called vulgar. I'll have you know I was the uncrowned queen of the music halls. I counted the Prince of Wales amongst my admirers – I had men falling at my feet.'

'And you'd have been flat on your back ready for them.'

'You take that back.'

'I only speak the truth.'

Breaking free from Sly, Lottie raised her arm as if to slap Sarah but the stranger, who up until this minute had stood silently observing the row, stepped in between them.

'Ladies, if I may have a word.'

'Who in hell's name are you?' demanded Sarah.

'Ma,' Joe said urgently, tugging at her sleeve. 'That's Mr Crowe.'

'You keep out of this, Jonas Crowe.' Lottie's eyes flashed angrily but she lowered her voice. 'Anyway, I wouldn't soil me hands on that woman.'

Rosetta moved closer, brushing Billy's restraining hand from her arm. It was as if some strange power in Jonas Crowe drew her towards him like iron to a magnet.

'A suggestion, ladies and gents,' Jonas said, addressing everyone in general. 'Since the location of the wake seems to be causing some bother, I suggest we all go back to my establishment in Raven Street. I'm sure you ladies would like a little drop of something to keep out the cold and the gents could probably do with something a bit stronger.'

Rosetta held her breath, willing them all to

accept the invitation. Ruby whispered something to Joe, but he shook his head, eyeing Jonas
with a wary expression on his face. Even Billy
was strangely silent, not like his usual cocky self
at all, and Aunt Lottie had calmed down all of a
sudden; it was obvious that she knew Jonas and,
like Joe, was a bit in awe of him. Rosetta shot
Jonas a sideways glance beneath her lashes; he
was speaking to Mum and Lottie, but she knew
instinctively that he was aware of her and a
frisson of excitement pulsed through her veins.

'I says we cut the cackle and go with the geezer
in the flash suit,' Granny Mole said, getting
slowly to her feet. 'I'm freezing cold and bloody
starving.'

'This is family business, Mr Crowe,' Sarah said,
her mouth setting in a stubborn line.

'And I respect that, Mrs Capretti. But you
might say that I'm a family friend and neigh-
bour.' Jonas angled his head towards Lottie.
'Isn't that right, Lottie?'

Whether it was the cold that finally won the
day or the fact that the fight had simply gone out
of both Sarah and Lottie after their battle of
words, somehow Jonas Crowe had his way.
Brushing aside the argument that it was too far to
walk to Raven Street, he sent Joe to summon a
fleet of hackney carriages to transport the entire
party. Despite a lot of pushing and shoving by
the cousins from Wapping, which caused Sarah

to wade in and sort them out with a few terse words, eventually everyone had a seat in a cab except Rosetta, Ruby and Billy.

'We can walk,' Ruby said, through chattering teeth, clutching Rosetta's old shawl tightly around her shoulders.

'I ain't walking all that way,' Rosetta said, loud enough for Jonas to hear. 'I got a performance tonight. Got to keep on me toes, so to speak.'

'No need to walk,' Billy said. 'I can give you both a lift on me cart.'

'I wouldn't hear of it.' Jonas offered his arm to Rosetta. 'You'll ride in comfort in my motor car.'

'That would be lovely.' Rosetta slipped her hand through the crook of his arm, smiling up at him. If only the girls at the Falstaff could see her now.

Jonas turned to Ruby. 'You'll come too, Miss Capretti?'

'I expect Ruby would prefer the cart,' Rosetta said, hoping that Ruby would get the message and go with Billy, who was standing with his fists clenched at his sides and his jaw sticking out as if he would like to punch Jonas on the nose.

'I'll take you, Ruby,' Billy said, scowling.

Ruby smiled apologetically. 'Ta, Billy, but I'd best go with Rose.'

'Suit yourself then.' Billy strode off, hunching his shoulders and stuffing his hands in his pockets.

As if the ride in the motor car was not enough to make her head spin, Rosetta had to bite the inside of her cheek to stop herself from gasping in awe at the grandeur of Jonas Crowe's establishment. Although it was part of the same terrace, situated slap next door to Lottie's rambling, ramshackle house, the exterior had been well maintained and the interior could not have been more of a contrast. A maidservant let them into the entrance hall that was richly decorated in crimson and gold with red Turkey carpet that stretched all the way up the polished mahogany staircase. Jonas switched on the electric lights, bringing gasps of amazement from everyone as they came in through the front door. Rosetta could see that Mum had begun to enjoy herself. It would please her to get one up on the cousins from Wapping, who could barely afford to buy candles let alone gaslight. Cousin Stan, who was a bit barmy anyway, was cowering behind Aunt Lil, squinting at the electric lights as if he expected the archangel Gabriel and a heavenly choir to burst out of the glowing bulbs.

'I never seen nothing like it,' Big Biddy whispered to Rosetta. 'He must be even richer than old Bronski. Play your cards right and you'll be in there, girl. You won't have to stitch another seam.'

'I won't anyway. I'm on the stage now and I

ain't never coming back,' Rosetta said, keeping her eye on Jonas. She didn't like the way he had led Ruby in first, keeping her at his side. He must, she decided, simply have got them muddled up. She tried to edge away, but Big Biddy had her by the arm.

'I don't understand,' Biddy said, closing her fingers round Rosetta's arm in a vice-like grip. 'What are you talking about, Rose? We sees you every day, don't we Winnie?'

Little Winnie nodded.

'Don't talk soft,' Rosetta said, wincing as she prised Biddy's fingers apart. 'I walked out before Christmas and I never come back.'

'But we seen you,' whispered little Winnie. 'I helped you thread your machine when you was poorly and lost your voice.'

'Lost me voice?' The truth dawned as Rosetta glared across the hall at Ruby. She would have words to say to her later, but she wasn't going to admit that she didn't know that Ruby had taken her place. 'That weren't me. I had a better offer so I sent Ruby in me place.'

'Why didn't you tell us?' Biddy's mouth worked as if she was about to burst into tears. 'I thought as how we was mates.'

Winnie shook her head. 'I knew there was something up.'

'No harm done,' Rosetta said, forcing a smile. 'Ruby needed the money more than what I did.'

'You don't know then,' Biddy said, frowning.

'We was robbed,' Winnie whispered, her lips trembling. 'One of them street gangs raided Bronski's and took all our wages. Beat up Mr Bronski something awful.'

Concentrating more on keeping an eye on Jonas and Ruby than on what was being said, Rosetta patted Winnie's shoulder. 'That's too bad. Maybe I can fix you up with complimentary tickets to see me on stage at the Falstaff.' As she hurried off, Rosetta could feel them staring after her. Well, what was she supposed to say? It was too bad they had lost their money, but it served Ruby right for sticking her nose in what didn't concern her.

Jonas and Ruby had gone on ahead, with the rest of the party following them up the staircase and Rosetta had to push and shove to catch up with them. Elbowing one of the Wapping cousins in the ribs, Rosetta managed to get a few steps closer to Jonas.

On the first landing, Jonas flung open double doors that led into a huge room, that smelt faintly of cigar smoke and brandy. Rosetta blinked as at the flick of a switch the room was flooded with light from crystal chandeliers. Wall lights hung with lustres sent prisms of colour dancing on the heavily patterned wallpaper. She had never imagined that such opulence could exist and, judging by the awed silence, neither had the rest of the party. The room was crowded with small tables, covered in green baize, set around with spindly gilt chairs, and at the far end, raised on a dais, stood a grand piano.

Standing next to Lottie, Rosetta tugged at her sleeve. 'What goes on here?'

'It's the gaming room,' Lottie said, raising her eyebrows. 'I won and lost a fortune in here.'

'But ain't that against the law?'

Lottie chucked. 'Of course it is, cara. That's what makes it exciting.'

'Make yourselves at home,' Jonas said, with an expansive wave of his arms. 'Normally I would have entertained you in the ladies' parlour but it's being refurbished as we speak. Refreshments will be brought shortly.'

'This is a bit of all right,' Sarah said, elbowing Lottie out of the way as she led Granny Mole to a table in the centre of the room.

'Where's the food and drink then?' demanded Granny Mole in voice that echoed round the room. 'A drop of gin would go down nicely.'

The cousins from Wapping gathered around a table in the corner, hovering expectantly like vultures round a dying animal. Lottie sailed past them all with her nose in the air and Billy strolled in with Sly, who stopped to light up a Woodbine and then headed for Lottie, who had taken a seat at a table directly opposite Sarah. Big Biddy and Winnie sidled in last and sat by the door, clutching their purses and looking a bit over-awed by the whole thing.

Waiting her chance to get close to Jonas, Rosetta moved towards him, but two maids carrying trays laden with sandwiches and cake distracted his attention. Following them into the room came a young woman who was anything but a servant. With suspiciously blonde curls piled high on her head in the latest fashion, and wearing a low-cut black gown that revealed more voluptuous curves than was modest, she was quite breathtakingly beautiful, and instantly Rosetta hated her. Watching Jonas incline his head to speak to the woman and noting the smile that softened his harsh features only added to Rosetta's yearning to rush over and scratch her eyes out. Startled and confused by the violence of her feelings, Rosetta dragged her gaze away from them and went to join Ruby and Joe, who stood apart from the rest, chatting to Billy. Before she had time to ask them what they were talking about, Jonas had led the woman in black to the grand piano. While she settled on the piano stool and opened her sheet music, Jonas clapped his hands and waited for silence.

'Ladies and gents, can I have your attention, please? It wouldn't be a wake without a bit of music and lovely Lily Lawson, the Shoreditch songbird, will be only too happy to entertain you while you enjoy a bit of light refreshment.' Jonas held his hand out to Lily, who struck up a chord and began to sing.

'Well, what a nerve!' Rosetta said, bristling. 'He might have asked us if we wanted the blooming Shoreditch sparrow to warble.'

'Hush, Rose,' Ruby said, blushing to the roots of her hair. 'Keep your voice down or he'll hear you.'

Rosetta tossed her head. 'I don't care if he does. If anyone was going to sing at Poppa's wake, it should have been me what was asked, not some brassy trollop what none of us knows.'

'Sounds to me like you're jealous,' Joe said, winking. 'But serious like, Rose, don't you go getting no ideas about Jonas Crowe, he's a dangerous bloke.'

'Says who?' demanded Rosetta.

Joe shook his head. 'Believe me, Rose, Jonas is nothing but trouble. He runs a street gang as well as an illegal gambling den. Don't get no funny ideas about him.'

Shrugging her shoulders, Rosetta couldn't help stealing a glance at Jonas as he strode around the room giving orders to the maids and making sure that the drinks were flowing. He strutted with the cocksure manner of a rooster in a farmyard, unselfconscious and arrogant. Entranced, Rosetta could only stand and stare; she jumped when Ruby pinched her arm. 'Ouch! What's that for?'

'To stop you making a fool of yourself,' Ruby whispered. 'He's a bad man, Rose. Listen to what Joe says.'

Billy nodded earnestly. 'Aye, and I second that. Steer clear of Crowe.'

'And you would know, I suppose?' Rosetta turned on him angrily. 'I suppose you and Joe couldn't just be a bit green with envy seeing as how he's so rich and successful and you two . . . well, Joe, you're just a printer's lackey, and Billy's a jumped up rag and bone man.' Rosetta broke off, biting her lip, knowing that she had gone too far this time.

'Rag and bone man!' Billy recoiled as if she had slapped his face.

Ruby nudged her in the ribs. 'Shut up, Rose.'

'No need to be so touchy,' Rosetta said, tossing her head. 'I just meant that Jonas Crowe is . . .'

'Shut *up*, Rose,' Joe said, turning pale. 'He's coming over.'

That night, Rosetta climbed into her narrow bed exhausted by performing on stage after the trauma of Poppa's funeral and the explosion of emotions brought about by her meeting with Jonas Crowe. She had not been able to get him out of her mind and had made so many mistakes in the dance routines that, at one point, Aggie had kicked her on the shins, and Madame had given her a right old telling off in the wings. She had pleaded a headache, but Madame had said that having a bad head didn't affect your feet and if she couldn't do better then she would be out on the street. Even in the darkness of her own room, Rosetta could feel her cheeks burning with shame, remembering how she had burst into tears, claiming that her poor performance was due to Poppa's funeral. Madame Smithsova had calmed down a bit then, but that didn't stop her delivering the lecture about how the show must go on even if your heart was breaking. A true artiste, she had said, would work their emotions into a heartrending performance that would bring the audience to tears. Rosetta had gone back on stage, gloomily anticipating Father Brennan's reaction at her next confession. How many Hail Marys would it take to absolve her from the multiplicity of sins that she had committed, from lying to lustful thoughts about a man she didn't even know?

However hard she tried, she simply could not fall asleep. Every time she closed her eyes she could see Jonas Crowe's face, hear his deep, slightly gruff voice and feel the tingle that had run up and down her spine when he had accidentally brushed against her. He had come over to express his condolences, addressing most of his remarks to Ruby and Joe, but he had been standing next to Rosetta and she had been so acutely aware of his physical presence that she was certain he had meant every word for her ears alone. Ruby had answered him politely, but frosty as a January dawn, and Joe had looked frankly terrified, as though he wanted to escape back to Fetter Lane as fast as his two feet would take him. Billy had acted like a sulky little boy, his usual cocky manner crumbling beneath the force of Crowe's overpowering presence.

Rosetta pulled the coverlet up to her chin, shivering as the temperature in the attic room plummeted now that the last glowing ember in the grate had burnt to ash. She was certain that Jonas had been about to give her his full attention, but Aunt Lottie had chosen that moment to stagger over to the piano with a glass of gin in her hand, announcing that she would come out of retirement to sing one of Aldo's favourite songs. She had knocked back the rest of the gin while Lily searched for the appropriate sheet music. Then, tapping her foot in time to the intro, Lottie had flung back her head, opening her mouth so wide that her face seemed in danger of splitting in two. Then, holding out her arms, she had done a swallow-dive, falling face down on the floor. The cousins from Wapping had whistled and cat-called and Sarah had leapt to her feet shouting abuse that would never have passed her lips if she had not drunk several port and lemons. Granny Mole, fuelled by gin, had jumped to her feet, lifted her skirts and begun to jig up and down like a drunken marionette. Cousin Stan had joined in, shrieking at the top of his voice, and Sarah had slapped him round the face, causing Great-aunt Lil, who was Granny Mole's younger sister who had married beneath her, to rush to his defence. Then the rest of the Wapping cousins had bundled on top of everyone with Big Biddy rolling up her sleeves and wading into the fray.

Rosetta could feel her cheeks burning with shame at the memory. Jonas had, with a click of his fingers, conjured up two giant minions who had knocked the men down like skittles and hefted the scratching, kicking women out of harm's way, one under each arm, dumping them outside the doors without a by your leave. The party had broken up after that. The humiliation and embarrassment were etched in her memory forever, but even stronger was the desire to see Jonas again. With sleep evading her, Rosetta struggled to think of a plausible excuse for calling at the house next door. Perhaps she should apologise for the rowdy behaviour of her family, but she abandoned that idea almost as soon as it formed. She would not demean herself by apologising for something that was not her fault. She could, of course, simply thank Mr Crowe for his hospitality, but that seemed a bit too obvious. What if the Shoreditch songbird should open the door? Did she live there and, if so, what was her relationship to Jonas Crowe? Rosetta felt her eyelids getting heavier and heavier as sleep began to overcome her. Tomorrow she would ask Aunt Lottie. After all, Lottie had vast experience in the world of men.

Next morning, Rosetta went into Aunt Lottie's bedroom carrying her breakfast tray and found her sitting up in bed, smoking a small black cigar and drinking seltzer water.

Lottie eyed her through a haze of cigar smoke. 'Where's Elsie?'

'That kid's worn to the bone,' Rosetta said, placing the tray on a side table. 'You and Uncle Sly work her too hard.'

'Hard work never killed no one and there are plenty more where she come from.' Lottie took a sip of seltzer, closing her eyes. 'Don't bother me now. Can't you see I'm poorly?'

Rosetta perched on the edge of the bed. 'You got a bad head from too much drink, so don't expect no sympathy from me.'

'You're a hard-hearted girl. Don't talk to your auntie like that.'

'You fell down dead drunk in the middle of Poppa's wake.'

Lottie inhaled a lungful of smoke and coughed. 'Did I, cara? I don't remember.'

'Well, you did, and then there was a fight. I'm mortified, Aunt Lottie. What can I do to make amends to Mr Crowe when he was so good to us?'

Lottie's eyes flew open and she stared at Rosetta. 'You keep away from Jonas Crowe, my girl.'

Rosetta shrugged her shoulders, pleating the coverlet between her fingers. 'I dunno what you mean. I was just being polite.'

'Ho, just being polite, were you? You can't bamboozle a bamboozler, Rosa. You got puppy love for Crowe, you better forget it; he's got a woman already. Compared to Lily you're just a bambina.'

'Lily's old,' Rosetta said, pouting. 'She got to be twenty-five at least.'

Lottie's cigar butt hissed and went out as she dropped it into the glass of seltzer water. 'Twenty-five, old!' She threw back her head and laughed. 'All right, Rosetta, seeing you're a lump off the old block, I'll give you some advice.'

'You mean chip.'

'I know what I mean, don't interrupt. You think you can handle Crowe, then you have a go, cara. Test your kitten claws on the big cat and see what you get.'

Undeterred, Rosetta grabbed Lottie's hand. 'Tell me how. What would you do?'

'You serious, Rosetta?'

'Deadly serious. I want him more than I've ever wanted anything in me whole life.'

Chapter Five

'Mr Crowe!' Holding the front door open, Ruby stared in astonishment.

'Miss Capretti.' Jonas tipped his hat.

'Mr Crowe!' Ruby repeated, too shocked to think of anything better to say. He was the last person she had expected to find on the doorstep of number sixteen Tobacco Court. The frosty air was filled with the distant sound of church bells summoning the faithful to Sunday service; above the grey-slate rooftops, fluffy white clouds chased like sheep across a winter-blue sky. For once, Ruby was lost for words.

'You could ask me in,' Jonas said, his lips twitching and a glint of amusement in his eyes.

'Ruby, who's that at the door?'

'Jonas Crowe, Mrs Capretti. Your daughter doesn't seem to want to let me in.'

'Go away.' Ruby lowered her voice, glaring at him. 'You ain't welcome here, Mr Crowe.'

'What are you thinking of?' demanded Sarah, dragging Ruby away from the door. 'Where's your manners, girl? Come in, Mr Crowe. Come in out of the cold.'

Taking off his hat, Jonas stepped inside. 'Good morning, Mrs Capretti. I hope I don't intrude.'

'Who's he?' Granny Mole asked, opening her eyes and squinting at Jonas.

'You'll have to excuse Ma, Mr Crowe,' Sarah said, wiping her hands on her apron. 'Her eyesight ain't too good these days. It's Mr Crowe, Ma. The kind gent what gave the wake for Aldo.'

'Oh, him! Well tell him I had heartburn something chronic after them potted-meat sandwiches. And the gin was watered down, I can always tell.'

'Don't take no notice of her,' Sarah said, with an embarrassed smile. 'You're very welcome, Mr Crowe. Ruby, fetch a chair.'

'Thanks, but I can't stay. I just came to give you this, Mrs Capretti,' Jonas said, taking a leather pouch from his coat pocket and pressing it into Sarah's hands. 'The lads passed a hat round when they heard what happened at Bronski's. We don't like to see a widow woman go short on account of the gangs.'

'We don't want charity,' Ruby cried, incensed by this barefaced lie. 'Give it back, Ma. We can manage.'

Sarah cast her a reproachful glance, shaking her head. 'Don't be ungrateful, Ruby.'

Speechless, Ruby could only glare at Jonas, balling her hands into fists behind her back. He must know that she could not say anything without revealing Joe's part in the robbery. How could he stand there, filling the small room with his presence, handing out conscience money and making himself out to be the hero of the piece, when in fact he was the black-hearted villain?

'I see you're dressed for going out,' Jonas said, meeting Ruby's angry gaze with a wry smile. 'I'd be honoured to give you a lift in my motor car.'

'It ain't far,' Ruby said, putting on her bonnet. 'I can walk, ta.'

'Ruby's going to Mass,' Sarah said. 'She goes every Sunday.'

'Popery.' Granny Mole spat into the fire. 'Don't hold with it.'

'We're Church of England ourselves,' Sarah said hastily. 'But we respect other people's beliefs.'

'I don't,' Granny mumbled. 'Don't hold with any of it, bloody mumbo-jumbo.'

'Ma!' Sarah wrenched the door open, smiling apologetically at Jonas. 'She's getting on a bit and don't know what she's saying, Mr Crowe.'

Jonas smiled. 'I'm sorry to say that I'm of the same opinion as Mrs Mole. I don't pretend to be a religious man.'

'Maybe he ain't so bad at that,' Granny said, looking him up and down. 'And I ain't deaf, Sal. I heard what you said about me.'

Sarah shut the door quickly, leaving Ruby and Jonas standing on the pavement staring at each other.

'So you speak the truth sometimes, then,' Ruby said. 'I dunno how you got the brass to come here, making out like you're doing us a big favour, when you was the one what stole the money in the first place.'

Jonas held up his hands. 'Not me!'

'I ain't simple, Mr Crowe. You was behind it and you got my brother involved in crime. I can't never forgive you for that.'

'D'you want the whole street to know your business?'

Following his gaze, Ruby saw curtains fluttering all along the street and pale faces pressed against the windowpanes, although most of them were gawping at the shiny black motor car parked outside her house. 'Leave us alone,' Ruby said, tossing her head and striding off down the street.

'Let me give you a lift.'

'No!' Ruby marched on, clutching her shawl tightly around her as the east wind whistled round the corner from Spivey Street. She heard the engine purr into action and quickened her pace as the motor car drew alongside her, moving slowly in time with her pace.

'You can get in, or we can go all the way to Raven Street like this,' Jonas said, smiling.

'I'm going to church.' Ruby marched on, head held high.

'You may have fooled your mum, but my guess is you weren't actually going to church.'

'You've got a nerve. Why would you think that?'

'Don't young ladies usually wear a bonnet and gloves when they're off to church, and maybe carry a prayer book?'

Ruby walked a bit faster. 'It ain't none of your business.'

'I think I was right in the first place and that you were on your way to see that charming sister of yours.'

'Go away and leave us alone.'

Driving slowly, Jonas leaned across and opened the passenger door. 'Miss Capretti . . . Ruby . . . we can go all the way to Shoreditch like this if you insist, but you'd be much more comfortable sitting up here beside me.'

Ruby paused, glaring at him. 'What do you want?'

'Maybe I want to right a wrong.' Jonas slammed on the brakes.

Aware that the whole street was watching them and a small crowd was gathering to gape at the unprecedented sight of a motor car in Tobacco Court, Ruby climbed in and sat with her hands folded on her lap, staring straight ahead. 'Why? I wouldn't have thought that was your style.'

Jonas was silent for a moment as he drove into Spivey Street, skilfully manoeuvring the motor into the chaotic crush of horse-drawn vehicles. 'You don't think much of me, do you?'

Ruby stared at his straight profile, confused by the serious note in his voice. 'What do you care?'

Jonas reached under the dashboard and brought out a leather pouch similar to the one that had been stolen from Bronski's. Keeping his eyes focused on the busy road ahead, he dropped the pouch in Ruby's lap. 'I take protection money from greedy buggers like Bronski who make a fortune out of the misery of their workers, but I don't steal the food from the mouths of women and children.'

'But that's just what you done.'

'The lads got it wrong and now I'm giving it back. I want you to see the women get it without old Bronski knowing. Can you do that?'

The money sat heavily in Ruby's lap. If he expected her to be grateful then he was in for a shock. All she could think about was the miserable Christmas that the women from Bronski's had suffered, and it was all his fault.

'Can you?' Jonas repeated.

'I can and I will, but you got to do something for me in return.'

Jonas turned his head, a fleeting look of surprise replaced by genuine amusement. 'You're bargaining with me?'

'I could take this to the police and turn you in.'

'You could, but Bronski wouldn't give evidence against me, Ruby. One thing you need to understand is that the likes of him hate the cops even more than they hate the street gangs.'

'I don't care about that,' Ruby said, not giving an inch. 'I want you to leave Joe out of your dirty deals. Leave him alone.'

'I'd like to oblige.' Jonas honked the horn at a costermonger who was about to push his barrow across the street. 'But Joe's a grown man. I can't stop him if he wants to play the tables.'

'Then I got nothing more to say to you. Set me down here. I'll walk the rest of the way.'

'And get mugged? Not a good idea. Sit tight, Ruby, we're nearly there.'

Barely waiting for the motor car to glide to a standstill, Ruby leapt out onto the pavement, slamming the door behind her. She could hear Jonas chuckling as she bounded up the front steps of Aunt Lottie's house but she did not look back. Seething inwardly and clutching the pouch of money beneath her shawl, Ruby hammered on the doorknocker. Shivering, and with her teeth chattering, Ruby stamped her feet in an effort to keep warm while she waited for someone to answer the door. Jonas strolled up the steps to his own front door and Ruby could hear the jingling of his keys, but he seemed in no hurry to let himself into the house. Although a low brick wall and iron railings separated the entrances to the two houses, Ruby was uncomfortably aware that she could have reached out and touched him. Sensing that he was watching her, she felt her hackles rise and was about to turn on him and tell him to go to hell when Lottie's front door opened.

A small, skinny girl stood in the doorway, staring at Ruby with her mouth hanging open and her pale eyes popping out like a codfish on a slab. 'How d'you do that?'

With one foot over the threshold, Ruby hesitated. 'Pardon?'

White and trembling, as though she had seen a ghost, the girl backed away down the hall. 'You can't be out there. You're upstairs with the missis.'

'No, no, you've got it all wrong,' Ruby said, slipping into the hall and shutting the door behind her. 'I'm Ruby, Rosetta's twin sister.'

'It's magic. Don't put the evil eye on me, miss. I ain't done nothing bad.'

'No,' Ruby said gently, 'you don't understand.' But the more she tried to explain, the more confused and frightened the girl became, and when Rosetta appeared at the top of the stairs demanding to know what all the noise was about, the terrified creature screamed and ran down the passage as though the devil were after her.

'Rose, it's me,' called Ruby, mounting the staircase. 'I scared the wits out of that poor girl.'

'That's Elsie. She ain't got much up top,' Rosetta said, staring hard at Ruby. 'Why'd you come, anyway? Has something happened at home?'

'No, everything's fine. I just wanted a word with Aunt Lottie.'

'You're not going to go on at her for falling down drunk at the wake?'

Ruby giggled in spite of herself. 'No, course not.'

'Then what's it all about?' demanded Rosetta, barring Ruby's way. 'You can't fool me, I know you too well. You wouldn't have walked all this way just for nothing.'

'It's Joe; he's been a bit daft and got himself into debt gambling. Aunt Lottie's been encouraging him and I just want to ask her not to lend him any more money.'

'He ain't in bad trouble?'

'Not yet, but he will be if he don't stop before the gambling fever gets in his blood.'

'There's something you ain't telling me.' Rosetta's mouth drooped at the corners. 'You can't fool me, Ruby. I know there's something up.'

Ruby hooked her arm around Rosetta's shoulders and gave her a hug. She couldn't bring herself to tell Rosetta that Joe had got involved with Jonas Crowe's gang. Rose had always looked up to Joe and the truth would only upset her. 'Joe got into debt but it's all sorted out now. Why don't you go downstairs and set the poor simpleton's mind at rest while I have a quick word with Aunt Lottie?'

'Oh, all right! But I still think you're keeping something from me.'

As Rosetta stomped off down the stairs, Ruby knew by the hunch of her shoulders that she wasn't convinced. She hated keeping anything from Rose, but at this moment it seemed more important to catch Aunt Lottie on her own. Bracing herself, Ruby went into Lottie's room.

'Ruby?' Lottie squinted at her through a haze of cigarillo smoke.

'Yes, it's me.'

'You ought to get yourself some new clothes, cara. You never catch a rich husband looking like a drab.'

Ignoring this remark, Ruby went to sit on a stool by Lottie's chair. 'Are you feeling better?'

Lottie stubbed the cigarillo butt onto a saucer. 'You never come to ask about my health. I ain't a fool, Ruby. I know you got something on your mind.'

'It's Joe. His gambling has got him mixed up with Crowe's gang. He's in trouble, Aunt Lottie.'

'So what d'you want me to do about it?' Lottie poured a generous measure of gin into a glass. 'Joe's a man now; he do what he wants to do.'

Slipping off her shawl, Ruby held up the

pouch, jingling the coins. 'Joe lost heavily at the gaming tables. When he couldn't honour the debt, Crowe forced him to join his gang in the raid on Bronski's. This is the money they took.'

'No, cara, Joe wouldn't do that. He's a good boy.' Lottie swallowed a mouthful of neat gin. 'But even if it's true, what can I do about it?'

'Don't give him no more money for gambling,' Ruby said, hiding the pouch under her shawl. 'And if you can, please pay off Crowe so that he's got no hold on Joe.'

'You got a bag full of money there,' Lottie said, giving Ruby a hard stare. 'Why don't you give that to Joe?'

'It ain't mine. It belongs to the women who worked hard for every penny of it.'

'So how you got it then?'

'Jonas Crowe give it me.'

'You crafty bitch!' Rosetta's voice rose to a shriek.

Ruby had not heard her come into the room and she gave a start, jumping to her feet and clutching the pouch to her bosom. 'Rose, you don't understand.'

Rosetta stormed across the floor, her eyes blazing and two spots of colour reddening her cheeks. 'I understand all right. Anyone could see that you set your cap at Jonas Crowe at the wake and today you turned up here riding in his motor car.'

'No, Rose, you got it all wrong.'

'Don't tell lies. Uncle Sly saw you getting out of Jonas's motor.'

'He give me a lift, that's all.'

'That's enough!' Lottie rapped on the floor with her ebony cane.

'She lied,' Rosetta said, pointing a shaking finger at Ruby. 'You said you walked all the way from Whitechapel.'

'I never did. You took it for granted that I walked here. I never told you that Crowe give me a lift because I knew you'd take it the wrong way.'

'And why would he give you a bag of money? What did you do to earn that?'

'The money is for the women at Bronski's what was robbed of their wages by Crowe's gang. Your friends, Rose, or have you forgotten them already?'

Rosetta blushed and bit her lip. 'Oh! Well, why would he give it you, then?'

'To give back to them, of course.'

'And why would he steal it in the first place if he intended to give it back?'

'It's a long story, Rose.' Ruby bit her lip, not wanting to tell Rosetta the whole truth.

'You must have made up some story to make him do that, but I tell you you're wasting your time. It's me he's interested in, not you,' Rosetta said, with a sulky shrug of her shoulders, and then her face brightened. 'You're still wearing my shawl. I'll bet he mistook you for me.'

Taking off the shawl, Ruby tossed it at Rosetta. 'Here, take your old shawl, but steer clear of Jonas. He's no good, Rose.'

'You're just jealous,' Rosetta said, clutching the shawl. 'Go away and leave me alone.'

'Stop this, both of you,' Lottie said, heaving herself to her feet. 'Give it back, Rose. You can't send her out in this weather without a shawl.'

'I'll fetch your rotten old shawl, but you keep away from Jonas. He's mine! I saw him first.' Rosetta ran from the room and her footsteps echoed on the bare boards as she raced up to her attic room.

'Better go, cara,' Lottie said, sinking back into her chair and reaching for the gin bottle. 'She'll get over it.'

Ruby made her way slowly downstairs. Facing the cold without a shawl was preferable to listening to Rosetta's hysterical ranting. Once Rose got an idea into her head, it was almost impossible to shift it. Mum always said you'd have to stick her neck on the block on Tower Green and chop her head off to change anything once Rosetta had made up her mind. As she rounded the bend in the staircase, Ruby could hear voices in the hall below. Leaning over the banisters, she saw Sly and Billy standing in the hall, chatting.

Billy looked up and saw her. 'Rosetta?' Then, as she came nearer, he grinned apologetically. 'No, it's Ruby, ain't it?'

'That's right, it's me.'

'Is your rich feller taking you home then, Ruby?' Sly asked, winking and tapping the side of his nose.

Before Ruby could answer, Rosetta came flying down the stairs clutching the old grey shawl. She came to a halt when she saw Billy. 'Oh, it's you, Noakes.'

Billy dragged his cap off. 'You ain't forgotten that you promised to step out with me today, Rosetta?'

Rosetta tossed the shawl at Ruby. 'Here, this is your one. Ta for the loan but I don't need it now, as you can see.' Placing her hands on her hips, Rosetta twirled around to show off her new dress.

'You look good enough to eat,' Billy said, licking his lips.

Rosetta frowned at him, pouting. 'Don't be vulgar. And I ain't in the mood to walk out with you. Anyway, it's freezing cold and I got to look after me voice. I got a solo in the second half tomorrow.'

Sly winked at Ruby. 'I got work to do,' he said, heading for the back stairs. 'Bye, Ruby.'

'I'd best be off too.' Ruby wrapped her shawl around her shoulders, suppressing a shudder as the matted wool scratched through the thin cotton of her blouse.

Billy pulled his cap on. 'So you don't want to come with me then, Rosetta?'

'I said so, didn't I?' Rosetta turned on her heel and started back up the stairs.

'In that case,' Billy said loudly, aiming his words at Rosetta, 'I'm going Whitechapel way, Ruby. Course I can't compete with a flash motor car, but if you ain't too grand to accept a ride on me cart, you're welcome.'

Rosetta stopped, turning her head to give Billy a searing glance. 'See if I care, Billy Noakes.'

'Ta, Billy, I wouldn't say no.' Following him out into the street, Ruby accepted a hand up onto the cart.

Billy threw the horse blanket over her knees and leapt into the driver's seat, flicking the reins. 'Straight home then, Ruby?'

Ruby thought quickly; she could hardly take a bag full of money into the house without Mum demanding to know everything. The first person that came to mind was Big Biddy. 'I got to take something to Rope Yard. Any chance you might be going that way?'

'Right ho,' Billy said cheerfully. 'Rope Yard it is and no questions asked, but it ain't the sort of place a young lady like you ought to go on her own.'

*

Rope Yard was, as Billy had said, a deprived area, so poverty-stricken and rough that it made Spivey Street look almost respectable. Tucking the horsewhip in his belt, Billy left his cart in Cable Street, giving a boy a halfpenny to mind the horse for ten minutes, with the promise of another when they returned. Ruby was glad to have a big fellow like Billy at her side as they walked through Rope Alley, a narrow passage between warehouses that opened into the twilight world of Rope Yard. The tenements were near derelict, one of the last remaining rookeries that had scarred the East End for a century or more, where the dregs of society huddled, sometimes twenty or more to a room, living more like sewer rats than human beings.

'Gawd, what a hellhole.' Billy linked his arm through Ruby's. 'Are you sure this is the right place, Ruby?'

Ruby nodded, unable to speak as the stench of raw sewage and rotting rubbish made her want to retch.

Barefoot children, with stick-like arms and legs poking out of their tattered clothes, hung about the doorways, staring at them like feral cats, ready to scratch and spit or to snatch a purse, a fob watch or anything that had the smallest street value.

'Here, you!' Billy beckoned to a girl who could not have been more than six or seven but was carrying a baby in her arms and had a toddler clinging to her ragged skirt. 'Come here.' Billy held up a penny.

The girl sidled over to them, her gaze fixed on the coin.

Ruby shuddered at the sight of the weeping sores that scarred the otherwise pretty face. This was poverty and neglect at its ugliest and her heart contracted with pity as well as anger at a society that could let the innocent suffer in this way. Billy squeezed her arm and Ruby's anger turned to fear as she saw the boys, grouped into a hunting pack, edging towards them. 'For Gawd's sake tell them who you're looking for,' Billy urged, snatching the horsewhip from his belt and wielding it over his head. The boys backed away, snarling, predatory and yet afraid.

'Big Biddy,' Ruby said, smiling at the girl, who stared back without a flicker of expression. 'Where can I find her?'

'Top floor.' The girl snatched the penny and ran into the building with amazing speed considering she was hefting a baby and dragging the smaller child by the hand. Some of the boys went to follow her but Billy cracked the whip and they slunk off into the shadows.

The interior of the tenement was even worse than the exterior. The air was foul and the bare floorboards were littered with rubbish, excrement from both humans and animals, and running with cockroaches. As they climbed the stairs Ruby could hear the scrabbling of rats and mice behind the skirting boards. The building echoed with the sound of wailing babies and adults shouting at each other in a confusion of different languages. It was, Ruby thought, hell on earth and something should be done about it.

They found Big Biddy's rooms on the top floor. When she got over her surprise at seeing Ruby, Biddy invited them in, apologising all the while for the state of the place. Shaken by what she had just seen, Ruby was deeply touched to see how much effort Biddy had put into making the room habitable. Although the floorboards were bare of any covering, not even a rag rug or a piece of drugget, they had been scrubbed bone white. The only furniture was a table and two chairs that had been roughly hammered together using old timber and orange crates and, in one corner, stood an iron bedstead where a man lay on a palliasse covered with one, thin blanket. Even though the temperature outside was close to freezing, there was no fire or evidence that there had been one for many days.

'Biddy!' A feeble voice called out from the bed. 'It's me husband, Mickey,' Biddy whispered. 'He's been bedridden since the accident.' She hurried over to him and held his hand. 'We got visitors, love. It's Ruby from work, and a gentleman friend, no need to get upset.'

'Perhaps we should leave,' Ruby said, casting an anxious glance at Billy.

Biddy tucked Mickey in with the tenderness she might have shown to a small child and dropped a kiss on his forehead. 'He'll be all right now.' She turned to Ruby with a tired smile. 'Don't go. It is nice of you to come visiting, Ruby. But where's me manners? Sit down both of you. Anyway, it makes my Mickey nervous to see people hovering.'

Billy went to sit down but the chair creaked so loudly beneath his weight that he jumped up again and moved to stand by the door.

Ruby perched cautiously on the edge of the chair. 'What's wrong with him?'

Biddy shook her head, sighing. 'Got crushed by falling barrels when he was working the docks. Can't move a muscle now; can't never work again neither. I'd like to do the same to them villains what stole our wages. I got six nippers to feed as well as taking care of Mickey. We've been reduced to begging from the Sally Army soup kitchen these past few days.'

Ruby brought the pouch from beneath her shawl. 'I got good news for you this time.'

Biddy's eyes widened in astonishment. 'Well I never! How did you come by that?'

'Mr Crowe had a whip-round in his club and they come up with the money. Now we got to get it back to the women at Bronski's. I can't take it home and I was wondering if I could leave it with you?'

'I wouldn't dare carry this much money about on me person,' Biddy said, shaking her head. 'Not that I ain't grateful for it, but as you can see, Ruby, we're in a poor way, what with one thing and another.'

'Ruby can't do it neither,' Billy said from the doorway. 'Them kids down below would tear her to shreds for a farthing.'

'Ta, Billy, but I can speak for myself. I would do it, Biddy, but I dunno where the rest of them lives.'

Mickey called out something that Ruby could not understand, but Biddy did and she threw him a grateful smile. 'Ta, love. You always comes up with good sense. Mickey says let our three eldest lads do it. They can slip out of the yard and no one would take a blind bit of notice.'

Ruby was not convinced. 'But won't they get beat up by the other kids?'

Biddy swelled with pride. 'Not my lads! They can stand up for theirselves. Leave it with me, Ruby, and bless you for getting the money back.'

Once outside the building, Ruby clutched Billy's arm, hanging on to him for dear life until they reached Cable Street. She breathed a sigh of relief when she saw his horse and cart waiting where they had left it, with the skinny little boy hunched up under the horse blanket on the driver's seat. Billy pressed a couple of coins into his hand and the child raced off, his legs going like the pistons in a steam engine.

'You all right, Ruby?' Billy asked, his face full of concern as he helped her up onto the cart. 'You look a bit pale.'

'I never knew people had to live like that,' Ruby said, shivering and shaking her head. 'We been through hard times and that's a fact, but we never starved.'

Climbing up beside her Billy picked up the reins. 'At least you done them a good turn and they'll all have full bellies tonight. You can't do no more, girl.'

Ruby said nothing as the cart moved off along Cable Street. Huddled beneath the horse blanket, she was deep in her own thoughts when they turned into Spivey Street and encountered a scene that was like arriving at the gates of hell. Smoke and flames were pouring out of the baker's shop on the corner. Men had already formed a chain with buckets of water from the pump, and women and children were running up and down the street screaming and shouting for help. A man staggered out of the burning building, his face blackened and his clothes badly singed, exposing the scorched flesh on his chest and forearms.

Shoving the reins in Ruby's hands Billy leapt

off the cart and grabbed the man by the shoulders. 'Is anyone left inside?'

The man's dazed look turned into one of anguish. 'Me wife and child. Oh, God, I got to get back in there.'

Hearing screams from an upper window, Ruby looked up and saw a woman and child hanging out, their faces contorted in terror. She leapt off the cart and grabbed Billy by the arm. 'Billy, look up there.'

'Take care of him.' Leaving Ruby to cope with the injured man, Billy raced across the road and charged into the building. Bits of masonry and burning wood were hailing down on the street below and thick, acrid smoke belched out of the broken windows, making it difficult to breathe.

'Billy, be careful,' Ruby screamed, but her voice was lost in the general noise and confusion.

'It's me wife and Lizzie.' The man pointed a shaking finger up at the window. 'I got to get them out.' He made a move to follow Billy, but he stumbled, doubling up and clutching his chest. His face paled, beads of perspiration stood out on his forehead and his eyes bulged from his head as he gasped for breath. Half dragging, half pulling him, Ruby managed to get him onto the cart. She loosened the necktie round his throat and undid the top buttons of his shirt; all the while she kept glancing up at the first floor window and the desperate woman and child screaming for help.

She tried to comfort the man but he seemed to be losing consciousness. A crowd had gathered in the street and there was a sudden roar of approval. Looking up, Ruby saw Billy pull the woman from the window and, lifting the child beneath one arm, he dragged them back into the billowing smoke. More men had appeared on the scene and a couple of them, with their jackets over their heads, charged into the burning bakery. Seconds later they emerged, sooty as chimney sweeps, coughing and gasping for air as they helped Billy with the unconscious woman and child. A loud cheer went up, echoing down Spivey Street, and the clanging of a bell made everyone scatter as the fire engine arrived.

They laid the woman in the cart beside her husband and child.

'You done well, mate,' one man said, slapping Billy on the shoulder.

'The bloke looks like a goner,' the other said, shaking his head.

'We'll get them to the hospital.' Ruby glanced anxiously at Billy, who was struggling to get his breath. 'Are you all right, Billy?'

Billy nodded, but it was obvious to Ruby that his hands and arms were badly burned and he was in no condition to drive the cart.

'C'mon, mate, let the little lady take you to the hospital.'

The men hefted Billy onto the passenger seat and Ruby leapt up beside him, picking up the reins.

'Can you drive a cart?' Billy gasped, his words punctuated with bouts of coughing.

'I dunno,' Ruby said, flicking the reins, 'but I'll have a bloody good try.'

Luckily, the horse did not seem to need much guidance, plodding along at his own pace and obeying the slightest tug on the reins when Ruby wanted him to change direction. Although he didn't complain, Billy was obviously in no state to help, and Ruby kept glancing over her shoulder to check on the casualties, praying that they would reach the hospital in time. The baker lay as though he were dead but the woman moved a bit, moaning every now and then, and fighting for each painful lungful of air. The little girl was deathly pale and barely breathing; Ruby urged the horse to a trot, shouting at pedestrians to get out of the way. Billy was slumped forward, slipping in and out of consciousness and, in a desperate effort to make the animal go faster, Ruby seized the whip, cracking it above the old horse's head. The wind had whipped her hair into a mass of curls, tumbling it about her shoulders and half blinding her as strands blew into her eyes. She was standing in the footwell, encouraging the horse to one last spurt of speed, as they turned into Whitechapel Road. She could have cried with relief as the arched portico of the London Hospital came into sight. Drawing in the reins, Ruby drew the cart to a halt outside its doors, and, leaping to the ground, she ran inside to get help.

Chapter Six

As she barged through the glassed doors into the main reception area, it seemed to Ruby that the world of pain and chaos outside had no place within these hallowed walls. The marble floors, high ceilings and polished mahogany, combined with the strong smell of disinfectant and a cathedral-like hush, enforced a sudden calm on her spirit. Nurses in grey uniforms with starched white caps and aprons moved quietly amongst the patients and visitors like well-mannered doves. A woman wearing sisters' uniform appeared in front of Ruby and began questioning her. Soothed and reassured by her air of authority, Ruby told her what had happened. The sister listened intently and then acted, setting things in motion, without so much as raising her voice. Within seconds, nurses and porters carrying stretchers were sent outside to bring in the injured.

This is where I want to be, Ruby thought, dazed but impressed, as she stood aside watching their expert handling of the casualties. There was no sense of panic, everyone seemed to know exactly what to do and Ruby felt her heart swell with admiration for the nurses. She knew now that she could never be happy until she was a part of this well-ordered, clinical world.

'See me old nag safe,' Billy murmured, as a nurse pushing a bath chair wheeled him past Ruby.

'I will,' Ruby said. 'Don't worry, I'll do it straight away.'

Outside the hospital, the raw reality of the East End hit Ruby like a slap in the face. Although she was used to it, the noise of the streets was suddenly quite deafening. The rumbling cartwheels, the clopping of horses' hooves, the cries of the costermongers and the endless marching of feet on stone pavements made her want to clap her hands over her ears to shut it out. Her knees were shaking and her hands trembling as she led the horse to a side street. She stroked his nose and he whickered as if in sympathy, rubbing his head against her shoulder. Leaving him tethered to a lamp post and munching from his nosebag, Ruby hurried back to the hospital.

There was nothing left for her to do now except pace the floor and watch the hands on the large, brass clock on the wall above the almoner's office tick away the seconds, minutes and eventually the hours. Fuming at the enforced inactivity, Ruby had nothing to do except to watch the nurses going about their duties. One nurse in particular caught her attention, a fresh-faced young woman with a pleasant smile, who came to escort patients to the treatment rooms. She went about her work as though she enjoyed every minute of it, offering words of encouragement to the sick people and comforting their anxious friends and relatives. Torn between admiration and envy, Ruby felt her ambition crystallise into a hard nugget deep inside her. The policy of all hospitals might be to take only middle-class young ladies with good educational backgrounds but it was time all that changed. She would make them accept her, or die in the attempt.

'Are you all right, miss?'

Ruby spun around to look into the smiling face of the young nurse. 'Yes, ta for asking.'

'You've been waiting for such a long time. How about a nice cup of tea?'

'I dunno . . .' Ruby shot an anxious glance at the stern-faced sister.

'Of course you would. Don't mind old fish-face; you come with me.'

Suppressing a giggle, Ruby followed her to a side room filled with steam from a spirit kettle.

'Sit down, before you fall down,' said the nurse cheerfully, as she made a pot of tea. 'We're not supposed to do this, but you look as though you could do with a little sustenance.' Adding two teaspoonfuls of sugar, she passed the mug to Ruby. 'My name is Pam, Pamela Chadwick, and you are?'

'Ruby Capretti.'

'Well, Ruby, you sit here and drink your tea and I'll go and find out what's happened to your people.'

'Oh, they ain't mine,' Ruby said, gulping down a mouthful of hot tea. 'I mean, Billy's a friend, but I don't know the others. We was just on hand at the right moment.'

'Then well done you! I mean, your prompt action probably saved their lives.'

Ruby felt the blood rush to her cheeks. 'Oh, I dunno about that.'

'Nurse Chadwick!' A voice echoed down the corridor.

'Coming, Sister.' Pulling a face, Pamela opened the door. 'I have to go or I'll be in trouble. Stay and finish your tea, Ruby, but don't let old fish-face see you.'

Ruby swallowed the tea as quickly as she could and then she tidied everything away so that Pamela would not get into trouble. Making sure no one saw her, she made her way back to the vestibule and took a seat next to a fat woman who had nodded off to sleep and was snoring with grunts and whistles. After waiting for what seemed like eternity, Ruby felt like stuffing a cork in the woman's mouth and was about to go

outside for a breath of fresh air when Pamela
returned with Billy. He was smiling but he
looked deathly pale and his hands and forearms
were swathed in bandages.

Ruby jumped to her feet. 'Billy, are you all
right?'

'Well, I ain't going to go ten rounds with the
champ,' Billy said, attempting a laugh and
ending up with a rasping cough. 'But they fixed
me up good, so I can't complain.'

'He's had a dose of laudanum for the pain,'
Pamela whispered. 'He'll be a bit dicky for a
while.'

'How is the baker?' Ruby asked anxiously. 'He
looked really bad.'

'He'll survive, but it may take a while for him
to get well again.'

'And his wife and the little girl?'

Pamela smiled. 'They'll be fine, thanks to you
and Mr Noakes.'

'I'm fine too,' Billy said, grinning stupidly and
hooking his arm around Ruby's shoulder. 'Let's
go to the pub. I'm parched and I really fancy a
pint.'

'Yes,' Ruby said, humouring him. 'We'll do
that, Billy, but first we ought to take your poor
old horse home.'

'He's a good chap, is my old horse. Best friend
I got.'

Pamela laid a hand on Billy's shoulder. 'You'll

need to get your doctor to change the dressings regularly, Mr Noakes.'

'If I can't work, love, I can't afford to pay the sawbones.'

'I know,' Pamela said, her smile fading. 'If I had my way all medical treatment would be free.'

'Maybe I could do it?' Ruby felt herself blushing. 'I mean, I'm sure I could, if you was to show me how. I've always wanted to be a nurse, just like you.'

'I'm sure you'd make a wonderful nurse, Ruby. Come back this time tomorrow and I'll show you how to change the bandages and put on a dressing. There's really nothing to it.'

'Nurse Chadwick, stop chattering and get back to work.' Sister's voice echoed off the high ceiling.

Pamela gave a guilty start. 'See you tomorrow then,' she whispered as she hurried off.

'There now.' Billy nudged Ruby in the ribs. 'Nurse Capretti.'

'Never mind that now,' Ruby said, leading him to the exit and holding the door open. 'Let's get you home.'

Stepping outside, Billy stopped, staring around with a dazed expression. 'Me cart's gone.'

'It's all right, Billy. It's just round the corner.'

Billy stared at his bandaged hands. 'Bugger it! I can't do nothing with me hands all trussed up like a Christmas turkey. I suppose I'll have to ask you to drive me home, Ruby.'

Billy's home turned out to be a loft above a stable that was situated next to a coal yard, close to the railway lines. Having unhitched the horse and settled him in his stall and, ignoring Billy's protests that he could manage on his own, Ruby took the key from him and ran up the wooden steps to unlock the door. Hesitating on the threshold, she peered into the gloomy interior. The room was clean but sparsely furnished with a narrow bed, a table, two chairs and a chest of drawers; the only source of light was a small roof window and that was coated with grime and bird droppings. Stumbling past her, Billy fumbled with a box of matches but the bandages made him clumsy and he spilt them all over the tabletop. He swore loudly and Ruby hurried over to help him.

'You're helpless as a baby,' she said, lighting the paraffin lamp. 'You oughtn't be here on your own, Billy.'

'Ta, but I'll be all right,' Billy said, sitting down suddenly as the drugging effect of the laudanum began to wear off. 'A good night's kip is all I need and tomorrow I'll be back to me old self again.'

'I don't see no food,' Ruby said, glancing around the room. 'You ought to eat something.'

'I ain't hungry. If I get peckish I can always go down the pie and eel shop.'

'Don't be so stubborn, Billy. Give us the money and I'll go down the pie shop for you.' Fixing him with a stern stare, Ruby held out her hand.

'Maybe I could manage some pie and mash. There's some money in the top drawer of the chest.' Billy waved his bandaged hand in the vague direction of the chest of drawers.

Ruby found the coins and was counting out the pennies when she dropped one and it rolled under the wooden pallet that served as Billy's bed. Getting down on her hands and knees, she lifted the coverlet and ran her hand over the bare boards. As she found the coin her fingers touched something soft wrapped in material. It was too dark to see but Ruby's experienced hands recognised the texture of a wax doll. Reaching beneath the bed, Ruby pulled out one doll after another. Jumping to her feet, she faced Billy, waving a doll by the leg.

'So you never sold them to the wholesalers!'

'You wasn't meant to find them.'

'But you gave Mum the cash for the dolls. You said they was sold to the warehouse.'

'Ruby, don't go on. I done it for the best. Your old man was sick and I knew that pious old sod of a priest wouldn't pay up.'

Ruby gasped in horror. 'Don't talk about Father Brennan like that. You'll end up in purgatory.'

Billy threw back his head and laughed. 'Get on

with you. You don't believe all that religious cant.'

'What I believe don't count,' Ruby said, laying the dolls out on the coverlet and smoothing their crumpled dresses. 'But I thank you for what you done and I'll pay you back somehow or other. You're a good man, Billy.'

'Leave it out, girl. I owed Aldo a favour. I'll sell them on and probably make meself a tidy profit. There's only one person what matters to me and that's Billy Noakes.'

'You never gave yourself a thought when you run into that burning building, so don't give me that.'

'Anyone would have done the same. You get on home, Ruby. I'm going to be just fine on me own.'

'I'm going, but not until I've seen you fed.' Ruby slipped the money into her pocket. 'I'm off down the pie shop but I'll be quick as I can. You sit there and don't move.'

'Yes, nurse,' Billy said, with a mock salute.

When Ruby returned to work after the funeral, the women at Bronski's had been a bit cool after they discovered that she had tricked them into thinking she was Rosetta. Big Biddy and little Winnie had stuck up for her, but Ruby got the feeling that she had broken their unwritten code of comradeship, and that the others were more hurt than angry. If she could have found another job quickly, she would not have gone back to Bronski's, but with Poppa barely cold in his grave, there was no alternative. On the morning after the fire Ruby went to work, determined to get off early so that she could visit Billy and make sure he was all right. The fire and Billy's injuries had put the business of returning the stolen money out of her head; Ruby was quite unprepared for the welcome she received and the heartfelt gratitude of the women, that was largely delivered in pats on the back, winks and whispers. All the same, she couldn't help wondering how they would all react if they knew that their benefactor was the person who had ordered the robbery in the first place. But she wouldn't think of that now. She had to find a way to get off work early and having confided in Big Biddy, Ruby realised for the first time the power of collective action. At a given moment, Ruby pretended to faint and the women did the rest. They buzzed around her like worker bees around the queen, giving Vinegar Lil no opportunity to examine her, and countering her protests that one faint did not merit being sick enough to go home with a tirade of angry catcalls. Within minutes, Big Biddy had hefted Ruby up on her shoulder and carried her outside into the alley.

'There now, you get off and see to Billy. We'll

sort out Lil and Bronski too, if it comes to it.'

'Ta, Biddy. You're a sport.'

Ruby ran all the way to Billy's place and found him lying on the bed, still fully clothed, flushed and feverish. For a moment she was seized with panic, uncertain what to do next. Billy groaned and opened his eyes but there was no recognition in them, just the fog of high fever. Knowing instinctively that she must get the fever down, Ruby seized the jug from the chest and went down into the yard to fetch water from the pump. The horse neighed at her from his stable, but she told him he must wait. She would see to him later.

After stripping Billy of the charred remnants of his shirt, Ruby bathed him and put a cold compress on his forehead. When he seemed to be quieter, she took what was left of the money in the drawer and ran down the street to the nearest chemist to buy quinine and a pennyworth of laudanum. Back in Billy's room, she dosed him with quinine mixed with a little water and gave him enough laudanum to ensure that he slept while she went to the hospital.

Ruby was relieved to find that Pamela was on duty in the vestibule, collecting patients and taking them to the treatment rooms, just as she had been on the previous day. As soon as she had a free moment, Pamela took Ruby to a treatment room and gave her gauze, lint and bandages and some salve to put on Billy's burns, with instructions on how to cut away the soiled dressings and a quick demonstration of how to bandage a hand.

'Can you remember all that, Ruby?' she asked, making a parcel of the dressings.

'I think so. I'll have a go, but I'm a bit worried about him.'

'I get off duty at eight o'clock. If you meet me outside the hospital you can take me to Billy's house and I'll have a look at him, although he really should be seen by a doctor.'

'I'd be ever so grateful.'

'Then that's settled.' Pamela handed Ruby the parcel of dressings. 'Put that under your shawl so that old fish-face doesn't see you taking anything out of the hospital. The way that woman carries on you'd think it all came out of her wages.'

'I can pay for the bandages.'

'Never mind that, you get back to Billy and I'll see you later.'

As she changed the dressings on Billy's hands, Ruby tried to remember all Pamela's instructions. He was still too feverish and drugged with laudanum to understand what she was saying, but Ruby kept up a one-sided stream of conversation while she worked, realising that the mere sound of her voice had a quietening effect upon him. Once or twice he called her Rosetta and she did not correct him. When she was done, she made him as comfortable as possible, lighting the paraffin lamp on the table before she left for home and telling him that she would be back soon and not to worry. There was no way of knowing whether or not he had understood and Ruby worried about him all the way to Tobacco Court.

'Where the hell have you been?' demanded Sarah. 'And don't tell me you was at work because that Vinegar Lil come round checking up on you.'

'Oh, no!' Ruby pressed her hands to her cold cheeks. 'That's put the kibosh on it.'

'Well, it would have if I hadn't been too quick for the old cow,' Sarah said, puffing out her chest. 'Now if it was Rosetta what had gone missing I wouldn't have been surprised, but when you miss an afternoon's work then I know there's something up, so I told Vinegar Lil that you was sick in bed.'

Granny Mole, sitting by the fire snoozing, opened one eye. 'You'll never go to heaven, Sal.'

'Maybe not, but it sorted that woman out good and proper. So come on, Ruby, out with it or there's no supper for you, my girl.'

Slipping off her shawl, Ruby moved closer to the fire. Her hands were numbed with cold and began to tingle painfully as she held them close to the flames; she couldn't even feel her feet. A pan of vegetable soup simmered on the hob and her stomach growled with hunger. There was nothing for it: she would have to tell Mum everything.

Ruby began by admitting that she had not gone to Mass on Sunday, explaining that Jonas Crowe had offered to take her in his motor car to visit Rosetta. She ended by telling them of Billy's heroic actions in the fire and of the injuries he had suffered.

'Well I never! The poor man!' Sarah said, ladling soup into a bowl. 'You oughtn't to have left him on his own. Ain't he got no one to care for him?'

Granny Mole choked on her soup. 'Don't you bring him here. I ain't giving up my bed for no one.'

'No one's asking you to, Ma. But all the same, I don't like to think of the poor bloke sick and all on his ownsome. He done us a good turn selling them dolls so close to Christmas.'

'Bah! I expect he made a bob or two for hisself. He's a chancer is Billy Noakes.'

'That ain't fair, Granny,' Ruby said, frowning. 'Billy's all right, he is.'

Sarah shot her a curious look. 'So what is he to you, Miss? It's Rosetta he's sweet on.'

'I know that, Mum, but we owe Billy. I found the dolls that he said the warehouse took under

138

his bed. It was his own money what he give us at Christmas.'

'Well, I never did! And you say he's sick with no one to look after him?'

'No one. He's living in a stable loft, with no heat and not even a cold tap in his room. His horse is stabled better than what he is.'

'Then that settles it. You got to get him here one way or another. It's cold enough for snow and he'll catch lung fever if he ain't looked after.'

'I said he can't have my bed,' repeated Granny Mole. 'I need me sleep.'

'No one's asking you to give up your bed, Ma. I'll move in with Ruby and Billy can have my bed just until he's well enough to go home.'

Ruby stood outside the London Hospital stamping her feet and shivering as lacy white snowflakes fell from a black velvet sky. Every time the doors opened she peered through the swirling snow looking for Pamela, only to be disappointed. Finally, when she had almost given up hope, Ruby saw Pamela come out of the hospital followed closely by a tall young man. They were laughing at some shared joke and Ruby could tell by the way Pamela angled her head to look up at him that he was someone special to her. Embarrassed and thinking that she must have been forgotten, Ruby was about to walk away when Pamela called out to her and came hurrying over, dragging the young man by the hand.

'Ruby, Ruby, it's me. Do stop.'

Ruby hesitated, suddenly very conscious of her bedraggled appearance.

'Ruby, I want you to meet my friend, Adam Fairfax,' Pamela said, tucking her hand through his arm with a proprietorial gesture. 'Adam, this is Ruby Capretti.'

'How do you do, Miss Capretti?' Adam doffed his hat and bowed. In the soft glow of the gaslight, snowflakes glistened like a halo on his guinea-gold hair.

Ruby swallowed hard and bobbed a curtsey. 'Pleased to meet you, Sir.'

'No, please, Miss Capretti. My friends call me Adam.'

His expensive clothes and manner of speaking set him apart as a gentleman, but Adam's charming smile made Ruby feel quite dizzy and her heart turned a somersault inside her chest. She barely heard what Pamela was saying.

'Adam is a doctor and he'll be happy to take a look at Billy's hands.'

'Hold on, Pam,' Adam said chuckling. 'I'm not a doctor yet. I've another year to go before I qualify.'

'Don't be such a tease.' Pamela tossed her head, pouting. 'You promised you'd help.'

'And I will, of course. I'd be happy to take a

look at your friend's injuries, Ruby, if you agree.'

Ruby nodded, shivering and staring mutely into his eyes that appeared to be the deepest chocolate brown, that is until he smiled, when they danced with golden glints.

'My dear girl, you're frozen stiff,' Adam said, his voice full of concern. 'And you're soaked to the skin. I'll call a cab.' Shrugging off his black cashmere overcoat, he wrapped it around Ruby and strode off into Whitechapel Road to hail a cab.

Ruby huddled into the folds of his coat that was still warm from his body. The satin lining touched her cheek like a soft caress and she closed her eyes, inhaling the scent of bay rum and freshly washed linen. No man had ever shown her such consideration and she had never before met anyone remotely like Adam Fairfax; he was a golden, god-like young man, socially out of her class and undoubtedly in love with Pamela. But her heart was beating a tattoo inside her chest and she felt weak at the knees; if this was love then it was a dangerous and impossible passion. Adam was utterly wonderful and completely unattainable.

'He's such a dear,' Pamela said happily. 'And Adam is a wonderful doctor. You mustn't worry about Billy. We'll have him up and well in no time.'

*

They found Billy as Ruby had left him, feverish and barely conscious. Having checked the dressings on Billy's hands and congratulated Ruby on her efforts, Adam gave him a thorough examination. When he had done, he folded his stethoscope and put it back in his pocket, looking thoughtful.

'Is he worse?' Ruby couldn't keep quiet a moment longer. 'He is worse, I know it.'

Adam shook his head. 'Billy must have inhaled a lot of smoke when he went into the burning building, which has affected his lungs, quite apart from the burns on his hands. He has a fever and I'm afraid it might turn to pneumonia. He needs proper care.'

'We can help you with medicine and dressings, can't we Adam?' Pamela cast him a pleading look. 'Can't we?'

Adam shook his head. 'He really ought to be in hospital.'

'Mum said I was to bring him home,' Ruby said quickly. Hospital treatment cost money; there were paupers' wards but they were grim places and she didn't fancy Billy's chances in one of them. 'I got medical books. I can take care of him.'

Adam stared at her thoughtfully and a slow smile lit his eyes. 'Ruby, I believe you could do anything you put your mind to, but this man is really sick. I don't think you realise just what an undertaking it would be.'

'I only know he ain't going into the hospital,'

Ruby said, standing her ground. 'Not in one of them paupers' beds.'

Pamela laid her hand on Ruby's shoulder. 'You must care an awful lot for Billy.'

'He done us a good turn and round here we pay our debts,' Ruby said, tossing her head. 'He comes home with me or I stays here and that's that.'

'I see there's no arguing with you when your mind's made up, Ruby,' Adam said, his frown melting into a boyish grin. 'The cabby will help me get Billy into the hackney. It was lucky that I told him to wait.'

Having settled Billy in Sarah's bed, Ruby sat with him throughout the first night, putting cold compresses on his brow and watching anxiously while he lapsed in and out of a fevered state, sometimes raving and at other times in a deep sleep induced by generous doses of laudanum. She did not go to work the next day and it was only when Sarah forcibly ejected her from Billy's bedside that she went to her own room and snatched a few hours' sleep. Firm footsteps coming up the stairs and the deep tones of a man's voice awakened her with a start. Half awake, Ruby thought at first that she was dreaming but she could still hear the voices and her eyes were wide open. Tumbling out of bed, she opened her bedroom door and came face to face with Adam.

'I'm sorry, Ruby. I didn't mean to disturb you.'

Realising that her hair hung loose about her shoulders and that her blouse and skirt were creased and crumpled, Ruby felt the blood rush to her cheeks. 'You didn't. I mean, it's very good of you to come.'

'Don't keep the doctor talking, Ruby,' Sarah shouted up the stairs. 'I've put the kettle on. I'm sure the young man could do with a nice hot cup of tea.'

'I could murder a cup of tea.' Granny's voice rose to a plaintive wail.

Ruby looked aghast at Adam and saw that his lips were twitching and his eyes were full of laughter. Suddenly she was giggling too and the feeling of embarrassment had gone.

'Let's have a look at the patient, shall we, Nurse?' Adam said, holding the door open to allow her to pass.

Ruby watched as Adam examined Billy, her admiration for him growing minute by minute. He was so cool and so professional, so capable and so thorough. No wonder Pamela adored him. Thinking of Pamela brought Ruby back to earth with a bump. Adam was spoken for, that was quite obvious, and she must be mad to let her thoughts run away with her.

Packing his instruments back in the black leather Gladstone bag, Adam stood up. 'You've done a good job, Ruby. His fever is down and he's making good progress.'

'He's not going to die?'

Adam shook his head, smiling. 'Not for a very long time. He's young and he's strong and it would take more than a lungful of smoke and some third degree burns to finish off this man. But I'll come again tomorrow.'

Adam came the next day and the next. When he arrived on the third day, Billy was downstairs in the living room, fully dressed and standing in the middle of the floor, arguing with Ruby. 'Don't think I ain't grateful to you, Ruby, nor you, Mrs Capretti, but I got to get back to my place and see to my horse.'

'I been every day,' Ruby protested. 'I fed and watered him like you showed me and he's fine. You can't look after yourself, Billy. Not with your hands still bandaged like one of them Egyptian mummies.'

'You'll get lung fever again if you goes back to that cold stable loft with no proper food,' Sarah said, turning to Adam. 'You tell him, Doctor.'

Adam shook his head. 'If Billy feels he's fit enough to go home, then we must leave it up to him. But you'll need to have your dressings changed every day, Billy.'

'That's all right, doc. Ruby will do it, won't you, love?'

'Of course,' Ruby said, fighting a bitter disappointment that Adam would no longer have

145

an excuse to call at the house. 'Of course I will.'

'She's a good nurse,' Billy said, hooking his arm around Ruby's shoulders. 'She's wasted working at old Bronski's sweatshop.'

'I doubt if I've got a job now.' Seeing the dismayed expression on all their faces, Ruby regretted the words the moment she had spoken them.

Adam's smooth brow crinkled in a frown. 'Ruby, I had no idea that you might lose your job. I could have made different arrangements if I'd known.'

'Young man, do we look as how we can afford a private nurse?' demanded Sarah.

Adam flashed her his most charming smile. 'I'm sure I could have persuaded one of the probationers to help out now and again.'

'Pity you never thought of that before,' Granny Mole said. 'Any more tea in the pot, Sal?'

Adam shrugged on his elegant cashmere coat. 'Billy is right about one thing, Ruby. You'd make a fine nurse.'

'Oh, I dunno about that,' Ruby said, crossing her fingers behind her back, praying that Mum wouldn't put in her tuppence-worth about the impossibility of a girl from Tobacco Court being accepted as a probationer nurse.

'If you change your mind just let me know and I'll speak to Matron. I'm sure she'd be delighted to give you an interview.'

Later that evening, when Mum and Granny Mole had gone to bed, Ruby sat by the glowing embers of the fire, thinking about what Adam had said. Although cold hard common sense kept telling her that it was impossible, a stubborn voice in her head urged her not to give up so easily. Poppa had always said that if you wanted something badly enough you had to fight for it and tomorrow she would begin that fight. Ruby yawned and stretched. She was tired after several disturbed nights tending to Billy and not even Granny Mole's snoring would keep her awake tonight. She was just about to turn off the gaslight when someone pounded on the doorknocker. No one called at this time of night, not unless there was a death in the family or a dire emergency affecting one of the neighbours. Ruby ran to the door and opened it just a crack.

'Ruby, let me in.'

'Joe?'

Unceremoniously, Joe pushed the door open and slipped inside, closing it behind him. 'Thank God you're up. I thought you'd all be asleep.'

'Joe, what's wrong?'

'You got to help me, Ruby. I'm in terrible trouble.'

Chapter Seven

Rosetta stood in the entrance hall of Jonas Crowe's premises clutching two complimentary tickets for the Falstaff in her gloved hand.

'What d'you want then?' The hall boy's freckled face puckered in a suspicious scowl, like a small bulldog.

Rosetta glared back. 'What's your name?'

'What's it to you?'

'You're rude, you are, and I'm going to tell Mr Crowe on you.'

'I'm Tucker, so who are you?'

'Well then, Tucker, tell Mr Crowe that Miss Capretti would like a word.'

'He's busy and he don't have time for your sort.'

'You'd best tell him I'm here,' Rosetta said, raising her hand. 'Unless you want a clip round the ear, you cheeky little sod.'

Tucker backed away towards the staircase. 'Ho, yes. I'll tell him a real lady wants to see him, shall I?' He raced up the stairs before Rosetta could carry out her threat.

He seemed to have been gone for ages and

Rosetta paced the tiled floor, pausing to examine her reflection in the gilt-framed wall mirror. Patting a stray curl back into place beneath the new fur hat perched on top of her curls, she adjusted the spotted veil so that it covered her eyes. Turning her head this way and that, Rosetta tried to decide which look was the most mysterious and alluring. She had spent all her wages on the hat and the short jacket with leg-of-mutton sleeves. She smiled at her reflection in the mirror, well satisfied. The end result was worth all the pain, hard work and ritual humiliation handed out by Madame. Rigorous days of rehearsal and late nights dancing and singing in the smoky music hall had not yet taken their toll of her looks, as they had with some of the girls. Jonas, she thought, would not be much of a man if he could resist her. Never mind the silly misunderstanding when he had mixed her up with Ruby. After all, Ruby was a dear, but sensible and serious, too much of a bluestocking to appeal to a man like Jonas Crowe.

'He'll see you now.' Tucker ambled down the stairs, jerking his head in the direction of the gaming room.

'Ta for nothing.' Rosetta swept past him, making her way up the stairs with as much dignity as she could muster. Tucker had left the door ajar and, pretending that she was going out on stage to do her solo, Rosetta waltzed into the room, but there was no thunder of applause from an appreciative audience. Jonas sat at the roulette table with a ledger open in front of him, a cigar clenched between his teeth. He did not look up.

'Ahem.' Rosetta cleared her throat.

'Take a seat, Miss Capretti. I'll be with you in a moment.'

This was not the greeting that Rosetta had wanted or expected. Here she was, looking simply stunning, and he could not even be bothered to raise his head to look at her. She marched over to the table and waited, tapping her foot on the floor. 'I call it rude to ignore a lady what's come to pay a call on you.'

Jonas did look up this time. He took the cigar from his mouth and his lips curved into an amused smile. 'Miss Capretti.'

'And it's common courtesy to stand up when a lady comes into the room.' Rosetta was furious now, angered more by his amusement than by his rudeness. 'I come to thank you for what you done for my poppa and to give you complimentary tickets for the show at the Falstaff. I wish I hadn't bloody bothered now.'

Rising to his feet, Jonas pulled out a chair. 'I don't get too many young ladies visiting my club, so you'll have to forgive my lack of courtesy, Miss Capretti.'

Rosetta shot him a suspicious look; it was hard to tell if he was laughing at her or whether this was a genuine apology. His expression was serious now, but there was a definite gleam in his eyes, like the glint of polished steel. She sat down. 'Well, I am a lady and I expects to be treated as such.'

'I'm glad we've got that straight.' Jonas perched on the edge of the roulette table, folding his arms across his chest. 'So, what brings a young lady to this house of ill repute?'

'You're laughing at me again.' Rosetta slapped the tickets down on the table in front of him. 'I come to give you tickets for the next show but I can see I was wasting me time.'

'It's Rosetta, isn't it?' Jonas picked up the tickets and slipped them into his breast pocket. 'I appreciate the generous gesture. Thank you for the tickets.'

Rosetta met his gaze and held it. 'I got a solo singing spot and it won't be too long afore I'm top of the bill.'

'You're ambitious; I like that.'

'I might be open to offers,' Rosetta said, angling her head. 'I can sing just as well as the Shoreditch songbird – better, in fact – and I'm years younger.'

Jonas threw back his head and laughed.

'That's it! I never come here to be laughed at.'

'So why did you come? To repay my

hospitality or to convince me of your great talent?'

Out-manoeuvred, humiliated and furious, Rosetta hissed at him like an angry cat. 'You wouldn't recognise talent, not if it jumped up and bit you on your bum.' She flounced out of the room and ran down the stairs, almost colliding with Tucker.

'Turned you down, did he?'

'Mind your own bloody business,' Rosetta said, wrenching the front door open and slamming it behind her.

'So what's got you in such a state?' Tilly sat in front of the dressing mirror, putting the finishing touches to her stage make-up.

'I ain't in a state.' Rosetta jabbed paper flowers into her piled-up hair.

'It's got to be a bloke,' Tilly said, grinning. 'Is it that Billy?'

'Billy! Don't make me laugh. I ain't seen him for a couple of weeks and I don't care if I never sets eyes on him again.'

'All right, I was only asking.'

Rosetta jumped up from the stool and smoothed down the frills of her costume. 'Get a move on, Tilly, or we'll miss our cue.'

Dabbing her face with a powder puff, Tilly got to her feet. 'He must be a bit of all right to get you in such a state.'

'Shut up, Tilly.' Rosetta pushed past Aggie who had obviously been listening and had opened her mouth to make a comment. 'And you can shut up too!' Rosetta slammed out of the dressing room and made her way to the wings.

Halfway through the opening number, Rosetta almost missed her step when she saw Jonas sitting in the box nearest the stage. Next to him was Lily, looking palely beautiful in a pink silk evening dress. Jonas turned to Lily, smiling and making a remark that brought the colour flooding to her cheeks, and Rosetta's moment of triumph dissolved into one of jealous rage. If she could have leapt across the limes and scratched Lily's eyes out, she would have done it and not felt a twinge of remorse. With her temper well and truly roused, Rosetta put every last bit of effort into her performance, so that even Madame congratulated her as she tripped off the stage.

Buoyed up with fury and drunk with anger, Rosetta upstaged everyone in the chorus during the second half of the show. Her solo brought roars of approval from the audience and dire looks from her fellow performers, even Tilly.

'Don't know what you think you're playing at!' Aggie hissed as they danced off stage having taken the final curtain after several encores and applause that shook the building. 'You may think you're the bleeding star but you're not. I hope Madame rips your ears off, you selfish bitch.'

'They loved me. You're just jealous.' Rosetta made her way to the dressing room, swallowing down tears that threatened to choke her.

The call boy met her in the doorway, carrying a huge bouquet of red roses. 'You got a rich admirer, Rose.'

'They must have cost a bob or two,' Tilly said, peering over Rosetta's shoulder. 'There's a card with them. Read it, Rose. Tell us who your mystery bloke is.'

Rosetta's fingers trembled as she opened the card. *Crowe*. No message, just the one word.

'Who's the mystery man then?' demanded Aggie. 'No, don't tell us, we can guess. It must be the Prince of Wales hisself.'

Everyone laughed and Rosetta felt her cheeks burning. How dare Jonas put her in such a position, especially when he had brought that woman with him. She tossed the bouquet into a wastepaper basket. 'Bleeding royals,' she said, determined to have the last word and put Aggie in her place by stealing the laughter. 'Always pestering me, but I says, "No, Prince, leave us alone, there's a good bloke." And then he sends me red roses! Well, did you ever!'

Stealing back to the dressing room after everyone had left, Rosetta picked up the bouquet and was about to leave when Madame burst into the room followed by Alf Ricketts, the theatre manager.

'There!' Madame said, turning to Alf. 'I tell you that Rosetta is a true professional. She no leave the theatre like it was on fire like the rest of the girls; she stays on and think about her next performance. Maybe do a little rehearsal on her own.'

'No need to pile it on, Smithy,' Alf said, dismissing her with a wave of his hand. 'I got the point. Now you can leave the details to me and Miss er . . .'

'Capretti,' Rosetta said, smiling. 'Rosetta Capretti, Mr Ricketts.'

'Well then, Rosetta, I saw you upstage the whole damn chorus tonight, and while I don't approve of such goings on I can see you've got talent, and what's more you've got push, girlie.'

'She could be a star, given the proper training,' Madame said, puffing out her chest.

'Yeah, yeah,' Alf said, taking a silk hanky from his breast pocket and mopping his brow. 'You said your piece, Smithy. Ain't you got a home to go to?'

'Are you all right, Mr Ricketts?' Rosetta cast an anxious glance at Madame. 'Should we send for a doctor, Madame?'

'It's just a touch of dyspepsia,' Alf said, belching. 'And you ain't making it any better,

Smithy, standing there looking daggers at me. You done your bit. Now sling your hook.'

'Well!' Madame made gobbling noises like a turkey in Smithfield Market. 'No one speak to Madame Smithsova like that.' She flounced out of the dressing room, slamming the door behind her.

'It ain't fair to tease her, Mr Ricketts,' Rosetta said, frowning. 'She's done a lot for me.'

'Never mind old Clara Smith,' Alf said, running his finger down Rosetta's bare arm. 'You and me got a little business to do, dearie.'

Now they were quite alone and Rosetta felt sick and suddenly quite scared. She tried to back away but Alf slid his arm around her waist and pulled her towards him. His breath stank of beer and onions and he was sweating profusely. 'I think I should go home, Mr Ricketts,' she said, using the bouquet to fend him off. 'It's getting late.'

Tightening his grip round her waist, Alf fingered one of the rosebuds, teasing the petals apart and allowing his finger to stray from the bloom to trace the swell of Rosetta's left breast. 'There's nothing to worry about, girlie; Alf wants to take care of you, that's all. Be nice to me, ducks, and next week you might get second or third billing, depending on how good you are, if you get my meaning.'

Rosetta did get his meaning; she stamped on his foot and hit him over the head with the roses, leaving him hopping up and down on one leg in a shower of red petals. Storming out of the dressing room, Rosetta left the theatre by the stage door and strode down Old Street, too angry to feel the cold or to be scared of walking home alone. If any man tried to assault her at this moment in time, Rosetta would have scratched his eyes out and enjoyed it.

She arrived back in Raven Street cold, tired and still fuming with outrage. Lights blazed from all the windows of Crowe's establishment. The front door opened and closed as a constant stream of shadowy figures came and went, vanishing into the night. In contrast, Lottie's house was in darkness except for a light from her upstairs sitting room. Rosetta let herself into the hall, ignoring lewd remarks from a couple of drunken men lurching down the steps of Crowe's place. She closed the door, leaning against it as her knees threatened to give way beneath her. It had been a horrible day and an even worse night. Jonas was a cruel beast who obviously enjoyed making a fool of her and Alf was a dirty old man. They wouldn't have dared to treat her like this if Poppa had been alive. He would have sorted them out good and proper. Tears welled up in her eyes, running unchecked down her cheeks as she remembered Poppa's loving kindness; he had called her his little canary and, no matter what she had done, she had always been able to go to him for help. If only Ruby were here. Rosetta rubbed her hand across her eyes, sniffing; she had only herself to blame for the rift with Ruby. She shouldn't have gone for Ruby like that just because Jonas had given her a lift in his motor car, and she hadn't meant those nasty things that had come tumbling out of her mouth. Why did she always let her sharp tongue run away with her? Choking back a sob, Rosetta ran up the stairs and burst into Lottie's room. The air was thick with a fug of cigarillo smoke and gin fumes.

Lottie gave her a bleary smile. 'How was the show tonight, cara?'

Slowly unbuttoning her jacket, Rosetta bit her lip, afraid that if she tried to speak she would burst into a fresh bout of tears.

Lottie reached for her drink, eyeing her shrewdly. 'Not good, eh?'

Tossing her jacket and hat onto the nearest chair, Rosetta flung herself onto the stool at Lottie's feet. 'It was horrible. I hate all men.'

'Take your time, Rosetta, and tell me all about it.' Sipping her drink and smoking, Lottie listened to Rosetta's impassioned account of the day's events, nodding her head but without making any comment. She laughed out loud when Rosetta told her how she had stamped on Alf's foot and walloped him with the bouquet of roses.

'It's not funny, Aunt Lottie,' Rosetta said, with a catch in her voice. 'He insulted me.'

Lottie tossed the butt of the cigarillo into the fire. 'You would be more insulted if he had said you were untalented and ugly.'

'What?' Rosetta stared at Lottie in amazement. 'You think I should be flattered?'

'There are ways, Rosetta, of dealing with men like Alfredo.'

Rosetta's head was spinning; the airless room was making her feel sick and faint. 'I don't understand.'

'You are such a child. You got to grow up a bit if you want to get on in this world. It's a hard place; take it from someone who knows.' Lottie refilled her own glass with gin and poured another for Rosetta, handing it to her. 'Have a drink, cara. Calm your nerves and listen to me.'

Rosetta sipped the neat gin, choked and pulled a face. She could feel the spirit burning her throat and making its fiery way down to her stomach. 'I ain't going back, not ever.'

'So what you going to do, then? You no work, you don't get no money. How you going to live?'

Rosetta took a mouthful of gin; this time it went straight to her head and she felt pleasantly muzzy. 'There are other music halls. I'll get another job.'

'Once Alfredo puts the word about, you don't

get no work in the East End and they won't look at you up West, take it from me. You want to end up back at Bronski's, you're going the right way about it.'

Shaking her head, Rosetta stared into her empty glass but her eyes wouldn't focus properly and she could see two glasses instead of one. Everything was so confusing. 'What shall I do?'

Lottie lit another cigarillo, blowing smoke rings over Rosetta's head. 'You go back to the theatre and you be nice to Alfredo.'

'Never.'

'Or you go back to Crowe and sweet-talk him into letting you sing. I hear that Lily is not always well and sometimes cannot perform. If Crowe sent you the roses then he got an interest in you, Rosetta, or at the very least it shows he's sorry for the way he treated you. Take advantage of it; go and see him again. Use your charms. You got to learn how to flirt and make men fall in love with you.'

'I wouldn't flirt with Jonas Crowe if he was the last man alive. He laughed at me. I hate him.'

Lottie's mouth curved in a wry smile. 'One thing you got to realise is that deep down all men are the same. You play them like a musical instrument. You give a little and then you stop. Tease them until you get your own way. How far you go depends on how far you want to get. Do you understand?'

Focusing with difficulty, Rosetta shook her head. 'I'm not a tart, I'm a good girl.'

'Of course you're a good girl, but bad girls get more furs and jewels and a lot more fun. You're like me, Rosetta. You want everything out of life and you want it now. You ain't going to sit around and wait for some dull, respectable young man to come and make an honest woman of you.'

'It's true, but I ain't going to end up on the streets neither.'

Lottie threw back her head and laughed. 'Course you ain't, not with Carlotta Capretti to tell you what to do. I been there, cara. I had more lovers than you got curls on your pretty head. I'd be a rich woman now if I hadn't had the little weakness for gambling.'

'But you didn't have to be nice to men like Alf Ricketts. I can't do it. And anyway, I'd probably end up in the family way.'

'Have another drop of tiddley,' Lottie said, slopping gin into Rosetta's glass. 'There are ways of not getting a baby and I can see it's time I give you the benefit of my experience.'

Shocked but fascinated, Rosetta tried to imagine Lottie as being young and desirable, and failed. 'But surely it was God's will that you never had children.'

Lottie choked on her gin. 'You been listening too much to that Father Brennan. He's a man and a priest, so what does he know?'

Rosetta gulped and crossed herself. 'You shouldn't say things like that. You'll go to hell.'

'Don't worry, Rosetta, the devil and me are old friends.' Exhaling smoke from her nostrils, Lottie lay back in her chair, her eyes half closed. 'My family back in Italy married me off when I was sixteen. At seventeen I had a baby.'

'You had a baby?'

'A boy, Gianni. My little Gianni.'

'But what happened to him?'

'I don't know. I was young, Rosetta, too young to be a wife and mother. I ran away to join a touring dance troupe.'

'You left your husband and baby?'

'And I never saw them again. When Aldo decided to come to England, I come too. The rest is history, but by that time I had learnt how to make men fall in love with me, and more important, how not to have more babies. Now you listen to me, Rosetta, and I pass this knowledge on to you. Then you make your own choice, cara.'

Standing outside Alf Rickett's office, Rosetta took a deep breath and knocked on the door. She had spent a sleepless night listening to the drunken revellers stumbling along the corridor outside her room and the street noises that went on into the early hours. She had lain awake struggling with her conscience. If she followed Aunt Lottie's shocking advice she would be going against her strict upbringing, and there was little difference between the edicts of Mum and Father Brennan when it came to morals. On the other hand, if she behaved like a good girl, she would end up back in Bronski's sweatshop working alongside Ruby, sharing the same bed as her sister and falling asleep to the sound of Granny Mole's snoring.

'Come in.'

Alf's voice jarred Rosetta back to the present. She straightened her fur hat, pulled the veil down a little farther over her eyes, bit her lips to make them red, and went into the office.

Alf sat behind a desk littered with playbills and papers. His expression darkened as he looked up and saw Rosetta standing in front of him. 'You've got a nerve.'

Rosetta forced her lips into a smile. 'Mr Ricketts, I dunno what come over me last night. I come to apologise for my behaviour.'

Alf's jaw went slack and his mouth hung open like a toad catching flies. He swallowed hard and his Adam's apple bobbed up and down above his starched collar. 'Well, now. Well, now!'

Seeing him at a loss for words, Rosetta perched on the edge of his desk with what she hoped was a seductive smile. 'I was a bit embarrassed, you see, Mr Ricketts. You got me all of a dither and I didn't know what to say. I may have been a bit hasty.'

Alf leaned back in his chair, squinting at her through narrowed eyes. 'Give me one good reason why I should take you back.'

'One, I got talent, and two, I can be very grateful, if you know what I mean.'

Alf's eyes nearly popped out of his head. He ran his finger round the inside of his collar. 'How grateful, girlie?'

Fighting panic and the desire to run away, Rosetta shot him a glance beneath lowered lashes. 'That depends on you, Alfie.'

Twenty minutes later, Rosetta left the office, flushed, breathless and triumphant. She stopped for a moment to button up her blouse; it wasn't so bad really, not if you kept things under control and only let the old goat go so far and no farther. She had been so nervous at first that she had been sure he could hear her heart hammering inside her chest, but then she had realised that Aunt Lottie had been right: once you got a man's interest, the rest was easy, as long as you kept control of the situation. She had left him greedy for more and the feeling of power was more intoxicating than gin.

'So you came back!'

Madame Smithsova's voice behind her made Rosetta jump and spin round. 'And why not?'

'Don't act all innocent with me, girl. It's all over the theatre what you did to old Ricketts.' Madame's granite features crumpled into a smile. 'Good for you. It's time someone put him in his place.'

'And I got third billing next week,' Rosetta said, unable to keep it to herself any longer.

Madame's smile widened into a grin that almost split her face in two. 'I knew you had it in you the first time I set eyes on you. You got talent, Rosetta, and you got brass.'

'What's happened to your voice, Madame?' Rosetta stared at her, realising suddenly that Madame's strong Russian accent had given way to pure cockney.

'You heard old Alfie. I'm Clara Smith from Plaistow.'

'So why pretend to be Russian?'

Madame shrugged her shoulders. 'Russian ballerinas were all the rage when I danced at the Paris Opera. Plain Clara Smith wouldn't have gone down too well in the theatre, so I became Clarissa Smithsova. I had brass too, in the old days, but now I got to turn great lumps of horseflesh into dancers. Beauty fades with age, remember that, Rosetta. Grab what you can while you're young.'

'I intend to,' Rosetta said, turning to go.

'And where d'you think you're going?'

Rosetta hesitated. 'Going home to learn me new act.'

'Oh no you don't!' Madame caught her by the shoulders, propelling Rosetta towards the rehearsal room. 'You got to work twice as hard now if you want to be a pro. You're going to dance until your feet bleed and practise your scales until you croak like a frog. Success don't come easy; you got to work for it and fight for it. Understand?'

At the end of the day, Rosetta limped out of the theatre, footsore and hoarse. Madame had worked her like an overseer on a sugar plantation; the only thing she lacked was a whip, although her sharp tongue could lash and hurt much the same. Rosetta was beginning to think that allowing Alf to fondle and squeeze her titties was the easy part of clawing her way to the top.

It was raining and large puddles had pooled on the pavements, gleaming like mirrors in the glow of the gaslights. If only she had thought to borrow an umbrella. Rosetta's sigh turned into a muffled scream as a man leapt out from a doorway and clapped his hand over her mouth.

'It's me, Rose. Don't scream.'

'Joe!'

'I didn't mean to frighten you.'

Joe's face was pale in the gaslight and his eyes lost in dark shadows, but Rosetta was too angry to feel sympathetic. Shaking all over, she punched him on the shoulder. 'You stupid bugger, you scared me half to death.'

Joe hooked his arm over her shoulders. 'Rose, I'm in trouble; I need money or I'm a dead man.'

'Oh, Joe! What have you done?'

'Nothing wrong, I swear it. I owe some money, that's all. Can you loan me some? I'll pay you back, honest.'

Rosetta shivered as the rain soaked through her jacket, running in icy rivulets down her neck and between her breasts. 'I'm stony-broke. I ain't even got the money for a cab.'

Joe struck his forehead with his hand. 'You're my last hope.'

Rosetta's knees buckled as he leaned his full weight on her and it was all she could do to hold him up. 'Let's get you home. You're soaked to the skin. When did you last eat?'

'Dunno,' Joe said, laughing weakly. 'Food ain't exactly my uppermost consideration at the moment, Rose.'

Somehow, with many stops on the way, Rosetta managed to get Joe back to Raven Street. Refusing to go in through the front door, Joe dragged her down the area steps, insisting that they go in through the servants' entrance.

Elsie was alone in the kitchen, stirring a pan of

stew on the range. She goggled at them, clutching the wooden spoon like a dagger. 'He's not allowed in here,' she cried, pointing the spoon at Joe. 'Mr Sly said he's not allowed.'

'It'll be all right,' Rosetta said, stripping off her wet coat and hat.

'She's right,' Joe said, backing towards the door. 'I don't want to cause you no trouble.'

'Take those wet things off and sit down,' Rosetta said firmly. 'I'll settle things with Uncle Sly.'

Reluctantly, Joe did as he was told and Rosetta hung their damp clothes over a clothes horse by the fire to dry. She set Elsie to cut bread while she ladled out a bowl of stew, placing it in front of Joe with strict instructions to shut up and eat.

Elsie scuttled about like a frightened crab, eyeing Joe warily and tugging at Rosetta's sleeve, repeating over and over again that Mr Silas wouldn't like it. When Silas came through the kitchen door, Elsie shot off into the scullery, howling.

'What's the matter with the daft cow?' Silas stopped, staring at Joe and frowning. 'And what are you doing here, boy? Didn't I tell you to make yourself scarce?'

Joe mumbled something with his mouth full of bread.

'You can't stay here,' Silas said, fumbling in his pocket and bringing out a packet of Woodbines.

'You know what Lottie said last time you got yourself in a fix.'

'I don't understand,' Rosetta said, staring from one to the other. 'What's going on?'

Silas lit a cigarette and inhaled deeply. 'You tell her, mate. Tell her how you fell foul of the Crowe gang and now they want your guts.'

'It's true, Rose. I lost me job and I've been living rough, scared out of me wits for fear of the gang. If I can't pay Crowe then I'm a dead man.'

'No, I don't believe it,' Rosetta said, shaking her head. 'Jonas ain't like that. You got to speak to him, tell him how you're fixed.'

'Like he'd listen!' Silas spat the words. 'No one messes with Crowe. Best thing you can do, son, is get as far away from here as you can and don't stop running.'

'It's too late,' Joe said, holding his head in his hands. 'I done a terrible thing.'

Rosetta threw herself down on her knees beside him, tugging his hands from his face. 'What have you done? Tell me, Joe.'

'I'm a poor apology for a man, Rose. I was too cowardly to go meself so I sent Ruby.'

Rosetta shook him, hard. 'Sent Ruby where?'

Joe stared at her, white-faced, with tears springing from his eyes. 'Crowe,' he whispered. 'I sent Ruby to beg Crowe to let me off. I got me own sister involved with the Raven Street gang. God knows what that bastard will do to her.'

Chapter Eight

'Oh, it's you again!' Tucker leaned against the doorpost, blocking the doorway.

Guessing that he had mistaken her for Rosetta, Ruby didn't bother to argue. She was not in a mood to exchange words with a cheeky boy and she pushed past him, heading for the staircase.

'Here, you can't do that.'

'Just try and stop me.' Ruby marched upstairs to the gaming room with Tucker following her, protesting loudly. The gaming room was empty. She stormed out onto the landing, looking up and down the dark corridors, wondering where Jonas had his private rooms – always assuming he slept in a bed like a normal human being. Ruby had visions of him climbing into a coffin at dawn like the vampires in penny dreadfuls.

Tucker barred her way. 'You got to go, miss, or I'll be in for it when he gets back.'

Ruby spun round and glared at him; she'd dealt with the Spivey Street kids often enough to know that you had to stand up to bullies. 'What's your name, boy?'

'Tucker, miss, but . . .'

'When is Mr Jonas due back, Tucker?'

Tucker's freckled face lost its belligerent scowl and a look of uncertainty spread across his face, giving him the appearance of a confused hobgoblin. 'I dunno, and anyway, it ain't none of your business.'

Before Ruby could put him in his place, a door opened at the far end of the corridor. 'Tucker, is that you?'

'Now you've been and gone and done it,' Tucker said, scowling.

'What is all the noise?' Lily Lawson came towards them, looking like a wraith in a white silk wrap, with her pale blonde hair hanging loose around her shoulders. She stopped when she saw Ruby. 'It's Miss Capretti, isn't it?'

'Ruby Capretti.'

Lily shivered and pulled her wrap closer about her body. 'Come to my sitting room. It's warmer there and we can talk.'

'But Miss Lily,' Tucker said anxiously. 'You're supposed to be resting.'

Lily turned to him with a smile. 'It's all right, Tucker. Be a good chap and fetch us some tea and toast, will you, please?'

Ruby saw Tucker's pug face transformed by a look of adoration. Nodding wordlessly, he ambled back down the stairs.

'He's not a bad boy,' Lily said, leading the way. 'You just have to know how to handle him.'

Lily's apartment was at the far end of a long corridor and her sitting room, in contrast to the rest of the house, was bright, warm and distinctly feminine. Ruby stared around her, drinking in the sheer luxury of blue-velvet curtains that exactly matched the upholstery on buttoned chairs and an elegant chaise longue. The walls were covered in floral wallpaper and hung with gilt-framed paintings of country scenes and still lifes depicting flowers and fruit. Ruby felt her feet sinking into the thick pile of a Chinese carpet; she could never have imagined that anyone, other than Queen Victoria herself, lived in such fine surroundings.

She came back to reality with a start as Lily sank down onto the chaise longue, racked by a fit of coughing. Covering her mouth with a white linen handkerchief, she motioned Ruby to take a seat. 'I – I'm sorry,' Lily gasped, in between spasms. 'It's this silly inflammation of the lungs. I suffer it every winter.'

'Are you all right?' Ruby asked anxiously as Lily hastily crumpled up the bloodstained hanky and stuffed it behind a cushion.

'I'll be fine in a minute.' Lily reached for a medicine bottle that stood on a side table and spooned some into her mouth. She collapsed against the cushions, her breathing ragged and her face deathly pale.

'You ought to see a doctor,' Ruby said,

frowning. Coughing up blood was serious and the most likely diagnosis was consumption; she knew that without having to refer to her medical books.

'I have, my dear,' Lily said, with a wan smile. 'He says I should get away from smoky old London and live in Switzerland or the south of France. But that's enough about me, tell me about yourself, Ruby. What brings you here today?'

Ruby had no intention of burdening Lily with the truth and she was about to make an excuse to leave when the door opened and Tucker came in carrying a tray of tea, followed by Jonas.

Jonas stared hard at Ruby and his expression relaxed just a fraction. 'A second visit from the Capretti sisters. I'm honoured.'

'You needn't be,' Ruby replied, jumping to her feet. 'It ain't a social call, Mr Crowe.'

'No? You surprise me!'

Lily raised herself on one elbow. 'Jonas, what's going on?'

'Nothing to bother your head about, Lily. Go back to bed and rest or you'll not be fit to entertain the punters tonight.'

'But Jonas . . .'

'Good God, woman. Do I have to carry you to your bed?'

'Oh, Jonas, don't fuss,' Lily said, getting wearily to her feet. 'I will have a lie down.

Goodbye, Ruby, it was nice to meet you. I see so few people other than punters in the club and I'd really love to have a friend close to my own age. You will come again, won't you?'

Ruby nodded. 'Of course, if you want me to.' She watched as Lily wandered into the adjoining room and, as the door closed behind her, Ruby turned on Jonas. 'You're a proper bully, you are. Can't you see she's really ill?'

Jonas stared at Ruby, eyebrows raised, eyes cold. 'Not that it's any of your business but yes, I do know, and how I take care of what's mine is my business.'

'What's yours?' Ruby almost choked on her indignation. 'You can't own a human being.'

'That's where you're wrong, but I don't have to explain myself to you or anyone.'

'You – you arrogant, hard-hearted brute! Can't you see you're killing her? Lily should be in a sanatorium, not singing her heart out in a smoke-filled room just to entertain your punters.'

'And you're a medical expert, are you, Ruby?'

'I'm doing me best to study and one day I'll get into nursing school, but it don't take a doctor to see the trouble here.'

'So that's your ambition, is it?' Jonas sat down, making the chaise longue look like a piece of doll's house furniture. 'You're so different from your sister. It's hard to believe you're twins.'

Ruby drew back, startled by the sudden

change in the conversation. 'You don't know Rosetta. You only met her at the funeral.'

'She came to me for a job. I'm surprised you didn't know that, being so close to your sister.'

There was no mistaking the irony in his tone and Ruby felt a stab of alarm. 'I don't believe you. Rosetta wouldn't do that.'

'Don't worry, I turned her down. I won't be corrupting her morals in my illegal gambling den.'

'You leave Rosetta out of this. You done enough harm to my family.'

'I suppose you're talking about your brother?'

'Yes, I'm talking about Joe. He's young and he's reckless and he's got hisself into debt by gambling right here in this building. I don't say it was your fault, but there's no cause for you to frighten him half to death with your threats and bullying. He's a good bloke deep down; he's just gone off the rails a bit and you're taking advantage of him.'

'Well,' Jonas said, leaning back against the cushions, a smile of genuine amusement playing on his lips. 'You are a spirited little thing after all. I took you for a bluestocking the first time we met. It seems you've got hidden depths, Ruby Capretti.'

Ruby stamped her foot. 'We're not talking about me, or Rosetta, who for some reason thinks that the sun shines out of your arse, we're talking about a young man whose life you're ruining just for the sake of a few bob.'

'A few bob?' Jonas pulled a face. 'My dear Ruby, your brother owes me two hundred pounds. I don't call that a few bob.'

Ruby swallowed hard and she sat down suddenly as her knees gave way beneath her. Two hundred pounds was a fortune; it would take her years to earn that much money working at Bronski's.

'He didn't tell you? I'm not surprised.'

Feeling as though the breath had been sucked out of her lungs, Ruby shook her head. 'We'll pay you back somehow or other. Just don't hurt him; I'm begging you, Mr Crowe, please don't hurt my brother.'

Staring at her for a moment, Jonas got up and taking Ruby by the hand, he pulled her to her feet. 'Maybe there's a way, but I'm not promising anything.'

Looking into the depths of his eyes, Ruby shuddered. 'I'll do what you want.'

'Anything?' Jonas fingered Ruby's thin shawl. 'Would you work for me to pay off your brother's debts?'

'What would you want of me?' Ruby met his eyes steadily; she wasn't a fool and she hadn't come down in the last shower of rain.

'I haven't quite decided, but surely anything would be better than working in that sweatshop.'

'I don't mind hard work, but I'm a respectable girl.'

'And your brother is well on the road to perdition. I can ruin him with one snap of my fingers. Do you want to break your mother's heart, Ruby? Do you want her to lose her only son, so soon after losing her husband?'

'You wouldn't!'

'Wouldn't I?' Jonas's eyes were chips of blue ice. 'I'm used to getting my own way. Don't go against me, Ruby.'

Licking her dry lips, Ruby felt suddenly quite faint. Joe had said he was in fear of his life and she had not really believed him. Now she did. 'What do you want me to do?'

'First things first. Did you walk here dressed like that?'

'What?' Startled, Ruby could only stare up into his impassive face.

Suddenly businesslike, Jonas grabbed her by the hand. 'Right, then. Now you're in my employ, the first thing you can do for me, Miss Ruby Capretti, is to let me buy you a proper damn overcoat.'

'What?'

'Don't keep saying that; you sound like an idiot and I know you're far from that.' Jonas opened the door and, pulling her along behind him, he went down the stairs and out through the back of the house into the yard where his shiny black motor was parked. 'Hop in, Ruby. We're going shopping.'

'I can't let you buy me clothes,' Ruby said, climbing reluctantly into the passenger seat. 'It ain't decent, it ain't respectable. My mum will kill me.'

'And I'll kill Joe if you don't,' Jonas replied amicably. 'You're no good to me or anyone else if you die of pneumonia, so sit tight and shut up. You're going to have a new coat and that's that.'

'I won't let you do this,' Ruby said, hanging onto the seat as Jonas drove out of the yard at a speed that made jumping out hazardous, if not impossible, and tooting the horn, he sped down the service alley that led into Raven Street.

'You said you'd do anything to get Joe out of trouble,' Jonas said, with a sardonic smile. 'I don't think being bought a new coat will send you tumbling into the fiery furnace. Seems to me that most girls would be delighted at the prospect of being treated to new clothes.'

'Then I ain't like most girls.'

'And that's your chief charm, Ruby. You aren't like most girls.'

Turning her head away, Ruby stared fixedly at the familiar streets flashing past. It seemed impossible that she was allowing Jonas to take her on a shopping trip and all because Joe had come to her last night, scared out of his wits and begging for help. She stole a surreptitious glance at Jonas's profile; somehow it was hard to believe that he would cause Joe actual bodily harm. Despite her loathing for him, Ruby could not convince herself that he was a killer. She really did not know what to make of him; sometimes he appeared brutal, and at other times he seemed quite human and even generous, as he had been when he returned the women's wages.

Seeming to sense her glance, Jonas turned his head to give her a quizzical stare and Ruby looked away. What had she got herself into, and all because of Joe. When he had turned up last night in a terrible state, Ruby had tried to calm Joe down, promising to help if she could, but he had been so distressed that he had gone off apparently unconvinced. She suspected that he would go straight to Rosetta, knowing that she was sweet on Jonas Crowe, hoping that she would intervene on his behalf. Maybe she ought to have left it to Rosetta after all, Ruby thought, clasping her hands tightly together in her lap. Rose was better with men. She knew how to flirt and she would have known exactly how to handle this situation.

'Bloomsbury,' Jonas said, steering the motor expertly between a stationary wagon and a brewer's dray. 'And on to Oxford Street when I can get through the traffic.'

Tempted to jump out and walk home, Ruby thought of her mother's distress if she discovered that Joe had got himself into a desperate situation, and she abandoned the idea.

'You know, Ruby,' Jonas said, as they came to a halt while a costermonger dragged his barrow across the street. 'You're the most silent woman I've ever met.'

'I got nothing to say to you.'

'Well, it makes a change from constant chatter about nothing in particular.' Jonas urged the motor forward, honking the horn.

'You don't like women much, do you?'

'Wrong again. I love women.'

'But not in the right way.'

'And what's the right way?'

'Not your way, that's for certain.' Hunching up into as small a space as she could, Ruby stared steadfastly at the now unfamiliar streets, but try as she might she could not quite crush the excitement of riding in a motor car. There were so few of them on the road and heads turned to stare at them all along their route. In spite of everything, she felt important and grand, just like the queen in her golden coach. Realising that they had stopped outside the imposing façade of a huge emporium that dwarfed anything Ruby had ever seen in the East End, she allowed the doorman to help her out of her seat and she followed Jonas into Peter Robinson's store without a murmur.

One look at Jonas in his expensive clothes and the shop assistants did treat them like royalty.

Completely overawed and not wanting to draw attention to herself by making a fuss, Ruby tried on coats, hats and kid gloves as soft as a baby's skin. Not satisfied with just the purchase of a pure merino winter coat, a matching hat and a pair of kid gloves, Jonas insisted on buying three ready-made dresses, one in dove-grey worsted, one in floral-print cretonne and, despite her protests that it was too fine and she would never wear it, a lavender silk afternoon gown. Ruby suffered in silence as the shop assistants laced her into whalebone stays and pushed and prodded her into the tightly fitting gowns, smooth across the stomach in the latest fashion and puffed out over pads to form a bustle at the back. Despite the deference shown by the staff, Ruby saw them glancing at her ring-free left hand and knew they were thinking the worst. Having to parade the new garments in front of Jonas for his approval made her blush with shame, but she held her head up high; whatever they thought, she was not his mistress, nor ever would be if there was any other way to save Joe from his vengeance.

'We'll take them all,' Jonas said, as Ruby emerged from the fitting room wearing a turquoise tussore evening gown that had been thrust upon her at the last minute.

'Not this one,' she said, glaring at Jonas. 'It's a waste of money.'

The shop assistant hastily turned a snigger into a sneeze.

'It's my money,' Jonas said, laughing. 'We'll take it and the chemise or whatever you call it that goes underneath.'

'Shut up!' Ruby felt the blood rush to her cheeks. She bent down to hiss in Jonas's ear. 'It ain't proper for a gent to know about such things.'

'I'm not a gent, so it doesn't count, Ruby my dear,' Jonas said, chuckling and running his finger down her cheek, caressing the slim column of her neck and stopping just above the swell of her breast exposed by the low neckline. 'Let them think what they like. It doesn't matter.'

But it does matter to me, Ruby thought bitterly as she stepped out of the beautiful gown in the privacy of the fitting room. The shop assistant, with her facial features well under control now, looped the dress over her arm and took it off to be packed. Putting on her own clothes, Ruby was even more aware of their shabbiness and the poor quality of the material. Even though she had hated being treated like a kept woman, deep down inside she had to admit the thrill of wearing new and expensive clothes that she had never thought to possess in all her wildest dreams. Rosetta would be green with envy and mad with jealousy. Perhaps she would give the evening gown to Rosetta and that would salve her conscience just a little. Looking at her reflection in the mirror, Ruby saw someone quite different staring out at her. They had piled her hair high on top of her head to show off the evening gown and there were bright spots of colour in her normally pale cheeks. Her eyes glowed with anger or maybe it was excitement, and Ruby found herself wishing that Adam Fairfax could have seen her in that lovely evening gown, looking like a real lady. She was instantly ashamed of having such a mean thought; Adam was all but engaged to Pamela. If she wanted to keep her sanity, she had better forget all about him and, if it came to that, her ambition to train as a nurse. When Jonas had finished with her, Ruby was well aware that her reputation would be ruined for ever. Oh, Joe, she thought, what have you done to us all? She jumped as the curtain was pulled aside.

'Get your clothes on, Ruby. We're off to the shoe department next. I won't be seen with a woman in down at heel boots two sizes too big for her feet.'

With the dicky seat piled high with bandboxes, Jonas drove back towards the East End. 'D'you want to go by way of the church so that you can confess your sins?' he said, chuckling.

Huddled in the warmth of her new coat, Ruby sat fuming at her own weakness in accepting such a handsome gift. 'You're laughing at me again.'

'Not really, Ruby. I'm not used to women with consciences.'

'What is it you want of me, Mr Crowe?'

Jonas turned his head to look at her. 'I'll let you know that when I've made up my mind.'

Lapsing into silence, Ruby became more and more agitated as they arrived in the familiar territory of the East End. Jonas may not have made improper advances towards her, but she was not so naïve as to believe that a man like Crowe would spend a small fortune on her and expect nothing in return. If he did not want her for himself, then perhaps he expected her to be available to the men who frequented his club. Ruby had read books about the white slave trade, courtesans and high-class prostitutes. Suddenly she felt sick.

'Here we are,' Jonas said, slamming on the brakes. 'Time for your confession, Ruby, my girl.'

Ruby had been so wrapped in her own thoughts that her surroundings had simply not registered in her brain. The motor car was parked outside her own home. Curtains fluttered in the windows all down the street and Jonas had already leapt out and was standing on the pavement holding his hand out to her. 'Are you coming in or are you going to sit in my motor all day?'

Sarah's face was a study in disbelief and amazement when Ruby walked into the living room followed by Jonas.

'What's he doing here?' demanded Granny Mole. 'And what's Ruby doing dressed up like a dog's dinner?'

'Ma!' Sarah said, shooting her a warning look. 'You'll have to excuse Ma, Mr Crowe, she says whatever comes into her head.'

'I appreciate honesty,' Jonas said, acknowledging Granny Mole's comments with a nod and a smile. 'No doubt you'll be a bit curious yourself, Mrs Capretti.'

Sarah smiled but Ruby could see that her hands were plucking nervously at her apron and her eyes were wary. 'I'm sure there must be a reasonable explanation for it, sir. Seeing as how you've brought Ruby home.'

'Consider me a friend of the family,' Jonas said, his voice smooth as buttercream. 'I've taken Joe under my wing so to speak and now, with your permission, I'd like to take Ruby into my employ.'

'You would?' Sarah looked from Jonas to Ruby, frowning.

Meeting her mother's anxious gaze, Ruby shrugged her shoulders. She had the uncomfortable feeling that the situation was spinning out of control, but what could she say, how could she explain without incriminating Joe?

'As what?' Granny Mole demanded, with a derisive snort. 'In my day that would have meant just one thing.'

'Ma!' Sarah said, a dull flush suffusing her face. 'Let Mr Crowe have his say.'

'I understand your very natural concern, Mrs Mole,' Jonas said, in a voice that sounded as if he had taken the cloth. 'But we all know that Miss Ruby is wasting her talents working in Bronski's sweatshop. I feel I owe it to her late father to offer her something more suitable to a young lady whose very worthy ambition it is to become a qualified nurse.'

'Well, now!' Sarah's eyes opened wide and she sank down onto the nearest chair, wiping her face with her apron. 'Well, I never did!'

'Nor I, neither,' added Granny Mole. 'Sounds like a load of poppycock to me. A man like him's got just one thing on his mind and it ain't Florence Nightingale and her bleeding lamp.'

'Ma!' A turmoil of emotions from shock to suspicion flitted across Sarah's face. 'Mr Crowe, you'll have to excuse Ma, but Ruby's a good girl, sir. I trust your intentions is honourable.'

Jonas sat down beside Sarah, taking her hand in his. 'You mustn't worry, Mrs Capretti. I understand a mother's feelings for her daughter and I can promise you that Ruby will come to no harm in my house.'

Ruby stared at Jonas in surprise. His mild

manner and concerned expression seemed totally alien to the blustering, swaggering style that he normally adopted. What a strange mixture of people seemed to be rolled up in the person of Jonas Crowe; one moment a bully, a gang leader and a man feared by the toughest men in the East End, and yet here he was holding Mum's hand and speaking in a mild way like a proper gent.

Jonas looked up, meeting Ruby's eyes with the hint of a smile. 'I want Ruby to nurse my poor wife in her battle with consumption. If you agree to Ruby coming to live in my house and taking up this employment, then I will personally see that she has free time to study her books on nursing. I can't say fairer than that, now can I?'

'Maybe you can't,' Granny Mole said, before Sarah had a chance to speak. 'But if you takes Ruby away, who's going to support me and my Sal now that Aldo has gone?'

'Be quiet, Ma,' Sarah said, shaking her head. 'I'm sure Ruby won't forget us and that Mr Crowe will treat her fair like any good employer.'

Jonas reached into his breast pocket and pulled out a fat wallet. He took out two crisp, white five-pound notes and placed them in Sarah's hand, closing her fingers around them. 'Consider that an advance on Ruby's wages. I'm a generous man to those who serve me well.'

Sarah's eyes widened and her mouth formed a circle of surprise, her lips working soundlessly. 'More than generous, sir,' she managed to gasp. 'More than generous.'

Ruby knew she was trapped. It would take her a year to earn this much money at Bronski's, and if she were to refuse now, then Mum and Gran would want to know the reason why and it would have to be a good one.

Jonas tucked his wallet back in his breast pocket. 'Then I take it that you have no objections to Ruby coming to live in my establishment, Mrs Capretti?'

Sarah stared at the money for a moment as if struggling with the decision. Ruby could see that Mum was unsure, but she also knew that ten pounds would make life a whole lot easier for her mother and Granny Mole.

Sarah raised her eyes to Ruby's face. 'Ruby? Are you sure this is what you want?'

Somehow, she couldn't do it. Ruby longed to cry out that she would rather die than be beholden to a man like Jonas Crowe, but there was Joe to consider and she couldn't pitch her family into disgrace and undoubted poverty. She managed a smile. 'Yes, Mum, I'm sure.'

Jonas got to his feet. 'That's settled then. Come along, Ruby. It's time we went home to poor Lily.'

'Lily's your wife?' Ruby said, as soon as the

front door closed behind them. 'You never said that you was married.'

Jonas opened the door to the passenger seat. 'Hop in.'

'Is she or isn't she?'

'Not in the eyes of the law.'

'Then why did you lie about it?'

'Do you think your mother would appreciate being told that I bought Lily from her villain of a father when she was just fourteen, half starved, beaten and up for sale to the highest bidder?'

Ruby swallowed hard, shaking her head. 'No.'

'And do you think your mother would let you come and work for me if she knew what sort of businesses I run?'

'No.'

'Then get in the motor car.'

'No.'

'No?' Jonas's eyebrows shot together and his mouth hardened into a straight line. 'Is that all you can say?'

'No, as a matter of fact I got quite a lot to say, but I ain't in a position to argue with you, Mr Crowe.'

'Good! Now get in the motor, please.'

'No,' Ruby said, squaring her shoulders. 'I'll work for you like you said and I'll be happy to care for Lily, but I got terms I want met as well.'

'You realise the whole street is watching this

conversation and straining their ears to hear what we're saying?'

Ignoring this remark, Ruby took a deep breath. 'I'll work hard for you but I want you to promise that no harm will come to Joe. We'll pay you back his debt somehow or other but it'll take time and I won't leave until it is paid off. Have we got a bargain?'

His rigid expression melting into one of amusement, Jonas held out his hand. 'You drive a hard bargain, Ruby Capretti.'

As they shook hands Ruby was conscious of a tingling sensation shooting up her arm, spiking in her chest and, when she snatched her hand free, she could still feel the impression of his fingers firmly gripping hers. She shivered.

'Come along now,' Jonas said, striding round the bonnet to the driver's seat. 'Get in before you freeze to death on the pavement.'

'No,' Ruby said, slamming the passenger door. 'I got a few things to do. I'll make me own way to Raven Street.'

'You what?' Jonas's black brows drew together in an ominous scowl.

'Don't try and bully me, Mr Crowe,' Ruby said, giving him look for look. 'I got things to do and people what I need to see.'

His foot on the running board, Jonas glared at her, almost growling with anger. 'What people?'

'If you think I'm going to leave without

making sure that Billy is coping all right then you got another think coming, and I got to see my friend at the hospital, not to mention letting old Bronski know that I ain't coming back.'

'What's Billy Noakes got to do with you?'

'It's a long story.'

'And who do you know at the hospital?'

'That's my business,' Ruby said, turning on her heel and walking off in the direction of Spivey Street, calling over her shoulder, 'and don't worry, Mr Crowe, I'll be at your place afore teatime.'

Billy's horse was not in the stable and the door to his room was firmly locked. Ruby was conscious that her smart appearance was attracting more attention than usual and this made her uncomfortable and wary. Young women dressed in expensive clothes did not usually walk round Whitechapel unaccompanied. She quickened her pace as she walked to Bronski's, arriving in the middle of their afternoon tea break. Suddenly hungry and very thirsty, Ruby realised that she had had nothing to eat or drink since a cup of tea and a slice of toast at breakfast. If she had expected a warm welcome she was doomed to disappointment. One glance at her clothes and their smiles of welcome faded into suspicious sneers.

'No need to tell us what you've come for, Ruby

Capretti,' Vinegar Lil said, arms folded across her flat chest. 'I always knew as how Rosetta would end up bad and I can see you're just the same.'

'That's not true,' Ruby said, looking from one hostile face to the other. 'I just come to say I got another job, and . . .'

'And we all know what that is.' Vinegar Lil's nostrils flared. 'Don't we, girls?' Stepping forward she fingered the pure wool merino of Ruby's coat. 'It would take more than a year's wages to pay for a coat like this. You never got this from the pop shop and there's only one way a girl like you could earn that sort of bees and honey, eh, girls?'

'Flat on her back,' chortled Mad Mabel.

'Here, steady on.' Big Biddy shot a sideways glance at Ruby with a hint of apology in her eyes. 'Leave her be.'

'Get off with you,' Vinegar Lil said, giving Ruby a shove. 'We don't want your sort round here. You always thought yourself a cut above us anyhow, so clear off.'

'It's not true,' Ruby said, turning to little Winnie, but she shrugged her shoulders and walked away.

'Tart,' carolled Mad Mabel, dancing up and down. 'Stuck-up tart.'

With the unkind words ringing in her ears and biting back tears of humiliation, Ruby left

Bronski's hurrying blindly in the direction of the hospital. She found Billy sitting in the waiting room. He looked up and the pleasure in his eyes faded as he took in her changed appearance. Her heart sank; how could she explain the situation to Billy when she did not fully understand it herself?

'Hello, Billy,' she said, sitting down beside him. 'How are you?'

'What's happened to you, Ruby? You robbed a bank or worse?'

'Nothing like that.'

Billy frowned but was prevented from questioning her by Pamela popping her head out of the treatment room and calling his name. She spotted Ruby and gave her a cheery wave.

'I'll speak to you in a minute,' Billy said, ominously, as he got to his feet.

'Can't stop now,' Pamela called, smiling. 'I'm due for a break soon. Do wait.'

Ruby sank back onto the hard wooden seat. At least Pamela didn't seem to think the worst, not like everyone else, even Billy. Pamela had been so kind and helpful while Billy was really bad; she had been unfailingly patient when she had shown Ruby how to deal with Billy's burns. She had been fun too. Pamela's abundant good nature and bubbling sense of humour made her a joy to be with and Ruby knew that, for some strange reason, Pamela had taken a liking to her.

Maybe it was because they laughed at the same things, evading the wrath of old fish-face, for instance. Maybe it was simply that Pamela was a thoroughly nice person with no side to her who seemed oblivious of the difference in their social standing. Ruby sat studying her hands, clenched in her lap; Pamela might behave differently towards her if she knew how she felt about Adam. Everything was so complicated – everything was going terribly wrong.

'Hello, Ruby. How nice to see you again.'

Startled, Ruby looked up into the smiling face of Adam Fairfax.

Chapter Nine

Adam looked and sounded really pleased to see her but then, Ruby thought, being a proper gent, he's probably like this with everyone. Hoping that he hadn't noticed her blushes, Ruby returned his smile. 'Hello, Dr Fairfax.'

'Now that's not fair,' Adam said, sitting down beside her. 'I can't call you Ruby if you won't call me Adam.'

'Adam,' Ruby repeated, savouring the sound like a mouthful of Fry's Chocolate Crème.

'I must say you look spiffing. Is that a new hat, by any chance?'

Ruby nodded. If he asked her how she had come by her new clothes she would be really stuck, but Adam was chatting away as if totally unaware that this type of outfit was normally well beyond her means.

'I've spoken to Matron about you, Ruby.'

Ruby jumped. 'Pardon?'

Adam smiled. 'She's willing to see you, that's if you still want to become a nurse.'

'Yes – of course, I do.'

'I wasn't sure. I mean, you look so prosperous,

I thought that you must have found yourself a new position.'

'I – well, yes.'

'But you still want to study nursing?'

'Oh, yes. I really do, it's just that I've been taken on by a gentleman with a sick wife. He wants me to nurse her but he says as how I can train to be a proper nurse in me spare time.'

Adam slapped his hands on his knees. 'Excellent. Although I think Matron might not like the idea of you studying in your spare time. However, we'll deal with that particular problem when we come to it. The first thing is to get you an interview with Miss Luckes.'

'Dr Fairfax, you're wanted on the ward round.' A ward sister came bustling over to them, bristling with efficiency.

'Coming, Sister.' Jumping to his feet, Adam gave Ruby an encouraging smile. 'I have to go, Ruby, but if you give Pam your new address I'll let you know when Matron can see you.'

Drowning in his smile, Ruby nodded, unable to speak. She watched him stride away into the depths of the hospital followed by a group of nurses fluttering after him like grey moths. Allowing herself to dream, Ruby imagined herself standing at Adam's side, helping him in his life's work of treating the sick and saving lives. The real world came crashing back as Billy erupted from the treatment room and came storming towards her, his face dark with suspicion.

'What's going on, Ruby?'

'Don't bully the poor girl,' Pamela said, coming up behind him. 'Ruby's been an absolute brick, looking after you when you were sick and helpless.'

Pushing a lock of hair back off his forehead with a bandaged hand, Billy grinned sheepishly. 'I know that, but something's up. I wouldn't be surprised if Rosetta walked in here dressed up to the nines, but not Ruby.'

'I'd say that was Ruby's business.'

'Stop talking about me like I wasn't here,' Ruby said, jumping to her feet. 'As it happens, I've come up in the world. I've been taken on to look after a poor lady sick with consumption.'

'She must be rich,' Billy said, staring pointedly at Ruby's clothes and scowling. 'Who is this old girl anyway?'

'You don't know her.'

Pamela slipped her arm around Ruby's shoulder. 'I say, good for you. You deserve better than slaving away in that horrible place making cheap clothes.'

'A rich lady who togs you out in new clobber?' Billy shook his head. 'Come on, girl, this stuff never come from Petticoat Lane.'

'You got no right to question me,' Ruby said, standing her ground. 'I ain't nothing to you, Billy, except a friend, so mind your own business.'

'Never mind him,' Pamela put in hurriedly before Billy had time to retaliate. 'I've got to get back on duty before old fish-face notices I'm not actually working. Let me have your new address, Ruby, and I'll come to call on you.'

Turning her back on Billy, Ruby whispered the address.

'Raven Street,' Pamela said, frowning. 'That's Shoreditch, isn't it?'

'Yes,' Ruby said, glancing anxiously over her shoulder to see if Billy had heard. Judging by the expression on his face, he had.

'Nurse Chadwick, get back to work.' Sister's voice echoed down the corridor.

'I'm in for it now. I'll see you soon, Ruby; we must keep in touch.' Pamela hurried away in the direction of the treatment rooms.

Ruby turned to go but Billy barred her way. 'That was Crowe's address.'

'Like I said, it's none of your business.' Pushing past him, Ruby hurried out of the hospital. She ran to the edge of the pavement, looking up and down Whitechapel Road, praying that a passing hansom cab would stop and save her from embarrassing explanations. But her luck was out and Billy caught up with her, grabbing her by the arm.

'You don't know what you're getting into, Ruby.'

'Look, Billy, you've been good to me and my

family but this don't concern you.' Snatching her arm free, Ruby waved frantically at the driver as a cab pulled up to drop off a fare. The London particular was creeping through the City like a thief, stealing the daylight and replacing it with a choking, smoky-green pall. Ruby leapt into the cab. 'Raven Street, please.'

Ruby had a room of her own just down the corridor from Lily's bedroom, linked by an electric bell so that Lily could summon her if she wanted something in the night. At first, Ruby was nervous of the bell, jumping when it rang and avoiding touching it fearing an electric shock. Gradually overcoming her fear of mighty electric power, now she could not resist switching her bedroom light on and off every time she went into her room, just for the pleasure of seeing it work. Mum still thought that gaslight was a minor miracle, and just having it in Tobacco Court made them a cut above the candlelit world of Spivey Street; Ruby couldn't help wondering how she would cope with electricity. With the luxury of a lamp on her bedside table, Ruby was able to study her medical books at night, although by now they were so well worn and dog-eared that the pages kept falling out and she knew each chapter almost by heart.

Looking after Lily was hardly challenging; in

fact, it was so easy that Ruby wondered why Jonas had insisted on hiring her. She had not heard from Joe, and that worried her, but Jonas had given his word that no harm would come to her brother as long as she stayed in his house and looked after Lily. If this was being held hostage, then it was definitely a gilded cage and that in itself made Ruby uneasy; she suspected that Jonas was playing a deep game and that one day he would show his hand. Until then, she had to be content to live in this velvet-lined world where her duties were more those of a paid companion than a nurse.

The doctor had instructed Lily to rest as much as possible and to eat nourishing meals, but Lily was forever on the move, refusing to rest and sending her meals away virtually untouched. The only delicacy that tempted her capricious appetite was chocolate, and Jonas kept her supplied with expensive boxes of chocolates decorated with crystallised violets, rose petals and silver dragées. Her sitting room was always bright with vases of flowers filling the air with their heady perfume, but in spite of all this luxury, Ruby sensed a deep sadness in Lily that had nothing to do with her illness. Even in such a short space of time, Ruby had grown fond of Lily; in fact, it would have been difficult to find anything to dislike about her. Lily was kind, gentle and funny; she told Ruby risqué stories about the gentlemen who frequented Jonas's club, making her laugh until her sides ached. She made light of her illness, never complaining and insisting on performing her songs every night to entertain the punters, in spite of the fact that the fuggy atmosphere brought on severe bouts of coughing that left her weak and exhausted.

Ruby had seen very little of Jonas in her first days at Raven Street. His visits to Lily's room were infrequent and brief and he treated her with casual affection, more like a brother than a lover and their relationship puzzled Ruby. Even from the first, she sensed that Lily was deeply in love with Jonas, and yet she slept alone in the huge four-poster bed. Sometimes Ruby caught a haunting look of sadness in Lily's eyes when they rested on Jonas and yet they seemed to be on good terms, never quarrelling or bickering like most couples.

One evening, Ruby was lacing Lily's stays, helping her get ready for her nightly appearance in the club, when a sudden bout of coughing produced telltale, bright red spots of blood on Lily's hanky.

'It's nothing,' Lily gasped, scrunching up the handkerchief. 'Just a nose bleed.'

'You should rest. I'm sure Mr Jonas wouldn't mind if you missed just one night.'

'He would hardly notice,' Lily said, lowering herself onto her dressing stool and patting rouge onto her pale cheeks. 'But that's not the point. I like to pay my way, Ruby. I'm not a kept woman.'

Meeting Lily's eyes in the dressing table mirror, Ruby shook her head, shocked. 'I never thought you was.'

'You must have wondered.'

'It ain't my place to wonder.' Ruby snatched up a silver-backed hairbrush and began brushing Lily's hair.

'We've been together for eleven years,' Lily said, half to herself, her long fingers toying with a powder puff. 'My father sold me to Jonas just before my fourteenth birthday. Did you know that, Ruby?'

Ruby nodded, concentrating on pinning swathes of Lily's blonde hair into a shining coronet on the top of her head.

'And you weren't shocked?'

'I know it happens.'

'Jonas is not a bad man at heart, you know. He was good to me, treated me like a human being and I fell in love with him.'

'Flowers or pearls? For your hair.'

Lily smiled at Ruby's reflection in the mirror. 'Pearls, I think. Have I embarrassed you?'

Fixing the long string of pearls in Lily's hair gave Ruby an excuse not to reply.

'Well, I have and I'm sorry. Have you ever been in love, Ruby?'

Adam's face danced before Ruby's eyes and

the pearls slipped out of her fingers. Bending down to retrieve them, she mumbled something that could have been taken for yes or no.

'Then you'll know how I feel,' Lily said, sighing deeply. 'At first it was wonderful, but something has changed. I don't know why, but he has lost interest in me and I'm scared, Ruby. I think he doesn't care for me any more and I don't know what to do about it.'

Next morning, having taken Lily's breakfast tray into her bedroom, Ruby went into the sitting room and was buttering a slice of toast when Tucker burst unceremoniously into the room. 'Got a letter for you, ducks.' Tucker waved a white envelope in front of her face. 'D'you want it or not?'

'Don't mess about, Tucker. Give it here.'

'And what's the magic word?'

'Tucker, I'll swing for you one day, you cheeky little beggar.' Dropping the butter knife, Ruby jumped to her feet, but Tucker backed away grinning like a mischievous monkey.

'What's it worth?'

'If you give it me now I won't tell Miss Lily on you.'

Scowling, Tucker tossed the letter at her. 'You would too.'

'Thank you, Tucker,' Ruby called as he left the room, slamming the door behind him.

Staring at the white vellum envelope, addressed to Miss Ruby Capretti in elegant copperplate writing, Ruby's knees gave way beneath her. She knew instinctively that this was Adam's handwriting and she ripped it open with trembling hands.

The London Hospital,
Whitechapel

30th January, 1899

Dear Ruby,
I hope this finds you well and enjoying your new position. I have spoken to Miss Luckes, the matron, who just happens to be a good friend of my mother, and she will be pleased to see you for an informal interview. Can you manage this afternoon at two o'clock? I'm afraid this is very short notice, but if it is inconvenient, please let me know and I will try to rearrange the meeting.
Yours sincerely
Adam Fairfax

At ten minutes to two, Ruby was sitting outside Matron's office, trying to control the butterflies that were whirling and fluttering in her stomach. Lily had been unwell, sending her breakfast tray away untouched, and opting to remain in bed all day. She had raised no objections when Ruby had explained why she wanted an hour off in the afternoon, nodding her assent, closing her eyes and drifting off into a feverish sleep. Ruby had suffered a few twinges of conscience on leaving her, but even if she stayed at Lily's bedside, there was little she could do. She had made Tucker promise to answer the bell if Lily should ring, safe in the knowledge that when it came to Lily's well-being Tucker would do his best.

'Miss Capretti?' A tall woman, all starch and uniform, stood in front of her.

Ruby leapt off the hard wooden seat, standing to attention. 'Yes, ma'am.'

'Come into my office if you please.'

Sitting on the edge of her chair, Ruby answered all the questions that Miss Luckes fired at her with the intensity of a woodpecker drilling a hole in a tree trunk. Sitting for a while in silence, steepling her fingers, Matron stared thoughtfully at Ruby. Seconds felt like hours as the wall clock ticked on inexorably towards Ruby's fate. She sat with her hands knotted together, barely daring to breathe; her whole future depended on Matron's answer.

'Well, Miss Capretti, I can see that you are sincere in your desire to become a probationer nurse and that you are an intelligent young woman, but I'm afraid I am going to have to disappoint you.'

Ruby stared at her blankly for a moment, barely able to assimilate the bad news. 'But why? I'd work ever so hard and study in every spare minute I got.'

A glimmer of sympathy lit Matron's eyes but she dropped her gaze, staring down at the sheaf of papers on her desk. Her square-tipped fingers toyed with a pen, tapping it rhythmically up and down on the tooled-leather desk top. 'I'm sure you would, but you must understand that we have to uphold standards. All our probationer nurses come from similar backgrounds to Miss Chadwick and, to be blunt, you would not fit in.'

Ruby shook her head, unable to speak.

'We have public wards, Ruby,' Matron said, gentling her tone. 'But we also have private wards and wealthy patrons who, quite frankly, wouldn't care to be treated by a young person who could not enunciate their own language.'

'You mean I don't speak proper.'

'That's exactly what I mean.'

'What if I learned to speak proper?'

'I know it sounds harsh, unkind even, but you would have to learn quite a lot more.' Placing the pen in its holder, Matron shuffled the papers with an air of finality. 'I'm sorry, but that's the way it is. I would be quite prepared to take you on trial as a ward maid, if you so wished.'

Ruby stood up, holding her head high and struggling to find a little dignity in this utter humiliation. 'Thank you, ma'am, but I mean to be a proper nurse, not a skivvy what cleans up slops and sluices. I won't take up no more of your valuable time.'

Hurrying from Matron's office with her head down, biting back tears of disappointment and frustration, Ruby almost cannoned into Pamela.

'Ruby? What happened?'

'It's no go,' Ruby said, swallowing a sob and sniffing. 'But I ain't giving up. I can learn to speak proper. I'm as good as the next person.'

Hooking her arm around Ruby's shoulders, Pamela pulled a hanky out of her pocket and gave it to her. 'Of course you are, dear. You're worth two of most people I know.'

Ruby blew her nose. 'Well, she don't think so.'

'Oh dear, Adam will be so cross,' Pamela said, sighing. 'He was so certain that you would be accepted.'

'Was he?' A spark of hope flared in Ruby's breast. 'Was he really?'

'Of course. Adam thinks a lot of you, Ruby, and so do I. You mustn't give up, you simply mustn't. And if there's anything I can do to help then I promise you I will.'

'Ta, but I ain't one to give up easily.' Wiping her eyes, Ruby managed a watery smile. 'Don't worry about me, Pamela. And thank Adam for me, will you?' She turned to go but Pamela caught her by the sleeve.

'Why not tell him yourself? He usually manages to drop in and have a cup of tea with me at this time of the day.'

'No, no, I got to go. Maybe another time.' Unable to bear the prospect of their combined sympathy, Ruby backed away. She had to get out of the hospital, away from lost hopes, shattered dreams and the painful sight of Adam and Pamela drinking tea together like an old married couple.

She walked back to Raven Street, barely feeling the icy shards of sleet pelting her from a lowering sky. The winter dusk had closed in on the city and the lamplighters were finishing their rounds, creating ragged yellow pools of light that glimmered on the wet pavements. Everyone seemed to be in a hurry, hidden beneath black umbrellas, moving forward like a river of mushrooms. Tears flowed freely down her cheeks but no one gave her a second glance. Arriving wet, tired and dispirited on the steps of Crowe's establishment, Ruby fumbled in her purse for her key. She couldn't help glancing up at Aunt Lottie's house and wondering if Rosetta was at home.

They had not spoken since the day when Rosetta had flown into a jealous rage because Jonas had given her a lift in his motor. Ruby had gone next door several times, but Rosetta was always at the theatre rehearsing or else performing, and she had never made a move to heal the rift between them. This saddened Ruby and she longed to sit and talk to Rose, sharing troubles as they had done in the past. Ruby understood only too well that, in her ignorance of the real world, Rosetta was harbouring romantic dreams about Jonas. She saw only the wealth that he had created, without understanding the criminal activities that had brought him his fortune. Rosetta and Joe both lived in a world created by their own imaginations, Ruby thought, turning the key in the lock. Joe always thought that the next bet would win back his fortune and Rosetta, like a spoilt child, was confident that she simply had to demand love and attention and it would automatically be showered upon her. If Ruby admitted the truth, that Jonas had a hold over her because of Joe's gambling debts, it would be a double blow to Rosetta. Ruby could not face telling her, and even if she did, she doubted whether Rose would listen.

Tucker was in the hallway, nodding off to sleep on his chair by the door. He snorted and jumped as Ruby shut the door.

'Oh, it's you, miss.'

'Is everything all right?'

'Not a sound. I put me head round her door a few minutes back but she was sleeping like a babe and beautiful as an angel.'

'Ta,' Ruby said, managing a smile. 'You're a good lad, Tucker.'

Cold, wet and dispirited, Ruby trudged up the stairs, pausing outside the gaming room and listening. It was unusually quiet. Although most punters came late at night, there were plenty of well-healed gents who came to pass an afternoon playing roulette, hazard, faro or chemin-de-fer. She could hear deep male voices and occasional bursts of laughter. Tobacco smoke seeped under the door in frayed skeins, like shredded fog. Perhaps Jonas would not need Lily tonight if things were quiet, or maybe there was something planned to be held later on in the brick confines of the back yard. Ruby had heard the baying and yelping of dogs in the rat catching contests and the roar of the crowd at illegal cockfights. She knew that men paid good money to watch the vicious and bloody bare-knuckle fights. Lily had told her that there were even contests between female wrestlers, who bared themselves to the waist, pulling each other's hair and rolling about in the mud, and all for the entertainment of the mob. Ruby shuddered; she would never have believed that such things existed before she left her mother's little oasis of respectability in Tobacco Court.

Opening the door to the sitting room, Ruby was relieved to see that Tucker must have been unusually thoughtful and seen to the fire, which burnt brightly, casting dancing shadows on the walls. Without stopping to switch on the light or pull the curtains, Ruby opened the door to Lily's room and went inside. Tucker had been right when he said that Lily was sleeping peacefully. Her long hair spilled over the pillow like molten gold; her face was pale and translucent as candle wax but her breathing was soft and even. Glancing at the bedside table, Ruby saw that the cork had been left out of the medicine bottle. Picking it up, she realised that Lily must have helped herself to a hefty dose of laudanum as it had been half full when she left and was now almost empty. Frowning, Ruby laid her hand gently on Lily's brow and was relieved to find that the fever had abated. Perhaps sleep was the best medicine of all, even if it was drug induced. She tiptoed from the room, closing the door softly. Lily would almost certainly sleep until morning but that thought did little to cheer Ruby; she would have liked to tell Lily of her humiliating interview with Matron Luckes. Lily would have understood how she felt and been sweetly sympathetic.

Taking off her sodden outer garments, Ruby spread them over the backs of chairs to dry. A feeling of exhaustion swept over her as she pulled the curtains, shutting out the dreary winter night, and she went to sit by the fire. It was comforting and soothing, sitting in the glow of the firelight and toasting her feet in front of the cheering blaze. She would not think about her disappointment now; tomorrow she would make plans, try other hospitals, approach different matrons, but now all she wanted was to be alone and to rest. Making herself comfortable, Ruby pulled the pins out of her wet hair, letting it fall loose around her shoulders. Her damp skirts sent clouds of steam billowing up the chimney and as the warmth permeated her chilled flesh, making her pleasantly drowsy, she undid the top buttons of her blouse. Closing her eyes Ruby relaxed against the velvet cushions and, clearing her mind of the dismal events at the hospital, allowed herself to drift into that pleasant place between waking and sleeping.

The sound of someone poking the fire followed by lumps of coal being shovelled from the brass coal scuttle made Ruby wake up with a start. The room was in semi-darkness, the fire having died down so low that it had almost gone out.

'You were asleep on duty.'

Blinking, Ruby realised that the tall shadow bending over the fire was Jonas.

'Is Lily . . .?'

'Lily is sound asleep, full to the back teeth with laudanum, but that's not such a bad thing in her condition,' Jonas said, giving the fire a poke and stepping back as the flames licked up the chimney. He laid the poker in the grate, eyeing

Ruby with brows raised. 'What happened to you?'

Startled and conscious of her dishevelled state and the fact that her blouse was undone, revealing the top of her shift, Ruby sat upright, fumbling with the buttons. 'I got caught in the rain.'

'And you went where?'

'Lily knew where I was going. Do I have to ask you every time I want to leave the house?'

'You're not a prisoner, Ruby.'

'You could have fooled me.' Rising to her feet, Ruby made a move towards the door but Jonas caught her by the arm, twisting her round to face him in the flickering firelight.

'You've been crying.'

Ruby shook her head. 'I told you, I got caught in the rain.'

'Don't take me for a fool, Ruby. I can tell the difference between rainwater and tears. For one thing, rainwater doesn't redden your eyes and nose.' Jonas ran his finger down her cheek. 'Or leave sooty streaks. You've been bawling your eyes out. What happened?'

Ruby met his gaze, ready to deny everything and storm out of the room, but she saw nothing but sympathy and concern in his eyes, and the sudden change in his normally imperious attitude was both disturbing and confusing. 'Nothing,' she said, looking away.

'Is it a man?' Jonas's voice was harsh, like steel on steel. 'Was it that Billy Noakes that you've been caring for? Did he do anything to you?'

'No! It weren't nothing to do with Billy. If you must know, I went to the hospital to see the matron and she turned me down flat.' Despite her struggle to appear unconcerned, Ruby heard her voice crack. Biting her lips to stop them from wobbling, she stared down at her feet.

'Turned you down! For God's sake, why?'

Tears flowed from Ruby's eyes, fast and unstoppable as a breached dam. 'She said I didn't speak proper and I weren't a lady.'

'The stuck-up bitch!' Guiding her gently to the sofa, Jonas sat down beside Ruby, holding her hand. 'You don't take that sort of crap from a dried-up old spinster. I'll go and see the old cow myself.'

'No!' Ruby snatched her hand away, wiping her eyes on her sleeve. The thought of Jonas storming into Matron's inner sanctum was so ludicrous that she giggled. 'No, please don't.'

Taking a large, white handkerchief from his pocket, Jonas handed it to Ruby, a smile crinkling the corners of his eyes. 'I made you laugh, Ruby. I've never seen you laugh before.'

'You ain't never given me anything to laugh about.' Ruby blew her nose in the hanky, glaring at Jonas over its white folds. 'All you done is to threaten me and Joe with violence.

That's your answer to everything, Mr Crowe.'

'Not everything,' Jonas said, brushing a lock of hair back from Ruby's forehead. 'I've given you a hard time, using you to get to your brother.'

'Are you saying you're sorry?'

'Am I sorry that I separated you from your worthless brother and selfish sister? Not in the least.'

'Here,' Ruby said, thrusting the crumpled hanky into his hand. 'Take it back and don't you dare say nothing about my family.'

Frowning, Jonas tossed the offending hanky onto the floor. 'Ruby, you're worth a dozen of them. Can't you see that?'

'I – I don't understand you,' Ruby said breathlessly. 'What do you want of me?'

For a moment Jonas was silent, his expression unreadable, but Ruby sensed a tension in him that made her suddenly wary. He seemed to be fighting some deep and dangerous emotion; she could feel it in the air like an approaching thunderstorm. She attempted to rise but Jonas was too quick for her and he laid his hands on her shoulders, looking deeply into her eyes.

'Ruby. You really don't know, do you?'

Alarmed by the timbre of his voice and the burning desire that clouded his eyes, Ruby pressed her hands against his chest in an attempt to push him away, but it was as futile a gesture as that of a mouse trying to escape from a cat and

Jonas drew her into his arms, holding her so that there was no escape. His mouth was hot and demanding, savage and yet strangely exciting. It was hard to breathe, impossible to think. The world was spinning as he released her just enough to hold her at arm's length.

'You're not used to being kissed, are you, Ruby?'

'I been kissed,' Ruby said breathlessly, remembering timid pecks on the cheek and bolder but brief excursions to her lips by boys who had occasionally walked her home from school or church. 'But not by a rotten swine like you.'

Instead of being angry, as she had expected, Jonas's eyes gleamed with amusement and he chuckled. 'I've always admired your spirit, Ruby. I recognised it the moment I set eyes on you at the funeral. You've got brains and beauty and I'd bet my last farthing that you've got depths of passion buried beneath that prim and proper exterior.'

'Let me go. I ain't one of your street women.' Ruby tried to get up, but he held her in an uncompromising grip. Panic seized her. 'I think I heard Lily call.'

'Lily's taken enough laudanum to knock out the whole street,' Jonas said, his smile fading and his eyes darkening. 'Have you any idea what a desirable woman you are, Ruby?'

'No, you've got the wrong sister. It's Rosetta

that the men go for, not me,' Ruby said, struggling to get free. 'I'm the sensible one. I ain't interested in you, Jonas Crowe. Now let me go.'

For a moment she thought he was going to release her, but his eyes held her in an almost hypnotic gaze; eyes so dark that they looked black and she felt that she was being drawn into them, drowning in their depths. Jonas stroked her cheek with one finger, sliding it down her neck. His hand was warm and moved seductively, tantalising, searching beneath her chemise, tugging at the thin cotton of her blouse and sending buttons flying in all directions. She tried to break away but his free hand moved swiftly behind her head, dragging her inexorably nearer until his mouth covered hers, devouring her with an urgency that sent her senses tumbling into a dizzying abyss. Dimly, Ruby felt the laces on her stays snap like cotton threads. The thin material of her blouse ripped as easily as tissue paper. All the while his mouth plundered hers and his hands moved expertly, cupping her breasts, caressing her taut stomach and entering the most secret, private place between her legs until a soft moan of pleasure escaped from her throat. This was not happening. A small voice in her head told her to fight, to bite, to scream, but even then she knew that resistance was useless. There was no one to hear her cries. And she did scream as he rose above her, freeing her lips but entering her with a primeval force that sent shards of pain searing through her body. Suddenly and without her willing it, their bodies were moving together in a wild rhythm, culminating in a breathtaking sensation that sent her senses soaring like fireworks into a black-velvet night sky. She could hear a woman sobbing and moaning with animal pleasure. Ruby realised, as he withdrew from her body, that the voice was her own.

Chapter Ten

'You got to get a job, Joe.' Rosetta sat on the edge of her bed buttoning her boots. 'Sly and Aunt Lottie would go barmy if they knew you was hiding in my room and I can't keep on pinching food from the kitchen. Even young Elsie is getting suspicious and you know how daft she is.'

Huddled in the wooden rocking chair by the fire, Joe stretched and yawned. 'Aw, come on, Rose. Don't nag.'

'Nag? I should throw you out on your arse,' Rosetta said, jumping to her feet. 'Look, I'm sorry you lost your apprenticeship but you got to admit that you asked for trouble.'

'Me heart weren't in it. I'm not cut out to work in a print shop.'

'Well, I ain't covering up for you no longer. You been here for over a week and if Aunt Lottie or Sly finds out we'll both end up on the street. You got to get work and find a room of your own, or else come clean to Aunt Lottie and admit that you still owe Jonas money.'

'Aw, Rosie, don't go on at me. Ruby's settled in next door looking after Lily and as long as she's there it keeps Crowe sweet. We got an agreement that so long as I don't run up no more IOUs he won't call in the debt.'

'I dunno why you had to go and drag Ruby into it. I could've done better.'

'You'd have ended up sitting on his lap and forgetting all about me,' Joe said grinning. 'Give us a break, love, and fetch us something to eat. I'm bloody starving and I haven't had a bite since breakfast yesterday.'

Arms akimbo, Rosetta stared at him in disbelief. 'I give you money for a pie or something. What did you do with it?'

'It was a sure thing, that is until the nag fell at the last fence.'

'I give up. You promised you'd stop gambling.'

'I never said as much.'

'You got a short memory, Joe. I seem to remember you snivelling and scared stiff what Jonas would do to you and feeling guilty because you sent Ruby to do your dirty work?'

'Yes, but she's landed on her feet, or so Tucker tells me.'

Rosetta stared at him in disbelief. 'You mean you spend half your time round there and you ain't even had the decency to see Ruby and make sure she's all right?'

'And get an ear bashing from her? No fear! She'd go mad if she found out that I still play the tables.'

'And Jonas lets you?'

Joe shrugged his shoulders. 'It's part of the deal, though Ruby don't know nothing about it. He lets me play the tables and I keep an eye on the punters to see no one cheats or looks like winning too much and breaking the bank.'

'I don't understand. Why would Jonas do that, and how is Ruby a part of it?'

'He's making me work off me debts. He lends me the stake money every night, which I have to pay back. If I win a bit I keep it, but if I lose I'm in dead trouble. Honest, Rose, I might as well be in the clink. He only wants Ruby there so that he's got a hold over me, but I don't think he'd ever do her harm. He just talks tough to scare me into doing what he wants.'

'So you end up doing what you like best – playing the tables – while Ruby is held hostage. You're rotten, you are, Joe.'

Shrugging his shoulders, Joe flashed her a winning smile. 'I never pretended to be a saint, Rose. But you've no need to worry about Ruby. She's got it easy compared to me.'

'And how d'you work that one out then?'

'Ruby's paid to look after Lily and that don't amount to what I'd call hard work. She's got a room all to herself and I hear that Jonas bought her a set of new togs that would make you turn pea-green with envy. You missed the boat there, you know.'

Incensed, Rosetta threw a pillow at him. 'And I keep telling you I ain't interested in Jonas Crowe. He can go to hell for all I care and if he don't treat Ruby right, then I'll go round there and scratch his eyes out. Which is what you should have done if you was a proper man.'

'Me fingernails ain't long enough,' Joe said, laughing and demonstrating his fingernails bitten to the quick. 'You can't fool me, Rose. I saw you making sheep's eyes at him during the wake. Anyway, I thought you wasn't speaking to Ruby since she's snatched your gentleman friend from beneath your nose?'

'That's right, we ain't talking, but that don't mean I don't still love her and it don't mean I'd let anyone harm a hair off her head.'

'You ain't as tough as you makes out, are you, Rosie?'

Tossing her head, Rosetta picked up her coat and hat. 'I got a rehearsal to go to and you can find your own breakfast. If you ain't out of my room by tonight, I'll tell Sly. I mean it, Joe.'

Down in the basement kitchen, Rosetta found Mr Wilby finishing a bowl of porridge. Scraping his plate clean he jumped up, tipped his battered top hat in her direction and scuttled off like a green-tinged beetle.

Elsie came in from the scullery and picked up his empty plate. 'Porridge is all gone,' she said. 'There's bread in the crock.'

'Where is Mr Silas?' Taking a mug from the dresser, Rosetta filled it with tea. 'Any milk?'

'He took the missis's breakfast upstairs and the milk is off.' Elsie put the plate back on the table, apparently forgetting why she had picked it up in the first place, and began to sweep the flagstone floor with a besom. 'I got so much work to do. I'll get a thick ear if it ain't done afore he comes downstairs.'

Rosetta wrinkled her nose as she sipped the strong, stewed tea. It was warm and wet and that was all you could say for it. 'Tell me, Elsie. Why don't I ever see any of the gents what lodges here, other than creepy Cyril Wilby that is?'

Elsie giggled. 'You'd best not say that in front of him, miss.'

'No, I'm not likely to be so daft. But you didn't answer my question.'

Elsie dropped the broom and picked up the plate. 'Oh, I got to get on. Got to get on. Oh dearie me.' She ran into the scullery, slamming the door behind her.

Rosetta took another sip of tea. At first, she had not thought it strange that the only lodger she had ever seen was Mr Wilby, but now she was beginning to wonder exactly what sort of establishment Uncle Sly was running. At night there was the constant passage of feet, loud and drunken voices and the sound of doors opening

223

and closing, and yet, by morning, all these men had disappeared like mist burned off by the sun. It was very strange. Glancing at the clock on the mantelshelf, Rosetta set her mug down on the table. If she didn't hurry she would be late for rehearsal and Madame was driving her even harder than ever. Tonight would be her first appearance as a solo artiste and she could not afford to give a bad performance.

Rosetta was about to open the front door when Sly came steaming down the stairs. 'Oy! You ain't paid last week's rent yet, Rose.'

'I'll give it you when I get me wages at the end of the week.'

'You'd better pay up, my girl, or I'll have to tell Lottie and she won't be best pleased.'

Rosetta blew him a kiss. 'Don't worry, you'll get your money.'

'And there's the matter of a knuckle of ham what went missing. I give Elsie a good thrashing for it but she swore it weren't her. D'you know anything about that?'

'Sorry, Uncle Sly. I got to go.' Opening the door, Rosetta fled.

At the end of the day's rehearsals, Rosetta slumped down on a chair with her head between her knees.

'You done good, Rosetta,' Madame said, coming to stand in front of her. 'You perform like that tonight and you'll be well on your way to star billing.'

Rosetta lifted her head, brushing the sweat from her eyes. 'You think so?'

'I'm sure of it. For one thing you've got talent and for another you've got Alfie wrapped round your little finger.'

'Maybe.'

'No need to be modest,' Madame said, winking. 'I seen the old goat leering at you. You've put Aggie's nose right out of joint. Anyway, I got to go and give her what for. She was late again this morning.'

Watching Madame marching off down the corridor, Rosetta couldn't help feeling pleased that Aggie was going to get a good telling off. She had arrived late for rehearsal, sour as a bag of lemons, and, during rehearsals, had danced like a duck wearing hobnail boots. The gossip was that Aggie had been out to supper with Alf Ricketts last night. Getting stiffly to her feet, Rosetta could hear Madame's shrill voice berating Aggie and she almost felt sorry for her. After all, if Alf was getting what he wanted from Aggie then, when it came to her turn, he might be satisfied with a lot less. Rosetta shuddered at the thought of allowing Alf anything more than a grope and a bit of a cuddle, but if that was what it took to get top billing, then that was what it took. She would show Jonas Crowe that she was someone to be respected, an artiste in her own right. When she was top of the bill at the Falstaff he would come begging her to entertain the punters in his club, and then she would have the pleasure of turning him down. That would show him that Rosetta Capretti was not a person to be overlooked, ignored or patronised.

The show had gone well and Alf was pleased. Rosetta had been prepared for an invitation for supper but she hadn't counted on eating in a pie and eel shop. She stabbed her fork into the white flesh of the stewed eel swimming in liquor and popped it into her mouth. She had thought that Alf might take her up West for a meal in an expensive restaurant, but by the time the show was over and the theatre closed up for the night, she was so hungry that she could have chewed the leg off the table and enjoyed it. Alf, sitting beside her in the booth with a chequered napkin tucked into his collar, was dipping bread into the liquor and sucking it into his mouth with moist, slopping sounds and grunts of pleasure.

'I like to see a woman with a good appetite,' he said, wiping his face on the napkin. 'You're a girl after me own heart, Rosie.'

'Rosetta. I don't like being called Rosie, it's vulgar.'

Slapping her on the thigh, Alf gave a deep belly laugh. 'Ho, and that song you sang tonight wasn't vulgar? Not a bit risky, like? Come off it, Rosie, you ain't no nun, so don't go putting on airs. I like you just as you are.'

Rosetta swallowed the last piece of eel and, reluctantly, left a potato on her plate, remembering Mum's strict instructions regarding manners. A young lady never finishes up everything on her plate; it makes her look greedy and it ain't polite.

'Right then, you ready for the off, girlie?'

'Don't I get no pudding? Not even a penny lick?'

'I'll give you more than a penny lick, my girl.'

Alf's beery breath made Rosetta feel sick, but she forced a smile, angling her head. 'Oh, you are funny, Alfie. But I could manage a bit of spotted dick and custard.'

Alf raised his hand to summon the waiter. 'Never let it be said that Alf Ricketts don't know how to treat a lady.'

Whether it was the combination of eels, spotted dick and custard or the proximity of Alf's sweating body in the hansom cab, by the time they reached Old Street Rosetta was feeling genuinely sick.

'Why are we stopping here?' she demanded as Alf banged on the roof and ordered the cabby to stop outside the theatre. 'Don't tell me we got a midnight show.'

'We could have our own little private show, dearie.'

'Alfie, dear, I really ought to get home to me beauty sleep. After all, you don't want me falling asleep during me number, do you?'

'Falling asleep is the last thing on my mind, Rosie.' Alf clambered out of the cab, paid the driver and held his hand out to Rosetta. 'Just got a couple of things I need to check in my office, Miss Capretti. If you'd do me the honour.'

Alf's mottled, beef-sausage fingers waved a cheery goodbye as the hansom cab drew away from the kerb. Rosetta stumbled, grabbed the iron railings outside the house and was sick down the area steps. Shivering and trembling all over, she dragged herself up to the front door and felt inside the letter box for the piece of string that was tied to the door key. Once safely inside, she went downstairs to the kitchen, treading softly so as not to wake anyone in the house. Elsie was curled up like a puppy on a rug in front of the range, sound asleep. Tiptoeing past her, Rosetta went into the scullery and filled a cup with cold water from the tap. She drank thirstily and splashed her face with water, intent on getting rid of the taste and smell of Alf Ricketts. She retched at the memory of his drunken, slobbery kisses, the stench of his breath and the final pain and degradation she had suffered when her protests were ignored and he took her on the office floor like a common slut. Aunt Lottie had made it all sound so easy, as if the act of love was a delight in itself and bringing men to it was all a game. For the first time in her life, Rosetta found herself envying Ruby. Ruby, she thought, would never have put herself in such an unenviable position. Rosetta had always teased her about her dry old medical books and her ambition to care for the sick and needy, but maybe Ruby had the right idea after all.

Creeping back past Elsie, Rosetta left the kitchen and dragged her aching body up to the first floor. She was still shaking all over, weak at the knees and her teeth clattered together like a busker playing the spoons. She paused. There was no telltale strip of light under Lottie's door and Rosetta went inside, fumbling her way in the dark to the small side table where Lottie kept her bottle of gin. She took off the stopper and put the bottle to her lips. The fiery spirit burnt her throat, made her gasp and her eyes watered. Smothering a cough, she took a deep breath and another swig of gin. It hit the lining of her now empty stomach like a lightning bolt, ricocheting upwards, dizzying her brain and blunting memory. Putting the bottle carefully back where she had found it, Rosetta made her way to the staircase and climbed the three flights to the attic. Pausing to catch her breath, she heard the now familiar sound of footsteps, male voices and tipsy laughter coming towards her. She ran to her room and dodged inside, looking anxiously over her shoulder to see if Joe was asleep in the chair. The room was empty and she breathed a sigh of relief. Maybe he had seen sense after all. Holding the door ajar, she peeped out and saw three men, one with a woman leaning on his arm. They had gone past her door and were now lurching drunkenly towards the staircase. Their voices were still audible long after the darkness had swallowed them up. Rosetta heard more doors open and close and then silence.

The gin had gone to her head, dulling the memory of losing her virginity to a disgusting pig like Alf, and the effects of the alcohol had made her bold. Determined to find out once and for all where these nightly revellers were coming from, Rosetta crept along the passage that ended, as she had always thought, in a blank wall. She was in total darkness but, amazingly, straight ahead of her there were threads of light outlining the shape of a door. Running her hands over the wall she could not find a handle, but what she had previously thought to be panelling now appeared to be the indentation of a doorway. On the other side, in Crowe's premises, she could hear the sound of voices and laughter and approaching footsteps. Panicking, she turned to run but caught her heel in a threadbare patch of carpet. There was a moment of silence, Rosetta kicked free of the cords but was pitched backwards as the door flew open, pinning her to the wall.

'What the hell?'

Rosetta almost fainted with relief. 'Joe?'

'For God's sake, Rose, what d'you think you're doing?'

'What was I doing? What are you doing coming through the wall like a bloody spook?'

'Shut up or someone will hear you.' Joe grabbed her by the shoulders and pushed her along the corridor.

'There's no need to shove,' Rosetta said, breaking away from him. 'Keep your stupid secrets if you must.' Strutting off towards her room, she could hear Joe padding along behind her.

'There!' Joe said, following her into the room and tossing a leather pouch on the bed. 'I won tonight. I told you me luck would turn.'

'And you paid off your debt to Jonas?'

'No, but I got enough to buy me a bit of time. One or two more runs of luck like tonight and I'll be able to get away from Crowe.'

'He'll skin you alive when he finds out.'

'I covered me tracks. I ain't stupid, Rose. One more big win and I'm a free man.'

Rosetta dashed her hand across her eyes as exhaustion washed over her in a great tidal wave. The way Joe talked about gambling was beyond all reason and he sounded just like Lottie: the big win was always just a bet away. Right now all Rosetta wanted was to get into bed and forget everything in sleep.

'You all right, Rose?' Striking a match, Joe lit a candle and held it close to Rosetta's face. 'You look a bit peaky.'

'Just tired. It's been a long day.'

'Get some sleep and forget what you saw tonight.'

'How can I forget it? Why is this house linked with Crowe's place?'

'It's a business deal between Sly and Crowe.'

'I don't understand.' Rosetta's knees gave way beneath her and the bedsprings groaned in protest as she slumped down onto the flock mattress. 'You'd better tell me, and I want the truth, mind. I'm not in a mood to listen to lies.'

Joe sat down in the rocking chair and kicked off his boots. 'You're a sport, you always was.'

'You ain't answered the question and I ain't stupid. Does Aunt Lottie know what's going on under her own roof?'

'Shouldn't think so.' Joe tapped the side of his nose, grinning. 'Sly by name and sly by nature! Letting rooms to tarts and punters is a good deal more profitable than looking after commercial travellers and a lot less work.'

'Turn your head,' Rosetta said, preparing to undress.

Obediently, Joe looked away, staring into the empty grate. 'I think that Sly done the deal without telling Lottie. And let's face it, she don't care about anything much as long as she's got a bottle of tiddley to keep her company. Old Cyril Wilby is the only real lodger. He's just there to make the place look respectable. Rose, are you decent? Me neck's aching something chronic.'

Down to her shift, Rosetta climbed into bed, pulling the covers up to her chin. 'Someone ought to tell her that Sly's running a knocking shop.'

'Well it ain't gonna be me,' Joe said, yawning. 'And if you take my advice, Rose, you'll keep your mouth shut too.'

Next morning when Rosetta woke up she found that Joe had gone, but on her bedside table he had left a shining golden guinea. She did not feel in the least little bit like going to the theatre and the thought of seeing Alf was nauseating, but Rosetta knew that if she missed a single rehearsal she would lose her solo spot. She must be nice to Alf, but this time she would take charge and there would be no repeats of the disgusting events of last night. Her head ached as the result of drinking Lottie's gin and the taste of vomit lingered in her mouth; she longed for a hot, sweet cup of tea to wash it away but she had little appetite for breakfast. On her way down to the kitchen, Rosetta took a peek into several of the rooms, first listening at the keyhole to make sure they were unoccupied. Each room was identical to the last, sparsely furnished with a double bed, a washstand and a single chair. There was no doubt left in her mind: Sly was running a bordello and more than likely keeping the profits to himself. Should she tell Aunt Lottie, or should she follow Joe's advice and say nothing?

Silas was sitting in his usual chair by the range, with his feet up on the brass rail, reading a copy of the *Daily Mail*. He glanced at Rosetta over the top of the paper. 'You wasn't in last night when I locked up.'

Shrugging her shoulders, Rosetta went to pick up the teapot.

'It'll be stewed. Breakfast was over an hour ago and I sent Elsie to the market.'

Without answering, Rosetta set about making a fresh pot of tea.

Silas put down his newspaper. 'I heard young Joe had a winning streak last night.'

Rosetta almost poured boiling water over her hand, missing the brown teapot and slopping it onto the flagstone floor. 'How do you know that?'

'I got it from young Tucker when I went out to buy a morning paper. It come from the horse's mouth, so to speak. Satisfied?'

*

When Alf did not put in an appearance during rehearsals, Rosetta began to relax. Madame put everyone through a rigorous practice session and, not wanting to draw attention to herself, Rosetta had to force her aching limbs to keep up with the rest of the girls. When at last it was over, she was in the middle of dressing and barely listening to the girls chattering about their male admirers, teasing each other and making lewd jokes, when Alf put his head round the door. There was total silence and Rosetta could feel everyone staring at her.

'Excuse the intrusion, ladies.' Alf cast around the room until his eyes lit upon Rosetta. He raised his finger and beckoned. 'Miss Capretti, please. I need to go over a clause in your contract. In my office, now!'

As he closed the door, everyone began to giggle.

'I wouldn't bother to pull them up, dearie,' Aggie said, jerking her head in Rosetta's direction. 'He'll have them off again in two ticks.'

Hastily buttoning her blouse, Rosetta felt her cheeks burning but she forced a smile. 'You'd know all about that, Aggie Brown.'

'Me and most of the girls in this room, but then we didn't get third billing. You must have got something that we ain't got.'

'It's called talent, Aggie,' Rosetta said, tossing her head. 'Something you definitely ain't got.'

Aggie flew at her with fingers crooked into talons, but Rosetta nimbly dodged her and left the room with her head held high. Let them talk and let them giggle behind her back. She was going to put Alf firmly in his place; there would be no repeats of last night's shenanigans.

She strode through the narrow corridors to Alf's office, rapped smartly on the door and went in without bothering to wait for an answer. 'Now, Alfie dear, you really shouldn't show me up in front of the other girls. It won't do and I won't have it.'

Alf got up from behind his desk, his teeth bared in a wolfish smile. 'Oh, I think you will, pet. That is, if you want to remain at number three. If you're a very good girl, we might even get you up as far as number one, but you'll have to be ever so good.'

Poised for flight, Rosetta curled her fingers round the doorknob. 'You got it all wrong. I ain't cheap and I ain't easy.'

'I've seen your sort come and go over the years, so don't put on airs and graces with me, girlie.'

Alf was coming at her, his lips parted like a dog salivating over its dinner. Rosetta tried to open the door but he lunged forward, slamming it with one hand, turning the key in the lock with the other, his portly body pinning her to the wooden panels.

'I'll scream,' she said, struggling.

'Don't worry, pet,' Alf said, lifting up her skirt. 'Scream away if you want. We're underground and there's a full orchestra rehearsal going on.'

Rosetta began to live in dread of Alf's frequent summonses to his office. Everyone knew what was going on behind his locked door. She found that almost as hateful as his seemingly insatiable lust. She was trapped by her own ambition and her need for money. Alf had threatened to make sure that if she refused to co-operate, she would never work in the London theatre again and Rosetta had no option but to believe him. She took no pleasure in their hurried couplings on the office floor – or, if he was feeling generous, in a cheap hotel room after an indifferent supper. But there seemed to be no way out. Aunt Lottie would not be sympathetic; after all, hadn't she told her that this was the one and only sure way to get to the top? Rosetta thought of confiding in Joe, but almost at once abandoned the idea. There was no knowing which way he would react; he might be shocked and angry, playing the part of the outraged elder brother and physically assaulting Alf. He might even think it funny or simply turn his back on her, saying that she had brought it upon herself.

Rosetta's thoughts turned to Ruby who was living just next door, although it might have been a hundred miles away with Jonas Crowe standing like a barrier between them. Once, what seemed like a lifetime ago, she had told Ruby absolutely everything. They had lain side by side in bed whispering confidences long into the night to the background noise of Granny Mole snoring. It had been so innocent, Rosetta thought sadly, although they had thought it shocking at the time, when Sammy Maloney had kissed her on the lips and tickled her tongue with his. She had been certain that this was how babies were made, but Ruby had said it didn't count unless you were lying down in bed; that's what Sukey Harris had told her and she should know, being one of ten children living in two rooms with their parents, and a new baby arriving regularly every year.

No, she couldn't tell Ruby. She couldn't admit what a stupid, over-ambitious fool she had been and that now she was trapped in this horrible situation, having to suffer physical intimacy with a man who revolted her, and whom she was beginning to hate so much that nightly she dreamed of killing him. Rosetta could just see Father Brennan's face if he knew just half the truth of her fall from grace. She had never been a conscientious churchgoer, and she could barely remember the last time she had been to confession, but she was certain that her catalogue of sins was so great that no amount of Hail Marys or penances could save her immortal soul.

To add to her burden of guilt, Rosetta had been short with Billy when he had come to call. Joe had told her all about his bravery in rescuing the baker and his family and how Ruby had nursed him until his burns healed, but Rosetta had long ago lost interest in Billy. Compared to Jonas Crowe he was little more than a cheap chancer, doing dodgy deals and living by his wits, who would never amount to anything. She could not imagine now what she had ever seen in Billy, and had made it clear that she did not want him to call again. When he had gone, Rosetta had to run to the privy in the yard and was sick. She had been sick that morning too, and the previous morning. She really must stop eating the chocolates that Alf now bought for her, having complained that she had grown too thin for comfort and needed a 'bit more meat on her bones'.

After almost three months, there was nothing that Alf did that either surprised or shocked her; she did not enjoy their physical union but Rosetta found that, by concentrating on something else, perhaps a new dance step or the words of a song, she could mentally detach herself from the sweaty, humiliating process. His demands on her had gradually eased, so that now it was just once or twice a week that she had to suffer his advances. For the rest of the time, he left her more or less alone. Rosetta was more than grateful for this, but she had her sights set on top billing and she couldn't help worrying a bit that she had lost some of her bargaining powers.

Walking to the theatre one morning in late April, Rosetta realised with a lift of her spirits that the bite had gone out of the wind and ragged puffball clouds were scudding across a baby-blue sky. The streets were just as grey and dirty as before, but the costermongers' barrows spilled over with golden daffodils and narcissi brought in from the country. Old women at street corners sold nosegays of violets and primroses and the scent of spring was in the air. Rosetta bought a bunch of violets, pressing the velvety purple flowers to her nose and inhaling the delicate scent. Pinning it to her lapel she paused at the stage door, studying a poster and revelling in seeing her name printed in large black letters just one line beneath the comedian who was top of the bill. If she could catch Alfie in a good mood, who knows, with a little cajoling, she might even get to the top very soon, and once she was a star she would have theatre managers falling over in their eagerness to sign her up. She could tell Alf to go to hell and never have to put up with his sweaty embraces ever again. Looking at the billboard outside the theatre, Rosetta could see her name in large, black letters. In her mind she had already achieved star billing and proper high-class gents were queuing up to drink champagne from her slippers.

'You're late,' Madame said, pouncing on her almost before she had got inside the door. 'Don't think you're too high and mighty to need rehearsals now that you're second billing. You still got to practise, practise, practise or you'll never get nowhere.'

'Yes, I'm sorry,' Rosetta said, hurrying towards the dressing room. She did not tell Madame that she was late because she had been sick again. It was happening so regularly that she was beginning to think she had something very wrong with her. To her dismay she found Aggie was in the dressing room, sprawled on a chair, smoking a cigarette.

'Oh, it's you. I thought it was old Clara come to get me.' Aggie took a drag on her cigarette and exhaled a plume of blue smoke.

Choking, Rosetta turned away, the too familiar nauseous feeling rising in her throat. 'No smoking in here. You know that.'

'Ooh, listen to her. Just because you're Alf's bit of skirt don't mean you can tell me what to do.'

Before Rosetta could answer, Tilly rushed into the room. 'Aggie, better come back quick. Madame's looking for you.'

'Bleeding hell,' Aggie said, stamping the cigarette end out on the polished floorboards.

'You'd best get a move on too, Capretti.'

Tilly moved closer to Rosetta, staring hard. 'You all right, Rose?'

Rosetta had discarded her coat and had her blouse half off, but the room had begun to spin round her as if she were doing pirouette after pirouette. Suddenly she was on the floor, looking up into Tilly's freckled face.

'You passed out,' Tilly said anxiously. 'Are you sick?'

Rosetta struggled to a sitting position, holding her head. 'Just a bit dizzy. Can't think why.'

'Don't be bloody stupid,' Aggie said, coming to stand over her, hands on hips. 'Been throwing up lately, Rose?'

'Sometimes, when I eat too much chocolate.'

Aggie let out a hoot of laughter. 'It ain't chocolate what's in your belly, ducks.'

'Shut up,' Tilly said, glaring up at Aggie. 'Don't listen to her, Rose.'

'So when did you have your last monthly?' Aggie demanded. 'Bet you can't remember. You're in the family way, ducks, good and proper.'

Chapter Eleven

Avoiding Jonas was comparatively easy. He seemed to be avoiding her. For days, after what had amounted to rape, Ruby had lived in a constant state of anxiety, shame and self-loathing. She had done so little to stop him; perhaps she had unintentionally given him some kind of encouragement? She hated him for what he was and what he had done to her and yet, deep down and to her eternal shame, Ruby had to struggle with the knowledge that her treacherous body had responded with a passion that she could never have imagined. It must, she thought, have been some kind of devil within her that allowed Jonas to play with her senses, exciting her body to a fever pitch over which she had no control.

Ruby lay in bed night after sleepless night unable to banish the memory of Jonas's hands caressing her bare flesh, his mouth demanding her response and the shameful climax when she had cried out, not in pain but in ecstasy. Mum had always told her that the intimate relations of the marriage bed were the curse that women had to bear, and that the act of procreation was not supposed to be pleasurable. It was a wife's duty to suffer in silence. Ruby's cheeks flamed in the darkness as she remembered the illicit pleasure that had been her downfall. She should have fought to protect her virginity; she should have screamed out, bitten, scratched, appealed to Jonas's better nature, but she had done none of those things.

Ruby thought of running away but she had nowhere to go. She could not return to Tobacco Court in disgrace, she could not leave Joe to face his fate, and now she had another tie in that she had grown fond of Lily who was desperately sick and needed her. Focusing her anger and despair on Jonas, Ruby convinced herself that she would never forgive him for what he had done: he had ruined her and no decent man would want to marry her now. She was used goods, second-hand, spoilt. She would never be able to look Adam Fairfax in the face again; not that a gentleman like Adam would look twice at her anyway, but any slight chance of that had been wiped out by that cataclysmic night when Lily lay in bed, drugged with laudanum and helpless in the grip of her illness.

With the coming of spring, Lily seemed to be recovering slowly from the exacerbation of the disease that was slowly consuming her body, and Ruby had to steel herself not to blurt out a confession, begging her forgiveness. She knew that it would be impossible to avoid Jonas for ever, but she had been unprepared for the violence of her reaction when he came unexpectedly into the sitting room while she was reading out loud to Lily. Ruby dropped the book, covering her confusion by going down on her hands and knees to retrieve it.

'Jonas!' Lily's pale cheeks flushed to a delicate pink and her eyes glowed with an inner light.

'How are you today, Lily?'

Scrambling to her feet, Ruby couldn't look Jonas in the eye. He was standing in front of Lily looking down at her as she lay on the chaise longue, so pale and thin that her flesh seemed almost transparent. By comparison, Jonas looked ruggedly healthy and his strength and vitality seemed totally out of place in a sick room. Backing away, Ruby made for the door.

'It's all right, Ruby,' Jonas said, in an even tone, as if nothing had ever happened between them. 'Don't go. I need you to hear this too.'

'What is it?' Lily said, reaching up to hold his hand. 'Is it something nice, Jonas?'

Jonas sat down beside her. 'I've spoken to the doctor, Lily. He says you should go away to convalesce. Out of London and preferably by the sea.'

'A seaside holiday?' Spots of colour appeared on Lily's cheeks, giving her the appearance of a painted wooden doll. Sparks of excitement flared in her blue eyes. 'I've never seen the sea.'

'It's all arranged. I've booked you into a hotel on the seafront in Southend. They say the air is bracing on the east coast. We'll soon have you back on your feet.'

Lily's smile faded. 'You've booked me in? Aren't you going to stay with me?'

'I'll take you there in the motor, but you know that I've got business here and I can't just leave things to run themselves.'

'I know that, Jonas.' Lily sighed, collapsing back against the cushions, closing her eyes.

'I'll come down as often as I can to see you,' Jonas continued in a voice he might have used to comfort a small child. 'You'll be well looked after, and I'm sending Tucker with you. He'll run your errands and see that no one bothers you.'

Lily's eyes flew open: two blue pools swimming in tears. 'But Ruby will come too?' She began to cough, holding a hanky to her lips.

Ruby made a move towards her but Jonas caught her by the hand. 'You have a visitor waiting in the hall, Ruby. You'd better go down and see what he wants.'

'Adam!' Ruby almost missed a step as she ran downstairs to greet him.

'Ruby, I had to come myself,' Adam said, his

boyish features creased into a grin. 'I've got some wonderful news for you.'

Seeing Tucker straining his ears to hear what they were saying, Ruby led Adam to the ladies' room where supper was served in the evenings and where the women gathered, eating and drinking while the men occupied themselves in the gaming room upstairs. Shutting the double doors behind her, she motioned Adam to take a seat. Perching on a chair opposite him, she struggled to gain control her of her breathing, folding her hands in her lap to stop them trembling. 'You – you said you had some news for me?'

Adam smiled. 'It's absolutely splendid, Ruby. Matron called me into her office and said that she had been reconsidering her decision in the light of a generous donation of a bursary from an anonymous well-wisher. The upshot is that she is willing to take you on as a nurse probationer.'

'She wants me? Are you serious, Adam?'

'Absolutely serious. I'm so pleased for you and so is Pamela. She wanted to come with me today but she's on duty at the hospital.'

For a shining moment, Ruby saw her dream about to come true, until the harsh reality of the situation hit her. 'Mr Crowe only said I could study in my spare time and it looks like I'm going to Southend with Lily.' Jumping to her feet, she turned away so that Adam would not see the guilty blush that burned her cheeks at the mere mention of Jonas's name.

'You don't understand, Ruby. Mr Crowe thinks it's an excellent idea.'

Spinning round, Ruby stared hard at Adam. 'You asked him?'

'I probably should have mentioned it to you first, but he wanted to know why I was here. A perfectly reasonable request in the circumstances, and he was most affable. You have a good employer there.'

A good employer? Ruby couldn't look Adam in the face. He was so blissfully unaware of the nature of things here in Raven Street. With his high ideals and comfortable background, Adam had no idea what it was like existing in the twilight of the London underworld.

'You are pleased, aren't you, Ruby? You haven't changed your mind?'

Ruby shook her head. 'No, of course not. It's just a bit of a surprise, that's all. When do I start?'

When Adam had gone, Ruby went in search of Jonas. He was not in the sitting room and Lily had fallen into a drugged sleep on the chaise longue. Determined to get things straight, Ruby looked for him in the gaming room, which was unusually empty of punters. She found him in the small room that he used as an office, sitting behind his desk with a ledger open in front of him. He did not seem surprised to see her.

'Did you mean it?' Ruby demanded. 'Are you going to let me attend the nursing school, or were you just playing games with me?'

'Why would I do that?'

'You made me come here because of Joe's gambling debts. Why would you release me to study nursing?'

'I'm not your jailer.'

'I'm supposed to be looking after Lily, so I should be going with her to the seaside.'

Closing the ledger with a snap, Jonas sat back in his chair, his face an impassive mask. 'The doctor told me that Lily's condition is serious. She needs complete rest under medical supervision. The hotel is really a sanatorium but I didn't want to frighten Lily by telling her the truth.'

'You're sending her away.'

'For her own good and only for as long as it takes to make her well again.' Jonas got to his feet. 'Lily will have the best care that money can buy.'

'She'll be lonely and frightened amongst strangers.'

'Which is why I'm sending Tucker with her. He's a useless piece of flotsam but he is devoted to Lily and I know I can trust him to see that she has everything she needs.' Jonas walked slowly round the desk to stand in front of Ruby, his expression softening. 'If you want to help Lily, then study hard and learn as much as you can about nursing so that you can care for her when she is allowed home.'

A worm of suspicion crawled into Ruby's brain. 'Did you donate the money to the hospital so that I could study?'

'Does that sound like something I would do?'

'I don't know,' Ruby said, shaking her head, confused by the sudden physical proximity to him that brought memories flooding back. 'I don't know you at all.'

Jonas leaned back against his desk, arms folded across his chest, his expression carefully controlled. 'I'm not a good man; you keep that thought in your head. I do things with a purpose and for my own benefit.'

'So why are you doing this for me?'

'Don't go running away with the idea that I'm a generous benefactor. I'm keeping you to your part of the bargain and I want you back here every night as soon as you finish at the hospital.'

'But they don't finish until late. It would be easier if I went home to Tobacco Court.'

'This is your home, that is until that good-for-nothing brother finishes repaying the money he owes me.'

'I thought I was working for you to pay off Joe's debts. What are you making him do?'

'Nothing illegal, so don't worry. While you're here I promise not to break his neck,' Jonas said with a grim smile. 'Don't look so alarmed, Ruby. I've got Joe where I want him, for now. He can meet you at the hospital every evening and bring you home in a hansom cab. I won't have you walking the streets of Whitechapel on your own after dark.'

'Thank you.'

'You have nothing to thank me for,' Jonas said stiffly. 'We both know that.'

Ruby met his gaze steadily, anger bubbling to the surface. 'You treated me like a common whore.'

'No!' Jonas almost spat the word at her, his brows drawing together in a frown. 'Never think that. You must never think that.' He turned away from her, bowing his head, his voice barely audible. 'Forgive me, Ruby.'

During the next few days, Ruby barely had time to think about her sudden change of fortune. Everything now revolved around getting Lily packed and ready for the journey to Southend. Tucker was sent on ahead by rail with the luggage and on a bright morning at the end of April, in between sunshine and showers, Ruby helped Lily into the motor car, wrapping her in a fur rug.

'Good luck with your nursing studies, dear,'

Lily said, her eyes filling with tears. 'I'm going to miss you so much, Ruby.'

Hugging her, Ruby tried hard not to cry. 'You'll have a lovely time by the sea. I wish I was coming with you.'

Lily turned to Jonas as he climbed into the driving seat, having started the engine with the cranking handle. 'That's a wonderful idea. You could bring Ruby down with you next weekend, Jonas. Oh, say you will. I should have something extra special to look forward to.'

'Ruby might not be able to get away from the hospital, Lily. We'll have to see.'

'Do try,' Lily called as the motor pulled out into the street. 'I'll send you lots of postcards, Ruby.'

As Ruby stood, waving until they were out of sight, it hit her all at once that from now on, except for the servants, she would be alone in the house with Jonas every night. She had been so busy getting Lily ready for her trip, and, in her spare moments, dreaming about working at the hospital and seeing Adam every day, that she had not given a thought to what Jonas might expect of her with Lily away. He had treated her with the utmost civility, bordering on aloofness, since his whispered apology that day in his office. Sometimes Ruby thought she must have imagined that he asked so humbly for her forgiveness; the odd thing was that she had forgiven him, almost.

On Sunday, with Jonas not having returned from Southend and the whole day ahead of her, Ruby decided to visit her mother and give her the splendid news that she was about to enrol as a probationer at the London Hospital. It was a glorious spring day, full of golden sunshine in between the showers, and the pavements gleamed as though they had been freshly scrubbed. Opting to walk rather than to waste good money on a hansom cab, Ruby set off for Tobacco Court feeling happier than she had for a long time. She had worked it out in her head that if Jonas had not donated the bursary, then it must have been Adam. There was no one else who would have her best interests at heart and Adam had shown her marked attention from the start. Of course, she knew that he was devoted to Pamela and she would never do anything to come between them, but it was just more proof, if she had needed any, that Adam Fairfax was a wonderful person.

Stopping at a shop on the way, Ruby bought bread, butter, boiled ham and a slab of fruit cake. She was halfway home when a voice hailed her from a passing cart, and, turning her head, she saw Billy waving to her.

'Going home, Ruby? Hop up, I'm going that way myself.'

The basket was heavy and Ruby didn't argue.

Sitting beside Billy, she saw that his hands, although scarred, were free from bandages.

Billy grinned, holding his hands up for her to see. 'Much better, thanks to you.'

'I'm glad, but I didn't do much, Billy. It was Pamela and Adam who looked after you.'

'No, I won't have that, girl. It was you who saw to me when I was out of me head with fever and it was you who took me to your home to be looked after.' Billy flicked the reins to make his horse move at a slightly quicker plod. 'As a matter of fact I was on me way to call on your mum, just to see how she was going on.'

'That's nice of you, Billy. But as for me, I only did what any friend would do,' Ruby said, holding onto her hat as a frisky breeze tried to tug it off her head. 'Rosetta would have done the same if she'd been at home.'

Billy's face darkened. 'She don't want to know me now.'

'Oh, Billy, I'm sure that's not true.'

'You ought to know. You lives next door to each other.'

'I haven't seen Rose for weeks. She's not too happy with me working for Jonas Crowe.'

'So that's it, is it? I knew it wasn't just that she's doing well in the music hall. She's got her sights set on a bloke with more money than I'll ever get me hands on.'

Ruby couldn't argue with that and she sat in

silence, clutching her basket, thinking about Rosetta and her impossible dream of becoming Mrs Jonas Crowe. One thing Ruby knew now for certain was that Jonas took what he wanted, when he wanted it, and if he had had the slightest desire for Rosetta he would have taken her, willing or not.

'Penny for 'em.'

Billy's voice cut through her reverie, making Ruby jump. 'I was just thinking about Rose. I worry about her, Billy. She's not as tough as she makes out.'

'I know that,' Billy said, steering the horse into Tobacco Court. 'It's just that she thinks she knows it all.'

Ruby leapt out as the cart stopped. 'Are you coming in?'

'Is that an invitation?'

Ruby laughed. 'Of course it is. There's enough food in my basket to go round and Mum and Granny Mole will be pleased to see you.'

Sarah's face lit up when she saw Ruby and Billy. Granny Mole gave them a nod, silent and unsmiling, but that was a welcome in itself. Ruby had never known Granny Mole hold her tongue if she had anything to say, good or bad.

'What a lovely surprise,' Sarah said, hugging Ruby with an unusual display of emotion.

Ruby put the basket on the table noting, with a

stab of conscience, that the midday meal already laid out was half a stale loaf and a pot of dripping. Looking round, she realised that the brass timepiece had gone from the mantelshelf, and as Sarah thrust her hands into the basket Ruby saw that her wedding ring was missing.

'This is a treat, Ruby,' Sarah was saying, as she set the food out on the table. 'Sit down both of you and I'll make a pot of tea.'

'Better than that,' Billy said, opening his coat and producing a quart bottle of ale from a poacher's pocket. 'I thought Granny might appreciate a drop of tiddley.'

'Fetch some glasses, Ruby,' Granny Mole said, sitting up alert and bright-eyed. 'I haven't had a drop since the wake and I'm so dry I'm spitting sawdust.'

'You're a good bloke, Billy,' Sarah said. 'We've missed you since you went back to your own place.'

Hooking his arm around her shoulders, Billy gave her a hug. 'And I've missed your cooking, Ma. Makes me wish I weren't a bachelor.'

'You won't have no home cooking if you get tied up to Rose,' Granny Mole said, darkly. 'She's a flighty little madam. We ain't seen hide nor hair of her since she joined them theatricals.'

'Then it's just as well I'm happy to be single,' Billy said, pouring beer into the tumblers that Ruby handed him.

Sarah looked up from serving the food and smiled at Billy. 'You're always welcome here whether you're courting Rosetta or not. She's like Joe, she'll come home when she's good and ready.'

'Never mind them, Sal,' Granny Mole said impatiently. 'Cut me a slice of that boiled ham before I dies of hunger.'

Later, when Granny Mole had fallen asleep in front of the fire and Billy had gone out into the yard to fetch a hod of coal, Ruby and Sarah were washing the dishes in the scullery.

'Mum, I wish you'd told me you was hard up. What happened to all that money that Mr Crowe gave you as an advance on my wages?'

Avoiding Ruby's enquiring glance, Sarah concentrated on the washing-up. 'There was expenses, love.'

'What are you talking about, Mum?'

'All right, if you must know, Joe was a bit hard up and I helped him out.'

'You never.'

'He finished his apprenticeship but the printer couldn't take him on so he's been out of work. But I'm sure he'll find something soon. He's a good boy.'

For a moment, Ruby almost let the truth slip, but she stopped herself just in time. Struggling with her anger, she decided that she would tell Joe a few home truths when she next saw him, but that would have to wait. She would not upset Mum now for anything; with a huge effort Ruby managed to control her inner rage. 'So how have you been managing, then? Has Rosetta sent you any money?'

'You know Rose; her head's up in the clouds most of the time. Anyway, you mustn't worry, ducks. What you've given me has helped and we've got by,' Sarah said, wiping her hands on her apron. 'Billy give us money for his keep while he was here and I done a bit of washing for the baker's wife down Spivey Street. Poor soul, she ain't right yet after that fire and her husband might never be able to work again. There's always someone worse off than you and that's the truth.'

'You should have told me, Mum. I wouldn't have let you pop your clock or your wedding ring, not for the world. But you should have hung on to the money that Mr Crowe gave you.'

Sarah's sallow skin flushed dull red and she turned away, stacking the dishes in a cupboard. 'I'll get it back when Joe gets a better job. He's a good son, Ruby. He just had a run of bad luck. It weren't his fault.'

'No, it never is.'

'And he's well in with Mr Crowe,' Sarah added hastily. 'He's doing all sorts of jobs for Mr Crowe, though Joe won't say what. But I expect that's how business is done in the City.'

'Is that what he says?'

'Well, you must know what goes on in that big house, you being the private nurse to Mrs Crowe and all that. I've told all the old busybodies in Tobacco Court how you come up in the world. I'm so proud of you, Ruby. And now you're going to train as a proper nurse at the London. Your dad would have been ever so pleased.'

Ruby had not intended to spend so long at home, but Sarah insisted that Joe would be coming and it would be nice if they all had tea together: after all, it would be a crying shame to waste that slab of rich fruit cake. To Ruby's surprise, Billy settled down in Poppa's chair by the fire, entertaining Mum and Granny Mole with stories about his dodgy dealings and his brushes with the law. It was dark by the time Sarah grudgingly admitted that Joe might not be coming after all. Even so, she cut a generous slice of cake and wrapped it in a piece of cloth to save for him.

With nothing to hurry for, Ruby had not worried about returning to Raven Street, but when she decided it was time to leave Billy insisted on driving her home. Nightfall had brought with it a cloudburst and Billy produced a large, black umbrella from the depths of the footwell. When they arrived outside the house, Billy sprang off the cart to help Ruby down and he held the umbrella while she searched her purse for the latchkey. She had just put the key in the lock when the front door of Lottie's house opened and Elsie appeared on the top step screaming and crying for help.

Vaulting over the iron railings, Billy took her by the shoulders, giving her a gentle shake and demanding to know what was wrong. Hampered by her long skirt, Ruby had to take the long way round, and by this time, Elsie had dragged Billy into the hall.

'What's wrong, Elsie?' Ruby hurried inside, closing the door behind her. 'Calm down. We can't understand a word you're saying.'

'She's out of her head,' Billy said, as Elsie scuttled off towards the basement stairs, crying and mumbling to herself.

'Something terrible must have happened.' Picking up her skirts, Ruby chased after Elsie with Billy close on her heels. The flickering gaslight turned their shadows into amorphous monster shapes on the walls that followed them along the narrow passages and down the stairs to the basement. As they neared the kitchen the sound of wild, hysterical screaming made Ruby's blood spike in her veins.

Pushing Elsie aside, Billy rushed into the kitchen. 'Bleeding hell!'

He stopped suddenly, causing Ruby to cannon into him. She stared in horror at the nightmarish scene. The kitchen was in darkness except for a pool of light from the fire as flames roared up the chimney; the range had been stoked with coal so that it resembled a fiery furnace. Wallowing in a tin tub filled to the brim with steaming water and completely naked, Rosetta clasped a gin bottle in her hand. Screaming hysterically, her skin reddened by the scalding water, she stared blindly at them as she writhed around, sending waves of water spilling onto the flagstones.

'Rose, stop that.' Slipping and sliding on the wet floor, Ruby threw herself down on her knees by the bath. 'Billy, we got to get her out of there.'

'Shut up, you silly girl, and fetch a towel,' Billy said, shaking Elsie until she stopped howling, and stood shivering and staring dumbly up at him.

Rosetta's screaming turned to wild laughter and Ruby plunged her arms into the hot water.

'No, no, leave me be.' Rosetta pushed Ruby away, putting the bottle to her lips and pouring gin into her mouth.

Grabbing the bottle, Ruby wrenched it from her hand and tossed it across the room, where it shattered against the wall. 'Billy, give us a hand, for God's sake,' she cried, struggling to keep hold of Rosetta, who was slippery as an eel and a dead weight.

Plunging his arms into the scalding water, Billy caught hold of Rosetta and, despite her biting and kicking, dragged her from the tub with Ruby hanging onto her flailing legs. In seconds they were both soaked to the skin but Billy had Rosetta firmly clutched to his chest. 'You can struggle all you want, Rosetta,' he said grimly. 'I ain't letting you go until you calm down.'

Ruby snatched the towel from Elsie's hands, attempting to wrap it around Rosetta's shoulders and receiving a savage kick in the stomach for her pains. Dropping the towel on the floor, Ruby clutched her belly, doubling up with pain.

'You stop that now,' Billy said, lifting Rosetta bodily and dumping her onto a chair. She struggled like a wild thing, trying to get back into the water, screaming and laughing until Billy slapped her across the face. Her head jerked back, her eyes widened in shock. In stunned silence, Rosetta stared at Billy. 'There now,' he said, picking the towel from the floor and wrapping it around her naked body. 'I never hit a woman before but you was acting like a mad thing, Rose.'

'What was you thinking of?' demanded Ruby, gasping for breath. 'You got to tell us why you done something so stupid. You frightened the poor dimwit half to death, and us too.'

At that, Elsie began to howl low and long like an animal in pain. 'She made me fill the bathtub. I never knew what she had in mind.'

'It's all right,' Ruby said, patting her shoulder. 'You go and fetch a glass of water for Miss

Rosetta. Everything will be all right, you'll see.'

Nodding dumbly, Elsie disappeared into the scullery.

Ruby brushed the tangled mass of hair back from Rosetta's forehead. 'Rose, can you hear me?'

Burying her face in her hands and shivering, Rosetta subsided into muffled sobs.

Elsie hurried back from the scullery, slopping water on the floor in her haste. She handed the half-full glass to Billy and he held it to Rosetta's lips. She drank a little, hiccupping and sniffing.

'That's better,' Billy said, setting the glass aside and wrapping his arms around her, comforting her as if she were a baby. 'We'd best get you to bed.'

'Where is Mr Silas?' Ruby asked, turning to Elsie. 'And Miss Lottie?'

'She's dead drunk as usual,' Elsie said, rolling her eyes. 'He went out. He'll kill me when he gets back.'

Ruby gave her a reassuring smile. 'Clear up this mess like a good girl and he won't know nothing about it. You won't get into trouble, Elsie, I promise.'

'In trouble,' Rosetta repeated, laughing hysterically. 'It's not Elsie what's in trouble.'

'That's enough, Rose,' Billy said, sweeping her up in his arms. 'You're going to bed now, and sleep it off.'

'No, Billy,' Rosetta cried, her laughter turning to tears. 'You don't understand.'

'I understand all right,' Billy said, taking the stairs two at a time in spite of his burden.

'She's out of her head with drink, Billy,' Ruby said, hurrying after them. 'Don't take no notice of what she says.'

Pausing at the top of the basement stairs, Billy turned his head to glance at Ruby, his face twisted with pain. 'Don't take no notice? All right, she may be a bit squiffy, but I'd say some bugger has got her in the family way and she's half killed herself trying to get rid of it.'

'Oh, Rose!' Ruby covered her eyes with her hands, leaning against the wall as a wave of nausea rose in her throat. She might have been in this sorry state herself after what had happened with Jonas, but she had been lucky; her monthly had come on just days afterwards and she had cried all night with sheer relief.

'Ruby, come on,' Billy said, heading for the main staircase. 'I need you to help me get her into bed.'

Rosetta was asleep almost before her head touched the pillow. Having tucked the coverlet firmly around her, Ruby's knees gave way and she would have fallen if Billy hadn't put his arm around her and guided her to a chair.

'I'm sorry. I don't know what come over me.'

'You've had a shock. Take it easy for a bit.' Billy went over to the fireplace and put a match to the pile of coal and sticks laid ready in the grate. 'Someone should stay with her tonight, just in case.'

Ruby understood only too well what he meant. 'Don't say that.'

'You got to be practical, Ruby. Maybe we ought to fetch a doctor.'

'No, not yet. I read about . . . you know what . . . in my medical books. I think I would know what to do. You done your bit, Billy. I can't thank you enough.'

Kneeling in front of the fireplace with the flames licking around the kindling, spitting and crackling, Billy looked up at Ruby and a slow smile wiped the worried lines from his face. 'I love Rose. I'd do anything for her even if she don't give a damn about me.'

'Oh, Billy, you're a good man. Rose is just a girl and she don't know her own mind, but she'll need friends and family, especially now.'

'And I'll stand by her, Ruby, no matter what. I'd just like to get me hands on the dirty scoundrel who got her in trouble. If that bugger Crowe is the father, I'll kill him.'

Ruby was about to tell him that the idea of Jonas and Rosetta together was the most ridiculous thing she had ever heard, but the words froze on her lips. Why not Rose? She had been determined to catch his eye and Ruby knew that there was not much that would stop Rosetta when she had her heart set on something. The idea of them together was shocking, nauseating and degrading; too horrible to contemplate.

'Did you hear what I said, Ruby? I'll kill Crowe if he's laid a finger on her.'

Billy's anxious voice penetrated the red mist that was circling round and round in her head.

'If it's true,' she said, 'I'll kill him myself.'

Chapter Twelve

Rosetta woke up with pains shooting through her head as if little men with picks were hammering inside her skull. Her mouth was dry and her tongue felt twice its normal size. The light hurt her eyes and, as she raised her head, she felt sick. The room was spinning in dizzying circles as if she had just climbed off a merry-go-round. She fell back on the pillow, closing her eyes and groaning.

'Rose, are you all right?'

Opening one eye, Rosetta thought that it was Ruby who was standing over her, pale-faced and with her hair flowing loose around her shoulders. But what was Ruby doing in her attic room? 'Ruby?'

Ruby laid a cool hand on her forehead. 'How do you feel?'

'I think I'm dying. Me head is splitting and I'm parched.'

'No pain anywhere else?'

Ruby's face swam in and out of focus. 'No. I don't know. Oh, God!' Rosetta sat up, holding her head in her hands. 'Tell me it was a dream. Tell me that Billy weren't there last night.'

'He was there all right and lucky for you. You was nearly boiled alive. Who told you to do such a daft thing?'

'Lottie said it would work. Maybe it has . . . or maybe it'll just go away.'

'Don't be bloody stupid!' Ruby said angrily. 'You got to face up to it, Rose. You got to tell the father and he should look after you.'

'I can't. I mean, he won't.'

'Who was it, Rose?' Ruby demanded, shaking Rosetta until her teeth rattled. 'Was it Jonas Crowe?'

'No, it weren't him. I wish it was.' Shutting her eyes tight, Rosetta could still see Alf's face leering at her. She could smell him, feel his hands on her body, taste the stale tobacco and whisky on his breath. But Alf already had a wife and six children; he would deny everything and sack her into the bargain. If only it had been Jonas who had wanted her so badly, he would have stood by her, she was certain. Now her life was in ruins, her career on the stage finished almost before it had begun. She wanted to die. 'Ugh! I'm going to be sick.'

Opening her eyes, Rosetta moved her head cautiously from side to side. Miraculously, the pain had stopped. Ruby had held the washbowl for her while she vomited, had washed her face and hands afterwards and had dosed her with some of Aunt Lottie's seltzer. She was so very sorry now that she had ever had bad thoughts about Ruby and that she had teased her about her ambition to become a nurse. Rosetta sank back against the pillows, wondering where Ruby had gone and hoping that she would return soon. The door opened and Elsie came in, carrying a tray. The aroma of chicken broth wafted up Rosetta's nostrils and she realised that she was starving. Giving her a lopsided grin, Elsie waited until Rosetta had raised herself to a sitting position and then laid the tray across her knees.

'There's more, if you wants it. Miss Lottie sent me out to the market to buy an old boiler special and Miss Ruby made the broth, even though I says I could do it, but I peeled the carrots and spuds and the onion too, even though it made me cry.'

'Thank you.' Rosetta raised the spoon to her lips. Realising that Elsie was waiting and watching her, eager for praise, she managed a smile. 'It's good.'

Apparently satisfied, Elsie shuffled out of the room, but the door had barely closed when it opened again and Lottie swept in, making a grand entrance.

'So, it didn't work. What went wrong?'

Rosetta swallowed a mouthful of soup. 'I dunno, Auntie. I done everything what you told me.'

'Well, it don't always work first time,' Lottie said, swaying a little and leaving a scent trail of lavender cologne and gin as she went to sit in the chair by the fire. 'But I can give you the address of a woman in Hackney. She'll get rid of your little problem for you.'

The broth had cooled and Rosetta's appetite disappeared. She pushed the tray away to the end of the bed. 'I've heard the girls at the theatre talking about that sort of thing. I don't think I could go through with it.'

Lighting a cigarillo from a spill, Lottie inhaled deeply, exhaling with a sigh. 'Then you go to tell the poppa and make him take care of you.'

'I can't, I just can't.'

'You got no choice, cara. Sly and me can't keep you and the baby. You won't be able to hide your condition for long and you can't go on stage looking like a big barrel. I'm sorry, Rosetta, but you going to have to go home to your mama and tell her you been a silly girl.'

Rosetta burst into Alf's office without knocking. He looked up from his work, scowling. 'Bloody hell, Rose! Where's the fire?'

'I'm in trouble, Alf.'

Alf's eyebrows shot up into his hairline and his

already florid complexion darkened to brick red. 'What sort of trouble?'

'You know what I mean. I'm in trouble. You got me in the family way.'

Beads of sweat stood out on Alf's brow. 'So what do you expect me to do about it?'

'Do about it?' Rosetta heard her voice rise to a mouse-squeak. 'You done it. The least you can do is help me out. Take care of me and the nipper.'

Jumping to his feet, Alf leaned across the desk, glaring at her. 'You can't prove nothing. A little trollop like you has probably had half a dozen blokes.'

'That's not true!' Rosetta stared at him in horror. 'You know that ain't true. You was the first and you got to help me.'

'I don't have to do nothing. It's your little problem, girlie.'

Seeing Alf's jaw harden in a stubborn line, Rosetta felt panic rising inside her like a stifled scream. 'I never been with anyone else. What if your wife was to find out? I bet she wouldn't be too pleased.'

Alf was round the desk before Rosetta could back away towards the door. His hands grasped her throat, pressing, constricting. She coughed and choked, feeling as though her eyes were about to pop out of her head. 'Don't threaten me, girlie, or you'll be sorry.' He released his grip, throwing her against the wall.

Clutching her throat, Rosetta glared back at him. 'You bastard. You will help me or I swear I'll tell everyone you're the father.'

'And I'll see to it that you will never work again. You're sacked, you little tart. Get out, and if you come near the theatre again I'll set the police on you.'

Terrified but desperate, Rosetta stood her ground. 'I'll go, but not until you hand over me wages, and a bit more to keep me going. It's the least you can do.' For a moment she was sure he was going to strike her to the ground and she did not care. He had ruined her, shown her the door, and now her world was crumbling. She was not afraid of him any more. She met his fierce gaze with her chin up, unflinching. 'I ain't leaving without what's due to me.'

'You're a one, you are, Rosetta.' Alf's face relaxed into a reluctant grin. 'Pity you wasn't a bit more careful. I'll miss you, but you're no use to me now.' Opening a drawer in his desk, he pulled out a roll of notes, tossing it on the floor at Rosetta's feet. 'Take it and don't say that Alf Ricketts isn't a fair man. But come near me again and you'll be more than sorry.'

When Rosetta arrived back in Raven Street, she found Sly standing on the front step smoking a Woodbine and at his feet she recognised her battered cardboard suitcase held together with a length of string.

'So you lost your job then?' He moved the Wood from one side of his mouth to the other. 'Thought that'd be the case.'

'I can still pay me way, Uncle Sly. I got money.'

Silas pushed the case towards her with the toe of his shoe. 'Sorry, ducks. Lottie and me can't keep you here, not in your condition. Your money won't last long and then we'd be stuck with you and the kiddie.'

'Please let me stay, just until I get fixed up.'

'The truth is that Lottie can't abide kids, especially babies. Reminds her of the one she left in Italy all them years ago. Take my advice and go back to your mum, there's a good girl.'

'Mum will kill me.'

Delving into his pocket, Silas produced a slip of paper. 'Lottie told me to give you this in case you change your mind. Said to tell you it was the woman in Hackney and you'd know what she meant.'

Rosetta stared at Lottie's spidery scrawl, shaking her head.

'Good luck, Rose,' Silas said, going inside. 'You'll need it.'

The door slammed in her face.

Staring at the door for a blank few seconds, unable to believe that this was happening to her, Rosetta scrunched the paper up and shoved it into her pocket. As she turned to go, a bout of dizziness swept over her and she clutched the iron railings to steady herself.

Down below in the area, the kitchen door opened and Elsie popped out like a small jack-in-a-box. 'Miss Rose.' She raced up the steps, sobbing, and flung her arms round Rosetta's neck. 'Don't go. Don't leave me.'

Pinned against the railings with Elsie clinging to her like a leech, Rosetta dropped the case. It bounced down the steps, spilling the contents on the pavement in a rainbow of bright colours. Breaking free from Elsie's frantic grasp, Rosetta ran down the steps, snatching up her scattered possessions and stuffing them back in the case. 'Don't just stand there, Elsie. Give us a hand.'

'Let me come with you. I'll work for you and help you take care of the nipper. I likes babies. There was lots of them in the workhouse.'

Rosetta's legs suddenly gave way beneath her and she sat down on the bottom step. 'I can't take you with me. I'm sorry, but at least you got a roof over your head.'

'There's always Miss Ruby,' Elsie said, pointing to Crowe's house. 'Maybe she'd take us both in.'

Ruby! Of course. Why hadn't she thought of her in the first place? They had patched up their differences and Ruby had been kindness itself when she was poorly. 'Go and knock on the door, Elsie. Ask for Ruby, or, if she's not there, ask for Miss Lily.'

Skittering up the steps, Elsie rattled the knocker until someone opened the door. Rosetta couldn't see who it was but the conversation only lasted a few seconds. When she came scurrying back, Elsie's face was more expressive than words. 'It's Miss Ruby's first day at the hospital. She won't be back until late tonight and Miss Lily has gone to the seaside to get better. I asks for Mr Jonas but they says go away, he don't want to be bothered with the likes of me.'

The world seemed full of closing doors. Rosetta sat with her head held in her hands. Why did Ruby have to be out today, of all days?

Elsie tugged at her sleeve. 'There's always Mr Joe.'

'I don't know where he is.'

'But I does.' With surprising strength for someone so small, Elsie dragged Rosetta to her feet. 'I had to help him back to his digs one night when he was too tiddley to walk straight. You come along with me, Miss Rose.'

They found Joe in a squalid basement room that he shared with several others in a rat-infested back alley near Spitalfields market. It was well past midday but he had obviously only just awakened from a heavy sleep. Bleary-eyed and tousled, he made them wait in the doorway while he shrugged on his jacket and thrust his feet into his boots. Rosetta could see several figures sleeping on the floor, huddled beneath coats or bits of sacking. The smell of unwashed bodies, human excrement and stale beer made her retch.

'This is a disgusting place, Joe. How could you sink so low?'

Joe hustled them outside into the area. 'You turned me out, remember?'

'It's raining,' Elsie said, shivering. 'I'm getting wet.'

'There's a coffee shop round the corner,' Joe said, pulling on his cap. 'Got any money, Rose?'

The scent of the coffee barely disguised the smell of closely packed humanity sheltering in the small café. Joe tucked into a plate of bacon and eggs, munching while he listened to Rosetta. She didn't spare herself or try to pretend that she was the innocent victim; Joe knew her too well and she had nothing to lose by telling the truth.

Swallowing the last morsel of bread and bacon, Joe licked his fingers, one by one. 'I'm sorry for you, Rose. But there's nothing I can do to help.'

'You always was a selfish sod, Joe.' Pushing her cup of tea away, barely touched, Rosetta leaned her elbows on the table. 'Look, I'm desperate, and I got a bit of money from Alf. Maybe we could set up together in some rooms. After all, you can't go on living in that pigsty. It ain't healthy.'

'And I can get work,' Elsie said, cramming the piece of cake into her mouth that Rosetta had nibbled and left on the side of her plate. 'Let me stay with you. I don't want to go back to Mr Sly. He beats me black and blue for nothing, he does.'

'Hush, Elsie, not now,' Rosetta said, keeping her gaze fixed on Joe's face. 'I know I wasn't much help to you before, when I threw you out of my room, but I had no choice then. You and me, we've both made a mess of things, so it would make sense to stick together now.'

'And it would, ducks, only I ain't going to be around much longer. You see, Rose, I never paid Crowe back. I was supposed to be watching the punters at the tables and using his stake money just to make it look right, but then I started winning. I thought me luck had turned and it had, for a while. Then I started losing and now I owes him more than ever.'

'Oh, Joe! You stupid fool.'

'Come off it, love. You're a fine one to call me stupid.'

'I know, I'm sorry, but if you get a job and I go back to Bronski's, I'm sure we could get by and repay Jonas too.'

'It would take twenty years to pay back what I owe. If I stick around I'll end up at the bottom of the Thames with a lead weight tied round me neck.'

'But if you run away, what happens to Ruby? You can't leave her to take the rap for you.'

'Ruby's well looked after. She's fallen on her feet, and Crowe won't hurt her. He's not that sort of bloke.'

'So where are you going, then?'

'The long and short of it, Rose, is that I've joined up.'

Rosetta stared at him in disbelief. 'You're going to be a soldier?'

'I'm leaving tomorrow for training camp. There's going to be more trouble in South Africa before too long. I'd rather fight a whole army of Boers than Crowe's gang.'

Rosetta was soaked to the skin by the time she had walked from Spitalfields to Tobacco Court. Elsie had trailed behind her, twittering like a fledgling bird fallen from its nest and crying to its mother for help. Rosetta had tried persuasion and downright bullying to make Elsie go home to Raven Street, but nothing she said had made any difference.

The living room was full of steam and the scent of freshly ironed cotton sheets. Granny Mole looked up from her ironing, eyebrows raised. 'Who's that?' she demanded, waving the flat iron at Elsie.

'Where's Mum?'

'Up West with her fancy man! Where d'you

think she would be? Out in the bleeding back yard breaking her back doing other folks' washing, that's where she always is these days. And me, at my age, still working me fingers to the bone.'

Too fraught to take on Granny in one of her more belligerent moods, Rosetta left her staring suspiciously at Elsie, who was standing dumbly by the door, as if poised for flight. The back door was open, and despite the rain Sarah was in the yard with a fire going beneath the copper, hissing and spitting as raindrops evaporated on contact with the flames.

'Rosetta?'

'Oh, Mum. I'm in terrible trouble.'

There was silence in the living room as Sarah digested Rosetta's news over a cup of tea. For once, Granny Mole seemed to have nothing to say as she dunked biscuits in her tea, sucking the soggy mixture through the gaps in her teeth. Elsie huddled in the corner by the fire, making herself small and keeping quiet.

After a while, Rosetta's nerves, which were already stretched taut as violin strings, began to snap one thread at a time. She slammed her cup down on the table. 'Holy Mother of God, how long are you going to take, Mum? Can I stay or not?'

'You ain't in no position to speak out,' Granny

Mole said, wiping her lips on the back of her hand. 'You're a disgrace, that's what you are.'

'I've been considering,' Sarah said slowly. 'I'm more sad than angry, Rosetta. You've let the whole family down and I blame Lottie for leading you on, but none of this would have happened if you'd stayed at home.'

'But, Mum . . .'

Sarah raised her hand, her face serious. 'I don't say this lightly, but I got a reputation to think of in Tobacco Court. We've always been respectable people and I'm not having them all tittle-tattling behind their doors, saying that my daughter ain't no better than she should be.'

'What are you saying?' Rosetta leapt to her feet, pacing the floor. 'You can't mean to throw me out on the street.'

'Calm down. Of course not. I'm sorry for you but you've done wrong, and if the man what got you into trouble won't marry you then you got to take the consequences. You can stay here tonight but first thing tomorrow morning I'm taking you to Wapping. You can stay with the Moles until your time comes.'

'You don't mean it!' Rosetta came to a halt, staring at her mother's set face. 'I hate the Moles. They live on bread and scrape and their place stinks.'

'You'll go to the Moles and like it.'

'I won't do it. You can't make me.'

'It's that or the street. I'm not having you bring shame on us.'

'That's right,' Granny Mole said, wagging her finger at Rosetta. 'You brought shame on us. Pass me another biscuit.'

Curled up with her arms wrapped round her knees, Elsie began to sob.

'That's enough from you too,' Sarah said, getting to her feet. 'Come into the yard, young Elsie. You can make yourself useful by helping with the washing. If I don't get it done, I don't get no money.'

'You mean you're going to let Elsie stay, but not me?' Rosetta stared at her mother, unable to believe that this was happening.

'She may be small and skinny but she'll earn her keep. I wouldn't send a cat back to live with Sly and Lottie.'

'But you'd send your own daughter away. It ain't fair, Mum. It just ain't fair.'

'Life ain't fair, my girl. And don't you go bothering Ruby now she's training to be a proper nurse; or Joe for that matter.'

'At least he's a credit to the family,' Granny Mole muttered, scowling.

Cold white fury roiled in Rosetta's stomach. 'That's all you know. You think your precious Joe is so wonderful; well, I can tell you he's no better than me.'

'What are you talking about?' demanded Sarah.

Rosetta bit her lip. She hadn't meant to tell, but Mum and Granny were staring at her and she knew they wouldn't be satisfied with anything that smacked of a lie. 'He's lost his job and got hisself into so much debt gambling that he's in trouble with the mobs.'

Sarah sat down suddenly, panting as if someone had punched her in the stomach. 'I don't believe you. My Joe wouldn't be so daft.'

'You're a wicked girl, telling such lies,' Granny said, shaking her finger. 'Pity you can't be more like your sister.'

Rosetta tossed her head; she wasn't going to take all the blame. 'You think Ruby's so good and clever, well let me tell you, she's no better than me.'

'What are you saying?' Sarah had paled alarmingly and she clutched her chest, a bemused expression on her face.

Having started, Rosetta found she could not stop. 'If you believe that Jonas Crowe has taken her on just to nurse Lily, then you're a bigger fool than I am.'

'Don't say things like that, Rose. Mr Jonas has been good to us all. You're just jealous.'

'You don't know the half of it, Mum. Jonas Crowe runs a high mob every bit as tough as the Odessians or the Essex gang, and he's bought you with money made out of poor sods like Joe. I bet it would be different if I was Ruby come home to tell you that it was Crowe who got me in the family way.'

'That's it. You've gone too far this time.' Jumping to her feet, Sarah gave Rosetta a shove towards the door. 'Get out, Rosetta. I won't have that sort of talk in my house.'

'I'm going, but I'll never forgive you for treating me so cruel. Never!' Grabbing her things, Rosetta slammed out of the house.

Outside on the pavement the rain had already soaked through her cotton blouse before Rosetta had time to struggle into her jacket. The curtains in the houses opposite fluttered and she poked out her tongue. Let them sneer; let them think what they liked. Holding her head high, she strode down the street, not having the slightest idea where she was going, but determined never to return to Tobacco Court as long as she lived. Stopping on the corner of Spivey Street, the realisation of what she had done hit Rosetta like a smack in the face. Why had she said all that to Mum? Why had she made trouble for Ruby and Joe? Her spiteful tongue had made it impossible for her to ask Ruby for help now; she really hadn't meant to say those horrible things about her and Jonas. She might be Ruby's twin in looks, so why couldn't she be more like her in nature? Ruby was so down to earth, trusting and trustworthy; Ruby would never have let herself be led astray by a man. Wiping her eyes on her sleeve, Rosetta couldn't tell whether it was tears or rainwater that ran down her cheeks, trickling into her mouth.

'How much, darling?'

Blinking, Rosetta found herself staring into the leering face of a man who had just staggered out of the pub. Too furious for words, she hit him with her suitcase, catching him off balance so that he sprawled on the wet pavement. Breaking into a run, she headed in the direction of Cable Street.

'Spare us a copper, lady.' A small girl, who could not have been more than five or six appeared from an alleyway, dragging a toddler by the hand. They were both filthy, covered in sores and so thin that their heads seemed too big for their bodies; their flesh was stretched taut over twig-like limbs giving them the look of living skeletons. Rosetta fumbled for her purse and dropped two pennies into the child's outstretched hand. Immediately she realised her mistake. Ragged children appeared as if from nowhere, holding out their hands and begging for money. Bigger boys came, kicking and lashing out at the smaller children; they advanced on Rosetta, their eyes gleaming like a hunting pack of wolves. Even though she was head and shoulders taller than most of them, Rosetta knew she was outnumbered and she tossed a handful of coins into their midst. Fighting, snapping and snarling, they fell upon the money as it rolled over the wet cobblestones and landed amongst the filth in the gutter. Seizing her chance, Rosetta broke into a run and did not stop until she reached the baker's shop on the corner. Leaning against the window, she gasped for each painful breath, doubled up with a stitch, and holding her side. The panicky feeling inside her subsided a little now that she was out of danger, but she had never felt so alone or lost. Perhaps, if she hurried, she could catch Joe at the station before he left for the training camp. Joe would have to stay and help her; he couldn't be so selfish or hardhearted as to leave her to struggle on alone. She was so deep in her thoughts that she barely noticed the familiar cart with the horse, munching the contents of its nosebag, as it waited outside the bakery.

'Rosetta!'

Brushing back the wet hair plastered on her forehead and blinking the rainwater from her eyes, Rosetta realised that it was Billy who had just come out of the shop. 'Hello, Billy.' She tried to sound casual, as if it was quite normal to be leaning against the shop window, soaked to the skin, with a suitcase at her feet. 'What are you doing in the baker's shop?'

'I've been keeping an eye on the family since

the fire. The poor bloke's not been able to do much since then and his wife is struggling to make ends meet.' Pushing his cap to the back of his head, Billy stared down at Rosetta's suitcase. 'What's all this then? Going on holiday, Rose?'

Fighting back the desire to fling her arms round his neck and beg him for help, Rosetta forced a smile. 'I was just on a visit home, in between jobs. I've got star billing in a music hall up north. I was just on me way to the station.'

'You're a poor liar, Rose,' Billy said, giving her a searching look. 'You're forgetting that I know you're in trouble.'

Rosetta bit her lip; she had been hateful to Billy when they last met and she was not going to give him the satisfaction of seeing her cry. 'I got rid of it. The gin and the hot bath worked a treat. Are you satisfied?'

Billy flinched, but he stood his ground. 'You're lying, Rose.'

'Let me pass, Billy. I've got a train to catch.' Picking up her case, Rosetta would have walked on, but Billy caught her by the shoulders, spinning her round to face him.

'I love you, Rose. You know you can tell me anything, so for Gawd's sake stop play-acting and tell me the truth.'

Chapter Thirteen

Exhausted but happy at the end of a long first day, Ruby took a deep breath of the cool night air as she stepped outside the hospital. It had been a wonderful day, despite the fact that everything was new and strange, but the best part of all was that Nurse Tutor had assigned her to a mentor, a more experienced nurse. When her mentor turned out to be Pamela, Ruby thought she had died and gone to heaven. Yes, it had been a marvellous day, even though the smell of disinfectant still clung to her hair and her clothes, and her hands were reddened and sore from being constantly in water and the use of carbolic soap. Her back and feet ached like nothing on earth, but the feeling that she had accomplished something constructive, and that at last she was on the way to achieving her ambition to become a proper nurse, made up for everything.

'Hey, Ruby.'

Looking round, she saw Joe leaning nonchalantly against a lamp post, smoking a cigarette. He tossed the butt on the pavement and ground it to shreds beneath his boot. 'I 'nearly gave you up,' he said, hooking his arm around her shoulders.

'I didn't think you'd come, Joe,' Ruby said, smiling. 'I haven't see you for ages.'

Joe's grin faded into a frown. 'I know, and I'm sorry, Ruby. I got something to tell you, ducks.'

Alarm fisted in Ruby's stomach. 'Oh, Joe, what have you done now?'

'There's a pub round the corner. You can buy me a drink.'

In the cosy fug of the public bar, over a pint of mild and bitter, Joe admitted that his gambling had once again got out of hand. Shame-faced and contrite, he told Ruby that his only way of escape was to join up. She listened in silence, her heart sinking at the thought of what Jonas would say and do when he discovered that Joe had run away owing him a small fortune.

'You'll be all right, won't you, Ruby? And you'll look after Rose?' Joe laid his hand over hers.

Staring at his long, slim fingers, smooth and unblemished by toil, in total contrast to her own small, capable hand, red and chapped by hard work, Ruby couldn't bring herself to tell him the truth. Whatever he had done, deep down he was still the same big brother who had protected her from the Spivey Street kids when they bullied her on her way home from school; he was still the same Joe who used to tell her jokes to make her laugh when she was sad. It had been Joe who had comforted her when she was going through the gangly-legged, coltish stage of adolescence, telling her she was lovely and one day she would knock the socks off all the lads for miles around. She met his eyes with a smile. 'Don't worry about me or Rosetta. We'll be all right.'

'Crowe treats you well, I can see that. And anyway, he wouldn't take it out on you. He may be a hard man but he wouldn't stoop so low as to harm a woman.'

Ruby sipped her port and lemon, saying nothing.

'As for Rose, well, she's gone home to Mum, who'll give her an ear-bashing, but she'll take care of her and the nipper. With you as a doting auntie, it'll be a lucky little bastard and that's the truth.' Supping the last drop of his pint, Joe slapped the glass down on the table

Staring at him, Ruby wondered how anyone who was so basically kind and loving could also be so completely self-centred and selfish. She loved Joe dearly but, at this moment, she really didn't like him at all.

'Come on, Ruby,' he said, getting to his feet. 'Don't look so serious. I'm sure army life will suit me down to the ground, so you don't need to worry about me. Let's get you back to Raven Street, and then I'm off to be a soldier of the queen.' With a mock salute and a bow, Joe held his hand out to her, grinning as though he had not a care in the world.

Throwing herself into her studies, Ruby had no time to worry about Joe or Rosetta. She had the comfort of knowing that Mum and Granny Mole would be surviving more comfortably now she had sent them the rest of her wages; it wasn't a fortune but at least they would have enough to eat.

Working a fourteen-hour shift meant that Ruby had little or no spare time, but somehow that didn't seem to matter. She worked alongside Pamela, who took great pains to explain every procedure and to encourage her, and, best of all, there were the wonderful moments when she had to assist Adam as he went about his duties. Ruby's admiration for him grew every time she watched him undertake a clinical procedure. He seemed to have the happy knack of being able to communicate with patients, whatever their social standing or their intellectual capacity. Ruby cherished the golden moments when she stood by his side, even though she might be holding a kidney dish filled with bloodied dressings, a vomit bowl or a smelly bedpan. She wondered at his easy-going, cheerful nature; nothing ever seemed to ruffle the calmness of his disposition and nothing seemed to matter except that she was helping Adam in his life's work of ministering to the sick. She took a secret delight in the knowledge that he had made it possible for her to train as a nurse. His generosity in donating the bursary made him even more special in her eyes. The more Ruby grew to know Adam, the deeper she fell in love with him and the more desperate she became to deny what she knew was a hopeless passion. Pamela had confided in her that she and Adam had become unofficially engaged, and that made Ruby even more determined to control her runaway emotions.

The weeks slipped by almost without Ruby noticing the passing of spring into summer. She left for the hospital at six-thirty every morning, returning well after nine o'clock every evening. She always walked home, the same way every night, enjoying the cool breeze on her cheeks after a long hot day working on the wards. Buying textbooks had used up the small amount of money she had saved from her wages for that particular purpose, leaving nothing for cab fares, but the summer evenings were light and Ruby saw no danger in walking the familiar streets on her own.

She had seen very little of Jonas since he had returned from Southend and Ruby made no attempt to seek his company. Lily sent postcards, sometimes two or three a week, and she seemed to have accommodated herself to life in an institution. Her notes were cheerful, optimistic and affectionate and Ruby sat up late at night, writing long letters in reply.

On her infrequent days off, Ruby always meant to visit Tobacco Court to see how Rosetta was getting along, but somehow there was always something that stopped her. Mostly she was simply too tired to walk all the way to Whitechapel and she would spend the day resting, reading and studying. In her determination to avoid Jonas, she also managed to shut herself off from what went on in the house. Ruby knew that bare-knuckle fights, ratting and cock-fighting took place nightly in the walled confines of the back yard, but it was surprisingly easy to close her mind to the illegal goings-on in Jonas Crowe's establishment. Gambling, drunkenness and prostitution were all part of life in the East End and Ruby knew that she couldn't change a thing; but when she was a qualified nurse, she could at least help alleviate the suffering brought about by poverty and disease. Single-mindedly, she concentrated all her efforts on her studies.

It was a warm night in July and the full moon hung like a golden ball in the darkening sky as Ruby walked home. She felt strangely restless, with a quiver of excitement fluttering inside her chest like a caged sparrow. Forcing her feet to go in the direction of Raven Street, Ruby tried to rationalise her disquiet, thinking that it must be the unexpected invitation to Adam and Pamela's engagement party that had unsettled her. She had known that they would make it official as soon as Adam had qualified, but now it had happened it was so final. In a few days they would be pledged to each other in front of family and friends. Ruby had not expected to be invited to the party at Adam's parents' house in Highgate and she did not want to go, but Pamela had insisted that she accept, challenging her to think of a reason why she should not attend. To admit that she would feel out of place in such an illustrious gathering would sound like inverted snobbery; Ruby knew that she would have to accept and put on a brave face.

She had one foot on the bottom step of the house in Raven Street when a hansom cab pulled up and Jonas sprang out. He paid the driver and caught up with Ruby before she had time to let herself into the house.

'I thought I told you never to walk home alone.'

'It's safe enough.'

Jonas's dark brows knotted across the top of his nose. 'I expect that's what the women thought who got carved up by the Ripper. I know that worthless brother of yours has done a bunk, but I told you to always get a cab home at night.'

'All right, I will next time.' Ruby could feel his breath hot on her cheek, bringing back vivid memories of that night months ago. Her hand trembled as she tried to insert her key in the lock.

Reaching across her, Jonas unlocked the door. He followed her into the hall. 'You will get a cab every night without fail. Do you hear me?'

'There's no need to raise your voice, Mr Crowe. I heard you.'

For a moment they stared at each other, locked in a battle of wills.

'If you've run out of money, you only have to tell me and I'll see you have sufficient for cab fares,' Jonas said, unbending a little.

'Thank you. Can I go now?'

'Yes, and change out of that hideous rag you're wearing. You look like a drab.'

'I'm proud of this uniform,' Ruby said, with a defiant lift of her chin.

'Maybe, but it doesn't do you justice. What happened to that blue gown I bought for you? Why haven't I seen you wearing it?'

Staring at him in amazement, Ruby shook her head. She had intended to give it to Rosetta but somehow she couldn't bear to part with something so beautiful. 'It's hanging in the cupboard.'

'Then go and put it on. I want to see you in it.'

Ruby hesitated, sensing danger. 'Why?'

'Why do you hide your good looks with

dowdy clothes and your hair scraped back into that hideous bun?' Jonas fingered a curl that had escaped from the combs that held Ruby's hair off her face. 'Dress yourself up, do your hair and have dinner with me.'

Suspecting the worst, Ruby tried to read his expression and failed. 'I – I don't think so.'

'Don't you trust me, Ruby?' A smile played around the corners of Jonas's lips and the steely look in his eyes was replaced by a disconcerting twinkle.

'No, I don't, and with good reason,' Ruby said, backing away from him.

'I can't lie and say I'm sorry for what I did – let's say the temptation was too much for me – but I promise I won't lay a finger on you. Humour me, Ruby. Change your dress and join me for dinner.'

'I'm tired. It's been a long day . . .'

'And you need to eat. I'll give you fifteen minutes to change and then I would appreciate it, Miss Capretti, if you would give me the pleasure of your company.'

It was an order rather than an invitation but Ruby was not going to submit to bullying, even when it was disguised by a velvet voice and a teasing smile. 'No, thanks.'

'And I want to talk to you about Joe,' Jonas said over his shoulder as he walked away.

This could not be taken as anything but an

ultimatum. Reluctantly, Ruby went up to her room and changed into the gown of shimmering, lavender-blue silk. Even to her tired eyes, the effect was astounding: a stranger looked back at her from the mirror, even before she had had time to pile her dark curls into a fashionable upswept style. For the first time in her life, Ruby wished that she had some jewellery, just a plain necklace or some earrings, to complete the transformation. I look like a proper lady, she thought, staring at her reflection, wide-eyed. If only Adam could see me now.

Wishing she were anywhere but here, Ruby walked into the dining room prepared to face the most unpleasant evening of her life so far. Anger simmered away beneath her outward appearance of calm: bitter, seething anger at Jonas for using threats against Joe to bend her to his will.

'Very nice,' Jonas said, eyeing her up and down. 'I always knew I had good taste.'

'I suppose it's all down to you then?' Ruby looked him straight in the eye. 'You think you're so blooming clever but you're really just a big bully, picking on people what can't defend themselves and sending your gang out to do your dirty work. Well, I ain't frightened of you because there ain't nothing left for you to do to me that you ain't already done. Now I'm starving, so either feed me or mash me up to a pulp to get even with Joe. At this moment, I don't particularly care which, just get it over.'

'Well then,' Jonas said, pulling out a chair. 'I'm glad you got that off your chest. Now sit down, please. I promise not to mash you to a pulp until you've got a good dinner inside you.'

Aware that he was laughing at her, Ruby sat down. She had not noticed, until this moment, that the food was already set out on the table, and his assumption that she would accept his invitation to dine with him made her even more cross and uncomfortable. Jonas seemed to be totally unaware of her discomfort, and he sat down, cutting a large slice from a pie that smelt tantalisingly of steak and kidney. Heaping her plate with potatoes and cabbage, he passed it to her with a jug of gravy.

'Mrs Bragg isn't the most ambitious cook,' he said, smiling, 'but she makes the best steak and kidney pie in London.'

Ruby would have liked to push the plate away, feigning loss of appetite, but she was too hungry to pretend and the pie tasted even more delicious than it looked and smelt.

'Good,' Jonas said, filling Ruby's glass with red wine from a cut glass decanter. 'I like to see a woman with a healthy appetite.'

'Oh, shut up,' Ruby said, gulping down a mouthful of the wine.

Jonas refilled her glass, saying nothing, and

they ate in silence until Ruby had cleared her plate.

'There's blancmange,' Jonas said, waving his hand in the direction of a fat, white, wobbly shape on a willow pattern plate. 'Or I can ask Mrs Bragg to make you one of her jam omelettes.'

Pushing her plate away, Ruby drank the last of her wine. 'I don't want a jam omelette. I want to know why you got me here?'

'The blancmange is very good,' Jonas said, scooping some onto his own plate.

'All right, I'll have some, but only if you tell me what you're planning to do about Joe. You do know that he's joined up, I suppose?'

Jonas heaped another plate with the dessert and handed it to her. 'Of course I do.'

'Why are you taking it so calmly? Joe was scared stiff of what you and your gang would do to him.'

'I have my reasons, Ruby. The army will be the making of Joe.'

Staring at him, Ruby tried to imagine what was going on behind his bland expression. Suddenly she wanted to make him angry, to provoke some reaction from him. 'And so you're holding me hostage until he comes back or pays you off, which he'll never do.'

'No, I don't make war on women.'

'Then why did you force me to come and live here, and why did you . . .' Ruby couldn't bring herself to put the deed into words; she stared down at her plate, hoping he could not see the blush that flooded her cheeks.

'I never intended that any harm should come to you, Ruby. I shouldn't have forced myself on you. It was unforgivable.'

Looking into his eyes, Ruby saw genuine regret and she knew she should have savoured this small triumph, but strangely she felt only disappointment. 'Is that why you made me come to work for you? Just so that you could use me and humiliate me?'

Jonas flinched as though she had slapped him across the face. 'No! That wasn't how it was at all.'

'So why did you make me come and live here, if it wasn't to get even with Joe?'

Jonas was silent for a moment, sipping his wine, as if carefully calculating his answer. 'I wanted you to care for Lily,' he said slowly, 'and I knew you wouldn't come unless I forced your hand. I'm not proud of what I did but, in the first place, it was purely for Lily's sake.'

'And now?'

'Lily is dying. The sanatorium is her last hope but it's a slim one. I've neglected Lily and taken her for granted.' Jonas pushed his plate away as if he had suddenly lost his appetite. 'I let her fall in love with me knowing that I could never return the feeling. She has no idea how ill she is and I just wanted her to have a friend, someone she could rely on. I knew from the first moment I saw you standing in the graveyard that you would be the right person.'

Ruby stared at him, amazed at the raw emotion in his voice and the tormented expression in his eyes. 'But why go through all that pretending that it was because of Joe and his debts?'

'Would you have come to live in this disreputable house if I hadn't made it impossible for you to refuse?'

'Probably not.'

Pushing his chair back, Jonas rose to his feet. 'You're free to go whenever you wish, Ruby. I can't make you stay if you don't want to, but . . .'

'But?'

'Lily will be coming home soon and the doctors tell me there's no hope of a recovery. Even if you hate me, it would be a kindness to her if you would consider staying on until – until the end.'

There was no mistaking the pain in his voice or the sincerity of his words. The situation had turned itself about and Ruby's anger was replaced by sadness.

Jonas poured two glasses of brandy from a decanter on a mahogany chiffonier. 'Drink this,' he said, putting a glass in her limp hand. 'You've had a shock. I'm sorry. I'm not used to breaking news gently.'

The fiery liquid burnt Ruby's throat, making

her eyes water and her head swim. She looked suspiciously at Jonas. 'This isn't just another of your fairy tales, is it?'

'No. I swear it's the truth,' Jonas said, sitting down on the chair next to her. 'Stay on, Ruby. You can name your own terms. You can continue your training at the hospital. Stay on please, for Lily's sake.'

Lily was dying. The words echoed in Ruby's head as she struggled to come to terms with the awful truth. Almost immediately, her thoughts turned to Adam. Surely he could do something to save Lily?

'Adam?' Jonas's voice cracked like a whip.

Ruby looked up, startled. Had she really spoken his name out loud? 'Dr Fairfax. I work with him sometimes. Maybe he could help Lily?'

'That would be the same young man who came to persuade you to take up your studies at the hospital.' Jonas smiled grimly. 'Don't look so surprised, Ruby. This is my house and I make it my business to know everything that goes on.'

'I got Adam to thank for the bursary. I bet you didn't know that.' Ruby's head was becoming pleasantly muzzy and, feeling more confident and relaxed, she drank the last drop of brandy.

Jonas refilled her glass. 'No, I didn't.'

'Well, he did and he's a fine doctor. And he's getting engaged to Pamela.'

Jonas lit a cigar. 'Is he now?'

'I'm invited to their engagement party at Adam's family home in Highgate, only I can't go.' Just why had she blurted that out to Jonas? Almost before the words were out of her mouth, Ruby wished them unsaid. It must be the wine and brandy taking hold of her brain and making her stupid.

'And why can't you go?'

Shaking her head, Ruby stared down into the amber liquid in her glass. 'I'd feel out of place among the toffs, and anyway I got nothing to wear.'

'Poor Cinderella,' Jonas said, chuckling.

Jumping to her feet, Ruby felt the room spinning round and she sat down again. 'I feel a bit dizzy.'

'Come on,' Jonas said, getting up and hooking her arm around his shoulders. 'Let's get you to your room.'

'I can manage, ta.' Pushing him away, Ruby staggered and clutched at the chair back. 'I'm a bit tipsy, but I don't need no help.'

'Of course you don't,' Jonas said, hoisting her over his shoulder. Having carried her up the stairs in this undignified manner, he dumped her unceremoniously on the bed in her room. Jonas stood for a moment looking down at her.

Focusing her eyes with difficulty, Ruby wagged her finger at him. 'No funny business.'

Lifting her skirt a little, Jonas slipped off her

satin shoes and dropped them on the floor. Sitting on the edge of the bed, he unrolled her stockings, peeling them off and holding one of her feet in his hand, he stroked it slowly and sensuously. The warmth of his fingertips and the unexpected thrill of his light touch on her bare foot sent a shiver of excitement through Ruby's body, but a warning voice in her head made her sit up and pull her foot away.

'You promised!'

For a moment, Jonas sat quite still, staring at her with a perplexed frown, and then his lips curved in a smile and his eyes darkened with desire as he took her in his arms. 'I warned you before, Ruby, I'm a bad lot.'

Confused and tormented by her own wicked lust, which would surely see her burn in hell, Ruby struggled against the treacherous response of her body, but the strong masculine scent of him filled her with a wave of desire. It was shocking and disgraceful, but it seemed that she was powerless to resist and Ruby wound her arms around Jonas's neck. His mouth was so close to hers that she could almost taste him. Closing her eyes, she parted her lips, waiting for his kiss. She felt the muscles of his arms contract and he released her so suddenly that she fell back against the pillows.

'I want you, Ruby,' Jonas said gruffly, 'but not like this.'

Ruby awakened next morning suffering from a thumping headache, a parched throat and mouth and toe-curling embarrassment as she remembered the events of last night. She had always known that Jonas was a dangerous man, but the real danger lay in her passionate response to his lovemaking; she was confused and bitterly ashamed of her wanton behaviour. How could you hate a man, as she most definitely hated Jonas, and yet respond to him as if it were the most natural thing in the world? And how could she bring herself to reveal all this to Father Brennan in the confessional? She could not understand why Jonas had left her so suddenly, but she was painfully aware that she had behaved like a common tart and she felt her cheeks burning with mortification and self-loathing. Ruby slipped out of the house before anyone else had stirred and she set off for the hospital.

No matter how many excuses Ruby thought up, Pamela always countered with a good reason why she must come to her engagement party. As the days slipped by, Ruby was running out of ideas, and had just decided to simply tell Pamela the truth when Adam cornered her in the sluice.

'Pam is really worried that you won't come to the party, Ruby.'

'I'm not sure if I can get the time off.'

Taking the bedpan out of her hands, Adam dropped it into the sink. 'We both want you to come. If there's a problem, I'm sure it can be overcome.'

Struggling to come up with a convincing lie, Ruby felt herself floundering. 'I – it's a long way to Highgate.'

A frown puckered Adam's high forehead. 'And a cab is expensive. How thoughtless of us, Ruby. I'll send a hansom cab for you and make sure that there is one to take you home. Please say you'll come. Pam is so fond of you, and so am I.'

Unable to resist his smile, Ruby nodded. She would walk barefoot from Shoreditch to Highgate just to hear Adam say he cared for her. She had nothing special to wear and no idea how a lady would dress to attend a fashionable garden party. But, as Granny Mole had always said to her, 'Who's going to look at you anyway?' She would just wear her print frock and hope she did not look too out of place.

Taking advantage of the spell of fine summer weather, the party was going to be held in the Fairfaxes' garden. Pamela had been chattering excitedly about the fact that fresh salmon and venison were being sent down from Scotland for the lunch, together with dozens of punnets of raspberries. There was to be a marquee, just in case it rained, and an orchestra had been hired to play all day and into the evening when there would be dancing. Caught up in all this, Ruby was in a state wavering between joy and despair. What good was it that Adam cared for her, if she was about to witness him getting engaged to someone else?

The evening before the engagement party, praying that by some divine intervention she would have a valid excuse for not going, Ruby went home to Raven Street. Matron, who for some reason was being unusually beneficent, had agreed to Ruby having the next day off, dashing her last hope of a reprieve. As she let herself into the house, she could hear music and laughter coming from the large dining room downstairs where the women were being entertained, and the low droning of men's voices as Ruby passed the gaming room on the first floor. Wearily, Ruby climbed the stairs to her own room. Switching on the lights, she blinked to make sure she was not imagining things. The entire surface of her bed was covered in bandboxes and a large hatbox from Peter Robinson's emporium. For a wild moment, she thought that the gifts might have come from Adam and she rummaged amongst the boxes looking for a card. She found one, tucked inside a deckle-edged envelope.

For Cinderella

Jonas! He had teased her, calling her Cinderella, and no one else would have known that her measurements were listed in Peter Robinson's order book. Disappointment clouded her mind. How stupid could she be, imagining that Adam might have made such a generous gesture? As for Jonas, his motive was far from clear; it could have been guilt or perhaps he wanted her to make a fool of herself at the party. Ruby ran her fingers over one of the satin-smooth cardboard boxes, torn between curiosity to see what was inside and the desire to fling them all back in his face. In the end, curiosity won. Tearing at satin bows, Ruby opened box after box, until her bed was covered in a froth of undergarments made of silk and lace, an exquisite dress that was finer than anything she could ever have imagined, shoes to match, gloves, a parasol and a wide-brimmed hat that was a confection of tulle and silk flowers. Of course she couldn't accept such an extravagant gift, but who could resist just trying them on to see the effect?

Leaving the comparative security of the hansom cab, Ruby trod the path up to the imposing red-brick Georgian house owned by Adam's parents. Sick with nerves, wishing that she were any-where but here, she took a deep breath and raised the gleaming brass lion's head knocker.

A parlourmaid opened the door and led her through the house and out into the back garden. Left alone on the paved terrace, Ruby clutched the handle of the lace parasol that exactly matched the lavish trimming of her turquoise silk gown, and peering beneath the wide brim of her hat, she searched for a familiar face in the crowd. Strolling in the sunshine on green-velvet lawns, the elegantly dressed ladies, leaning on the arms of gentlemen in tailcoats and top hats, appeared delicate and colourful as butterflies. Aware that her presence was attracting curious stares, Ruby could only think that it was her lone state that was causing such interest. Everyone seemed to be in pairs or family groups and she prayed for the ground to open up and swallow her. Miss Luckes, almost unrecognisable out of her starched uniform, was sipping champagne and chatting to a distinguished-looking man. Ruby recognised him immediately as Lord Knutsford, Chairman of the Board of Governors of the London Hospital. Overcome with nerves, Ruby was about to retreat through the French windows into the drawing room when Pamela came rushing towards her, arms outstretched, cheeks flushed and her eyes sparkling with happiness.

'Ruby! I'm so glad you came. You look absolutely beautiful. Come and say hello to Adam.' Without waiting for an answer, Pamela slipped her arm through Ruby's and dragged her down the steps onto the lawn. 'Adam, darling! Look who's just arrived.'

Breaking away from a group of men, some of whom Ruby recognised as consultants from the London, Adam came towards them, a genuine smile of pleasure lighting his face. 'Ruby, how good of you to come and how absolutely stunning you look.'

Ruby managed a smile. 'Congratulations to you both.'

'See my ring; isn't it just too gorgeous for words?' Pamela waved her left hand in front of Ruby's face so that the sunlight caught the solitaire diamond, turning it into a ball of white fire.

'I never seen nothing like it,' Ruby said, blinking.

'It is rather splendid, isn't it,' Pamela said, gazing fondly at Adam. 'I'm so lucky.'

Adam bent down to drop a kiss on her forehead. 'No, I'm the fortunate one. Don't you think so, Ruby?'

Swallowing an egg-sized lump in her throat, Ruby could only nod.

'Darling, we're neglecting poor Ruby,' Pamela said, slapping him playfully on the hand. 'Fetch her a glass of champagne, will you, please?'

'Of course,' Adam said, flashing a smile at Ruby. 'Why don't you introduce her to our parents, Pam?'

Watching Adam stroll off in the direction of the marquee, Ruby felt as though her heart was being ripped out of her body with a pair of surgical forceps. She had always known there was no hope for her but this was truly the end of her dreams. Adam and Pamela officially belonged together now and this was their world, a world in which she felt totally alien.

Bubbling over with happiness, Pamela did not seem to notice Ruby's discomfort, guiding her from group to group of people, making introductions until the faces and names registered nothing but a blur in Ruby's mind. She was aware of stretched smiles and penetrating looks from the ladies, as though they were mentally totting up the cost of her outfit and wondering how a common girl from the East End could afford such luxuries. The gentlemen were less severe, most of them openly admiring and some of them downright saucy; one of Pamela's uncles, who appeared to have drunk a bit too much whisky, actually pinched her bottom. Ruby got away from him as quickly as possible.

When Pamela made for the group around Miss Luckes, Ruby drew back. 'No, really. I'd rather not, Pam.'

'Good heavens, why ever not?' Pamela's delicate eyebrows formed arcs of surprise.

'It's Matron.'

'Of course it's Matron, silly. And that's Lord

Knutsford and Sir Frederick Treves but they won't eat you. They're all friends of the family.'

'Sir Frederick Treves, the surgeon what took care of the Elephant Man?' Ruby couldn't help staring at him, amazed that he looked so ordinary when he was considered little short of God at the London where, until recently, he had been such an eminent surgeon.

'Yes, of course. He's a dear and terribly funny,' Pamela said, chuckling. 'Adam used to attend his lectures and said he was always making risqué jokes. You simply must meet him.'

'Ah, there you are. I've been looking for you both,' Adam said, weaving his way through the throng with two glasses of champagne in his hands. 'Ruby, you must be exhausted with all this how-do-you-doing.'

Gulping a mouthful of champagne, Ruby's eyes watered as the bubbles went up her nose. She managed a smile and a nod, wishing that someone had warned her that 'pleased to meet you' wasn't the proper greeting amongst the toffs. No wonder some of the fusty old matrons had looked down their beaky noses at her.

'Ruby has borne it all like a real trouper,' Pamela said, sipping her champagne. 'I simply can't think of anything worse than having to meet all my ghastly relations in one go, let alone yours, Adam.'

Pulling a face, Adam grinned. 'I know, but one

has to do these things. We'd better circulate a bit, Pam. Will you be all right, Ruby?'

'Don't worry about me,' Ruby said, stifling a hiccup.

'Just watch out for Uncle Bertie,' Adam said, taking Pamela by the hand. 'He's a bit of a one with the ladies.'

'Ta, but I think we already met.' And I've got a bruise to prove it, Ruby thought, watching them walk away hand in hand. Out of the corner of her eye, she saw Uncle Bertie advancing on her with a glass of whisky in his hand and a leering look on his face. Taking evasive action, Ruby ducked into the shrubbery, making her way between the bushes to a shady part of the garden where some of the older ladies sat on spindly gilt chairs, chatting to each other. She had successfully dodged Uncle Bertie but the only way out of the shrubbery would bring her into the middle of the ladies' circle. Hardly daring to breathe, Ruby waited, hoping that Uncle Bertie would tire of looking for her and walk away.

'We're so lucky with the weather, Joan.' Ruby recognised Mrs Chadwick's clipped tones.

'You know what they say about the sun shining on the righteous, Blanche.'

That sounded like Mrs Fairfax, Ruby thought. Adam's mother had given her a very hard stare when they were introduced. She longed to get away but she could still see Uncle Bertie waiting and watching, like a fat black spider in the middle of his web. Ruby prayed that he would finish his drink and go to the marquee for a refill.

'I'm so looking forward to having Adam as a son-in-law.'

'And I'm just relieved that Adam had the good sense to pick a lovely girl like Pamela. I shudder to think that he could have fallen for someone like the common little girl from the hospital that they insisted on inviting. She may have a pretty face but when she opens her mouth she speaks like a costermonger.'

'I feel quite sorry for her, Joan. She must feel terribly out of place.'

'Not that sort, my dear. Have you stopped to wonder how a girl like that would be able to afford such an outfit unless she were – you know, up to no good? You'd better have a quiet word with Pam, warn her not to get too friendly. Even the most upright men can give in to that sort of temptation.'

Stuffing her hand into her mouth to stop herself from crying out in protest, Ruby picked up her skirts and ran, barging into Uncle Bertie and knocking him off balance. Racing through the house, she pushed past an astonished maid, sending a tray of glasses flying. Wrenching the front door open, Ruby stumbled out onto the tiled path and ran.

Chapter Fourteen

Unable to sleep for the heat, the sound of Granny Mole's snoring and the baby kicking her in the ribs, Rosetta got up and went downstairs to the living room. The first hint of the summer dawn was streaking the sky above the houses across the street, and Rosetta went to sit by the window, opening it to try to get a little air into the stuffy room. This was the dawn of her wedding day, a day that was supposed to be happy and special and she was going to be a radiant bride: but that was so untrue that it made her want to cry. Leaning her hot forehead against the cool glass of the windowpane, Rosetta closed her eyes, thinking back to the events that had brought her to this sorry state.

But if she were honest, she had to admit that there was no one to blame but herself. She had gone willingly with Billy that dreadful night when she had left home rather than go to live with the Moles until her baby was born. She remembered every incident clearly, from the moment when she had opened her eyes, staring up at the rafters in the unfamiliar stable loft that was Billy's home . . .

Rosetta sat up in bed – Billy's bed. Her stomach churned and the now familiar wave of nausea made her retch. 'Billy?'

The room, which was little more than a stable loft, was empty. The bed was narrow, just big enough for a single person; wherever Billy had slept it had not been at her side. Rosetta sank back onto the pillow, closing her eyes, waiting for the sick feeling to subside. Now the memories came flooding back to her, the angry scenes with Aunt Lottie and Alf and the final indignity when Uncle Sly had turned her out of the house in Raven Street. She could still hear the disappointment and disapproval in her mother's voice and Granny Mole's uncompromising condemnation of her behaviour. If Billy hadn't taken her in she would have had to sleep in a doorway or worse. One moment she had been Miss Rosetta, up and coming star of the Falstaff Music Hall, and now she was pregnant, homeless, sleeping on a truckle bed in a spider-filled loft, and even Billy had deserted her. Scalding tears forced themselves between her closed eyelids and trickled down her cheeks.

'Hey, hey, what's all this?'

Opening her eyes with a start, Rosetta saw Billy standing beside the bed, his face puckered in concern.

'I don't feel well, Billy.'

'You just need some grub inside you, girl,' Billy said, waving a package wrapped in newspaper in front of her nose. 'Breakfast, that's what you need. A bacon doorstep and a cuppa will set you up a treat.'

Rosetta turned her head away. 'I told you, I feel sick. I can't eat.'

'Suit yourself, then,' Billy said, pulling out a chair and sitting down at the table.

Sneaking a peek at him, Rosetta's mouth watered as she watched him unwrap two doorstep sandwiches, taking a bite out of one as he poured tea from a tin pail into two mugs. The smell of bacon and hot tea was too much for her. She sat up. 'Maybe just a cup of tea.'

Billy spooned sugar into one of the mugs and handed it to her. 'That's the ticket.'

Swinging her legs over the side of the bed, Rosetta sipped the tea, and as the sick feeling began to pass she realised that she was starving. Reaching out, she snatched a sandwich and bit into the thick wodge of bread, marge and crispy bacon.

'That's right,' Billy said, nodding in approval. 'You got to eat for two now.'

Rosetta swallowed a mouthful. 'Not for long. Don't think I'm going through with this, Billy. I'm going to get meself fixed up.'

Dropping his sandwich, Billy leapt to his feet and grabbed her by the arm, his face dark with fury. 'Don't you never say such a thing again, Rose. Don't you even think about doing something so bloody stupid.'

'Let me go. It ain't nothing to do with you.'

Billy tightened his grip. 'Now you listen to me, Rosetta. You go to one of them back street butchers and you'll end up dead. I know, because I seen it happen to someone I cared about.'

'Was you the father?'

'No, but the girl was me sister. I watched her die and there weren't nothing that anyone could do to save her.'

'I'm sorry, of course I am, really sorry, but that don't give you the right to tell me what to do.'

Taking her by the shoulders, Billy shook her hard. 'It is my business because I'm going to take care of you and the nipper. We're going to get spliced all legal and proper – unless you got any objections, that is.'

It was not the most romantic of proposals. Looking into Billy's eyes, Rosetta saw that he was in deadly earnest, and although her instant reaction was to refuse him, she could not think of one single reason why she should not accept.

'So what d'you say, Rose? Will you marry me?'

Rosetta shrugged her shoulders. 'Don't mind if I do.'

Billy wrapped her in his arms, his mouth seeking hers in a long, slow kiss. Recoiling at first, with the memory of Alf's beery breath and wet mouth still uppermost in her mind, Rosetta found to her astonishment that Billy's kiss was something quite different. His lips were firm, teasing and yet tender, patient and yet demanding. He slid his fingers through her hair, holding her head so that she could not escape, and to Rosetta's surprise she found that she did not want to. Sliding her arms around his neck, she relaxed against his firm young body, parting her lips with a sigh.

'I love you, Rose.'

Billy's mouth was hot on her neck, kissing the column of her throat while his hands caressed her breasts. She could feel the buttons of her blouse popping open beneath his eager fingers and the cold air chilled her naked flesh. Suddenly it was not Billy but Alf who was kissing her with mounting desire; it was Alf and not Billy who slid his hand beneath her skirt, feeling for the private place between her legs. Wild with panic, Rosetta pushed him away. 'No. No. I can't.'

Sitting back and running his hand through his hair with a perplexed frown, Billy stared at her then he smiled ruefully, shaking his head. 'You're right, Rose. This ain't going to be a hole in the corner affair. I want you like I've never wanted anyone before but we'll do it proper and wait until we're legally wed.' Getting to his feet, he picked up her blouse from the floor where it had fallen in a crumpled heap and laid it on the bed beside her. 'Get dressed, ducks. We're going round to see your mum.'

Once again, Rosetta felt as though her life was being taken away from her and organised by those about her, as though she were a child without a say in her future. Mum and Granny Mole wholeheartedly supported Billy's intention to make an honest woman of her. Sitting in her mother's cramped living room, unable to get a word in edgeways as Mum and Billy made arrangements for the wedding with Granny Mole throwing in her usual unhelpful remarks, Rosetta was beginning to feel as though she must be invisible. It was decided that Lottie should be made to pay for the whole thing, since she was always so keen to show off and it was all her fault anyway. Granny Mole said it was not to be one of them Roman Catholic dos with Father Brennan insisting that the nipper had to be brought up in the Faith like it had been when Sarah and Aldo were married. Billy said he didn't mind if the ceremony was conducted by a witch doctor, so long as it was legal. No one bothered to ask Rosetta what she wanted, and before she had time to protest, Sarah had decided that she would go and see the local vicar and then sort the rest out with Lottie. Of course it had to be done quickly, before Rosetta began to show; after all, there were plenty of seven-month babies in Tobacco Court, which was quite respectable, not like them in Spivey Street who dropped babies like litters of puppies, never knowing who had fathered them. Naturally, Rosetta would need a new dress, and again Lottie would have to pay. Granny Mole and Sarah, once started on a theme, were as unstoppable as the Thames at flood tide.

'I got business to do,' Billy said, winking at Rosetta and backing towards the door. 'Can't hang about now I've got a family to support.'

Rosetta got up, intending to follow him.

'And where are you going, Rose?' Sarah turned on her with a fierce frown.

'With Billy, Mum.'

'Sit down,' Sarah said, wagging her finger. 'There'll be none of that there until you're married.'

'But, Mum . . .'

'No,' Billy said, hooking his arm around Rosetta's shoulders. 'Your mum's right, ducks. Anyway, my place ain't fit for you to stay in. You'll be better off here.'

'That's right,' Sarah said. 'And when you've tied the knot you'll both live here. I'll move in with Ma and Elsie and you two can have the bed that me and Aldo shared for thirty years.'

'What?' Rosetta heard her voice rise to a shriek. 'Don't I get no say in all this?'

'No,' Granny Mole said, pointing a finger at

her. 'Girls what ain't no better than they should be get what they deserve.'

Rosetta turned to Billy, who was already halfway out of the door. 'Billy!'

'Don't worry, love. It'll all come right. Trust Billy Noakes.'

The door closed behind him. Rosetta turned on her mother. 'I'll not be treated like this.'

'There's always the workhouse,' Granny Mole said darkly.

'Think yourself lucky that you've got a decent bloke what's prepared to take on another man's bastard,' Sarah said, snatching up her shawl and bonnet. 'I'm going to have it out with Lottie and you, miss, can stay here and make a bit of dinner for your gran.'

'I'm not a skivvy,' Rosetta said, tossing her head. 'Where's Elsie? Ain't that her job?'

'Elsie went out early delivering the clean washing and she'll be bringing back the soiled things. She's been a good help to me, Rose, and when the baby comes she can look after it while you go out and get yourself a proper job. We'll have no more of that theatrical nonsense.' Slipping her shawl over her shoulders, Sarah marched out of the house, closing the door with an emphatic bang.

'Prancing about on the stage,' Granny Mole said, glowering. 'Just look where it's got you.'

Struggling to hold back a torrent of harsh

words, Rosetta snatched up her jacket and slammed out of the house. Let the old witch get her own dinner.

Ruby! Rosetta's first thought was to find her sister. She arrived at the hospital hot and breathless, desperate to see Ruby and quite unprepared for the cold reception she received from the senior nursing sister. No matter how much she pleaded and wheedled, Rosetta came up against a solid wall of officialdom. Probationer nurses were not allowed visitors during working hours and Nurse Capretti was not due off duty until nine o'clock in the evening. Personal matters must be conducted out of the hospital and on her own time. Determined not to go home, Rosetta walked back to Billy's place and, finding the door locked, she sat down on an upturned bucket in the empty stable, waiting for him to return.

She had lost count of time, but it seemed as though she had been sitting in the smelly stable for hours. Getting to her feet, Rosetta paced the floor, raging inwardly at the stroke of misfortune that had brought her to this. Just a couple of days ago she had been heading for stardom in the theatre, earning good money and independent of her family, and now she felt as though her life had come to an abrupt end. She could imagine no worse punishment for her folly than having to live back at home, with Mum, Gran and Elsie, not to mention Billy and the baby, with the daunting prospect of yearly pregnancies to follow. Never had the future looked so bleak.

'Miss Rose.'

Rosetta stopped pacing and spun round to see Elsie standing in the doorway. 'If they've sent you to bring me home you've wasted your time.'

'No, I guessed where you was and him in the baker's shop told me where Billy lived. I brung you this.' Shyly, Elsie held out a scrap of cloth wrapped round a hunk of bread and cheese.

It was a long time since breakfast and Rosetta was ravenous. 'Ta, Elsie.' As she bit into the bread, she realised that Elsie couldn't take her eyes off the food. Suddenly guilty, Rosetta divided the bread and cheese in two, handing a share to Elsie. 'This was for your dinner, wasn't it?'

'You was always good to me in Raven Street. I wanted to do something for you.'

'Well, you can,' Rosetta said, smiling. 'You can go home and tell me mum that Billy's looking after me now so she's not to worry. I'll come and see her when I've got me wedding band to flash in front of the neighbours. Can you remember all that?'

With her mouth full of bread and cheese, Elsie nodded.

Billy had not returned by the time Elsie set off for Tobacco Court and Rosetta decided to go looking for him. It should be easy enough to find him if she kept her eyes open for his old piebald horse and brightly painted cart. It didn't take her long to track him down in a pub at the end of Cable Street. Rosetta found him in the public bar doing a deal with a shifty-looking man over a pint of bitter.

'Rose, what the bleeding hell are you doing here?'

Rosetta flashed him a dazzling smile. She could feel all eyes upon her and hear the murmurs of admiration as she strolled up to the bar. Sensing the appreciative audience, it was almost like being on stage at the Falstaff. Standing very close to Billy, Rosetta fluttered her eyelashes. 'I couldn't bear to be away from you, darling.'

A small cheer rippled round the bar, with a few whistles thrown in.

Pushing his cap to the back of his head, Billy took a bow. 'Keep your mince-pies off her, lads. This lady's took.' Grabbing Rosetta by the arm, he pulled her to one side. 'Are you mad? Walking out alone in this area? I thought you was staying at your mum's.'

'Well you thought wrong,' Rosetta said, snatching her arm free.

'Come outside.' Still smiling, Billy wrapped his arm around her waist and walked her out into the street. 'Now then, Rose?'

'I ain't going home and you can't make me.'

'But I thought we agreed . . .'

'No, Billy. You and me mum agreed, but I never.'

'What am I going to do with you, girl? You can't stay at my place and that's that.'

Spotting a glimmer of sympathy in his eyes, Rosetta cuddled up to him. 'Let's not wait for the wedding band, Billy. Find us a nice cosy room with a proper feather bed and a coal fire and bugger the rest of them.' Reaching up, she brushed his set mouth with butterfly kisses until his lips parted in a reluctant smile.

'Well,' Billy said, drawing her closer. 'I just done a good deal. I can afford it, although I was going to save the money for our honeymoon.'

'Why wait?' Rosetta whispered in his ear. 'Let's have the honeymoon first, shall we?'

Billy grinned. 'There's me trying to make an honest woman of you and now you're leading a poor bloke astray. What am I going to do with you, Rosetta?'

'I expect you'll think of something, Billy.'

'Saucy mare!' Laughing, Billy lifted her onto the cart. 'We'd best collect your things first. Don't want to offend a respectable lodging house by turning up without any luggage.'

'And a ring,' Rosetta said, waving her left hand in front of his face. 'I got to look the part.'

The lodging house in Aldgate was not exactly what Rosetta had in mind, but the room was clean and reasonably comfortable. Mrs Wilkins, the landlady, took them in without asking any questions, having insisted on a month's rent in advance. Small and wizened like a brown monkey, her hooded eyes were shrewd and button-bright.

'No cooking in the room,' she said, pointing to a list of house rules pinned to the back of the door. 'No smoking and no spitting. Evening meal at six sharp. Those what turn up late don't get nothing.'

'Understood,' Billy said, nodding. 'I'm sure this will suit us fine.'

'You won't get no better, if I say so myself.' Turning to go, Mrs Wilkins shot a piercing glance at Rosetta. 'Breakfast is at seven, but I'll make allowances for a woman in your condition. If he's willing to bring it upstairs, you can have tea and toast in your room.'

Wondering how the woman could possibly know such a personal detail, Rosetta's hand flew to her stomach.

'Don't worry, dearie. I ain't no witch,' Mrs Wilkins said, with a glint of humour in her dark eyes. 'I just seen it all before. Just one thing though: no babies in this house. Nasty, squally things, babies. I can't abide 'em.'

'Well!' Rosetta said, giggling as the door closed behind their new landlady. 'I bet she is a witch.'

Lifting her off her feet, Billy carried Rosetta

over to the bed. 'Never mind the old girl, let's give the bed a go and see if it's as comfy as it looks.' Dumping her down on the coverlet, Billy sat on the edge of the bed, kicking off his boots.

'Not now, Billy,' Rosetta said, struggling to a sitting position. 'You heard the old bat. Supper is at six sharp and I'm starving.'

'Come on, love. We got a good quarter of an hour to get downstairs. You can't act all coy and virginal now.'

Pressing her down amongst the feather pillows, Billy tried to kiss her, but Rosetta turned her head away. 'Get off me.'

'Don't act soft,' Billy said, holding her down and unbuttoning her blouse. 'You wanted this, Rose, you said so. You can't go back on it now.'

His mouth sought hers, his kisses laced with anger and frustration as Rosetta struggled, attempting to push him off. She knew that she had flirted outrageously, had given him the idea that she wanted him to make love to her, but she was not ready. This was not how it was supposed to be; she wanted romance, just like in the penny dreadfuls. She wanted lover-like words, wine and flowers. She didn't want to be treated as Alf had treated her, like a whore; she wanted to feel like a beautiful lady, not a tart. In the end, there was nothing she could do but lie still, waiting for Billy's pent-up passion to reach a climax that she could not share. He was telling her again and again that he loved her, but it was too late, the words meant nothing now. When it was over he lay beside her, stroking her hair and promising her that he would always love and take care of her. Turning her head away, Rosetta felt hot tears sliding down her cheeks. She knew then that she did not love Billy; she had deluded herself, confusing liking with loving.

Billy sat up, patting her on her bare flank. 'Come on, love. I thought you was starving. I know I am.'

They were to be married on 28 July in the local church with Ruby, Sarah and Granny Mole in attendance. Billy had managed to persuade Sarah that a quiet wedding was the best option, although how he had done this Rosetta did not know. She had kept well out of the way until she was certain that a visit home would not incur long arguments and lectures. Surprisingly, Granny Mole had backed Billy up. He had related the story to Rosetta on his return, mimicking Granny's voice with deadly accuracy. Father Brennan's nose, she had crowed, would be put well and truly out of joint, and leaving her out of things would be a slap in the face for that Carlottie, the Eyetie tart. It would show her, once and for all, that the Moles had more pride than to accept her ill-gotten gains.

*

'Rosetta! What are you doing up so early?'

Opening her eyes with a start, Rosetta looked round to see Mum standing at the foot of the stairs, wearing her nightgown and a worried frown. 'I couldn't sleep, Mum. It was too hot and Granny snores like a stuck pig.'

Sarah's brow cleared and she smiled. 'I know, ducks, but I've had a lifetime to get used to it. You are feeling all right, aren't you?'

'I'm fine,' Rosetta lied. 'But I could murder a cup of tea.'

'Of course you could,' Sarah said, bustling over to the fireplace. 'I'll soon get the fire going and we'll have some tea and toast. Got to keep your strength up on your big day. I wish your dad was here to see you get married, Rose. He'd have been proud of you in spite of everything.'

'Yes, Mum.' Biting back tears at the mention of Poppa's name, Rosetta went to get up but Sarah motioned her to sit.

'You stay there and rest, there's a good girl. You're going to be the prettiest bride that Tobacco Court's ever seen and I don't want you looking peaky.' Riddling the embers of the fire, Sarah chattered on. 'We're going to see you get hitched in style, all proper like so that the gossips haven't got anything to talk about. If I'd left it to you and Billy, you'd have bowled up together for the wedding and everyone would have known you'd been living in sin. As it is you're not

showing too much, not if we drape Lottie's
Spanish shawl round your shoulders.'

'Yes, Mum,' Rosetta said, thinking that she
would rather die than be seen in that hideous
black thing, never mind what the neighbours
said about her.

Wearing the floral-patterned cretonne dress that
Sarah and Granny Mole had run up for her,
Rosetta walked down the aisle on Billy's arm,
forcing her lips into a smile when all she really
wanted to do was cry. Casting a sideways glance
at Billy she saw, with a stab of irritation, that he
was grinning like an idiot. Rosetta was still
fuming inwardly, having discovered that Billy
had bought himself a sharp, chequered suit for
the occasion, topped with a brown bowler hat.
He must have spent a small fortune on it and yet
she, the bride, was walking down the aisle in a
homemade dress made out of material bought
from a stall in Petticoat Lane. She had refused
point-blank to wear the black shawl, declaring
that she would faint with the heat, but that was
not much consolation. Rosetta had barely heard
the vicar's words as he droned through the
marriage ceremony. She had responded to her
vows in little more than a whisper, with Billy
squeezing her hand and making his responses in
a bold, clear voice that bounced off the stone
pillars in a mocking echo.

Outside the church, Billy tossed a handful of pennies, halfpennies and farthings to a crowd of street urchins. 'Now you're properly Mrs Noakes,' he said, kissing Rosetta in front of the whole street.

'Give over, Billy. You're making a show of me.' Rosetta tried to break free, but Billy laughed and drew her hand through the crook of his arm.

'I want the whole world to see what a lucky chap I am, Rose. You'll feel better when you've had something to eat. Come on, everyone. Dinner's on Mr and Mrs Billy Noakes.'

Leaning on his arm, clutching a posy of white carnations, Rosetta felt as though she were in the middle of a bad dream. The baby was jiggling around inside her belly as she walked beside Billy, her husband, and Rosetta knew that she was well and truly trapped. Life from now on would be the all too familiar struggle that she had seen her mother endure and from which there was no escape.

'You look beautiful, Rose,' Ruby said, quickening her pace to catch up with them. 'It was a lovely wedding ceremony.'

Rosetta could hardly bear to look at her sister. Ruby was living with Jonas Crowe, simply because he had picked the wrong sister; it must have been a case of mistaken identity. Ruby was dressed in a shop-bought grey silk gown that was the very latest fashion, with a jaunty little matching hat perched at an angle on her piled-up curls. Ruby's trim figure was a sharp reminder that her own was spreading rapidly, her swollen breasts straining at her bodice above the tightly laced stays that could barely disguise her bulging belly. It was not fair, Rosetta thought, shutting her ears to Billy's cheerful banter. It was just not fair.

'Where are we going?' demanded Granny Mole, hobbling along behind them. 'I can't walk much farther and I'm faint with hunger.'

'Just round the corner, Granny,' Billy said, over his shoulder. 'I've booked a table at a chophouse. No one can say that Billy Noakes is a skinflint.'

Seated round the table that Billy had booked for the party, everyone except Rosetta tucked into the meal of brown Windsor soup followed by lamb chops with onion sauce, mashed potatoes, boiled cabbage and plenty of gravy.

'If you don't want your chop, pass it here,' Granny Mole said, pointing her fork at Rosetta's plate.

'Ma, that ain't good manners,' hissed Sarah. 'This ain't a pie shop.'

'Bah!' Granny Mole's hand shot out, stabbing the chop on her fork. 'I hates to see good food go to waste. Rose is just like I was when I was carrying you. I lost me appetite, couldn't look at food.'

'All my eye and Betty Martin!' Billy whispered in Rosetta's ear.

Ignoring him, Rosetta pushed her plate across the table. 'Eat it all. I don't want it.'

'Are you all right?' Ruby asked anxiously.

'I'm fine, ta. You needn't come over all professional now you're a nurse.'

'Hey, Rose,' Billy said, a slight edge in his cheerful voice. 'Come off it, love. Ruby was just trying to help.'

Jumping to her feet, Rosetta knocked over a tumbler of water.

'Sit down,' Billy said, pulling her back onto the seat while Ruby did her best to staunch the flow of water with a starched white napkin. 'It's you who's behaving badly, Rose. This is supposed to be our special day and you're spoiling it.'

'It's all right. No harm done.' Ruby handed the soggy napkin to a passing waitress.

'I dunno what's got into you, Rose,' Sarah said, glancing anxiously around to see if any of the City gents eating their midday meals had seen the unfortunate incident.

'Wedding nerves, Mum.' Ruby put her arm around Rosetta's shoulders, giving her a hug. 'Just leave her alone for a bit.'

Sucking the chop bone, Granny Mole gave it up reluctantly as the waitress cleared the table, but her eyes lit up as the pudding was brought in on a big white dish: a steaming mound of suet pudding with a glistening treacle cap, sitting in a pool of thick yellow custard. 'Oh, my,' she said, licking her lips. 'Treacle pud. Me favourite.'

Serving Granny Mole first, Sarah divided the pudding with scrupulous attention to fairness, slicing it in geometrical triangles, but Rosetta refused hers, protesting it would make her sick. There was a strained silence as everyone else ate their dessert, Granny Mole and Billy having seconds, while Rosetta sat, silently staring into space. When the last of the pudding had been consumed, Billy insisted that they must have a toast and he ordered a glass of port for himself, port and lemon for the ladies.

Raising his glass, he turned to Rosetta, his face split in a huge grin. 'I ain't one for speeches, but I'd just like to thank my beautiful bride for agreeing to take me on. I'm the luckiest man alive. Here's to us, Mrs Noakes.'

A round of applause from the other diners brought the colour flooding to Rosetta's cheeks. Raising her glass, she downed the port and lemon in one gulp.

'Here, steady on, girl,' Billy said. 'You'll make yourself poorly.'

The wine on an empty stomach was already playing hopscotch in Rosetta's brain. 'If you don't want yours, Ruby, I'll have it.'

Before Ruby could protest, Rosetta had swallowed the contents of her glass too. She smiled, feeling the lead weight that had been pressing down on her lifting, leaving her light-headed and pleasantly muzzy. 'Cheers.'

'Well, it is our wedding day,' Billy said, lighting a cigar. 'Drink up, Mother Capretti and Grandmother Mole. We're celebrating.'

Granny Mole jerked her head in Rosetta's direction. 'I think she's had enough.'

'I'll have another, Billy,' Rosetta said, tossing her head. 'And a cigarette if you've got one on you.'

'A cigarette!' Sarah almost fell off her chair. 'You don't smoke, Rose.'

'I do,' Rosetta replied, with a careless shrug. 'Sometimes I do. All the girls at the Falstaff smoked.'

With an indulgent smile, Billy took out a packet of Argosy cigarettes. 'Go on then, ducks, let's see you smoke one of these.'

It was all Rosetta could do to prevent herself from coughing as she sucked in the pungent smoke. She had only tried a Woodbine once and that had made her feel sick, but the look of shock on the faces around her made it worthwhile. She blew a plume of smoke into the air, holding the cigarette between her fingers, mimicking the actions of Aggie and the other girls in the chorus.

Leaning across the table, Sarah's face was a picture of outrage. 'You can just give up that disgusting habit, Rose. Married or not, you won't smoke under my roof and that's that.'

'Lucky we got our own place then, ain't it?' Rosetta said, flicking ash into the ashtray. 'We got a really nice landlady. She lets me do just as I please, so it's as well we don't have to live with you.'

'That's what you think,' Granny Mole said, glowering at Rosetta over the top of her glass.

'What?' Rosetta turned to Billy for an answer. 'What's she saying?'

'Er, well, I was going to tell you later, love.' Billy ran his finger round the inside of his starched collar. 'You see, I had a lot of expenses lately and I been spending time with you when I should have been out working.'

'What he's trying to tell you,' Sarah said, folding her arms across her chest, 'is that he can't afford the rent where you've been staying. You're both coming to live at Tobacco Court with us.'

'No! It ain't true.' Rosetta turned to Billy, clutching his arm. 'I only stayed last night for the look of things. This is a joke, ain't it?'

Shaking his head, Billy's face crumpled into a worried frown. 'Sorry, pet. All this cost an arm and a leg. I wanted to do it in style . . .'

Without waiting to hear the rest, Rosetta jumped to her feet and stormed out of the chophouse.

Chapter Fifteen

'Leave her, Billy,' Ruby said, getting up from the table. 'It's all been too much for Rose in her condition. Let me talk to her.'

'I dunno what I did wrong,' Billy said, shaking his head. 'She's been acting queer all day.'

'Needs a good slapping,' muttered Granny Mole.

'I was like that with Joe,' Sarah said, staring gloomily into her port and lemon.

Hurrying out of the building, Ruby found Rosetta outside, sitting on the edge of an ornate, stone horse trough with the cigarette burning away between her fingers. Taking it from her hand, Ruby ground the dog-end into the cobbles. 'Calm down, Rose. There's no need to get in such a state.'

'How would you know? You've got it easy, living with your fancy man. Just look at you, Ruby, all dressed up to the nines and me in this cheap rag.'

Sitting down beside her, Ruby resisted the temptation to put her arms around Rosetta, knowing that, at this moment, any show of sympathy would only make things worse. 'First off, Jonas isn't my fancy man. I just work for him, Rose, as you well know. And you look beautiful, you always do. You could wear a flour sack and make it look good.' Rewarded by a watery chuckle, Ruby patted Rosetta's hand. 'What's up? You can tell me. Remember? We always told each other everything.'

'I'm a bad person,' Rosetta said, stifling a sob. 'I let Alf Ricketts have his way with me because I wanted to get out of the chorus. I made Billy think I was in love with him when there was someone else and now I'm stuck. I'm hitched to a man I don't love and I got to go back and live with Ma and Gran.' Flinging her arms around Ruby's neck, Rosetta burst into loud sobs. 'I wish I was dead.'

Ruby held her, patting her back and murmuring words of comfort that sounded feeble even to her own ears, allowing Rosetta to cry until she subsided against her shoulder exhausted. Billy had come out of the chophouse and was about to cross the street but Ruby shook her head, signalling him to leave them alone. He paused, looking uncertain for a moment before retracing his steps. Understanding only too well the pain of loving someone totally unobtainable, Ruby stroked Rosetta's damp curls back from her forehead.

'If it's Jonas you're thinking about, Rose, then best forget him.'

'You want him for yourself.' Rosetta jerked herself upright, staring at Ruby with undisguised hostility.

'No, no, of course not.' Ruby grabbed Rosetta's cold hands. 'He's not the man for you. He's bad news, Rose. He doesn't care for anyone but himself.'

Wiping her eyes on her sleeve, Rosetta hiccuped and sniffed. 'I can't help it. I love him.'

'You don't know him.'

'I know he's rich and successful. He's exciting and dangerous. I know he'd want me too, given half a chance. Billy is – just Billy.'

'He's a good man in spite of his shady dealings and at heart he's decent. Billy loves you, Rose. Don't throw that away for something that doesn't exist.'

Jumping to her feet, Rosetta stared down at Ruby, her bottom lip quivering and her eyes brimming with tears. 'You've never been in love. You don't know how I feel.'

'You're so wrong. I know exactly how you feel.'

'Ruby?'

Glancing across the road, Ruby could see pale faces staring at them through the window of the chophouse. Rising swiftly, she grabbed Rosetta's hand and began to walk. 'I'll tell you a secret,

Rose, but only if you swear you'll keep it to yourself.'

Ruby had confessed everything to Rosetta, everything that is except the truth about the night when Jonas had taken her by force and the second occasion when, to her everlasting shame, she had wanted him, but he had walked away from her. Jonas had left her alone since then, passing the time of day if they happened to meet in the labyrinth of corridors in the house, but never going out of his way to seek her company. For this, Ruby was relieved, and yet a small part of her was hurt and angry. She had been humiliated and used but it shamed her even more to remember that there had been excitement and illicit pleasure in the shocking act. Then Jonas had surprised her, yet again, with the handsome present of an outfit for Pamela's engagement party. Ruby knew that she ought to have thrown it back at him, but she had not; she had worn it and enjoyed the luxury of being dressed like a real lady. Perhaps her punishment had been the way the toffs had seen through her, knowing at once that she was not one of them. Rose was not the only one who would be doomed to perdition. Ruby was only too glad that living in Raven Street she was far away from Father Brennan's parish and the confessional. It would take a river of tears to wash away her sins.

Ruby found some relief in throwing herself into work and study. There were examinations to be taken, instituted by the formidable Miss Luckes, and Ruby studied hard, passing with respectable marks. While she was studying, Ruby saw very little of Pamela and even less of Adam. She was grateful for the fact that Pamela did not appear to have noticed her early departure from the engagement party. In fact Pamela had apologised profusely for getting so involved with her other guests that she had completely neglected her friend. Having set the wedding date for the following June, Pamela was full of plans, even going as far as suggesting that Ruby might like to be one of her bridesmaids. Deeply touched, Ruby knew that Pamela was speaking out of simple affection and straight from her kind heart, but to accept would be inviting a fiasco similar to that at the engagement party. They had become firm friends during the time when Pamela was Ruby's mentor, but that did not alter the fact that socially they were poles apart; Pamela might be able to overlook the incontrovertible truth, but Ruby never could.

Apart from Pamela's constant preoccupation with wedding plans, the talk in the hospital was mostly about the threat of fresh hostilities in South Africa. As the weeks went by and summer drifted into autumn, Ruby read the newspapers and listened to the war-mongering chat of the young medical students and housemen, but the fight with the Boers was a world away from Whitechapel and family problems. She made a great effort to visit Tobacco Court when she had any free time but Rosetta seemed to be in a permanent sulk, Granny Mole made things worse with her tactless remarks and constant carping, her mother looked strained and exhausted and Elsie flitted in and out like a pale moth. Billy was never in, supposedly going about his business but more likely, Ruby thought, keeping out of the way. With a house full of squabbling women, who could blame him?

Late one evening at the end of October, Ruby left the hospital, wrapping her coat tightly around her. An autumn gale shredded into shards by the city buildings hurled itself down the street like a hooligan on the rampage, picking up rubbish from the pavements and hurling it in the face of anyone unfortunate enough to be out on such a wild night. Holding onto her hat, Ruby was about to hail a cab when she saw a soldier approaching her. For a moment she thought it must be a visitor to the hospital but a familiarity in the walk wrenched a cry of surprise and joy from her throat. She ran towards him, flinging her arms around his neck 'Joe. Oh, Joe!'

'Hold on, ducks. If you strangle me I won't be no use in fighting them Boers.'

'No, not you, Joe?' Ruby stared into his face, pale in the gaslight. 'They're not sending you all the way to Africa? Not you?'

Joe grinned. 'I'm a trained soldier now. Got to do me duty, and to tell the truth I can't wait to get into the fray, but I had to come to see you first.'

'This is terrible. When do you have to go?'

'Got to catch the troop train for Southampton first thing in the morning.'

'Have you seen Mum?'

'Couldn't face it, Ruby. Thought it might come better from you.'

Hailing a passing cab, Ruby grabbed Joe by the arm; this was not the time for arguing. 'You'd best come to Raven Street with me, then.'

Joe shook his head. 'Not me. I'm steering clear of Crowe. I just wanted to make sure he was treating you right. I know I run out on you, ducks. I ain't proud of it.'

'Jonas has gone to Southend to see Lily. He's not due back for a day or two. Get in the cab, Joe.'

Unlocking the front door, Ruby went into the hall and switched on the electric light. 'It's all right, Joe. He's not here, I promise you, and there's no gaming allowed while Jonas is away. The place is empty except for the servants below stairs.'

Taking off his peaked cap, Joe stepped over the threshold, looking uncertain. 'It don't feel right, me being here.'

'Don't be daft. You'll be long gone before Jonas gets back and I'll not turn my own brother out on the street. Come on up to my room.' Without waiting to see if he was following, Ruby ran lightly up the stairs, leading the way to Lily's sitting room, which she had grown used to using as her own.

Leaving Joe to make up the fire, Ruby went down to the kitchen to collect a tray of supper. Cook had the night off and, taking advantage of the situation, the kitchen maid was entertaining her young man. They both jumped guiltily as Ruby walked into the kitchen.

'Don't worry about me,' Ruby said, picking up a tray. 'I won't say a word.' With the maid too engrossed in flirting with her boyfriend to see what she was doing, Ruby was able to pile the tray with as much food and drink as she could heft up four flights of stairs.

'This is the life,' Joe said, washing down the last of the cold pie with a glass of beer. Leaning back in his chair, he glanced round the elegantly furnished sitting room, nodding in approval. 'You got a comfy billet here all right, Ruby. Seems I needn't have worried about you.'

'I'm all right,' Ruby said, smiling. Any lingering resentment that she had felt melted away at the sight of seeing Joe looking tanned and fit, all traces of his past corrupt lifestyle honed away by hard training and discipline.

'And you're a proper nurse, like you always wanted to be,' Joe said, lighting a cigarette. 'You've done well, even better than Rose. How is she, by the way? Did she get that bastard theatre bloke to make an honest woman of her?'

'She's married, but not to Alf Ricketts.'

Joe listened in silence while Ruby told him what had happened since he left, carefully omitting the part about Rosetta's hopeless infatuation with Jonas. She had barely finished when the sound of approaching footsteps made her break off in alarm. There should not be anyone in this part of the house at this time of night.

The door flew open and Jonas strode in. He stopped, glaring at Joe. 'What the hell is he doing here? The maid told me you were entertaining a gentleman, Ruby, but I didn't think *he'd* have the gall to turn up here.'

'I can explain,' Ruby said, jumping to her feet. 'I didn't think you would be back so soon.'

Joe stood up, smoothing down his tunic, a belligerent look in his eyes. 'Don't blame her. It was my fault.'

'You don't have to tell me that.' Jonas snatched up Joe's cap, flinging it at him. 'Get out.'

'Jonas, have a heart,' Ruby said, making a superhuman effort to control her rising anger. 'Joe is my only brother and he's leaving in the morning for South Africa and the war.'

'You'll be cannon fodder, boy,' Jonas said, his

lip curling. 'I've tried to save you from yourself, but you're a worthless bastard who'd sell his own sister to preserve his lousy skin. Good riddance, I say.'

Incensed, Ruby grabbed Jonas by the arm. 'Don't talk to Joe like that.'

'Get rid of him.' Shaking her hand off, Jonas stormed out of the room.

For a frozen moment, Joe and Ruby stared at each other as they listened to Jonas's footsteps echoing through the silent building.

'He's right,' Joe said, at last. 'He's dead right. I should never have dragged you into this, Ruby.'

'No, I won't have that. You had no choice.'

'I'd better go,' Joe said, picking up his cap. 'I'll kip next door. Sly will give me a bed for the night.'

'Joe, I'm so sorry.'

'I don't like leaving you with him,' Joe said, giving Ruby a hug. 'Will you be all right, ducks?'

'Don't worry about me. I can take care of myself.' Standing on tiptoe, Ruby kissed Joe on the cheek. 'Write to me when you can and take care of yourself, Joe.'

Wiping his eyes on his sleeve, Joe managed a feeble grin.

Having seen him out of the house, and after a last, wordless embrace, Ruby's grief bubbled into anger. A thin splinter of light shining under the door to Jonas's office gave away his where-abouts. Ruby marched in without knocking.

'That was cruel and uncalled for. My brother's going off to fight for Queen and country, which is a damn sight more than you'll ever do.' The words tumbled out before Ruby realised that Jonas was sitting behind his desk, his head held in his hands. His silence frightened her more than his previous violent outburst. 'Jonas?'

Without looking up Jonas shook his head.

For a moment, Ruby thought he was simply angry and ignoring her, but there was something about the hunch of his shoulders and the whiteness of his knuckles as his fingers raked through his hair that told her otherwise. 'Jonas, what's wrong?'

Raising his head, Jonas stared at her blank-eyed. 'It's Lily.'

'She's worse?'

'She's dead.'

The words hit Ruby like a punch in the stomach, knocking the wind from her lungs. Dizzied by the maelstrom of emotions that had raged within her since Joe's unannounced arrival, Ruby's knees gave way beneath her and she sank down on the nearest chair. 'But – but she was getting better.'

'She had a sudden haemorrhage this morning.' Pushing the chair back, Jonas stood up, pacing the floor, his voice breaking. 'She died in my arms.' Coming to a halt in front of Ruby, Jonas dragged her to her feet, gripping her by the shoulders. 'Do you understand, Ruby? She died in my arms.'

'I'm so sorry,' Ruby said, forgetting everything in the face of such agony. 'I'm truly sorry.'

'But I'm not, you see.' Jonas buried his face in her hair and she felt his whole body shaking with emotion. 'I can't mourn her. I'm glad she's dead and out of her pain. I hated seeing that bloody disease eating her until she was a living skeleton. I'm glad she's gone. What does that make me, Ruby?'

Stroking his hair, Ruby held him. 'It makes you human.'

How long they stood there, wrapped in each other's arms, Ruby couldn't tell. Time seemed to have stopped, leaving them in a vacuum of shared anguish. There was no passion in their embrace and no remembrance of past anger. It was Jonas who broke away first, avoiding meeting Ruby's eyes, turning from her with an embarrassed shake of his head.

'You'd better leave. I'm not fit company.'

'Of course. I'll go first thing in the morning.'

'What?' Jonas stared at her, shocked. 'No. I didn't mean you should leave this house.'

'I only stayed for Lily's sake. I must go now.'

His face an unreadable mask, Jonas lifted his hands in a gesture of supplication, letting them fall with a hopeless shrug. 'You'll stay for the funeral?'

'Of course I will.'

It was the greyest of grey November days. Standing in the churchyard with the cutting east wind slicing at her black veil, Ruby glanced at Jonas who stood opposite her, the open chasm of the grave yawning between them. Less than a year ago they had gone through a similar ceremony, although in a different church, when they had buried her father. Barely hearing the vicar's words as he tossed a handful of earth into the grave, Ruby stared at the burnished mahogany coffin with its shining brass handles. It was chilling to imagine beautiful, kind Lily, lying there alone in her permanent sleep, her lovely voice stilled for ever. Choking back a sob, Ruby glanced up at Jonas and saw the muscles in his throat working as though he too were struggling with unshed tears. There were only a few mourners gathered around the grave. Lily had no close family and it was shocking to realise that her life had been wholly centred on Jonas. Aunt Lottie and Silas had come and they were standing a little behind Ruby, but Rosetta, who was now heavily pregnant, had refused to attend.

'It's a sad occasion,' Lottie said, sniffing into a lavender-scented handkerchief. 'So young and so beautiful.'

'That's the truth,' Silas said, attempting to light a cigarette in the teeth of the wind.

'Are we invited back for a drink?' Lottie whispered in Ruby's ear.

Ruby shook her head. 'No, no one is.'

'Bit mean I call it.' Using his coat as a wind-break, Silas managed to strike a match and light his Woodbine. He inhaled deeply, allowing a trickle of smoke out through his nostrils. 'Bloody mean, as it happens. Shouldn't wonder if we all comes down with lung fever after standing around in this weather.'

Lottie dropped her handful of soil onto the coffin and wiped her hands together. 'May the poor soul rest in peace. She never had much of a life with him.'

As Jonas moved away from the grave Ruby made to follow him. 'I'd better go, Auntie.'

Lottie's thin fingers snagged Ruby's sleeve like a bramble. 'You'll be moving out, then?'

'Are you offering me a room, Aunt Lottie?'

'Take my advice, cara. Move as far away from Raven Street as you can. Jonas Crowe is trouble and you're a good girl. You don't want to end up like your sister.'

Freeing her arm, Ruby looked Lottie straight in the eye. 'There's nothing wrong with Rosetta. She was just unlucky, and she'd never have got into trouble if you hadn't put the ideas into her head.'

'Sly, are you going to let her talk to me like that?' Lottie grabbed Silas's arm.

'Leave it out, Lottie,' he said, exhaling a plume of smoke into the frosty air. 'Let's get out of this place. It's giving me the creeps.'

Leaving them nattering and grumbling, Ruby walked over to where Jonas stood waiting for her. 'They're all expecting to be invited back for a bit of a do,' Ruby said, indicating the group of mourners, hovering like crows over carrion.

'I'm not in the mood; they can want all they like. Are you coming?' Jonas held out his arm.

Ruby hesitated, knowing that everyone was watching. She slipped her hand through his arm. 'I'm coming, but only to collect my things and then I'm moving out.' Holding her head high, she walked with him to his motor car. Let them talk and make up stories; at this moment she really did not care.

Handing her into the motor, Jonas cranked the starting handle, and when the engine kicked into action he leapt in beside her. 'You don't have to leave. You can stay for as long as you like and I won't bother you.'

Holding on to her hat as the motor surged forward, Ruby stared at his set profile. 'I don't think so.'

'Are you afraid of what the gossips will say?'

'No. I expect it's already been said a hundred times or more.'

'You needn't be afraid of me. I'm not a monster.'

Angling her head, Ruby gave him a sideways glance. 'Tell that to the poor people who've suffered at the hands of your street gang.'

Honking the horn at a cart obstructing their way, Jonas turned his head to look at her. 'That really bothers you, doesn't it?'

'I despise your way of life and what you do. Oh, I know most of it is just petty crime – the gambling, the illegal fights and the other things that go on in Raven Street – but what your thugs do to ordinary people struggling to make a living is unforgivable and detestable. You live your way, Jonas, and I'll live my own way.'

'Poor but honest?' Jonas said, with wry twist of his lips.

Turning her head away, Ruby didn't answer. When he pulled in at the kerb outside the house, she jumped down without waiting for him to help her. Running up the steps, she let herself in at the front door, acutely conscious that Jonas was only a couple of steps behind her. Turning, she handed him the key. 'I shan't be needing this any more.'

'You can still change your mind.' Jonas stared down at the key lying in the palm of his hand.

'I've arranged to share a room with some of the other probationer nurses.'

'Please yourself.'

'I will.'

'And don't worry, I'll continue to pay for your tuition until you qualify.'

Ruby stopped with one foot on the stairs, jerking her head round to stare at Jonas in horror. 'You never paid. It was . . .'

'The handsome young doctor?' Jonas let out a crack of laughter that echoed around the high ceilings in a mocking echo. 'Sorry, my pet, but it was paid for with some of the ill-gotten gains that you so disapprove of.'

'You're lying.'

Jonas shook his head. 'Sorry to disappoint you, but it's true.'

The magnitude of what he had just said stunned Ruby into silence. All the time she had been thinking that it was Adam who had made it possible for her to pursue her dream of becoming a nurse. It had never occurred to her that Jonas had lied when he had denied being her bene-factor. The thought made her feel physically sick. She had just berated him for the way he made his money, but she had been benefiting from it all along. Too angry, mortified and disgusted to speak, Ruby walked slowly up the stairs to collect her suitcase.

She had considered leaving all the clothes that Jonas had bought for her, but she had come to the conclusion that such an empty gesture would hurt her more than it hurt him. Instead, she had just left the lavender-blue silk gown neatly laid out on the bed, together with the outfit that she had worn to Pamela and Adam's engagement party. Ruby picked up her case, taking a last look round the room that she had come to love, in spite of everything, and made her way down the stairs for the last time. Jonas was nowhere in sight and Ruby let herself out, closing the door behind her. It was raining.

The room she shared with two other probationer nurses was small, cramped and shabby. The linoleum on the floor was cracked and draughts whistled up through the exposed floorboards. The fire smoked and they had to stuff newspaper in the window frames to stop them rattling. At night the temperature dropped so alarmingly that Ruby had to pile her spare clothes on top of the thin coverlet and even then she was chilled to the bone, curled up in bed with her teeth chattering until she fell asleep from sheer exhaustion. In the morning, the windowpanes were iced up on the inside and the water in the jug on the washstand had formed a small skating rink. The one advantage of the lodging house was that it was close to the hospital, but it was hardly home from home and Ruby hated it. She hated the lack of privacy and, although she didn't like admitting it, even to herself, she missed the luxury of her room in Raven Street.

Silently grieving for her friend, Ruby's conscience constantly reminded her that Lily had loved Jonas. She had betrayed Lily when she had wanted Jonas to make love to her for a second time. On the first occasion it had been against her will, but on the evening when they had dined together and she had drunk too much wine, she had wanted him – Jonas had walked away.

The rain had turned to sleet, covering the pavements with shimmering pearls of ice that melted instantly, leaving pools of black slush. Slipping and sliding, Ruby was relieved to have reached the hospital without injury. Almost immediately, she was aware of a tension in the atmosphere like the twanging of a plucked violin string. The whole hospital was buzzing with talk of the continued siege of Ladysmith. Ruby had read about it in the newspapers and, although she was sorry for the people besieged in the town, it was almost impossible to imagine the reality of their plight in a land so far away. Hurrying through the groups of people chatting in the vestibule, she found Pamela in the nurses' room, her face crumpled in the first stages of a good howl.

'What's happened?' Ruby placed her arm round Pamela's shaking shoulders. 'What's the matter?'

'I've begged him not to go but he won't listen to me.'

'Who won't listen to you?' Ruby's stomach muscles contracted in fear.

Fumbling for her hanky, Pamela blew her nose. 'Adam is leaving for South Africa to work in a field hospital with Sir Frederick Treves. I've pleaded with him not to go but he says it's his duty. Can you believe that, Ruby?'

'When?' Ruby licked her dry lips, her heart pounding inside her chest. 'When is he leaving?'

'Tomorrow. He only told me last night because he was too much of a coward to tell me before. We're supposed to be getting married in June. How could he do this to me?'

'Nurse Chadwick!' Sister Tutor stuck her head round the door. 'You're supposed to be on duty in Female Medical.'

Bristling and ready to defend Pamela, Ruby frowned. 'Nurse Chadwick has had some bad news, Sister.'

'And you're supposed to be in Outpatients, Nurse Capretti.'

'Her fiancé is about to leave for the war in South Africa.'

'We all have to do our bit and Dr Fairfax knows his duty. Now get back to work, Nurse Chadwick, or I'll have to report you to Matron.'

'I'm going, Sister,' Pamela said, wiping her eyes. 'Sorry, Sister, it won't happen again.' She hurried out of the room, blowing her nose.

Sister Tutor held the door open glaring at Ruby

with her lip curled like a terrier about to snap. 'Nurse Capretti.'

'Yes, Sister.' Ruby scuttled past her, heading for Outpatients, but once she was out of sight, she made a detour to Men's Surgical where she knew she would find Adam.

He was checking the dressing on an amputation stump when Ruby found him. He looked up with a smile that made it seem to Ruby that the ward was awash with sunshine, although outside it was still dark with sleet being tossed against the windowpanes like handfuls of gravel. 'That's splendid, Tom,' Adam said, placing a piece of gauze over the wound. 'Nurse will put a clean dressing on in a minute.' Pulling the curtain around the bed, Adam signalled to the young nurse hovering with a tray of bandages and lint. He turned to Ruby, smiling. 'What can I do for you, Ruby?'

'Tell me it's not true. You aren't really going to South Africa?'

Adam's smile puckered into a frown. 'I know Pam's upset, but it's something I have to do. You'll look after her for me, won't you, Ruby?'

'You don't have to go, Adam. There must be hundreds of other doctors who could take your place.'

'You are so sweet to worry about Pam,' Adam said, laying his hand on her shoulder. 'I couldn't wish for her to have a better friend than you, Ruby.'

She could feel the heat of his hand searing into her flesh through the thin cotton of her uniform. Choking with emotion, Ruby bit her lip to stop herself from blurting out the truth. She was no more a friend to Pam than she had been to Lily. Her concern for him was purely selfish. How could he not know how much she loved him?

'Nurse Capretti, this is not your ward.' The ward sister had come up behind them without Ruby noticing. 'Kindly leave.'

'It was my fault, Sister,' Adam said, flashing her an apologetic smile. 'I asked Nurse Capretti to run an errand for me.'

'You ought to know better, doctor.' Sister folded her arms across her chest, waiting.

'Goodbye, Adam,' Ruby whispered. 'Please take care of yourself.'

It was late afternoon when Ruby saw Pamela again. She came from the direction of Matron's office and she was actually smiling.

'Pam?' Ruby's heart gave a great leap inside her chest. 'Have you talked him out of going?'

'No. Once Adam has made up his mind to something there's no stopping him. I've done better than that, Ruby.'

'What have you done?'

'I've volunteered to be one of the nurses that

the Princess of Wales is sending out to help in the war effort. I want to be with Adam and I don't care about the danger.'

Ruby stared at her for a moment and suddenly she knew that she had to go too. Joe and Adam, the two men she loved, were risking their lives, and if a delicate flower like Pam had the courage to do it, then so could she. 'I'll go and tell Matron to put me on the list too. I'm coming with you and no one is going to stop me.'

Chapter Sixteen

'How could she do this to me?' wailed Rosetta. 'How could Ruby leave me at a time like this? The selfish bitch.'

'Now, Rose, don't go upsetting yourself,' Billy said, kneeling down in front of her, anchoring her flailing hands in a firm grasp. 'Think of the baby.'

'I'm sick of the baby and I'm fed up with people telling me how to behave.'

'I always said that Sarah was too soft on you,' observed Granny Mole from her chair by the fireside. 'A good slapping when you was little would have sorted you out, my girl.'

Pushing Billy away, Rosetta struggled to her feet. 'You're a nasty old woman and I hate you. I hate all of you, especially Ruby.' Taking a step backwards and bumping into Elsie, Rosetta turned on her in a fury. 'Get out of my way, you stupid girl.'

With a loud wail, Elsie fled into the scullery, almost knocking Sarah down as she came hurrying into the living room, her face crumpled into an anxious frown. 'What now?'

'It's all right, Mother Capretti,' Billy said. 'Rose is missing Ruby, that's all.'

Turning on him in a fury, Rosetta scowled at Billy. 'I can speak for meself and I ain't missing Ruby.'

'You should be proud of her for what she's doing,' Sarah said, wiping her hands on her apron. 'Ruby's done a brave thing going out there to help our boys.'

'She's gone gallivanting off to South Africa. She should have stayed to nurse me when me time comes. I need her more than them blooming soldiers.'

'You wouldn't say that if it was Joe what got wounded in battle,' Sarah said, casting an anxious glance at Billy. 'Best take her upstairs to your room, Billy. She'll do herself harm if she carries on like this.'

'You're doing it again; talking about me like I wasn't here.' Shrugging off Billy's arm, Rosetta snatched up her shawl. 'I need some air. I'm suffocating cooped up in this rabbit hutch.'

'You can't go out on a wild night like this,' Billy said, barring her way. 'Don't be stupid, Rose.'

'Get out of me way. I'm going for a walk and you can't stop me.'

'It gets them like this sometimes,' Granny Mole muttered. 'I seen it all before. She's near her time, that's for sure.'

Rosetta opened her mouth to scream and Billy

held up his hands. 'All right, Rose, have it your own way but I'm coming with you.'

Making a dive for the door, Rosetta stopped suddenly, doubling up and clutching her swollen belly. With one stride, Billy caught her in his arms, and helped her to a chair.

'Told you so,' Granny Mole said, grinning widely. 'I ain't never wrong.'

'Get her up to bed, Billy,' Sarah said, rolling up her sleeves. 'I'll send Elsie for the midwife.'

It was finally over, after what seemed liked hours of unimaginable pain and torture. Rosetta did not believe the midwife when she said that it was one of the easiest confinements she had ever attended. If that was easy, she thought, as she lay back exhausted against the pillows, then heaven help the poor souls who had a hard time. She took one look at the purple-faced, squalling morsel of humanity in the midwife's arms and turned her head away.

'Isn't she beautiful, Mrs Noakes? You've got a lovely little daughter.'

'I never seen anything so ugly. Take it away.' Rosetta closed her eyes, wanting nothing but sleep. She heard Billy's voice calling her name but it seemed far away. The midwife was answering him in hushed tones, telling him not to worry, that everything would be all right; it took a lot of new mothers that way. Mrs Noakes would be fine once she had had a rest. I'll never be fine again, Rosetta thought, drifting into the oblivion of sleep.

She was up and about within days, refusing to stay in bed for the lying-in period. Sobbing with frustration when she could not get into her old clothes, Rosetta raged at Billy, blaming him for everything, but his tolerance and seemingly endless patience only made things worse. She would have given anything for a full-blown quarrel with someone, but they were all tiptoeing around her, being kind and understanding until she wanted to scream. Worse still, everyone in the house seemed besotted with the baby and even Granny Mole said she was a pretty little thing and good too, for a newborn. Apart from feeding her, which she did reluctantly and only because there was no immediate alternative, Rosetta had as little to do with her daughter as possible, leaving it all to Elsie and Sarah. The house was filled with clouds of steam from washing hanging up to dry in the scullery, over the backs of chairs and on a clothes horse placed in front of the fire. Rosetta could not get the smell of baby sick and soiled nappies out of her nostrils. As if having to feed the baby every two or three hours during the day was not bad enough, it seemed as though she had just fallen asleep when the mewling cry penetrated her dreams, dragging her back to the reality of broken nights and boring days ruled by the demands of a small tyrant. Trapped in a house full of women, Rosetta yearned for the bright lights and excitement of the theatre. She missed the gaiety and sharp repartee of the girls in the chorus, even Aggie Mills, and that was saying something.

Billy was out most of the time, insisting that he was doing an important deal but refusing to say anything more. He seemed so different now from the dashing figure he had been when she first met him; that Billy Noakes had been full of swank, a charming chancer with a twinkle in his eye. To make things worse, Rosetta knew she was behaving badly but somehow she couldn't stop herself. If she had driven Billy away, then it was probably her own fault. Acutely aware that her figure had not yet returned to normal, Rosetta agonised about her lost looks, fearing that no man would look at her again but, when Billy reached out for her in bed at night, she turned her back on him.

The only sign that Christmas had been and gone was a withered sprig of holly stuck in a spill jar on the mantelpiece. Rosetta sat by the fire, fuming inwardly as she suckled the baby. She longed to share her pent-up emotions with someone sympathetic. If only Ruby had stayed on a bit longer, instead of going off to Africa to tend the wounded soldiers. Ruby would understand what she was going through; she might not approve, but she would understand. Gritting her teeth and feeling no pleasure as the insistent little mouth tugged hungrily at her nipple, Rosetta stared gloomily into the fire; this was how it was going to be from now on, with every day much the same as the last. She was caught like a rat in a trap, stuck in this tiny, overcrowded house with no hope of escape until they carried her out feet first. Everybody else seemed happy with their lot, content to carry on as usual, with Granny Mole dozing in her chair and Elsie placidly folding squares of cut up sheeting to use as nappies, while Sarah was preparing supper in the scullery. Sighing, Rosetta barely looked up as Billy came in from the street bringing with him a gust of frosty, smoke-laden night air.

'Well, now,' he said, taking in the scene with a happy smile. 'This is a sight for sore eyes. Just what a bloke needs at the end of a hard day.'

Shifting the baby to her left breast, Rosetta scowled at him.

Seeming not to notice, Billy took off his hat and coat, hanging them on a peg behind the door. 'How are my two best girls?'

Not trusting herself to speak, Rosetta remained silent.

Billy's smile faded into a concerned frown.

'Are you feeling all right, pet? You know you should have stayed in bed like the midwife told you. You got up too soon, in my opinion.'

'She always was wayward,' Granny Mole said, opening one eye. 'You're too good for her by half, Billy.'

'Nothing is too good for my Rose,' Billy said, chuckling. Perching on the arm of Rosetta's chair he stroked the baby's head with the tip of his finger. 'Ain't she just the pretty one? She's going to be a stunner, just like her mum.'

'Leave it out, Billy,' Rosetta said, covering her bare breast with her shawl. 'Don't disturb her. I want to get this over so that Elsie can put her down to sleep.'

'You know, pet, we can't keep calling the baby "her" and "it". We got to give the poor little moppet a name.'

'Yes, so?'

'So as you ain't come up with anything yet, I thought we might call her after my sister, Martha. She even looks a bit like her.'

'Don't talk soft, Billy. How can she look like your sister when you ain't the father?'

Twisting a lock of Rosetta's hair around his finger, Billy dropped a kiss on her forehead. 'It don't matter to me, Rose. I'll love her just as much as if she were me own and she'll never know the difference, not if we have half a dozen more little 'uns to keep her company.'

'There won't be no more, not if I can help it.' Rosetta pulled a face as the baby hiccuped and spewed out a mouthful of milk. 'I ain't going through this again. Anyway, the midwife said I was delicate. Another baby could be fatal.'

'Poppycock!' Granny Mole snorted. 'You're as strong as a horse. You could drop one a year and not notice the difference.'

'It seems to me that babies turn up when they want to,' Billy said, taking the baby from Rosetta's arms, hitching her over his shoulder and gently patting her back. 'The more the merrier, I say. We don't want little Martha to grow up lonely, now do we? Martha Noakes, me little princess.'

'Martha, that's a pretty name,' Elsie said, stroking the baby's head. 'I love Martha best in the world.'

'Put her to bed, Elsie,' Rosetta said, hastily buttoning her blouse as Billy's gaze travelled to her swollen breasts. 'I'll help Mum with the supper. I'm starving.'

'No need,' Sarah said, coming into the room with a tray of bread, cheese and pickles. 'Did I hear you say you've picked a name for the little one?'

Relieving her of the tray, Billy set it down on the table. 'It's Martha, after me poor dead sister. And how about Sarah as a second name, after you, Mother Capretti? The third most beautiful woman in me life.'

'Get away with you,' Sarah said, going red in the face and giggling.

'Don't I get a say in all this?' Rosetta jumped to her feet. 'She's my daughter, not yours.'

Still smiling, Billy placed his arm around Rosetta's shoulders. 'You've had a hard time, pet, and I know you was upset having to crowd the family by coming here, but I've got plans. This time next year we'll be set up for life.'

Granny Mole let out a cackle of mirth. 'You going to rob a bank then, Billy?'

'Better than that, Granny. I'm going straight. I've done me last shady deal and I've made enough money to buy a business. We're going to be in trade.'

'Well I never.' Sarah sat down suddenly. 'In trade.'

'What are you talking about?' demanded Rosetta.

Sitting down, Billy pulled her onto his lap. 'The baker in Spivey Street, the one what got burnt out, is selling up. His hands are so badly afflicted that he can't properly work no more. The long and the short of it is that I've bought him out. There's living accommodation above the shop, just right for a growing family.'

Rosetta stared at him aghast. 'But you don't know nothing about being a baker.'

'I can learn, ducks. Ted is going to stay on and teach me the business. I've watched him work and it don't look too hard. I'm a good learner.'

'But a baker's shop? You're having a laugh, aren't you?' Rosetta felt her heart racing as panic rose in her throat.

'No, cross me heart and hope to die,' Billy said, making the sign of a cross on his chest. 'That's what I been doing all these weeks, in between scraping up the money to buy the business.'

Closing her eyes, Rosetta pinched herself, thinking this must be one of her bad dreams. It hurt. It was real. 'I can't believe you'd do such a thing. Didn't it never occur to you to ask me what I wanted?'

'I'm doing this for you, darling, and for baby Martha. No more shady deals, no more dodging the cops. I'm a respectable tradesman now. What d'you think, Mother Capretti?'

'I think it's a fine idea, Billy.'

'Of course, I'll have to rely on you to give us a hand,' Billy said, smiling. 'No one makes a better bit of cake than you, or a lighter pastry. You'd get a share of the profits, of course.'

'Fine,' Rosetta said, struggling free from Billy's arms and getting to her feet. 'So where's my part in all this grand plan?'

'Why, sweetheart, you're my best asset. You can serve in the shop and charm the customers while Elsie looks after Martha.'

Speechless with rage, Rosetta stared down at him, her hands fisted behind her back.

'So what can I do, Billy?' demanded Granny Mole.

'You can give us the benefit of your good advice, Granny.'

'Bah! As if anyone listens to me.'

Making a huge effort to keep calm, Rosetta glared at Billy. 'So when is all this supposed to happen?'

'We'll move in on New Year's Eve, that's Sunday, and I'll bake me first loaves for Monday the first of January, 1900,' Billy said, slapping his hand on his knee. 'The start of a new century and the beginning of a new life.'

'Never!' Rosetta cried, stamping up the stairs. 'Never, never, never. I ain't going to live above no bloody bakery.'

The shop was small, but spotlessly clean, with a faint aroma of freshly baked bread. The living accommodation upstairs was roomy. Although workmen had repaired the fire damage and repainted the woodwork, the lingering stench of smoke and charring was not completely disguised by the sharp smell of turpentine and the distinctive odour of linseed oil emanating from the newly laid linoleum. Standing in the middle of the living room, all Rosetta's worst fears were realised. Empty except for a deal table and four kitchen chairs, the room was bleak and cold.

'It'll be fine when we get some proper furniture

in, pet.' Billy hurried over to open the sash window. 'It still smells a bit when it's been shut up, but that will go as soon as it's lived in.'

'It's horrible,' Rosetta said, shuddering. 'How could you bring me here, Billy?'

'I got a mate down Stepney way what's in the furniture business and he's sorting out a sofa and a couple of armchairs. We'll get a few rugs in the market and once we've got the fire going it will seem more like home.'

'Home! It's a hovel, Billy. I'd rather live in your old stable than here.'

Wrapping his arms around her, Billy gave her a hug. 'Come and see the bedrooms, pet. At least I got us a nice comfy bed with that feather mattress you've always wanted.' Billy took her by the hand leading her down a narrow strip of landing. Opening a door, he ushered her in. 'This is our room.'

Rosetta glanced around, her lips folded in a tight line. The room was much bigger than the bedroom in Tobacco Court, furnished with an iron bedstead, a chair and a washstand.

Billy eyed her nervously. 'And there's more.'

Saying nothing, Rosetta followed him across the landing.

'Now then, this is the big surprise,' Billy said, flinging the door open. 'What d'you think of that?'

Looking over his shoulder, Rosetta saw a white

but rather rusty bath standing on claw feet, a washbasin with hot and cold taps and a lavatory with a cast-iron cistern and a pull chain.

'Not half bad, eh?' Billy said, pulling the chain in demonstration. 'I bet the queen herself don't have a better bathroom in Buckingham Palace.'

'I suppose it would be nice not to have to go out in the yard at night,' Rosetta said grudgingly.

'And a hot bath whenever you want one. I knew you'd like it when you'd seen everything.'

'How do I do the cooking, then?' Rosetta demanded, refusing to be pleased. 'And the washing? Or do I do that in the bathtub?'

Running his fingers through his hair, Billy frowned. 'Don't be difficult, pet. There's a scullery upstairs and the bakehouse downstairs with a washhouse in the back yard. All right, it ain't a palace, but like I said it's a start. Give me time, love, just give me time.'

Seeing his crestfallen expression, Rosetta hated herself. She knew that Billy was doing his best, but these days there seemed to be a devil inside her that made her say and do things to hurt him. 'I daresay it will be all right,' she said, smiling and patting his hand. 'Show us the rest.'

'Right then.' Dragging her along behind him, Billy sprinted up the steep and narrow stairs to the attic rooms. 'I thought this one would do for Elsie.'

Rosetta peered into the room beneath the

eaves, dimly lit by a roof window. A truckle bed occupied most of the floor space, leaving just enough room for a chest of drawers. 'I daresay it's a lot better than anything she's ever had before.'

'And this one,' Billy said, throwing the door open to a much larger and brighter room, 'we'll make this into a room fit for a princess. Just for Martha.'

'Babies don't have rooms all to themselves. You'll spoil her rotten.'

'She'll have everything she wants. And so will you, Rose.'

Turning away, Rosetta made for the stairs, but Billy caught her by the hand, drawing her to him. 'I know it's not perfect, but I love you, Rose, and I just want you to be happy.'

Closing her eyes and imagining for a brief moment that it was Jonas who was pledging his love for her, Rosetta relaxed against Billy's tense body. 'I'm sorry, I know I've been a bit difficult lately. I don't mean to hurt you, Billy.'

Holding her so tightly that she could hardly breathe, Billy's mouth claimed hers with the hunger of a starving man. Sliding her arms around Billy's neck, Rosetta opened her lips with a sigh, responding to him for the first time in months, but all the time her heart was crying out for another man. If only it was Jonas who was kissing her with such need and urgency, she would not turn away from him at night in the marriage bed. Repeating her name over and over again, Billy's voice was thick with desire and his fingers shook as he unbuttoned her blouse. Burying his face in the soft swell of her breasts he pinned her against the wall, his hands searching beneath her skirt, stroking, caressing and tantalising until Rosetta gasped with pleasure. Blotting Billy out of her mind, she tried to convince herself that it was Jonas who was arousing her to a frenzy of desire. She did not protest when Billy lifted her in his arms and carried her down the stairs to their bedroom, throwing her down on the feather mattress and taking her roughly with all the pent-up emotion of enforced abstinence. Coming too late to her senses, there was nothing Rosetta could do to stop him and her struggling and fighting only seemed to excite him further, until he climaxed with an exultant shout. With silent tears running down her cheeks, she prayed that her mistake would not result in another unwanted pregnancy.

Afterwards, Billy held her to him, his lips pressed against her breast. 'This is the new beginning, sweetheart. We'll be all right now. You'll see.'

'Let me up, Billy. Mum and Granny will be here in a minute. What will they think?'

Lying back on the pillow with his hands behind his head, Billy's face split in a satisfied grin. 'Hell's teeth, Rose, they've both had husbands. They know what it's all about.'

'Don't be disgusting.' Swinging her legs over the side of the bed, Rosetta slipped on her chemise and bent to retrieve her corsets from the floor. 'Lace me up, quick. Tight as you can.'

'I like you better as you are,' Billy said, raising himself on his elbow.

'Don't talk daft. There's work to do.'

Rosetta had just finished dressing when Sarah arrived armed with a mop and bucket, followed by Granny Mole, grumbling as usual. Martha was howling dismally like a small, purple-faced banshee and Elsie was plainly agitated.

'Baby's hungry,' Elsie said, thrusting Martha into Rosetta's arms. 'Been crying all the way down Spivey Street with folks staring at me like I was sticking pins into her.'

'I'll get on with the chores,' Sarah said, rolling up her sleeves. 'You see to the baby.'

'Get on with it for Gawd's sake,' muttered Granny Mole. 'Can't stand listening to that noise. And why haven't you got a fire going, Rose? What have you been doing all this time?'

'Leave her be, Ma,' Sarah said, getting down on her hands and knees in front of the fireplace. 'Let Rose see to baby and I'll light the fire. Elsie, go and fetch coal and kindling while I clean out the grate.'

Shamed into working by Sarah's gallant efforts, Rosetta spent all day scrubbing floors and cleaning out cupboards while Elsie looked after the baby and Granny sat by the fire, issuing instructions. Billy kept out of the way, remaining in the bakehouse with Ted, using the excuse that he was getting to grips with the ovens as he prepared for his first solo attempt at baking bread.

Collapsing into bed that night in a state of exhaustion, Rosetta fell into a deep sleep. It was still dark when she woke up next morning, and Billy's side of the bed was cold and empty. She had been dimly aware that he had risen in the early hours of the morning to start the day's baking and she stretched out, luxuriating in having the bed all to herself. But her pleasure was short-lived as her warm feet touched the ice-cold sheets and she curled back into a ball, listening to the rumbling of carts and the clip-clopping of horses' hooves coming from the street below. The tramp of hobnail boots on cobbles sounded like an army marching as the factory workers headed for work. Rosetta stretched and yawned, thinking of the women at Bronski's who would be waiting in the dank alley for Vinegar Lil to let them in to start their daily grind. At least, now she was married to Billy, she was spared from returning to that particular hell.

A thin mewling wail from upstairs told her that Martha had awakened and she could hear Elsie's bare feet pitter-pattering across the floorboards as she went to pick up the baby. Rosetta sat up in bed, reaching for her shawl and shivering. Her breasts were heavy with milk and she could feel warm trickles oozing from her swollen nipples. There must be something seriously wrong with her, she thought, sighing heavily. She was a rotten mother and she had hated everything about being pregnant and giving birth. If she was one of those rich women she read about in the penny dreadfuls, then she would have been able to hand the baby over to a wet nurse and a nanny. But she wasn't rich and no one seemed to be interested in how she was feeling. Billy was so daft about Martha you'd think she was his kid, and that made Rosetta feel even worse. She could hear Elsie coming down the stairs, chatting to Martha as though the baby could understand every word, but then Elsie was doolally and she probably expected Martha to answer her.

The door opened and Elsie scuttled in with the baby swaddled in a shawl. 'Are you ready for her, miss?'

Reluctantly, Rosetta uncovered a breast, wincing as Martha latched onto her sore nipple like a hungry leech. 'Fetch me some tea, Elsie, with lots of sugar, and then you can light the fire in the living room.'

Billy dashed upstairs at midday, flushed and triumphant, having sold out of everything and wanting Rosetta to mind the shop while he and Sarah prepared a fresh batch of loaves and cakes. In the middle of feeding Martha, Rosetta sent Elsie down in her place, but she returned almost immediately, sobbing and shaking, terrified of being left alone to deal with strangers.

Hoisting Martha over her shoulder, Rosetta turned to Granny Mole for help.

'I ain't working in no shop; I'm too old for that lark,' Granny said, glowering. 'And anyway, I can't do nothing on an empty stomach. Here we are in a bakery and I ain't had no nourishment since breakfast. I'm fading away and no one cares.'

Biting back an angry retort, Rosetta jumped to her feet, thrusting Martha into Elsie's arms. 'Here, you look after baby. I'll sort this out once and for all.'

Marching into the bakehouse, Rosetta stopped as the heat hit her in the face, sucking the air from her lungs. Inhaling the fine white flour, Rosetta sneezed and coughed. Sarah was up to her elbows in cake mixture and Billy, looking more like a snowman than a baker, was kneading bread dough.

'I can't look after baby and see to the customers,' Rosetta said, arms akimbo. 'Elsie is useless in the shop and Granny is grumbling because she's hungry.'

Snatching up a tray of buns, Sarah thrust it into Rosetta's hands. 'Here, give them these and a cup of tea. I been so busy I forgot all about food.'

'It's only our first day, pet,' Billy said, wiping his brow with the back of his hand. 'We'll work it out.'

Rosetta stared at him. Where was the dapper, good-looking Billy Noakes who was good for a laugh and always seemed to have money to spend? This red-faced, sweating man with his face streaked with flour looked like a circus clown. Hating him and hating herself even more, Rosetta went into the shop to serve.

As she had known she would, Rosetta hated having to serve the poorest of the poor in White-chapel. Slatternly women, snotty-nosed kids and old people smelling like bad cheese wandered daily in a raggle-taggle procession through the door, with nothing but farthings, halfpennies and pennies to spend. Rosetta knew she ought to feel compassion for the half-starved urchins who came in begging for stale bread, but it was hard to love the poor when they dropped fleas in showers onto the sawdust and scratched lice-ridden heads with filthy fingers. It was worth the odd crust or stale bun simply to get them out of her shop.

There were plenty of disasters in the bake-house when the yeast refused to rise or the oven was too hot or too cold and the bread was ruined. On those days, when all she had to stock the counter were Sarah's cakes, customers grumbled but they queued outside for hours waiting for the fresh batch of bread. Some chose to walk to the nearest bakery in Spitalfields but many were too old, sick or weak from near starvation to make the distance. Rosetta grew to dread those mornings, when the line of white-faced, bone-thin women and children peered at her through the window with reproachful eyes.

Billy worked harder than anyone, getting up long before dawn and going to bed late, too exhausted to make any demands on Rosetta. She had waited anxiously for the start of her monthlies, terrified that she might have conceived again, and weeping tears of relief when she discovered one morning that she had worried for nothing. Having washed and dressed, Rosetta tiptoed downstairs to the small kitchen behind the shop, treading on the edge of the stairs to avoid loud creaks that might disturb Martha, who slept so lightly that a bat's sneeze would wake her. She had just made a pot of tea when the shop door rattled, and Rosetta hurried to let Sarah in before she rang the doorbell.

'You look more cheerful this morning,' Sarah said, angling her head like an inquisitive robin.

It was still pitch dark outside, with feathery flakes of snow swirling in the yellow shafts of gaslight. Rosetta shut the door and locked it. 'Where's Granny?'

'Took to her bed. She says she's caught her death coming out in the cold every morning so I told her to stay in the warm.'

'It is a bit parky. Come and have a cup of tea before you start.'

Taking off her bonnet and shawl, Sarah followed Rosetta through to the kitchen. 'You'll never guess what, Rose. I found a letter from Ruby on the mat when I got home yesterday. All the way from South Africa it come. Can you believe that?'

'From Ruby? What did she say? Let's see it, Mum.'

As she fumbled in her pocket, Sarah's face crumpled with dismay. 'Bother! I must have left it on the mantelpiece. I put it there special so I would bring it this morning. I was so busy running up and downstairs to your gran that I must have left it behind.'

Pouring tea, Rosetta handed it to her mother. 'Never mind. What did she say? Is she all right? Has she seen Joe?'

Clasping the mug in her chilled hands, Sarah gave one of her rare smiles. 'No, she ain't seen Joe, but Africa's a big place. It weren't a long letter but she said she's well and with them friends of hers, Pamela and that young doctor, what's his name?'

'Adam, the one she fancies! Adam Fairfax.'

'No, ducks, you're wrong there, he's engaged to that Pamela. Anyway, they're on the hospital train what Princess Christian sent out to look after the troops, waiting to go to that place what's under siege and I can't for the life of me remember its name.'

'You mean Ladysmith? I read about it in the newspaper.'

'That's it. Ladysmith. Funny old name for a town, I thought. Anyway, I hope it's all over soon so that Ruby and Joe can come home safe. I can't sleep at night for worrying about them.'

Before Rosetta had a chance to ask more questions, the door to the bakehouse opened and Billy came in on a gust of hot air. 'Mother Capretti! I thought you wasn't coming.'

Casting an irritated glance at Billy's flushed face, running with sweat, Rosetta frowned. 'Give her a chance. She's only just put her foot through the door.'

'I'll take me tea into the bakehouse,' Sarah said, getting to her feet.

'Give us a cup, Rose,' Billy said, slipping his arm around her waist. 'I'm parched.'

Rose wriggled free. 'Help yourself. I'll open up.'

'Good girl. We'll catch the dockers on their way to work. You've got a good head for business, ducks.'

By mid-morning the snow had melted into slush and the first rush of the day was over. Rosetta had shut the door to the stairs so that she did not have to listen to Martha's outraged yelling as Elsie attempted to wean her on to cow's milk. The shop was empty and, taking advantage of the temporary respite, Rosetta sat down on a stool behind the counter to study a copy of yesterday's *Daily Mail* that someone had left behind. She was engrossed in an article about a meeting held in Mile End to protest at the war against the Boers that had ended in uproar, when the shop bell tinkled. Annoyed at the interruption, Rosetta glanced up and the newspaper slid to the floor as she jumped to her feet.

'Good morning, Mrs Noakes,' Jonas said, tipping his hat.

'Mr Crowe!' Rosetta could hardly speak; her heart seemed to leap into her throat, almost choking her. 'What – I mean, can I help you?'

Tapping his kid-gloved hand with the ivory handle of his umbrella, Jonas looked around at the display of loaves and buns with a wry smile. 'I haven't come to buy a loaf. I need to contact your sister. Can you give me a forwarding address?'

Suffocating with jealousy, Rosetta could barely speak. 'She's gone to Africa.'

'I know that, but there must be a forwarding address.'

'If there is, then I don't know it.'

'Perhaps Mrs Capretti has it? I really do need to contact Ruby; it's important.'

'She won't be interested in anything what you've got to say, specially now she's got herself engaged.' The spiteful words were out before she could stop herself, but Rosetta had the satisfaction of seeing Jonas's face frozen with shock. Having started, she couldn't stop. 'He's a doctor, you know, from a well-to-do family. They're madly in love and she said they might not even wait until they get back to England. In fact, they might have tied the knot already.'

Chapter Seventeen

It had all happened in such a rush. One minute it seemed to Ruby that she had been happily working on the wards at the London and the next she had found herself on a steam ship bound for South Africa. Strictly speaking she should not have been included in the ranks of the qualified nurses, but Sister Tutor had made an exception in recommending her. Still smouldering at the revelation that it had been Jonas and not Adam who had been instrumental in her being accepted as a nurse probationer, Ruby took some comfort from the knowledge that this time she had been chosen on her own merits. Justifying her reasons for wanting to be included on this dangerous mission, Ruby convinced herself that she would be a poor friend if she stayed safely at home while Pamela was risking her life to help the sick and injured. Adam would need people around him he could trust to keep to his high standards and Ruby knew that she had to be there, working at his side, no matter what personal danger she had to face. She might never be able to live with Adam as his wife, but she would gladly give her life for him.

She had said a hurried goodbye to the family, saddened by Rosetta's stubborn refusal to speak to her or even wish her well. Billy had given her a brotherly hug and Mum had cried a lot, saying it was bad enough to lose a son to the bloody war let alone a daughter. Surprisingly, it had been Granny Mole who had told her she was a brave girl and doing the right thing, and that her poppa would have been proud of her. After that it had all been hustle and bustle, packing a few things in a suitcase and being taken to the docks to board the ship, finding the cabin she was to share with Pamela and two other nurses deep below the waterline and getting used to the way of life on board.

Ruby was one of the lucky ones who had found her sea legs by the time the ship reached the turbulent waters of the Bay of Biscay, but Pamela had succumbed to seasickness almost as soon as the ship was under weigh. Ruby had tried to help, but when the weather was bad around the Cape Pam had been certain that she wanted to die, and it was only when they approached the calmer waters of the Indian Ocean that she had begun to recover just a little. Although conditions were hardly those of a cruise liner Ruby had enjoyed the trip, taking guilty pleasure in Adam's company while Pamela was suffering in martyred silence in their stuffy, overcrowded cabin.

On the last leg of its voyage, the ship was steaming towards Durban, expected to make landfall the following day. Ruby went for a walk on deck after the evening meal, hoping that she might – by accident, of course – meet Adam. The sun was plummeting like a fireball behind a purple stripe of coastline to the west, turning the sea to molten bronze. Seabirds wheeled and cried overhead and, for the first time since they left England, Ruby could smell land. Her stomach churned with excitement at the prospect of reaching their destination, but she was sorry that this voyage would soon be just a bittersweet memory. Tomorrow they would have to leave the well-ordered routine of living on board ship and face the grim realities of war. But whatever was to come, she knew that nothing could erase the pictures in her mind of a world where the sea met the sky in endless shades of green and blue. She would take to her grave the thrill of standing on deck with Adam watching dolphins swimming and leaping playfully out of the water. She would always treasure the conversations they had shared when he had told her of his hopes and dreams for the future. All this seemed a million magical miles from the filth and poverty of Whitechapel and the hell of the battlefield that was to come.

She saw him, leaning on the ship's rail, gazing out across the vast, violet expanse of the Indian Ocean and her heart did a somersault inside her chest. How fine Adam looked in army officer's uniform, with the last rays of the sun glinting on his golden hair.

Almost as though he sensed her presence, Adam turned his head and his smile pierced her heart like an arrow. 'Ruby, come and watch our last sunset at sea. We should arrive in Durban late tomorrow afternoon.'

'So soon?'

'Are you afraid?'

'Yes, a bit.'

'Me too.'

'No!' Ruby stared up into his face. 'I don't believe it.'

'It's not something I would admit to just any-one,' Adam said, smiling ruefully. 'I hate violence and I don't believe that fighting a war will solve the basic problems.'

'But you've got to stand up for what you think is right.' Ruby stared at him, shocked by his words, struggling with the thought that Adam wouldn't last long in the East End if he couldn't handle himself in a rough-up.

'I agree, but I'd rather do it with diplomacy than the sword.'

Puzzled, Ruby frowned. 'Then why did you come? Why didn't you stay safe at home?'

'Do you think I'm a coward, Ruby?'

'No, but sometimes you've just got to fight,' Ruby said, remembering the violence of the street gang attacking Bronski in his sweatshop, and Joe knocked to the ground and barely conscious. Big Biddy hadn't been afraid to have a go, even if she had landed on the wrong bloke. 'Sometimes you've got to show a bully what's what.'

'I patch people up – that's my job. I leave the bloodletting to prizefighters, soldiers and men like Jonas Crowe. You were well out of that house, Ruby. I didn't like to say anything at the time because it really wasn't any of my business, but I could never understand what a nice girl like you was doing working for a man like Crowe.'

'Maybe nice girls like me don't have much choice,' Ruby shot back at him, feeling the blood rushing to her cheeks. 'We can't all be born with a silver spoon in our mouth.'

'Now I've offended you. I'm sorry, Ruby.'

Shaking her head, Ruby turned away. The difference in their backgrounds had never seemed so unbridgeable, and she couldn't bring herself to look him in the face.

'Look, Ruby. Just look at that sunset.' Abruptly changing the subject, Adam pointed at the dying sun as it plunged below the distant hills. 'Have you ever seen anything so beautiful?'

'I've never even seen the sea before. I've never been to Southend, let alone Africa.'

'Life is strange, isn't it?' Adam said slowly, staring into the distance. 'But for the war we wouldn't be standing here on this ship, miles from home, watching the sun setting over the African continent. It feels like a world apart, don't you think?'

Ruby gripped the iron railing and felt the throb of the ship's engines beating like her own heart. Adam's candid blue eyes searched her face for an answer; the warmth of his body enveloped her like a cloak as a cool breeze ruffled the surface of the sea, snatching playfully at her long skirt. She swallowed hard. 'It isn't Whitechapel and that's for certain.'

Adam's laughter broke the tension between them. 'Ruby, you are such a breath of fresh air. Don't ever change.'

'Oh well, I'm glad I've got some uses,' Ruby replied, staring down into the sucking swell of the water as the hull sliced through the waves. She looked up, startled, as Adam took her hand and tucked it in the crook of his arm.

'I'm sorry. I'm saying all the wrong things tonight, but I truly meant it; you are so refreshingly honest. Most of the girls I know simper and smile and say things they think I want to hear. You're different: you speak your mind.'

'Pamela isn't like that.'

'Pam is the sweetest girl in the world and I love her dearly but you're a chum, Ruby. I can say things to you that I would never say even to Pam. You don't mind, do you?'

Allowing herself the luxury of leaning against him as the ship changed course slightly, Ruby shook her head. 'No, of course not. I'm glad we're friends, Adam.'

Making landfall in Durban next day, they were transported to Maritzburg and the military hospital at Fort Napier. Ruby couldn't quite grasp the idea that it was the middle of January and nearing the end of summer, whereas they had left England shivering beneath a blanket of grey clouds that threatened snow. By contrast it was very hot during the day in Durban, much hotter than Ruby had ever experienced in England, but mercifully a lot cooler at night. The nurses were set to work almost immediately, tending the sick and wounded soldiers brought in by train. They were such young men, little more than boys, some of them with terrible injuries but many of them were ill with typhoid fever, which had spread with alarming and deadly rapidity. She had no idea where Joe was, but each one of the men in her care was some- one's son, brother or perhaps a father, and but for the grace of God, could have been Joe. Ruby worked tirelessly and, being one of the least qualified, hers were the dirtiest and most mundane tasks, all of which she did willingly. The hours worked by all the medical teams were long and at the end of each shift, all Ruby wanted to do was collapse on her bed, but she managed to compose a letter to her mother, writing a few lines every night before she fell into an exhausted sleep.

Sharing a room with Pamela and half a dozen other nurses, there was no privacy and no time to sit and think or to worry about what was happening six thousand miles away in London. In her few free moments, Ruby tried to escape the ever-present smell of carbolic, the stench of sickness and death and the draining heat by walking in the comparative cool of the tree-shaded hospital grounds. In these precious, quiet moments, she thought about her family at home and in particular about Rosetta, wondering whether her baby was a girl or a boy. She hoped that Rose was happier now and had become resigned to being married, putting aside her feelings for Jonas and recognising Billy for the good bloke he was beneath the brash exterior.

While the horrors of war that Ruby witnessed daily made everything and everyone at home in London fade into a hazy blur, like an old sepia tint, Jonas Crowe leapt into her thoughts with terrifying clarity. Late at night when she was drifting off to sleep, thinking of Adam, who had been summoned away to work in a field hospital under Sir Frederick Treves, Jonas would appear, his dominant personality wiping out everything else like the sweep of a board rubber on chalk. She had left London to get away from Jonas. She was in love with Adam, who was a good man and a fine doctor; she was desperately, deeply and hopelessly in love with him, but it was Jonas who haunted her subconscious. No matter how hard she fought against him, it was Jonas, a self-confessed villain, who made love to her in dreams from which she awakened night after night, aroused, sweating and having to creep out of the dormitory to the bathroom where she sponged herself down with cool water. Silently cursing and hating him, Ruby was shamed and disgusted by the lustful demon within her that no amount of water could wash away.

Despite the backbreaking work, the monotonous routine seemed to go on for ever as they waited for the order to board the sparkling white, luxuriously appointed hospital train donated by Princess Christian. Summer was slowly drifting into autumn and everyone at Fort Napier waited eagerly for the arrival of despatch riders with details of the push towards Ladysmith. The rainy season had started and nerves were stretched to the limit when the news finally came; the relief column had got through and the siege of Ladysmith was at an end.

After weeks of waiting, they were on their way at last and the train sped through the night, arriving at Ladysmith early next morning. Ruby thought they had been ready for the influx of sick and injured but she had not been prepared to see so many half-starved women and children who, in spite of their five-month long ordeal, were lining the track, waving, smiling and cheering their arrival. The stretcher cases were carried aboard and Ruby worked without stopping except for the occasional cup of tea and a bully beef sandwich. Working with a medical orderly, she was given the task of identifying and listing the patients, going from one end of the train to the other. By midnight, the names and faces began to blur and her ears rang with the soft groans of badly wounded soldiers and hoarse voices demanding water or begging for a cigarette.

Just as they thought they had finished, a fresh contingent of soldiers arrived bringing their most seriously injured.

Corporal Lewis, the nuggety Welsh orderly, took out his penknife and began sharpening his stub of a pencil. 'I thought it was too good to be true. Looks like we got a long night ahead of us, cariad.'

'I'll go and take a look,' Ruby said, stifling a yawn. 'Maybe there won't be too many.'

She found Pamela checking the men in and

assessing the severity of their injuries. She looked white and drawn, with dark blue smudges beneath her eyes, and her fresh blonde complexion had yellowed in the heat of Africa. Anxiety shafted through Ruby at the sight of her friend looking so spent and fragile like a wilting, white rose and, for a brief moment, she was ashamed of her own good health and resilience. 'Pam, you should have a break.'

Pamela looked up. 'Another twenty,' she said, sighing. 'Poor souls, some of them are in a sorry state.'

'Not me, nurse. I'm ready to take you out on the town.' A young soldier with his leg roughly splinted, grinned up at Pamela and winked.

'If you're that well, soldier, then maybe you're on the wrong train,' Pamela said, smiling. Having given his leg a quick examination, she made a note on his chart. 'I think the surgeon had better take a look at that leg.'

The young soldier's cocky grin changed to a worried frown. 'I won't lose it, will I, nurse?'

'Of course not, but I'm afraid it may need resetting. Don't worry, Private, we have the best surgeons on board.'

'Not to mention the best physicians.'

A voice from the darkness outside the train made Pamela spin round with a cry of delight. 'Adam!' She jumped off the train into Adam's arms.

'And I thought I was in with a chance.' The soldier grinned up at Ruby. 'How about you, nurse? Or are you spoken for too?'

Swallowing the lump in her throat, Ruby stared down at the list of names in her notebook, unable to bear the sight of the tender reunion as Adam held Pamela in his arms. 'Your name and number, please, Private.'

'Going to write it in your address book, love?'

'For the record and so that the authorities can let your folks know you're alive and well.' Ruby scribbled down the details, keeping her head bent over the page. She could not see Adam and Pamela but neither could she blot out the joyous sound of their voices. Out of the corner of her eye she saw the young private's face contort with pain and she laid her hand on his arm, forcing a smile. 'Maybe we'll meet up again in London, soldier. Good luck.'

He blew her a kiss as the orderlies carried him away, clearing the table for the next stretcher case that was already waiting at the foot of the steps. The bearers climbed onto the train hefting the stretcher onto the examination table.

Pamela came running in after them, dragging Adam by the hand. 'Look who's arrived, Ruby. Isn't it wonderful?'

'Hello, Adam.' Ruby flashed him a smile but her heart ached to see him looking lean and bronzed but bone-tired.

'It's good to see you, Ruby.'

'This one looks serious,' Pamela said, leaning over the inert body on the stretcher. 'Can you take a look, Adam? I think we may be losing him.'

Adam's smile faded. 'You're right. This one needs immediate surgery.'

'Yes, doctor,' Pamela said, snapping to attention. 'I'll see to it if Ruby will take down his details.' Without waiting for an answer, she hurried off in the direction of the operating theatre.

In spite of the bloodstained bandages that obscured the soldier's face, there was something terrifyingly familiar about him. 'Is he . . .?' Ruby's breath hitched and she couldn't say the word.

Shaking his head, Adam felt for a pulse. 'Alive. Just.'

'I'll need a name. Has he any identification?' She had seen dead and dying men, but this one was different and Ruby had to bite her lip to prevent herself from crying.

Feeling inside the man's ripped tunic, Adam found the piece of linen sewn inside detailing the soldier's particulars. 'Dear God!'

'Adam?' Seized by terror, knowing the answer but not daring to ask the question, Ruby closed her eyes. 'No!'

'It could be a terrible coincidence,' Adam said, taking her by the hand.

Trembling all over, Ruby lifted the bandages

on the soldier's face. She would have known him anywhere, even with half his face shattered by a bursting shell. She collapsed onto her knees, burying her face in her hands, wracked with sobs. 'Joe. My Joe.'

Lifting her to her feet, Adam wrapped his arms around her. 'He's not dead, Ruby. There's still a chance that we can save him.'

Although Pamela sent her off duty immediately, Ruby refused to leave Joe's side. He was deeply unconscious and for that fact she was truly grateful. Sitting beside the stretcher, she held his hand, keeping up a constant stream of chatter about anything that came into her head until the orderlies came to take him into the operating theatre. Beyond tears, Ruby paced the narrow corridor, wringing her hands and praying as she had never prayed before. Outside the brightly lit compartment, the world was a black void, and this part of the train was eerily silent. The sweet scent of chloroform mixed oddly with the odours of carbolic and Lysol, filling her nostrils and making her feel sick. She lost all sense of time as she paced, forgetting her fatigue, focusing all her willpower on Joe and willing him to survive.

Leaning her forehead against the cold glass of the window, Ruby was dimly aware of thin streaks of grey light cracking the black bowl of the sky. A movement behind her made her spin round and she saw Adam coming out of the operating theatre. She knew at once by his expression that it was all over, and everything went dark.

The hospital train travelled down the line to Mooi River, but at least Ruby had been able to attend the mass funeral service before it left. Saying goodbye to Joe and leaving him buried in a foreign land had been heartbreaking enough, but trying to write a letter home was almost impossible. They would have received notification of Joe's death from the official sources by now, but Ruby tried to find the words to soften the blow. Joe had died a hero's death; he had given his life for his country; no man could do more. The piece of writing paper was grazed by rubbing out words that seemed unsuitable, pockmarked with dried tears and creased by folding and unfolding as Ruby gave up the attempt and put it away to try again another time. She finished it eventually in a rare quiet moment in the nurses' dormitory at the Military Hospital in Mooi River.

Sighing with relief, Ruby felt as though a great burden had been lifted from her. Putting it all down on paper was her last goodbye to Joe. Despite the undeniable weaknesses in his character and his fatal addiction to gambling, Joe had had enough charm for ten men, and she had loved him dearly. She would always remember the laughter they had shared and forget the tears. Joe was and always would be her much-loved big brother, and at least now he was safe: safe from his own failings and safe from men like Jonas Crowe who had exploited them. Sealing the envelope Ruby got to her feet, pushing the memory of Jonas to the back of her mind. With Joe and Lily both gone there would be no reason for her ever to see Jonas again; his hold over her had ceased to exist.

Putting the envelope in the mailbag for home seemed like the last goodbye and she stood, for a moment, biting back tears and feeling desperately homesick. Hoping there might be a letter from her mother, Ruby was checking the incoming mail when Adam came to stand by her side.

'No letters?'

'I wasn't really expecting any. There was one from Mum waiting when we arrived.'

Rifling through the envelopes, Adam paused, giving her a searching glance. 'Not bad news, I hope?'

'Not at all. My sister had a little girl. They called her Martha Sarah and Billy has bought a bakery. I just can't imagine Rosetta serving in a baker's shop,' Ruby said, chuckling.

'I haven't heard you laugh since we were on board the ship.'

'It's been a hard time for all of us.'

Laying his hand on her shoulder, Adam's eyes were full of sympathy. 'Harder for you, Ruby. I'm truly sorry about your brother.'

Gazing into the depths of his blue eyes, Ruby was deafened by the blood drumming in her ears. The touch of his hand on her shoulder sent an electric charge through her whole body. 'Th-thank you.'

'Adam, there you are.'

Pamela's voice shattered the moment and Adam dropped his hand to his side, a dull flush spreading across his face. 'Pam.'

'I've been looking for you, darling.'

Quick to hear an unusually peevish note in Pamela's voice, Ruby shot her a curious glance. 'Are you all right, Pam?'

Brushing her hand across her forehead, Pamela nodded. 'I'm perfectly fine, except for this beastly headache.'

Feeling her brow, Adam frowned. 'I think we'd better get one of the other doctors to take a look at you, Pam. You ought to be in bed.'

'Don't be silly. I told you, I'm perfectly all right. Ruby, I know you're off duty but with so many of the nurses down with fever we need you now.'

Exchanging worried looks with Adam, Ruby followed Pamela as she marched off towards the sluice.

'These bedpans need washing out and dis-
infecting,' Pamela said, thrusting a mop into
Ruby's hand.

'You really don't look well.'

'For heaven's sake, don't you start. I told you
I'm perfectly well.'

Ruby saw her eyes roll upwards and made a
grab for Pamela as she fell to the floor in a dead
faint.

Pacing the corridor outside the side ward, Ruby
waited for news. It seemed like hours before
Adam came out, his face deathly pale beneath his
tan.

'It's typhoid fever. She's very sick, Ruby.'

'But she will recover? She must.'

Adam sank down on a chair by the door and
held his head in his hands. 'She must,' he
repeated dully. 'I pray to God she will.'

Sitting down beside him, Ruby put her arm
around his shoulders. 'She's young and strong
and she'll have the best care possible.'

'I don't know what I'll do if she dies,' Adam
said, raking his fingers through his hair. 'I love
her so much. I can't imagine life without her.'

Wrapping both her arms around him, Ruby
cradled his head against her shoulder. At any
other time, hearing him utter those words with
such devastating sincerity would have broken
her heart, but the thought of losing Pamela so

soon after Joe's death was even more unbearable.

'You do love her, don't you?' Ruby whispered.

'I do, I do. I didn't know how much until the second opinion confirmed my worst fears.' Raising his head, Adam met Ruby's eyes with a stricken stare. 'If I lose Pam, I don't think I can go on.'

Holding him close, Ruby stroked his hair back from his forehead. If she had ever had the slightest doubt, she knew now that Adam truly loved Pamela and there was no room in his heart for anyone else. The pain of realising that her own love for him had been a beautiful but impossible dream was as nothing compared to Adam's obvious suffering. 'She won't die, Adam. We'll get her through this no matter what. We won't let her die.'

The sister-in-charge was reluctant at first to allow Ruby to work in the isolation ward, insisting that only fully qualified nurses should be given such responsibility. Ruby argued that, as a probationer, she was the most expendable of all the nurses and that she was perfectly capable of carrying out instructions. In the end she won, and she was sent to the isolation ward to tend the mounting number of typhoid cases.

She nursed Pamela through delirium and stupor that within ten days lapsed into coma. Too busy to worry about her own health, Ruby spent all her free time with Adam. If she had thought him a god, she soon discovered that he was very much a human and Pamela's illness had affected him so badly that he was barely able to function. She had thought him a tower of strength, but she soon realised that he had relied almost entirely on Pamela who was his rock and without her he was like a man drowning.

At the beginning of the third week of Pamela's illness, she opened her eyes, recognising Ruby for the first time since her collapse. She was skeletally thin, so weak that she could not lift a cup to her mouth to drink, but she was fully conscious. Ruby went into the little kitchen and cried. When she returned to the ward, she found Adam sitting by Pamela's bedside with tears of joy running unashamedly down his thin cheeks. Neither of them had seen her and Ruby hurried away to answer the call of a patient in a bed at the far end of the ward.

For several days Pamela appeared to be recovering well, but late one evening when Ruby was on night duty, she found her feverish again and having difficulty in breathing. The duty physician shook his head, diagnosed pneumonia and sent for Adam. There was nothing anyone could do. Either Adam or Ruby stayed at her bedside and, although Pamela fought valiantly, she grew weaker and weaker.

Ruby was snatching a few hours' much-needed rest in the middle of an afternoon, having been on duty for twenty-four hours without a break. Typhoid was now endemic in the hospital and more soldiers had died of the disease than of their injuries. Shaken awake by one of the nurses, Ruby struggled into her shoes and hurried as fast as she could to the isolation ward. Adam was already at Pamela's bedside, clutching her hand in his. The duty doctor held a stethoscope to her chest, listening intently. He looked up at Ruby, his expression bleak, but the agonised look in Adam's eyes conveyed more than any words. Silently, Ruby pulled up a chair to sit beside him. Pamela's skin was almost transparent as she lay propped up upon several pillows, her breathing shallow and rasping. Her eyelids fluttered and she opened her eyes, a smile of recognition transforming her face. Her lips moved but no sound came out.

As he clasped her hand to his cheek, Adam's voice was thick with tears. 'Save your strength, darling. Don't try to talk.'

Pamela's blue lips curved into a shadow of her old smile. 'I love you, Adam,' she whispered. 'Don't forget me.'

Bending his head over her hand, Adam's shoulders shook silently.

'That's foolish talk, Pam,' Ruby said, struggling to keep her voice steady. 'You'll soon be up and about. You're getting better every day.'

'I'm dying, Ruby.'

'Don't leave me, Pam.' Adam's voice broke on a sob.

'Look after him for me, Ruby.' Pamela closed her eyes and sighed.

Feeling for a pulse, the duty doctor shook his head. 'She's gone. I'm so sorry.'

Adam collapsed onto the bed, his body racked with agonising sobs. Exchanging helpless looks with the duty doctor, Ruby tried to comfort him, but his grief was so intense that he was deaf to everything and everyone.

Getting to her feet, Ruby bent double as jagged shafts of pain tore into her belly. Dimly she could hear the duty doctor's voice as he made her sit down again.

As the pain subsided, Ruby sighed with relief. 'I'm all right, doctor.'

'You're far from all right, Nurse Capretti. I can't say without a proper examination but I'd say you're in the first stages of typhoid fever.'

Chapter Eighteen

Seeing Jonas again had only made things worse. However hard she tried, Rosetta could not get him out of her mind. His prosperous look and powerful presence had made her plight seem even more wretched. If she had been Jonas Crowe's woman, she would not be expected to stand behind a counter all day, serving poverty-stricken people who could barely afford the price of a loaf of bread. She would be dressed in fine clothes, pampered and adored like the heroines in *The Princess's Novelettes*: a complete story for only one penny. Of course, the beautiful heroine had to suffer dreadfully before the handsome hero finally saved her, but he always came through in the end. Ruby had been a fool to give up her comfortable life in his house to follow a ridiculous dream. You wouldn't catch me doing anything so daft, Rosetta had thought bitterly, as Jonas left the shop. Tense to the point of screaming, she had struggled through the rest of the day, but in doing so she had managed to upset everyone from Elsie to Billy. Refusing to keep the shop open any longer than was necessary,

Rosetta had shut the door and stamped up to the bathroom where she had locked herself in and wallowed in a chin-deep bath. The one good thing about the hateful flat above the shop was the luxury of having a proper bath instead of a zinc tub, filled laboriously with kettles of hot water, and set in front of the fire once a week, when everyone had to take turns. Here at least there was always plenty of hot water, providing Billy had remembered to stoke the boiler with coke.

As she stared at the brownish stain where the constant drip of water from the taps had left a rusty streak, Rosetta felt the cold chill of the cast iron through the thinning enamel on the bottom of the bath and she shifted her position. Jonas wouldn't have an ancient, rusting bathtub. He would have the best and it was so unfair that Ruby had been enjoying all that luxury when she didn't even like him. In fact, Rosetta thought, frowning, Ruby actually hated Jonas; she was hankering after that toff of a doctor who wouldn't give her a second look. Reaching for the cake of Pears' soap, Rosetta closed her eyes, sniffing its scent. Lillie Langtry herself used Pears'. She might have been just as famous as the beautiful Lillie if she hadn't fallen for Martha. Opening her eyes, Rosetta soaped her flannel and scrubbed her body until her flesh turned bright pink. However hard she tried to ignore her conscience, she couldn't help feeling just a bit guilty for lying to Jonas about Ruby being engaged to Adam. Maybe she had gone too far in saying they were actually engaged, but the shocked look that had flashed across Jonas's face had been a bit of a surprise. Surely he wasn't interested in Ruby, at least not in a caring way? He might have thought that Ruby was easy, but he would have soon discovered that she was not.

Splashing the rapidly cooling water over her exposed breasts, Rosetta chuckled out loud at her own stupidity. Ruby was a good sort, the best really, but she was too serious and straight-laced to be attractive to a man like Jonas. He needed someone who could entertain his punters, someone vivacious and charming. Someone like me, she thought, snapping upright and sending a wave of water splashing onto the linoleum. Suddenly, Rosetta knew what she must do.

Someone rattled the door handle. 'Why have you locked the door? Are you all right in there, pet?' Billy's anxious voice crashed in on her dream, bringing her rapidly back to earth.

'Can't a girl have a bath in peace? Leave me alone.'

'Sorry, Rose. I just thought . . .' Billy's voice trailed off miserably.

'I been on me feet all day. I just want a bit of time for meself.'

'Martha needs her bedtime feed, pet.'

'Tell Elsie to give her some cow's milk.'

'Elsie's scrubbing the bakery floor and Martha's crying.'

Rosetta reached for a towel. 'All right, I'm coming.' Stepping out of the bath, she came to a sudden decision.

Rosetta was wide awake but she feigned sleep as Billy clambered out of bed long before dawn to start the day's baking. Giving him time to reach the bakehouse, Rosetta leapt out of bed, her heart racing with nervous tension and just a little thrill of excitement. Today was the start of her new life, a life far away from the drudgery of the bakehouse and away from the shabby rooms above the shop. Martha would be well cared for by people who loved her, although, quite unexpectedly, Rosetta felt a twinge of conscience at the thought of deserting her child. Throwing her things into a cardboard suitcase, she tried to put Martha out of her mind. She had never wanted a baby, especially Alf's baby, and she had done her utmost not to bond with the dark-eyed little girl who already looked ridiculously like Ruby and herself. Some women were made for motherhood and some were not; that didn't make her a bad person, and when she had money she would see to it that Martha never wanted for anything.

Creeping out of the building by a side door,

Rosetta couldn't help taking one last glance at the attic window. Martha would be sound asleep in her wooden cot with the rag dolly that Granny Mole had made for her tucked in at her side. For a brief moment, Rosetta hesitated, and then bracing her shoulders she stepped out onto the wet pavement. Already people were hurrying to work in the docks or the manufactories that had grown up alongside the wharves and the railway lines. No one took any notice of her as she put her head down and turned in the direction of Shoreditch. There was only one place where she could go and be reasonably sure of being taken in off the street.

'So,' Lottie said, holding her hands out to the warmth of the fire. 'You left your husband and baby and you expect me to take you in?'

'Only for a while,' Rosetta said, shivering in her damp clothes. 'I got plans but I need somewhere to stay for a bit.'

'You got money?'

'Enough for my keep.'

Lottie's lined face crinkled into a smile. 'Then take off those wet things and sit by the fire. You're a chip off the old tree after all, Rosetta.'

'Block, Aunt Lottie,' Rosetta said automatically. 'I ain't proud of leaving Martha but I know she'll be better looked after than if I stayed on. I ain't the motherly sort.'

'Like I said, cara, you're so like me. I left my little Gianni more than thirty years ago.'

'And were you sorry you left him?'

'It was a long time ago. I don't remember.'

'But you never wanted to go back and find him?'

'Cara Rosa, can you imagine me as a mother?' Lottie shrugged her shoulders, chuckling. 'Now tell me this big plan of yours. You going back on the stage?'

'Yes. Well, not exactly. I thought with Lily gone that Jonas might need someone to entertain the punters.'

Reaching for the gin bottle, Lottie poured a generous measure into her glass. 'You want some to keep out the cold?'

'Ta, but it's a bit early for me.'

'It ain't never too early for me.' Taking a mouthful, Lottie rolled the neat spirit around her gums and swallowed. 'You still got a fancy for Jonas?'

'I might have.'

'Well, so far as street gossip goes, he ain't had no woman since Lily. You might be in with a chance.'

'He came to the bakery, wanting Ruby's address.' Rosetta hesitated, wondering why she had said that, but having started she couldn't stop. 'I told him that Ruby was engaged to her doctor friend, Adam Fairfax.'

Lottie's shrewd eyes glinted. 'So, that sounds like the good idea to me. You don't want no competition.'

'Ruby hates him, she said so, and she don't like the way he makes his money.'

'Ruby is a nice girl; too nice. You and me, we're bad girls, Rose. You get on with your life and let her get on with hers the way she wants. As for Crowe, there's something not right. He don't send the punters round here for a night's lodgings no more and we've had to take in commercial travellers. That means hard work and Sly don't like hard work. You get in with Crowe, find out what's going on, and maybe we get our business back.'

'I'll do it, but I wish I knew why he wanted to get in touch with Ruby.'

'Only one way to find out. Put on your Sunday best and a bit of slap to make your cheeks rosy – you too pale, by the way – and you go and get him. A pretty woman can get any man she like.'

'You won't tell anyone I'm here, will you?'

'You get our business back and I promise I won't tell no one, not even your Billy.'

Corseted so tightly that she could scarcely breathe, Rosetta had just managed to squeeze into one of her gowns from her theatrical days. Wearing a silver fox fur cape borrowed from Lottie, and disguising the smell of mothballs

413

with a generous sprinkling of cologne, Rosetta fixed her hat at a jaunty angle over one eye, and went to knock on Jonas's door. She could hear footsteps approaching and she closed her eyes in an effort to control her breathing, which was difficult with her lungs constricted by tightly laced corsets.

Tucker opened the door and his face lit up with a huge grin but, as he stared at Rosetta through narrowed eyes, his smile faded into a frown. 'Oh, it's the other one. I thought it was Miss Ruby come back.'

'I've come to see Mr Crowe. Is he in?'

'Might be.'

'Well go and see, there's a good chap. Tell him Mrs Noakes would like a word.'

'Hoity-toity,' muttered Tucker, shambling off and leaving Rosetta standing in the hall.

Primping in the hall mirror, Rosetta waited impatiently, her nerves stretched taut and vibrating like plucked harp strings. She had been rehearsing what she would say ever since she woke up that morning but now her mouth had gone dry, and when Tucker left her outside the door to Jonas's office she was afraid that her voice would come out strangled and high-pitched.

Looking up from a pile of papers on his desk, Jonas raised his eyebrows. 'Mrs Noakes, what can I do for you?'

Annoyed that he did not get to his feet, as any gentleman should, but determined not to let him see that she was ruffled, Rosetta perched on the edge of a chair facing him. 'It's more what I can do for you, Mr Crowe.'

Resting his elbows on the desk, Jonas steepled his fingers. 'I'm intrigued.'

'You need someone to entertain the punters and I'm available.'

'You get straight to the point, I admire that, but what makes you think I need an entertainer?'

'You still run the gaming club, don't you? You need someone classy to take the punters' minds off stale sandwiches and watered-down booze.'

Jonas threw back his head and laughed.

'What's funny?' Rosetta demanded, bristling.

'Why, Mrs Noakes, I believe you're just as much a crook at heart as I am.'

Jumping to her feet, Rosetta glared at him. 'Don't laugh at me. I'm offering to work in your lousy club but I can see I'm wasting my time.'

Jonas was silent for a moment, observing her with a thoughtful look in his eyes. The sudden leap to her feet had made Rosetta's head spin and she would have stalked out of the room, but she was afraid that if she made a move she might topple over. She had not eaten since yesterday's midday meal, which had been a bun and a cup of tea, and now she was feeling light-headed. Sticking out her chin, she gave him back stare for stare.

'Sit down,' Jonas said, adding, 'please.'

Rosetta sank gracefully and thankfully onto the seat. 'Well?'

'What I don't understand, Rosetta, is why you would want to leave your husband and child to come and work for me?'

'Maybe I ain't cut out for domestic life.'

'And what does Billy think about all this?'

'That ain't none of your business. All right, you want the truth? I only married Billy because I was in the family way. I was all set to be a star at the Falstaff and you'd be a fool to turn me down, but if you do there are plenty more music halls in the East End.'

'Then it would be my loss,' Jonas said, shrugging, 'and their gain.'

'You was quick enough to take Ruby in and set her up like a lady.' Jumping to her feet, Rosetta leaned her hands on the table, looking Jonas straight in the eye. 'All I'm asking for is the same chance.'

Holding her breath, she clenched her fists, digging her nails into her palms. For the first time, Jonas dropped his gaze, staring down at his hands. 'And you're still in contact with Ruby?'

'No, I told you that, but Ruby would want you to help me, you know she would.'

'Things have changed round here since Ruby left. The police have made it too difficult to carry on my former line of business and I'm running a legitimate gambling club now. If I agree to take you on, I want you to understand that.'

'When do I start?'

'Whenever you like.'

'And I can move into Ruby's room, so that I'm here on the premises?'

Jonas's black brows knotted together in a frown. 'No. You must make your own arrangements. And when you next hear from Ruby, I want to be told.'

Disappointed that she could not have Ruby's room, but determined not to be put off by his casual manner, Rosetta let herself out of the front door. It had barely closed behind her when she spotted Billy striding along the street towards her. He was bareheaded and still wearing his white apron: his hair and eyebrows were frosted with flour, making him look like an angry Christmas-card Santa Claus. She might have laughed at his appearance if he had not looked so furious. Seized by panic, Rosetta ran down the steps but Billy caught up with her before she could reach the door to Lottie's house, grabbing her by the arm, his fingers digging into her flesh.

'What the bloody hell d'you think you're doing, Rose?'

'Let me go.'

'You're coming home with me.'

'You can't make me.'

'You're my wife. You've got a baby at home, crying for her mummy.'

Realising that a small crowd had gathered on the pavement at the bottom of the steps, Rosetta stopped struggling. 'You're making a show of me. Shut up, Billy.'

The sash window directly above them flew up with a bang and Lottie stuck her head out. 'Get inside and stop that noise. You're bad for business.'

'Do as she says,' Billy said, through clenched teeth. 'I haven't finished with you yet.'

Sly met them in the hall, his sleeves rolled up and a scowl on his face. 'What's going on?'

'You keep out of this,' Billy roared. 'Now, Rose, are you going to tell me what this is all about?'

Shaking off his hand, Rosetta backed away from him. 'I've left you, Billy. Can't you get that into your thick head?'

'Why, Rose?' His angry expression fading, Billy held his hands out to her. 'I done everything I could for you. I've tried to make you happy.'

'Take her home and give her a good hiding,' Sly said, taking a packet of Woods from his pocket. 'We ain't running a charity institution. She can't stay here.'

Rosetta turned on him. 'Aunt Lottie says I can stay. I've got money and a job. I ain't asking for charity.'

Appearing at the top of the stairs, looking like a spectre in her white nightgown with her hair flying about her head in a nimbus cloud, Lottie clutched the banisters. 'Don't be a fool, Sly. She's working for Jonas.'

'What?' Billy's voice echoed off the high ceiling. 'You never. Tell me you didn't go crawling to that crooked bastard.'

'I never crawled to no one in me life,' Rosetta said, drawing herself up to her full height. 'You watch your tongue, Billy Noakes. I got me a proper job, entertaining in Mr Crowe's gambling club, which is all legal and above board now.'

'We'll see about that,' Billy said, heading for the door. 'I'll have it out with Crowe and put a stop to that lark straight away.'

Running after him, Rosetta caught him by the sleeve. 'If you do that, Billy, we're finished for ever.'

Breathing heavily, his faced flushed beneath the white film of flour, Billy's shoulders sagged as if she had punched him in the stomach. 'Have it your own way for now, but this ain't the end of it, Rose.' He stamped out of the house, slamming the door behind him.

The premises had changed beyond recognition. Rosetta had only been in the gaming room once, when Jonas had invited everyone back after Poppa's funeral, but now it looked quite different. Huge mahogany chiffoniers, set with crystal decanters on silver trays, had replaced the taproom bar. Card tables were set about the room surrounded by button-back, leather chairs. The garish red and gold walls had been stripped and hung with more subtle art nouveau wallpaper and deep-pile carpet concealed the floorboards. The downstairs room, that had been the meeting place for punters and tarts, was now a smart salon where the wives of respectable merchants, lawyers and bankers could meet, have supper and be entertained. Far from entertaining the gentlemen upstairs, Rosetta found herself in the salon with the ladies, competing with the rising volume of female voices, so that more often than not her singing went completely unheard. Risqué music hall songs were out and her new audience demanded sentimental ballads. Accompanied by a pianist and a fiddler, Rosetta sang until the fog of cigarette smoke made her cough and her throat went dry. This was not how she had imagined it to be and, worst of all, she saw very little of Jonas. Even though she was working until the early hours of the morning, he refused to allow her to sleep in Ruby's old room. Rosetta slept alone in one of Lottie's better rooms, for which she paid a grossly inflated rent. When she awakened in the middle of the day she had only to go next door, but no matter what time she arrived Jonas always seemed to be out. When questioned, Tucker was always vague, saying that Mr Jonas had business in the City. Whatever the business matters were, it seemed that they were extremely profitable. The house reverberated to the sound of workmen, chipping, sawing, plastering and painting. The smell of turpentine and gloss paint cancelled out the odours of stale tobacco and alcohol. The below stairs servants were no longer slatternly in their dress and casual in their manner. They wore neat uniforms and their faces and fingernails were clean, inspected daily by a new housekeeper who disciplined and drilled them with the vigour of a sergeant major.

Rosetta came and went much as she pleased and Jonas paid her well, but none of this made up for the fact that he was completely indifferent to her. He was always polite and treated her like a real lady but that was not at all what she wanted. She wanted him to notice her, to look at her with that sparkle of desire that came into most men's eyes when they met her. She wanted Jonas to listen to her, to value her opinion and to realise how much she could help him improve his business. She had achieved her independence but, if she couldn't make Jonas love her as she loved him, then she had nothing.

Lottie was unsympathetic, more interested in the gin bottle than in Rosetta's heartache. She told Rosetta bluntly that she had been a fool to fall in love with Jonas. If you wanted to stay ahead of the game then you didn't let your emotions become involved. You made men think they were in love with you, but you kept your heart locked in a hard little shell so that when the affair ended you did not get hurt. If she couldn't do that then she would be better off at home, working alongside Billy in the bakery.

Sly tolerated her presence but never failed to make sarcastic comments on her failure to restore his business link with Jonas. Depressed, and lonely for the first time in her life, Rosetta lavished money on clothes and trinkets but, after a while, even the thrill of spending began to pall. After his initial visit, Billy had not come near her again, and Rosetta dared not go home, either to the bakery or Tobacco Court. She could not face the anger and disappointment that she knew she must expect from Mum and Granny. Martha wouldn't know her and Billy probably hated her, and with good reason. If only Ruby was here, she thought miserably. Why had Ruby had to go off to that stupid war in Africa? Ruby was the one and only person who would understand. Everything else paled into nothing compared to the separation from her sister.

Closing her umbrella, Rosetta stepped inside the entrance hall almost tripping over a plank and a large pot of paint. Apologising profusely, a workman scooped up the offending items and scuttled off towards the back of the house, doffing his cap to Jonas who had just come from the direction of his office. As usual, the mere sight of him sent Rosetta's pulses racing; she thought he was going to walk past her, but he stopped, looking thoughtfully at a rolled copy of *The Times* in his hand.

'This war with the Boers has gone on far longer than anyone thought it would. You must be worried about your sister.'

'Good morning, Jonas.'

'You're soaking wet. You won't be able to sing if you catch cold.'

'I wouldn't be soaked to the skin if you let me have Ruby's old room.'

Jonas hesitated, eyebrows raised. 'Aren't you comfortable living with Lottie?'

'I can't see why you won't let me use me sister's room. Ruby wouldn't mind.'

'The papers are full of this business at Mafeking coming so soon after Ladysmith. Have you heard anything from Ruby?'

Something inside Rosetta's head seemed to snap like overstretched elastic. 'Why are you so interested in what Ruby is doing? What is she to you?'

'That's none of your business.'

Jonas made to leave but Rosetta grabbed him by the coat sleeve. 'It is my business. You are my business.'

Turning on her, Jonas stared into her eyes, his expression guarded. 'You just work for me, Rosetta. I pay your wages, don't forget that.'

'I work for you because I love you,' Rosetta cried, seizing his hand and pressing it to her cheek. 'Can't you understand that, Jonas? I love you.'

'You don't love me,' Jonas said, snatching his hand free. 'You don't even know me.'

'I do. I do know you. You're strong and you're powerful. People look up to you. You need a woman like me to stand by your side and . . .'

'No!' Gripping Rosetta by the shoulders Jonas shook her. 'You don't know what you're talking about. Go back to your husband and child, Rosetta. Go back to the family who love you.'

'But I love you.'

'Then I'm sorry for you.' Jonas walked towards the door but Rosetta ran after him, barring his way.

'I've never begged anyone for nothing, not in me whole life, but I'm begging you to give me a chance. I could be really good to you. You might even grow to love me, Jonas.'

'Not in a million years, my dear. My worthless black heart belongs to someone else.'

'Who?' Rosetta heard her voice rise to a scream. 'I'll scratch her eyes out.'

'It would be a wasted effort; the lady is pledged to another man.'

Feeling as though the air was being sucked out of her lungs, Rosetta clasped her hand to her chest. 'You don't mean . . . You can't mean . . .'

'I'm sorry, Rosetta, but I love your sister and have done right from the beginning. Impossible though it may be, I love Ruby.' Lifting Rosetta bodily out of the way, Jonas slammed out of the house.

Aware that the workmen were hanging off their ladders enjoying the spectacle, Rosetta fumbled blindly with the latch, opened the door and ran down the steps just in time to see Jonas hail a passing cab.

'Jonas, come back. Come back.' With tears streaming down her cheeks, Rosetta ran alongside the cab until it picked up enough speed to leave her standing on the pavement, panting and sobbing. Aware of the curious looks from passers-by, Rosetta gulped and sniffed, wiping her eyes on her sleeve. The sun had chased the rain clouds away and the pavements sparkled, wet and clean after the heavy shower. There was the hint of spring in the air but to Rosetta it was icy midwinter. Shivering, and with her teeth chattering, she wrapped her arms around her body. Jonas loves Ruby, she thought, catching her breath on a sob. He loves Ruby and not me. Jonas loves Ruby and I hate her. No, I don't, Rosetta thought miserably; I hate myself for being such an idiot. I should have realised when Jonas came looking for her that it was Ruby he wanted all along. I've been a blind, stupid fool, yearning after a man who never gave me a second look, and turning my back on the one who truly loved me. Billy must hate me now, but he can't hate me more than I hate myself.

Standing in the middle of the pavement, hugging herself and crying, Rosetta felt as if the whole world was collapsing around her. What would she do now? Where would she go? Her golden dream of love and life with Jonas had burst like a soap bubble, leaving her with nothing except pain and humiliation. Hunching her shoulders, she put her head down and began the long walk home to Tobacco Court and Mum.

'Rose!' Sarah dropped the basket of washing that she was carrying and rushed over to Rosetta, flinging her arms around her. 'Oh, Rose, thank God you've come home.'

Rosetta had expected a cool reception, but there was something in her mother's expression that terrified her. Cold fingers of fear ran up and down her spine.

'What's happened, Mum?'

'Not that you'd care,' snorted Granny.

'Shut up, Ma,' Sarah said, tears spurting from her red-rimmed eyes. 'This ain't no time for family feuds.'

'You're frightening me,' Rosetta cried, grasping Sarah's work-worn hands.

'Joe's dead.' Granny Mole spat the words out like pips stuck between her teeth. 'Killed defending Ladysmith, and your sister's gone down with the typhoid.'

Rosetta's knees gave way beneath her and she sank down onto the nearest chair. 'No! I don't believe it. There's got to be some mistake.'

Curling her fingers round Rosetta's cold hands, Sarah sat on the seat next to her. 'He died a hero, Rose. My bad boy ended up a hero. Wouldn't he have had a laugh about that?' Sarah's voice broke on a sob.

Slipping her arms round her mother's shaking shoulders, Rosetta held her close. 'Why didn't anyone tell me? I would have come at once.'

'Because you're a selfish little cow,' Granny said, heaving herself up from her chair by the fire. 'You left your husband and baby and went off to live with that old soak Lottie. You don't have no thought for no one until you're in trouble yourself.'

'That's not fair, Ma,' Sarah said, wiping her eyes on her hankie. 'Rosetta's here now, ain't she?'

'Probably got herself into trouble again,' Granny muttered, heading for the stairs. 'I'm going for me nap.' Her heavy tread made the stairs creak and groan in protest as she hauled herself up to her room, slamming the door behind her.

'Tell me it ain't true about Ruby and Joe. There must have been a mix-up somewhere along the line.' Rosetta looked to her mother, desperate for a denial.

Sarah shook her head with fresh tears spurting from her eyes. 'It's true. Ruby was nursing the troops; she was with Joe at the end. She wrote me a letter saying that he didn't know nothing about it and went real peaceful. Then she come down with typhoid.'

'But how do you know? It could be a terrible mistake.'

Sarah pulled a crumpled telegram from her apron pocket, handing it to Rosetta. 'It's from that doctor friend of hers. He says she's being sent home on a hospital ship.'

'This is dated weeks ago. Why didn't you let me know? Why didn't I know anyway?' Rosetta buried her face in her hands. 'Me and Ruby used to be so close. I should have known there was something wrong.'

Sarah laid her hand on Rosetta's shoulder. 'You ain't kids now, Rose. You got your own life to lead and so has Ruby.'

Brushing the tears from her eyes, Rosetta lifted her head. 'This says the ship will be arriving soon. I'll make it up to her, Mum. I've been wrong about so many things and I've been hateful to everyone who loves me, but I'm going to change. I swear on Poppa's grave that I'm going to be a better person. I'll see that Ruby gets the best treatment that money can buy.'

'Oh, Rosetta, my little Rose, you always had big ideas. We'll manage somehow, but we just ain't got the money for doctors and fancy convalescent homes.'

'We haven't, but I know someone who has. Ruby deserves the best and by God, I'm going to see that she gets it.'

Chapter Nineteen

The journey home had seemed to go on for ever, the days drifting endlessly through a fogbank of laudanum-induced sleep. Ruby knew that she had been very ill and was lucky to have survived but, as her mind became clearer and memory returned, so did the pain and grief of losing Joe and then Pamela. In the first days of her illness she had only been dimly aware of her surroundings. Adam had been at her bedside, holding her hand, offering words of comfort and encouragement that sometimes she understood but, when the fever was at its peak, it was just the sound of his voice that she had heard. It was only when she had begun to recover that Ruby realised she had lost three weeks of her life. By that time they were at sea and she was lying in a bunk on a hospital ship, out of danger but too ill to do anything but sleep the days away.

She was still weak and listless and even the news that they were nearing England had done little to raise her spirits. She had left Adam behind in Africa, coping alone with his grief, and she was powerless to help him through his lonely ordeal.

It would be winter now, adding to the dangers and discomforts of life on the front line. On deck, reclining on a steamer chair and muffled in blankets, Ruby watched the grey-green waters of the English Channel roll and break against the side of the ship, sending plumes of spray and spume onto the decking. Long before they reached the quiet waters of the Thames estuary, she had made up her mind to return to Africa as soon as she had regained her strength.

They docked in London early in the morning. Ruby was not expecting anyone to meet her; she had vaguely thought she would take a cab home but it was difficult to think clearly. She had managed to dress herself but it had taken a long time, with short rests in between struggling with buttons and laces. She had lost so much weight that her clothes hung off her and when she was done she had to lie down on her bunk as the cabin spun round her in dizzying circles. Of the three other nurses who had shared the cabin with her during the voyage, two had gone up on deck to watch the ship dock and the other girl was too sick to leave her bunk. It was not much of a surprise when two orderlies entered the cabin carrying a stretcher. When she realised that they meant to lift her onto it, Ruby protested that she was fit enough to walk off the ship. The orderlies disagreed and she had to suffer the indignity of being stretchered ashore.

'There she is. Ruby, Ruby, over here.'

Lifting her head, Ruby could see Rosetta waving frantically from the quayside. Dazzled by the bright sunlight, she shaded her eyes with her hand. For a moment she thought she was hallucinating and the fever had returned. Smartly dressed and smiling, Rosetta and Jonas stood in front of his motor car, looking for all the world like a prosperous City merchant and his wife. Too weak to hold her head up, Ruby lay back on the stretcher. So Rosetta had got her wish and captivated Jonas with her charming ways. She ought not to have been surprised, but the sight of them together was more of a shock than she could ever have anticipated.

'Ruby, how thin you are,' Rosetta said, a worried frown puckering her smooth brow. 'You mustn't worry about a thing, dear. We're going to look after you, aren't we, Jonas?'

The orderlies set the stretcher down on the ground and Jonas thanked them, pressing what had to be a generous tip into their palms, judging by the way they grinned and touched their caps.

'We've come to take you home, Ruby,' Jonas said, bending over her.

To protest meant using her last scrap of energy; Ruby hooked her arm around his broad shoulders as he lifted her into the passenger seat of his motor car.

Ruby had expected to be taken home to

Tobacco Court but she soon realised that they were heading towards Shoreditch. 'Jonas, where are you taking me?'

'Home, my dear,' Jonas said, turning his head and smiling. 'Rosetta and I have it all worked out between us. We'll have you fit and well again in no time.'

'Yes, and Mum and Granny will visit tomorrow, after you've had time to rest,' Rosetta said, leaning over the front seat and almost smothering Ruby in a cloud of expensive perfume. 'Jonas and me have worked so hard getting your room ready. Just wait until you see it.'

As Jonas drew the motor to a halt outside the house in Raven Street, the front door of Lottie's house opened and she came down the steps, beaming at Ruby. 'Welcome home, cara. We've all been so worried about you.' Wrapping her arms around Ruby, she brushed her cheek with paper-thin lips.

Amazed by all this attention, Ruby could only nod and smile.

Lottie released her, taking a step backwards as Jonas came round to open the door. 'She's as thin as a sparrow, Jonas. You got to take good care of her.'

'I can get out by myself,' Ruby protested as Jonas lifted her from her seat.

'From now on, Nurse Capretti, you'll do as

you're told.' Jonas carried her up the steps as easily as if she had been a small child.

Tucker opened the door, his face split in a huge grin. He thrust a bouquet of yellow roses into Ruby's hands. 'Welcome home, miss.'

'Oh, Tucker, how lovely.' Ruby buried her face in the scented blooms. 'Thank you so much.'

'Not at all, miss. It's good to have you home.'

'I'll come and see you later,' Lottie called from the doorway as Jonas carried Ruby up the stairs with Rosetta following close behind.

'Please put me down,' Ruby said, as Jonas mounted the second staircase. 'I'm not a complete invalid.'

'Yes you are,' Rosetta said, slipping past them and hurrying on ahead up the last flight of stairs. 'Jonas has put me in charge and I'm to look after you until you're fit and well again.'

Ruby leaned her head against Jonas's shoulder, closing her eyes. So much seemed to have changed since she left for South Africa. She couldn't wait to get Rosetta on her own to ask her what had happened between her and Billy. Where was baby Martha? Why was Lottie sober? How long had Rosetta and Jonas been a couple? Why did that thought disturb her so very much?

Dancing on ahead, Rosetta opened the door and Jonas carried Ruby into a room that was bathed in sunlight and filled with the scent of summer flowers.

Setting her down on a chaise longue, Jonas took Tucker's roses from Ruby and passed them to Rosetta.

'We've filled every vase in the house,' Rosetta said, chuckling. 'I think Jonas must have bought up the whole of Covent Garden this morning.'

Ruby managed a weak smile. 'Thank you, Jonas. That was kind.'

'I'll leave you to settle in,' Jonas said, making for the door. 'Don't wear her out, Rosetta. Remember you're the nurse now and Ruby needs to rest.'

As the door closed on him, Rosetta pulled a face. 'God, he's a bossy devil, but then you know that, you've lived with him.'

'And you're living here now?'

'I'm here to look after you, Ruby. I'll make up for how I treated you before, I promise. We won't never fall out again.'

'Never?' Ruby raised an eyebrow. 'Perhaps. But I'm tired, Rose. This is all lovely but it's too much. All I wanted to do was to go home and sleep in our old room. Mutton stew for dinner and Granny Mole grumbling by the fireside.'

'You got to be looked after properly, Ruby.' Crossing the room, Rosetta opened a door that led into a bedroom. 'This is yours and I'm just next door. You've only to ring the bell and someone will come day or night.'

Ruby stifled a yawn. The sudden change from

being on board the hospital ship and the strangeness of her surroundings made everything seem unreal and nothing made sense. 'I could have had my old room. Why is everything so different?'

'Jonas said your old room would be too noisy. He's gone respectable, Ruby. The club is all legal and proper. Jonas is a bony-fidy businessman now – none of that dodgy stuff.'

'And you live here now?'

'I work here. I entertain the punters' wives in the supper room.'

'And Billy? How does he feel about all this?'

'Don't you worry your head about my problems. You just concentrate on getting strong again. Have a nap and I'll be back later with something to tempt your appetite. I don't mean to be unkind, Ruby, but skeletons have got more meat on them than you have.' Covering Ruby with a soft woollen blanket, Rosetta dropped a kiss on her forehead. 'I'm glad we're friends again, Ruby.'

As the door closed behind Rosetta, Ruby lay for a moment gazing round the newly decorated room and admiring the delicate, flower-patterned wallpaper. The swagged curtains and thick-pile Chinese carpet sculpted in pink and pastel green could have been taken straight from an illustration in *The Lady's Pictorial*. Jonas, she thought sleepily, must have done all this with Rosetta in mind. It had been a shock to see them so obviously together but Rose seemed a different person from the unhappy, heavily pregnant girl she had been before Ruby had left for South Africa. She knew that she should have been happy to see Rosetta with the man she loved, but the idea of Jonas and Rose together was deeply disturbing. Ruby had tried hard to hate Jonas just as she had tried to forget him, and she had failed on both counts. The memory of the night when he had forced himself upon her was imprinted on her body as well as in her mind, and his physical nearness aroused her senses to fever pitch. Being close to Adam had never affected Ruby in that way. Her love for Adam had been in her head like a beautiful dream; Jonas had command of her darker side and Ruby knew well what Father Brennan would have said about that. As soon as she was strong enough, she would go home to Tobacco Court and, when she was completely recovered, she would ask to be sent back to South Africa. Ruby closed her eyes and the chaise longue seemed to rise and fall with the swell of the waves as she drifted off to sleep.

There was an emotionally charged visit next day, when Mum and Granny Mole came all the way from Whitechapel in a hansom cab, which for them was an adventure in itself. Having been refreshed with endless cups of tea, they settled down to listen to Ruby's account of Joe's last hours. Leaving out the goriest of the details and emphasising that he had died a hero's death, Ruby told them as much as she thought they could bear. Sarah wept openly and Granny sat tight-lipped, but with tears in her eyes.

'At least you was with him at the end,' Sarah said, mopping her eyes on a very soggy hanky. 'That's a comfort. I couldn't bear to think of my boy dying all alone in a foreign country.'

'Well, he wouldn't have gone into the army if he hadn't gone and got hisself into so much debt,' Granny said darkly. 'I blame that Carlottie for leading him astray.'

Ruby opened her mouth to tell them that it had been fear of Jonas that had made Joe join the army, but somehow the words would not come. In her heart she knew that it had been the fatal weakness in Joe's character that had led him into such desperate straits. She could never forgive Jonas for involving Joe in his street gang, but she also knew that Jonas had let Joe get away with unpaid debts of honour, a crime for which any other man would have ended up wearing lead boots at the bottom of the Thames.

'Have another cake, Granny,' Rosetta said, offering the plate of cakes to Granny Mole, whose beady eyes lit up as she selected a chocolate éclair.

'Hmm,' Sarah said, biting into a slice of Madeira cake, 'we'd soon lose all our customers in Spivey Street if we served up dry-as-dust cake like this.'

Rosetta bristled like an angry hedgehog. 'We got a damn good cook, Mum. Our suppers are very well received.'

'Watch your language, young lady,' Granny said, licking cream off her fingers. 'You may think you come up in the world by leaving your Billy, but you're no better than a kept woman.'

Rosetta went very red in the face. 'I ain't no kept woman. I'm a chanteuse if you must know.'

'You're living with a gang leader and that makes you a moll,' Granny said, snagging another éclair from the plate.

'That's enough, Ma,' Sarah said, frowning. 'Keep your opinions to yourself. You're upsetting Ruby and you know she's got to be kept quiet.'

Scowling, Granny slurped her tea, swallowing noisily.

'It's all right, Mum,' Ruby said. 'It's Rose who should be upset, not me. I don't think Gran is being fair to her.'

'You don't know the half of it, Ruby,' Sarah said, pushing her plate away. 'You been away for months and you ain't seen poor Billy suffering like I have.'

'Give over, Mum,' Rosetta protested. 'Don't drag all that up again.'

'He's a good man, Rose. And how you could abandon your baby, I just don't know.'

'Don't start on me,' Rosetta cried, tears springing to her eyes. 'I'll live my life as I see fit and what goes on between me and Billy is our business.'

Ruby could stand it no longer. 'Stop it, all of you. You're making my head ache with your constant bickering.'

Rosetta jumped to her feet. 'There, see what you've done. You've upset Ruby and I'm supposed to be looking after her.'

'Sit down, Rose,' Sarah said. 'You're making things worse.'

'You can't tell me what to do in my house.'

'Your house?' Lottie's voice from the doorway made everyone jump. She sailed into the room in a flurry of black ostrich feathers. 'Jonas went and married you, did he?'

'I'm still married to Billy.'

'Yes, cara, and you do good to remember that.' Lottie swept over to Ruby, bending over her so that the ostrich feathers tickled her nose, making her sneeze. 'You look tired, Ruby.'

'She can do without you adding your tuppence-worth,' Granny Mole said, curling her lip. 'What d'you want, Carlottie?'

Fending off another tiff, Ruby smiled up at Lottie. 'Why don't you sit down, Auntie, and have a cup of tea?'

'I won't stay where I'm not wanted.'

'Give over with the play-acting,' Sarah said,

frowning. 'Sit down and spit it out. You've obviously got something to say.'

Lottie collapsed on the end of the chaise longue, narrowly missing Ruby's feet. 'All right, I'll tell you. I've lost everything and I'm going to be thrown out on the street. Not that you'd care, Sal. You never liked me.'

Ruby shifted her feet as Lottie made herself comfortable. 'Why would you be thrown out on the street?'

'It's Silas. He's done a bunk, took all me cash and left me with a pile of bills. I'm ruined.'

'Serve you right, you gin-swigging, Eyetie trollop,' Granny said, sniffing.

Rosetta clasped her hands together, her eyes wide with dismay. 'That's not fair. Poor Aunt Lottie. I never did like that Sly.'

'I'm so sorry.' Ruby reached out to pat Lottie's hand.

Sarah put her head on one side, considering. 'But the house belongs to you, don't it?'

Lottie shook her head. 'I already borrowed on the house. Don't look at me like that, Sal. I know I got a weakness for the horses but some of it was to stake Joe. Poor boy, he inherited the Capretti gambling streak and now he's dead. It won't be long before I join him.' Burying her face in her hands, Lottie broke down and sobbed.

'Bah! Theatrical balderdash,' snorted Granny.

'Give her a glass of gin, Rosetta, that'll shut her up.'

'How can you be so cruel, Granny?' Rosetta put her arm around Lottie's shoulders and began to cry.

Everyone started speaking at once and, looking from one to the other, Ruby realised that not one of them was capable of doing anything useful. Struggling to her feet, she managed to get as far as the side table where Jonas had thoughtfully provided a decanter of brandy and one of sherry, but then dizziness overtook her. Clutching the edge of the table, she closed her eyes as the room and everything in it spun around her like a merry-go-round. Suddenly she was back in the ward surrounded by sickness and the dying. The overpowering smell of carbolic and the sickly sweet odour of chloroform filled her nostrils, mingling with the putrefying stench of death. Swaying on her feet, she would have fallen if Jonas had not come into the room at that moment and caught her in his arms.

'What the hell is going on? You are all supposed to be looking after Ruby.' Settling Ruby in an armchair he poured brandy into a glass and handed it to her. 'Sip this slowly.'

The brandy made her cough, but Jonas's presence was reassuring and Ruby managed a smile. 'I'm all right now, really I am. Lottie's had some bad news and I was trying to get a drink for her.'

Silenced, Rosetta, Sarah and Lottie looked mutely up at Jonas.

As usual, Granny Mole found her tongue first. 'Her bloke's run off with all her money. I always said that Sly was no good.'

'I'm ruined, Jonas. He took the lot,' Lottie wailed.

'He should be strung up,' Sarah said. 'I'm sure you could do something, Mr Crowe.'

'Yes, you must help her,' Rosetta added.

Jonas held up his hand for silence. He bent down to whisper in Ruby's ear. 'Would you like me to send them away?'

Feeling as though his mere presence had lifted a huge weight from her shoulders, Ruby slipped her hand into his. 'No, I'm all right. But you must do something to help Aunt Lottie.'

'I will, if that's what you want.' With a reassuring squeeze, Jonas disengaged Ruby's clutching fingers. He went to the chiffonier and picked up a decanter. 'Tell me exactly what happened,' he said, pouring brandy into a glass and placing it in Lottie's outstretched hand.

'I could do with a drop of brandy,' Granny Mole said, clasping her chest. 'Me heart, you know, it's weak.'

'Rosetta, give your mum and granny a drink,' Jonas said, perching on the arm of Ruby's chair. 'I'm listening, Lottie.'

Rosetta opened her mouth, as if to protest, but

she did as Jonas asked, handing the drinks to Sarah and Granny Mole, and then she sat down primly on the edge of the sofa.

Drinking the brandy down in one gulp, Lottie blew her nose loudly and tucked the hanky back up her sleeve. 'There's nothing more to tell. Sly must have been pocketing money for a long time. He just took off with every penny I had.'

'It ain't the first time you've been dumped,' Granny said, grinning. 'You'll get over it.'

'At least I had a good life,' Lottie shot back at her. 'I was the toast of London. I had princes at my feet.'

'In yer bed you mean, you hussy.'

'That's enough,' Jonas said. 'That sort of talk won't get us anywhere.'

Lottie threw him an appealing glance. 'I'm ruined, Jonas. What shall I do?'

'Everything will be all right. Just leave it to me.'

Although it was Rosetta who was supposed to be attending to her needs, Ruby was hardly surprised when it was Tucker who brought her meals to her room and answered the summons of the bell if she needed anything. It was Tucker who sat with her, making her laugh with his sharp cockney wit, and Tucker who kept her informed of the gossip below stairs. Rosetta wandered in at some point every day, usually when she was dressed up for her evening performance in the supper room. When questioned about Lottie, Rosetta said she didn't know what was happening; Jonas was handling everything. She was obviously bursting to tell Ruby something and it didn't take much persuasion for her to blurt out that a theatre manager had seen her performance and she was sure he was going to make her an offer. What did Jonas think of that? Rosetta admitted that she hadn't told him, not yet. She would tell him when the offer was confirmed and not before. She danced off, bubbling with excitement, obviously determined to give the performance of her life. Ruby lay back against her pillows, wondering what Jonas would say when he knew that Rosetta was about to desert him as well as poor Billy, who was so far in the background as to be almost invisible. When she was well enough, Ruby made up her mind to visit Billy in his bakery and to see, for the first time, her baby niece, little Martha. How Rosetta could leave her child was something that Ruby would never understand; if Martha had been her baby then nothing and no one could have separated them.

Ruby closed the textbook that she had been reading, or rather trying to read, but the print had blurred out of focus and she found she could not concentrate on the medical terms. Outside the window, she could see the evening sunlight glinting off the top floor windows on the houses across the street. A thin stripe of azure sky streaked with sunset red and gold was just visible above the chimney tops, reminding her of the sea voyage to Africa and the evening strolls on deck with Adam. He had never seemed so far away or so unreachable. Trying to picture his face, Ruby felt a surge of panic; all she could conjure up was a blurred image. He had not written to her, but then there was no real reason why he should. They were separated not only by several thousand miles of land and sea, but also by the rigid barriers of social class.

'Good God, what are you doing sitting in the dark?'

She had not heard Jonas come into the room and Ruby opened her eyes, realising that twilight had turned into purple dusk.

He strode about the room, switching on lamps. 'I'll have a word with Rosetta. She's so wrapped up in this new admirer of hers that she's been neglecting you.'

'You know about the theatre manager?'

'Of course I do. Rosetta is a born performer, she's never happier than when she's the centre of attention. I daresay he'll make her an offer she can't refuse.'

'And you don't mind?'

Turning his head, Jonas stared at Ruby, eyebrows raised. 'Why would I mind?'

'I – I thought that you two were . . .' Ruby

stared down at her hands resting on the blanket that covered her legs.

'You thought wrong then.' Jonas's voice had a sharp edge that made Ruby look up. 'There's nothing between your sister and me,' he said more gently. 'Don't get me wrong, Ruby, I'm fond of Rose, but any man who falls in love with her is in for a rough time.'

'That's not fair and it's not true.'

Pulling up a chair, Jonas sat close to Ruby, his eyes searching her face. 'I know you love Rose, but she's a beautiful bundle of selfishness. She'll go far but she'll walk over any man who lets her get away with it. You know that's true.'

'Rose does love someone and I thought he loved her.'

'She never loved me.' A sudden twinkle lit Jonas's eyes and his mouth curved into a smile. 'Rosetta fell for my money and my dubious reputation. Now I'm a reformed character she finds me quite boring, I promise you.'

Lost for words, Ruby could only shake her head.

Taking her hands in his, Jonas stared down at them. 'You are the one person who is important to me, Ruby. You are going to get back your strength and then . . .' he raised her hands to his lips, brushing them with the lightest of kisses, 'then we'll see.'

'Jonas, I . . .'

Laying a finger on her lips, Jonas shook his head. 'I shouldn't have spoken out so soon.' Clearing his throat, he got to his feet. 'Now, you need your rest. Rosetta is down in the supper room so I'll send one of the maids up to help you to bed.'

'I can manage by myself,' Ruby said, attempting to get up.

'If you don't do as you're told, I shall have to put you to bed myself. And we both know how that ended up on one notable occasion.'

'I thought you'd given up being a bastard,' Ruby said, chuckling in response to the laughter in his voice. 'You wouldn't force yourself on a sick woman.'

'You're right.' Jonas held out his arm. 'We'll compromise. I'll walk you to your room and you'll let the maid run your bath and help you into bed.'

Unable to resist his smile, Ruby relaxed and slipped her hand through his arm. If she were truthful, she was glad of the support as her legs had turned to jelly and her heart was thumping so loudly that the drumming in her ears almost deafened her. It was just weakness, of course, nothing more.

'And tomorrow,' Jonas said, leading her towards the bedroom, 'I'll take you for a ride in the motor car. We'll go out to Epping Forest and maybe the fresh air will put a bit of colour back in your cheeks.'

'And Rose can come too?'

'Are you afraid to be alone with me?'

'No,' Ruby said, leaning on his arm. 'No, of course I'm not.'

With a picnic hamper wedged in the dicky seat and Ruby dressed in a motoring coat complete with hat and veil that Jonas had procured from apparently nowhere, like a conjuror producing a bouquet of paper flowers from his sleeve, they set off in the middle of the morning. Leaving the jostle and bustle of the East End and its refuse-littered streets jumbled with costermongers' barrows and the polyglot crowd milling in and out of the horse-drawn traffic, the leafy, tree-lined suburbs came as a pleasant relief. Away from the city stench and the smoke and noxious fumes spilling out of the manufactories, the air in Wanstead was fresh and clean. Jonas drew the motor to a halt in a small clearing on the edge of Epping Forest. The sun was high in the sky and Ruby was glad to shed the thick linen coat and shake the dust off her hat. The air beneath the trees smelt delicious, like rich plum cake, and there was just enough breeze to cool the heat of approaching midday. She sat on a fallen tree watching Jonas as he laid out the picnic lunch on a gingham tablecloth.

He paused, cutlery in his hand. 'What's funny?'

'Watching you doing something so homely,' Ruby said, smiling. 'Jonas Crowe, the tough gang leader, making a picnic.'

'Reformed gang leader,' Jonas said, with a responsive twinkle. 'My business is on the straight now.'

'Truly?'

Jonas grinned. 'Well, mostly.'

A cloud passed across the sun, throwing them into deep shade. Ruby shivered. 'Pity it's too late for poor Joe.'

Sitting back on his haunches, Jonas gave her a searching look. 'You blame me for Joe's death?'

'Not entirely, but he wouldn't have joined the army if you hadn't held his gambling debts over him.'

'Is that what you think?'

'It's what he told me.'

'It's true I tried shock tactics to bring him to his senses and stop his obsession with gambling, but I wouldn't have laid a finger on him, Ruby.'

'You made him join your gang.'

'Only to show him what the rotten side of life was like. Joe was just a boy; I wouldn't have dragged him down to street level. It was just to teach him a lesson.'

'So why did you make me work for you? And why did you set up a bursary just so that I could train to be a nurse? It wasn't just for Lily's sake, was it?'

Getting to his feet, Jonas brushed dead leaves and dust from his knees. 'In the first place,' he said slowly, measuring his words, 'because I wanted to take care of you and Joe.'

'I don't understand. Why would you care what happens to a bunch of people you don't know?'

Jonas stood for a moment, looking down at her, his expression serious. 'I wasn't entirely truthful before, when I told you that I wanted you to look after Lily.'

Biting back a sharp retort, Ruby realised that this time he was speaking the truth. 'Go on.'

'I've never done much good in my life, Ruby. I've lived selfishly and with one aim and that was to make money. I cared for nobody and nobody, except poor Lily, cared for me. My father was long dead and my mother had abandoned me when I was a baby. Then I discovered that I did have a family, who quite honestly meant nothing to me at first . . . that is, until I met you.'

'I don't understand.'

Jonas sat down beside her, close but not touching, his eyes intent on her face. 'My name is not Jonas Crowe. My birth name is Gianni Aldo Ravenna and Lottie is my mother. You, Joe and Rosetta are my cousins – you are my family, Ruby.'

Chapter Twenty

If Jonas had slapped her in the face, Ruby could not have been more thunderstruck. 'Are you joking?'

'I've never been more serious in my life.'

'I – I don't understand. I didn't know that Lottie had a child. You can't be her son . . . it's impossible.'

'It's a long story,' Jonas said, taking her hand and raising it to his lips. 'I knew nothing of my parents until my guardian took me aside one day to tell me that my father had died in Italy. Up until that moment, I thought I was Jonas Crowe, an orphan, taken in by a distant relative when I was just a baby. I didn't even speak a word of Italian.'

'I can't take this in.' Pulling away from him, Ruby got to her feet, pacing the hard-baked forest floor, her feet crunching the beech mast and dried leaves. 'I don't know why you're making this up, but it's too ridiculous to be true.'

Watching her warily but not moving from his seat on the log, Jonas shook his head. 'Nevertheless it is true. Lottie left my father just weeks after I was born. He hired an English nanny to look after me and, when I was one year old, he married her. My stepmother apparently didn't appreciate having a ready-made son and heir and she produced a baby every year just to prove a point. I don't know how she did it, but before I was two, she had persuaded my father to send me to England under the guardianship of her brother, Roger Crowe, a miserable old skinflint if ever there was one.'

'And you grew up not knowing any of this?' Ruby eyed him suspiciously. 'Do you really expect me to believe this story?'

'You might if you'll stand still long enough to listen to me.' Catching her by the hand, Jonas pulled her down beside him. 'The first time I met my half-brothers and sisters was at my father's funeral. I wasn't a welcome guest.'

'I don't suppose they believed you either.'

'We were total strangers. The family had closed ranks and written me out of the history books. They were wealthy enough to have had the marriage to Lottie declared null and void, making me a bastard.'

'And you've lived up to your reputation ever since.' Ruby made an attempt to get up but Jonas held her firmly by the hands.

'Are you going to let me explain or not?'

'Only if you let me go.' He did and Ruby folded her hands in her lap, frowning, but she remained seated.

'I've never pretended to be a good man, unlike your honourable doctor friend. No, don't get angry again,' Jonas said, laying his finger on her lips. 'To cut the story short, I had no ties in Italy and there was no reason to stay. My guardian died a bachelor and, surprisingly, he left me his house in Surrey and a modest sum of money. I set myself up in business.'

'As a criminal?'

Jonas threw back his head and laughed. 'Not quite. I sold the house, bought the one in Raven Street and went to work for a stockbroker in the City. I learned how to play the market and how to make money both legally and illegally.'

'So how did you find Lottie?'

'Once I knew who my mother really was, I began to take an interest in Lottie's career, which wasn't difficult as her name was never out of the newspapers.'

'Why didn't you get in touch with her?'

'She'd abandoned me once and I wasn't going to give her the opportunity of doing it a second time. She was a big star then, feted by society, and I didn't think she would be too pleased if I turned up and introduced myself as her long lost son.'

'Then how did she come to buy the house next door to yours? Are you telling me that that was a coincidence?'

'Of course not. I'd bought it as an investment

but when I found out that Lottie had lost a small fortune gambling and fallen on hard times, I sold it to her, through a third party of course, at a knock-down price.'

'You wanted to gloat over her misfortune. You wanted to hurt her as she'd hurt you. That's terrible, Jonas.'

'I may be bad but I'm not evil. I wanted to be sure that Lottie had a roof over her head. I never trusted Silas and I kept the leasehold because I didn't want to see my own mother end up in the gutter.'

'You could have told her the truth.'

'And do you think she would have thanked me for telling her that her latest lover was a two-faced piece of shit? One thing I do understand about the Caprettis is their stubbornness and pride. I inherited most of it from Lottie.'

'Why are you telling me all this now?'

'What happened before I met you doesn't matter. I had to tell you the truth.' Jonas paused, looking deeply into Ruby's eyes. 'The fact is, Ruby, the first moment I saw you, I fell in love.'

'You love me?'

'I adore you.'

Ruby jumped to her feet, staring down at him in horror. 'How can you say that? After everything you've done to me and my family, how can you say you love me?'

'I do love you.'

Anger flamed in her belly. 'You raped me. You don't know the meaning of love.'

'I'm ashamed of what I did, but I can't honestly say that I'm sorry. I knew then that you were the only woman I could ever really love.'

'That wasn't love,' Ruby said, shuddering. 'Was it some kind of revenge against women for what Lottie did to you?'

'No!' Jonas got slowly to his feet, shaking his head. 'I'd never hurt you, Ruby. I admit that I lost control, but in that moment I saw myself as I really was. I knew afterwards that I would have to change my whole way of living if I wanted to win your love.'

Ruby met his eyes with a straight gaze. 'And did you force yourself on Rosetta too?'

'I swear to you that I never laid a finger on her.'

'I know Rosetta and she's been soft on you for a long time. You'd have to be a saint to resist her when she's got her heart set on something.'

'A saint I'm not,' Jonas said, his eyes crinkling at the corners. 'After she left Billy, I gave Rosetta a job to stop her selling her talents to some sleazy music hall manager. She stayed next door with Lottie and only moved into my house to look after you.'

This time, there was no doubting his sincerity. In her heart Ruby knew that being in love with Jonas had been Rosetta's fantasy. She wanted to believe him, but suspicion clouded her mind.

'You encouraged Joe and Lottie to gamble, did you really hate the Caprettis so much that you wanted to ruin them?'

'Gambling is in their blood. If they hadn't done it in my club they would both have gone elsewhere.'

'You expect me to believe that when you destroyed my brother?'

'I tried to save him from himself, believe me, Ruby.'

'By allowing him to gamble away a fortune?'

'Letting Joe gamble in my club gave me a certain amount of control over his losses. I knew Lottie was a hopeless case, but I hoped by scaring the living daylights out of Joe I could bring him to his senses. It didn't work, as it happened, but don't ever think that I enjoyed it. I may have gone about it the wrong way but all I wanted to do was to protect all of you, especially after Aldo died.'

'You didn't know my father.'

'No,' Jonas said, speaking softly. 'But I would like to have known him. Maybe I would have been a better man if I'd known my uncle.'

'I thought I knew you so well, Jonas. Now I realise that I don't know you at all.'

'This must all have come as a shock to you,' Jonas said slowly, measuring his words. 'I promise you I'll make everything right with Lottie and I'll help Rosetta and Billy in any way I can. I'm a respectable businessman now. That will please your mother.'

'What are you saying?'

Taking her hands in his, Jonas held them to his heart. 'I'm trying to tell you that I love you and I want you to be my wife. I'll do everything in my power to make you happy, Ruby, if you'll just give me a chance.'

'Marry you? After everything you've done?' Snatching her hands away, Ruby stared at him in anger and disbelief.

'I know what I've done but I've turned my life around and it's all been for you, Ruby. I love you. Can't you believe that?'

'Like you loved Lily? You don't think I've forgotten poor Lily, do you? You got tired of her and left her in the sanatorium to die.'

'You know bloody well that's not true.'

'I've hit a nerve, haven't I? I believe you have got some feelings, deep down, Jonas, but you can't change what you are.' Turning on her heel, Ruby marched off towards the motor car. 'Take me home.' She could hear his feet echoing on the dried mud as he caught up with her.

'Are you still in love with the doctor?'

'I don't know,' Ruby said, giving him back stare for stare. 'That's the honest truth. I just don't know.'

Taking her roughly in his arms, Jonas kissed her with a passion that was more savage than tender. Barely able to breathe, Ruby closed her eyes; this was the stuff of her dreams during those hot nights in Africa: the racing of her pulses, the thudding of her heart against her ribs, the spiralling sensations that blotted out thought and memory. Her mind told her to fight him off, but her body was perfidious in its response. Her knees were weak, her lips opened, the taste of him was sweet on her tongue and her arms slid round his neck. Ruby knew that she was losing to the hot, aching sensation of longing that made her want him to take her, even as she felt his hardness pressed against her. Her emotions were in turmoil as he released her lips, staring into her eyes, his arms banded around her like steel.

'You don't love him, Ruby, you love me. Stop lying to yourself and admit it.'

Staring at him blurrily, Ruby struggled to control her erratic breathing and gather her splintered thoughts. She pulled away, shaking her head. 'I won't let you bully me into saying something I'll regret. Take me home, Jonas.'

The sun was still shining, the plane trees leafy-green and alive with birdsong, the air in the suburbs was sweet with summer scents, but the atmosphere in the motor car was cold and gloomy as a November day. They drove back to Shoreditch in tight-lipped silence and Ruby climbed out of the motor almost before Jonas had drawn it to a halt outside the house. Tucker let her in and even his broad grin faltered when he saw her face. She went straight to her room and began flinging her clothes into a suitcase. Anger tinged with panic had given her a burst of energy and she barely looked up as Rosetta entered the room.

'Good God, Ruby. What the hell is going on?'

'I'm going home,' Ruby said, snapping the locks shut on the case. 'Something I should have done weeks ago.'

'But why? I thought you were happy here?'

'I'm going home,' Ruby repeated. 'I've been lazing around for too long. It's time I got back to work at the hospital.'

Sitting down on the edge of the bed, Rosetta stared at her, frowning. 'Have you had a row with Jonas?'

'No. Well, yes, in a manner of speaking.'

'Then you're a fool, that's all I can say. Can't you see that Jonas is in love with you?'

'He asked me to marry him.'

'What?' Rosetta's mouth dropped open in surprise. 'Don't tell me you refused him. You did, didn't you?'

'Jonas isn't what he seems to be. There's something you should know.' Sitting down beside Rosetta, Ruby gave her the story as told by Jonas.

Rosetta's eyes widened and her hand flew up to cover her mouth, stifling a giggle. 'Blimey!

460

We've got a rich relation.'

'Rose! Can't you think about anything but money?'

Throwing her arms around Ruby, Rosetta gave her a hug. 'Honestly, no. But I don't see why you're so upset. I'm the one he rejected but I've got over it and, even though I can't have him I quite like the idea of Jonas being in the family. It's legal for cousins to marry, you know, Ruby.'

'Rose, you're the end,' Sighing, Ruby got to her feet. 'It's the lies and deceit I can't stand. It's Jonas's whole way of life.'

'But he's a reformed character. He did it all for you. Give him a chance.'

Picking up her suitcase, Ruby went to the door. 'I don't see myself as being kept by any man and I want to finish my nursing training.'

'And you're still hankering after your doctor friend?'

'Adam is everything that Jonas isn't. To be honest, I don't know how I feel. All I do know is that I need to get away from here so that I can think straight.'

'So you're running away. That's not like you.'

'I'm not running away. I'm going home, and I think you ought to come with me, Rose.'

'Not me,' Rosetta said, grinning. 'I'm not going back to the bakery and that's final. I'm going to stay and watch the fun when Lottie finds out she's got a grown-up gangster for a son.'

Cocking her head on one side, Ruby stood listening. 'I think it's just started. Come on, Rose,' she said, with an irrepressible chuckle. 'I'll beat you downstairs.'

Lottie had collapsed into the hall porter's chair and Tucker was fanning her vigorously with a copy of *The Times*. Jonas stood, arms folded, staring down at her and frowning as she went up and down the scale of hysteria.

'Shall I slap her face, guv?' Tucker asked, making such a draught with the newspaper that Lottie's grey hair flew about her head in a wild tangle like a frosted briar patch.

'You'll do no such thing,' Ruby cried, running down the last few steps. Dropping her suitcase on the marble tiles, she snatched the newspaper from Tucker's hand. 'Fetch her a drop of brandy.'

Lottie stopped howling and opened one eye. 'Make that gin, Tucker, a large one.'

'Do as she says,' Jonas said, nodding to Tucker, who scampered off in the direction of the dining room.

Ruby turned on Jonas. 'This is all your doing. Couldn't you have let her down gently?'

'Why do you always put me in the wrong?'

'Because that's where you live. You've dealt with filth for so long that it's ingrained in your heart and soul, Jonas. You couldn't change, even if you wanted to.'

Rosetta let out a gasp of dismay. 'That's just not fair, Ruby.'

'I'm going home,' Ruby said, picking up her case. 'And if you've any sense, Rose, you'll come with me.' Opening the heavy oak door, Ruby walked out of Jonas's house and out of his life, she thought, hailing a passing cab. The further away she was from Jonas Crowe, and everything he stood for, the better.

At first, Matron Luckes was reluctant to take Ruby back on the wards, but eventually she agreed that she could work just a few hours a day, using her free time for resting and studying. Ruby's request to be sent back to South Africa was turned down flat and she knew better than to argue with the indomitable Miss Luckes. Even so, once she started back on the wards, Ruby realised that she was not as fit as she had thought. She tired easily and was glad when her shifts ended and she could put her feet up and open her books to study.

At home, Ruby was alarmed to see how exhausted her mother seemed to be at the end of each day. Getting up at first light and going to the bakery was obviously beginning to take its toll on her health. Ruby worried to see her mother looking paper thin, with bruise-like shadows beneath her eyes and skin the colour of parchment, but telling her to slow down was as useless as ordering the Thames to stop flowing. Granny Mole was as obstreperous as ever, sitting in the corner demanding food like a fledgling gannet and just as noisy. Rosetta remained in Jonas's house in Raven Street and it was only when Tucker came to bring a few things that Ruby had left behind that she found out that Jonas had paid off Lottie's creditors and was having major alterations done to the interior of her house. Lottie had moved in with Jonas, and here Tucker had grimaced horribly, suggesting that this had not found favour with him. Mr Jonas had locked up all the booze, making it impossible for Miss Lottie to get a drink. There'd been ructions at first but, he said, she was calming down a bit now.

Ruby had not dug any deeper but Tucker had volunteered the opinion that it was a pity she had not stayed on, as things hadn't been the same in Raven Street since she left. Mr Jonas was rarely at home, off doing business in the City, and when he was there he shut himself in his office, probably in Tucker's opinion, to keep away from two women who could talk the hind leg off a donkey.

Ruby had tried to put Jonas out of her mind, concentrating all her efforts on work and study, but still the memory of that last searing kiss haunted her dreams, coming back to her unexpectedly at quiet moments during the day and filling her heart and body with a savage longing that made her blush. He had not tried to contact her and, illogically, that hurt too. If he had truly loved her as he had said, then surely he would have tried to see her at least once. And if he had, she would have sent him away, wouldn't she? Her feelings for Adam had dulled with the passing of time; his face was a blur in her memory and the sound of his voice like a half-forgotten song. There had been no letter from him, but then she had hardly expected that he would write. With Pamela gone, there was nothing left for them to say to each other. Then, one morning on duty, she overheard two young registrars chatting and, when Adam's name cropped up, Ruby almost dropped the kidney dish filled with soiled dressings that she was taking to the sluice. They had passed by her but she ran after them, catching one of them by the sleeve.

'Excuse me, doctor, but did I hear you mention Dr Adam Fairfax?'

'You know him, Nurse?'

'I served with him in South Africa. He was engaged to my best friend.'

'Ah yes, bad business that. Very sad.' He smiled down at Ruby. 'Adam was badly wounded by shrapnel from a bursting shell. He's at home recuperating, poor old chap.'

She had to see him. There was nothing for it

but to risk being humiliated by the stuck-up servants who protected the Fairfax family like snarling bull terriers. Ruby knew in her heart that she had to see Adam again, if only to convince herself that she had got over him. A tumult of confused emotions kept her awake at night; first it would be Adam's clean-cut, handsome face that came to her but then, like the rumblings of an approaching storm, Jonas would come striding into her dreams; dark and satanic, but with the ability to turn her blood into fire sending common sense and decency straight out of the window.

On her day off, Ruby put on her best print dress over a petticoat of bright moreen, trimmed with frills of glacé silk so that it rustled as she walked. The petticoat had cost Jonas the massive sum of eight shillings and sixpence, and was a shocking extravagance, but wearing it made Ruby feel like a real lady. Fixing her straw boater at a jaunty angle, she felt ready to face anything, even the awesome Mrs Fairfax, should she be unlucky enough to bump into Adam's mother.

Ruby set off for Highgate, walking at a brisk pace but, having reached the Monument and beginning to feel the effects of the hot August sun, she threw economy to the winds and caught an omnibus to Regent's Park. Making an effort to keep to the shade of the trees, she stopped only once to sip water from a drinking fountain and then set off again, trudging up the hump of Primrose Hill. Pausing for a moment on the top, her hot cheeks fanned by a light breeze, she wiped a trickle of sweat from her face, but at least it was not far now to the Fairfaxes' home in Highgate. By the time she reached the impressive house in the tree-lined avenue, she was perspiring freely and she could feel the cotton of her frock sticking between her shoulder blades with damp patches spreading beneath her armpits. Even the glacé silk frills on her petticoat were wilting and had lost some of their rustle.

The butler stared at her impassively and for a moment Ruby thought he was going to turn her away, but then he nodded and stood aside for her to enter the cool, encaustic-tiled entrance hall. 'Wait there, Miss, and I'll see if Dr Fairfax is at home.'

Catching sight of herself in a wall mirror, Ruby's hand flew up to straighten her hat that had tipped to one side at a rakish angle. Her face was flushed and trickles of sweat ran down her cheeks. Wiping them off with the back of her gloved hand, Ruby was horrified to see that she had smudged a sooty smut making it run in a long streak down the side of her face. She was scrubbing at it with her hanky when the butler reappeared and signalled her to follow him. A quick glance in one of the gilt-framed hall mirrors reassured her that the smudge had gone;

squaring her shoulders, Ruby followed the butler through the spacious drawing room.

The conservatory was filled with ferns and exotic flowering plants and the scent of white stephanotis and tiger lilies was almost suffocating. Adam lay on a couch with an electric fan whirring noisily at his side.

'The young person, Sir.'

'Ruby.' Adam held out his hand, smiling. 'How nice to see you again.'

'How are you, Adam? I heard that you'd been wounded.' Ruby stood awkwardly, hands behind her back, eyeing him and wishing suddenly that she had not come. Adam's lean face was tanned to walnut brown, his eyes startlingly blue against his dark skin. His hair, bleached white by the sun, flopped down over his forehead making him look ridiculously young; quite suddenly she felt shy.

'It was so good of you to come, Ruby. Do sit down. You're making my neck ache staring up at you.'

Pulling up a rattan chair, Ruby sat down beside him, folding her hands in her lap. 'How are you, really?'

Adam shrugged, glancing at his heavily bandaged leg propped up on cushions. 'My leg took the blast. It's a bit of a mess but it'll heal in time. How are you, Ruby? Although I don't really need to ask. You look blooming.'

'I'm quite better now. I'm doing some hours on the wards and studying the rest of the time.'

'You're a splendid nurse,' Adam said, wincing with pain as he pulled himself to a more comfortable position. 'You were wonderful to Pam and I'll never forget it.'

'Can I get you anything?' Ruby asked, eyeing him anxiously.

'No, I'm fine, but what sort of host am I? You must be hot and thirsty. Would you like something cold to drink?'

Ruby shook her head. It all seemed so strange and stilted, as if they were strangers now. The closeness they had shared on the outward sea voyage and during those terrible days of death and disaster in war-torn South Africa seemed like another lifetime. She barely knew what to say. 'I won't stay long. I don't want to tire you.'

'Stay for a while at least.' Reaching over to a side table, Adam picked up a silver-framed photograph of Pamela, kissed it and set it gently back in its place. 'You are the one person who knew Pam almost as well as I did. Everyone else clams up when I mention her name, afraid they're going to upset me. I know I can say anything to you, Ruby.'

'Yes,' Ruby said, swallowing hard. 'Yes, of course.'

'But you must have some refreshment.' Raising himself up on one elbow, Adam tugged on a bell pull. 'We'll have some tea and muffins and you can tell me everything you can remember about Pam. You know, the things that you girls used to talk about when you were on your own.'

Ruby relaxed a little and smiled. 'I'm not sure that would be such a good idea, but I'll do my best.'

Over tea and muffins dripping in butter, Ruby talked until she was hoarse. Lying back against satin cushions, Adam listened quietly and then began to speak unashamedly of his love for Pamela and his terrible grief at her loss. Worn out with emotion, Ruby was just thinking it was time to leave when Mrs Fairfax swept into the conservatory. Memories of the humiliating events at the engagement party made the blood rush to Ruby's cheeks.

'Mother, you remember Ruby,' Adam said, not seeming to notice the strained atmosphere. 'Ruby was at our engagement party and we were all together in South Africa. Ruby was there at the very end.' Adam's voice broke on the last word.

Mrs Fairfax smiled with her lips but her eyes were cold. 'How do you do?'

Getting to her feet, Ruby bobbed a curtsey. It seemed the right thing to do in the circumstances. Mrs Fairfax, in her cream silk afternoon gown, overflowing with lace and pearls, and with her hair piled high in fashionable curls on the top of her head, looked so like photographs of the Princess of Wales that Ruby felt she was in the presence of royalty. 'Nicely, thank you, Mrs Fairfax.'

'It was kind of you to call,' Mrs Fairfax said, raising her delicate blonde eyebrows so that they almost disappeared into her curly fringe. 'But my son needs to rest. He is still far from well.'

'Mother, I am a doctor. Ruby has done me more good than all the patent medicines put together.'

With her patrician nose in the air, Mrs Fairfax stared at Ruby as if she were looking down the double barrel of a shotgun. 'I'm sure she has.'

'I really must go,' Ruby said, backing towards the French windows that led into the garden.

'You will come again?' Adam said anxiously. 'Please say you will, Ruby.'

Her fingers twined round the door handle, Ruby hesitated. 'Yes, if you want me to.'

'Not that way.' Mrs Fairfax swooped on the bell pull, giving it a sharp tug. 'Jenkins will show you out. We can't have a guest leaving through the tradesmen's entrance.'

Feeling like a naughty child sent home from school by an irate headmistress, Ruby was escorted to the front door by the disapproving butler, who seemed to suspect that she might well pinch the family silver on the way out. At the end of the path, she paused, taking a long look at the elegant house surrounded by a well-kept garden. The air was filled with birdsong and the jewel-bright colours of butterflies attracted by the honeysweet scent of buddleia and roses. With the uncomfortable knowledge that she was as unwelcome and out of place here as a sparrow in an aviary full of hummingbirds, Ruby knew for certain that this wealthy, well-ordered world belonged to Adam. If she had harboured any doubts beforehand, Ruby realised that she would never fit into this stultified way of life, and her love for Adam had been nothing more than infatuation. She had fallen in love with a handsome face and an impossible dream. She had mistaken his kindness and good manners for affection, and Ruby knew now that Adam had always belonged heart and soul to Pamela. Although how Pam could have contemplated taking on Mrs Fairfax as her mother-in-law, Ruby could not even begin to imagine. She turned resolutely in the direction of Primrose Hill and started walking.

By the time Ruby reached home, Tobacco Court was drowned by deep shadow, even though there were still several hours until dusk. As she turned the corner from Spivey Street, Ruby knew that there was something wrong. Neighbours were huddled in their doorways and they stopped talking when they saw her. Breaking into a run, Ruby arrived outside the house to find the front door open.

She went in and found Billy standing in the middle of the room, tousle-haired and flushed, as if he had just come straight from the bake-house.

'What's wrong?' Ruby cried, alarmed by his grim expression. 'What's happened?'

'It's your mum. She had a funny turn. I brought her straight home and sent Elsie for the doctor. He's with her now.'

'Holy Mother of God.'

Ruby made for the stairs, but the doctor was already on his way down.

His taut features relaxed into a smile. 'Ruby, I'm glad you're here.'

'How is she, Doctor? Is it serious?'

'It's her heart, I'm afraid. I've done all I can, my dear, but I think you'd best send for your sister.'

Chapter Twenty-one

'Tell Billy to go away. I don't want to see him.' Rosetta pushed her plate away, the food barely touched.

Tucker stood his ground. 'He says it's urgent, Miss, and if you don't come out and see him, he'll come and get you.'

'Bloody cheek!' Pushing her chair back from the table, Rosetta jumped to her feet.

'Best hear what he's got to say,' Lottie said, wiping her lips on a napkin.

'I'll soon sort him out.' Rosetta strode out of the dining room, slamming the door behind her. Billy came towards her, his cap clutched in his hand. Alarmed by his sombre expression, Rosetta went on the attack. 'I told you not to bother me again.'

'I've got some bad news.'

Her hand flying to her throat, Rosetta felt the air being sucked from her lungs as if someone had punched her in the stomach. 'Martha?'

'No, not Martha, she's fine. It's your mum, Rose. She's very poorly and the doctor says you must come quick.'

'I don't believe you. You're lying, Billy, just to get me to come home.'

'Honest to God, I'm telling you the truth, you silly cow.'

'What's all the noise?'

Rosetta turned to Jonas as he came from the direction of his office. 'It's Billy, telling me lies, trying to make me go home.'

'I ain't telling lies, Jonas. It's Ma Capretti. She's took bad and the doctor wants Rose to come home right now.'

'You're just saying that,' Rosetta said, fighting down panic. 'Tell me it ain't true.'

'What happened, Billy?' Jonas laid a steadying hand on Rosetta's shoulder.

'Ma was took poorly in the bakehouse. The doctor says it's her heart.'

'It'll be nothing,' Rosetta said, clasping her hands to stop them shaking. 'She often has little spells and then she's fine again.'

'You got to come, Rose,' Billy said, casting an appealing look at Jonas.

'She'll come if I have to carry her. Is Ruby with Mrs Capretti?'

'Yes, and Granny Mole. I sent Elsie back home with Martha.'

'I'll get the motor car,' Jonas said. 'Rosetta, stop acting like a halfwit and wait for me outside.'

'Blooming cheek!' Rosetta said, staring after him as Jonas disappeared into the depths of the house. A cold chill of fear made her shudder and she rounded on Billy. 'I'll kill you if this is a trick.'

Placing his arm around her shoulders, Billy gave her a hug. 'I wouldn't lie to you about something like this, Rose.'

Leaving Billy and Jonas in the living room, Rosetta ran upstairs to the tiny front bedroom that her parents had shared for more than twenty-five years. Sarah lay beneath the coverlet, grey-faced and barely conscious, with Ruby perched on the edge of the bed holding her hand. Granny Mole huddled on a chair in the corner, dry-eyed but unusually silent.

Ruby looked up and smiled through her tears. 'Rose, thank God you've come.'

'Billy said she'd had a funny turn.' Rosetta stood at the bedside, folding her arms across her chest, cold fear gripping her insides. 'Is she going to die, Ruby?'

'Shut up, you fool,' Granny Mole muttered from the corner of the room. 'You never had no sense, Rosetta.'

'Please, Gran,' Ruby said, sending her an appealing look. 'That kind of talk isn't going to help.'

Rosetta gazed anxiously at her mother's white face, so like one of the waxen doll heads that Poppa used to make. 'Tell me the truth, Ruby.'

'Mum's had a bit of a do with her heart. The doctor says she's been working too hard.'

'And I wonder whose fault that is?' Granny said, glaring at Rosetta. 'If you'd stayed with your man instead of running off like a common trollop, this wouldn't have happened.'

Sinking down onto her knees at the bedside, Rosetta buried her face in her hands and sobbed. 'It is my fault. Please don't die, Mum.'

'She's got to be kept quiet,' Ruby whispered, stroking Rosetta's hair. 'Bear up, Rose. You got to be brave.'

'Crocodile tears,' Granny Mole said, getting stiffly to her feet. 'I'm going downstairs to make a pot of tea. You sort yourself out, young Rose. You got a lot of making up to do.'

'I'm a bad person,' Rosetta sobbed. 'I've committed every mortal sin there is and I'll go to hell for sure.'

'Stop it,' Ruby said, in a low voice. 'Stop feeling sorry for yourself; it's Mum we got to think about now and you weeping all over her won't help.'

Sarah made a faint noise and her eyelids fluttered open and then closed again.

'Mum, can you hear me?' Ruby said, leaning close to her. 'We're here, me and Rose, we're both here.'

'And I'm sorry I've been such a disappointment to you,' Rosetta said, sniffing and wiping her eyes on the back of her hand. 'Dear God, I'll do anything you want if you'll just make our mum better. I'll give up the theatre and I'll even go home to Billy and work in the shop if that's what you want. I'm really, really sorry I've been so bad.'

'Oh, Rose, you're such a big kid,' Ruby said, with a watery smile. 'Do you really think you can make everything better by just saying sorry?'

Rosetta shook her head. 'I can't be like you, Ruby. You're so prim and proper and goody-goody and everything I do seems to turn out wrong. But if Mum gets better, I swear I'll try to be more like you and make her proud of me.'

'You make me sound such a prig. I'm not what you think. I'm not good at all.'

Startled, Rosetta stared at Ruby. 'How can you say that? What have you ever done that weren't right and proper?'

'I thought I was in love with Adam even though he was engaged to Pamela.'

'I know you did, but you can't help your feelings any more than I can help mine. I know that Billy is a far better man than Jonas will ever be but – well, you know how it is.'

'Yes, Jonas,' Ruby said, lowering her gaze. 'I can't get him out of my mind either, Rose.'

'But you hate Jonas.'

'I don't know. I just don't know.' Ruby raised her head, her face contorted in pain. 'He raped me and I hated him, but even then it stirred something in me that was like nothing else I'd ever known.'

'Ruby, he never did! You're making it up.'

'It's true. And another time when I was tipsy and he carried me to my room, I wanted him to make love to me but he didn't. He left me there, wanting him and humiliated. I used to dream about Jonas when I was in South Africa, even though I knew we'd done wrong and it made me a wicked woman. I hate everything he stands for, and yet he's in my blood, Rose, like a fever.'

Staring at Ruby, Rosetta felt as though she were seeing a different person from the sister she knew and had always loved, even when they had fought each other. She had never dreamed that Ruby could be anything other than strong and sensible; had never imagined that she could be swept away by such a tide of emotion. Reaching across the bed, she laid her hand on Ruby's. 'He loves you, Ruby. He told me so but I thought you hated him.'

Ruby shook her head. 'I do. I mean I did. I don't know how I feel, but it doesn't matter now. All that matters is getting our mum better.'

'Ruby, Rose.'

'Mum!' Rosetta and Ruby spoke together.

Sarah managed a weak smile. 'I'd like a cup of tea.'

'You must rest,' Ruby said, clasping Sarah's hand to her cheek. 'The doctor says . . .'

'A cup of tea won't kill me, ducks.'

Sighing with relief, Rosetta leapt to her feet. 'I'll fetch you a cup of tea, Mum, just as you like it.'

'No, I'll go,' Ruby said. 'You stay with Mum.'

As the door closed on Ruby, Rosetta raised herself to perch on the edge of the bed. 'Are you really feeling better?'

Sarah's bloodless lips sketched a smile. 'I'll be all right. You mustn't worry.'

Taking her mother's hand, Rosetta shuddered at the cold, clammy feel of the clawed fingers and she chafed them gently in a desperate effort to pass on some of her own vital warmth. 'You got to rest. That's what the doctor says and I'll make sure you do. I've been a selfish cow leaving you to slave away in the bakery.'

'Billy's a good man, Rose, and he loves you.'

'He must hate me now.'

Sarah squeezed her hand. 'Give him another chance, ducks.'

Blinking back tears, Rosetta kissed her mother's hand. 'You promise me not to die and I'll promise to try and sort things out with Billy.'

'You got a baby to think of too,' Sarah said, closing her eyes. 'She's a proper peach, just like you was.'

Terrified for a moment that Sarah had slipped away, Rosetta clutched the frail hand to her cheek and wept with relief when she felt a thready pulse of life. She looked up as the door opened, expecting to see Ruby, but it was Granny Mole who came in, carrying a cup of tea.

'She's asleep,' Rosetta said, seeing Granny's startled expression.

'Thank God. I thought she was a goner.' Granny staggered to the chair and sat down, slopping tea from the cup as she placed it on the chest of drawers. 'It's all right, Rose, you get on downstairs. I'll sit with her for a bit.'

Impulsively, Rosetta got to her feet and went over to hug her gran, giving her a kiss on her walnut-wrinkled cheek. 'You're an old fraud, Granny.'

'Course I am, ducks. I wouldn't have survived so long if I'd been a mimsy-pimsy thing what burst into tears at the first sign of trouble. Get yourself downstairs and sort it out with that man of yours. I ain't too feeble to give you a thick ear, young Rose.'

The presence of two large men made the living room seem even smaller than usual. Ruby sat by the fireplace, her hands folded in her lap, her head turned away from Jonas. Billy looked up as Rosetta came down the stairs and his lips smiled but the expression in his eyes was guarded. With her emotions already heightened to screaming pitch, Rosetta felt a further wave of guilt as she met Billy's gaze. When they had first met she had thought him handsome and dashing, a likeable scallywag and a bit of a laugh. With a sudden flash of insight, Rosetta realised for the first time that she had been responsible for the changes in Billy. Staring into his good-natured, puzzled face, she knew that she had hurt him badly. He had stood by her in her time of trouble, had given his name to another man's child and had tried his hardest to provide for them all. In return, she had rejected his love, turned her nose up at his efforts to earn an honest living and she had gone chasing off after a silly dream. Glancing at Jonas, who stood by the door looking out of place in his expensive clothes, his towering presence dwarfing the room and making everything in it look shabby and tawdry, Rosetta knew for certain that she did not love him; had never loved him. She turned back to Billy with a nervous half-smile. 'I'd like to see Martha, if that's all right with you.'

'What about . . .' Billy glanced up the staircase.

Ruby jumped to her feet. 'I'll stay with Mum. You take Rosetta home to see the baby.'

'Billy?' Rosetta laid her hand on his arm. 'I can see my child, can't I?'

'It was you who walked out,' Billy said warily. 'I never said you couldn't see Martha.'

'I'll drive you home,' Jonas said. 'I'll come back here, Ruby, to make sure everything is all right.'

'I can manage.' Ruby shot him a sideways glance, her cheeks flushing pink. 'I mean, thank you, Jonas, but I really can manage.'

Watching Ruby and Jonas treating each other like polite strangers, Rosetta willed Jonas to stand his ground and argue, but he simply shrugged his shoulders and went out into the street.

'We'll be back later, Ruby,' Billy said, with an encouraging smile.

Rosetta hesitated, torn between wanting to see Martha and fear that Mum might take a turn for the worse. 'Perhaps I ought to stay.'

Ruby shook her head. 'Go, Rose. It's what Mum would want, you know that.'

Kissing Ruby on the cheek, Rosetta lowered her voice so that Billy couldn't hear. 'And you should sort things out with Jonas. He was only trying to help.'

'You sort your own life out,' she said. 'Leave mine to me.'

The shop and the flat above it looked even more shabby and dilapidated than Rosetta remembered. In sharp contrast to the luxury of Jonas's home, the cheap linoleum and second-hand furniture only added to the general air of neglect and poverty. The faint smell of charred wood lingered on and, although it was warm outside, the living room felt cold and unwelcoming.

Elsie cried out with surprise and pleasure on seeing Rosetta, bursting into tears and rushing across the room to give her a hug. Martha, now nearly nine months old, was sitting on a rag rug in the middle of the living-room floor playing with some wooden bricks. She looked up at Rosetta with big, curious brown eyes but without a flicker of recognition. With a lump in her throat, Rosetta bent down to pick up her daughter.

'Martha, it's me, your mummy.'

Martha tugged at a lock of Rosetta's hair and then, spotting her gold earrings, made a grab for one, howling with rage when Billy came to the rescue and prised her fingers open. He took her in his arms and Martha buried her face in his shoulder, sobbing with outrage.

'She doesn't even know me,' Rosetta said, close to tears.

'What do you expect, love?' Billy said gently. 'You left when she was just a few weeks old.'

'But I am her mother. I thought she would just know it.'

'We've made a mess of things between us, haven't we, Rose?' Billy said, handing Martha back to Elsie.

Elsie cleared her throat nervously. 'Shall I take Martha to the kitchen for her tea? Or do you want to give it her, Missis?'

'You take her, Elsie. I'll come and say goodbye before I go.'

Elsie's bottom lip quivered. 'Ain't you staying?'

'Just go and feed her.'

With a reproachful glance, Elsie carried Martha out of the room, stomping her feet as if to underline her disapproval.

'What are you going to do?' Billy said, eyeing Rosetta warily. 'I don't suppose you'd want to come home?'

Avoiding his gaze, Rosetta stared down at her hands clasped in front of her. 'Do you want me back, Billy?'

'Not unless you mean to stay.'

That was not the answer Rosetta wanted to hear. She wanted to believe that he still loved her, but it seemed as though a shutter had blanked his eyes. He was staring at her, unsmiling. She had thought it would be easy, but it was not, and her confidence wavered. 'I . . . well, I don't know.'

'That's not good enough for me. Of course I want you, Rose. I love you, and I think I always will, but I'm not going to put up with you flitting in and out just because you feel like it. I only want you back if you mean to make a go of it. I can't give you a life of luxury like Jonas, so if it's him you'd rather choose, then you got to be honest with me.'

Hurt by the ultimatum, Rosetta stared at him, scowling. 'I've had other offers. I been working in Jonas's club, entertaining the punters. I got a theatre manager offering me third billing at the Hackney Empire.'

'If that's what you really want, I can't stop you, and I ain't going to try. You fair tore me heart out when you left, Rose. And it wouldn't do no good for little Martha to get fond of you and then you light off again when you get itchy feet.'

'Well, then, maybe I'd better just go before I upset you any more.'

Billy nodded, his expression guarded and his voice harsh. 'I'll see you home.'

'No need. I can take care of myself, thank you.' Rosetta stormed out of the living room, ran down the narrow staircase and let herself out of the shop. She heard Elsie call out to her but she took no notice. It was all Billy's fault, she thought, slamming the shop door behind her. He hadn't put up a fight, so he couldn't really love her. She had met him halfway but Billy was stubborn and unbending. She turned her back on the baker's shop and strode off in the direction of Tobacco Court.

Arriving home, breathless and angry as a wasp trapped in a jam jar, Rosetta entered the house to find the doctor in the living room talking to Ruby. Anger was wiped away by fear and Rosetta could hardly breathe the words. 'Has she been took worse?'

The doctor turned to her with a reassuring smile. 'No, I just came to give her a dose of laudanum to help her sleep. I'll come again tomorrow morning, but if you're worried in the meantime just send for me.'

'Thank you, doctor,' Ruby said, showing him to the door. 'I really appreciate you coming again like this.'

'Don't thank me, my dear; it was Mr Crowe who suggested it. And you have no need to worry about the bill, he's taking care of that too.' Putting on his battered old top hat, the doctor went out into the gathering dusk.

'Well!' Ruby said, closing the door behind him. 'What a cheek! Going over my head like that – he's got a nerve.'

'Hold on, Ruby. Seems to me he was just trying to help. After all, I suppose he thinks he's the head of the family now that Poppa and Joe have gone.'

'He can think what he likes. I won't have him telling me what to do.'

'Can we afford to pay the doctor's bills?'

'No.'

In spite of everything Rosetta couldn't help grinning. 'You haven't got the hump with him because he's helping us out, have you?'

'I don't know what you're talking about.'

'I know you too well, Ruby. You're in love with him but you don't want to admit it because he don't match up to your knight in shining armour, Doctor bloody Fairfax.'

A dull flush spread from Ruby's throat to her

cheeks. 'And you're too pig-headed to admit that you made a mistake thinking you were in love with Jonas. You liked Billy well enough before Jonas came on the scene but you had to throw it all away to follow your stupid dream.'

'And what about you? Going all the way to South Africa and nearly dying of the fever just to be with your stuck-up doctor.'

Ruby opened her mouth to answer back but Granny Mole's head appeared round the bend in the stairs and she hissed at them like a cat cornered by a bulldog. 'Shut up, you two, or do I have to come down and bang your blooming heads together? Your poor ma is trying to sleep and you're carrying on like a couple of fish fags.'

Silenced, Ruby and Rosetta stared at each other and Granny Mole stumped back up the stairs. Rosetta's bottom lip trembled and Ruby held out her arms.

'I'm sorry, Rose.'

'I'm sorry too.'

Hugging each other with tears flowing freely, they pulled apart sniffling and laughing through their tears.

'We mustn't fight,' Rosetta said, wiping her eyes on the back of her hand.

'What happened to us, Rose? We used to be such good friends.'

'And still are. It's them bloody men that have got us going.'

'To hell with them both, I say,' Ruby said, picking up the teapot from the hob and filling two mugs.

They clinked their mugs together and drank a toast in stewed tea.

Having decided to take it in turns to sit by their mother's bedside, Rosetta took the first watch. As she sat by the bed listening to Sarah's gentle breathing, terrified that each fluttering sigh might be her last, Rosetta thought hard about her life and she was not proud of herself. In the dark small hours, she saw herself as unloving and selfish; she had hurt those who loved her and now even Billy had grown tired of her. If only she could claw back time and change the past, she thought, fisting her hands and digging her nails into her palms. She had committed so many mortal sins that Father Brennan would need a couple of days to hear her confession and even then he might be hard put to give her absolution. Falling onto her knees at the side of the bed, Rosetta prayed as she had not prayed for years. Please, God, make Mum better and I promise to be good. I've made a terrible hash of things and I'll do whatever I can to put things right, if you'll just give me another chance.' Closing her eyes, Rosetta fell asleep.

She awakened with a start when Ruby shook her by the shoulder. Cold and cramped, Rosetta struggled to her feet.

'Go to bed,' Ruby whispered. 'Get some proper rest. I'll call you if I need you.'

Flinging her arms around Ruby, Rosetta gave her a silent hug. With one last glance at her mother, who appeared to be sleeping peacefully, she went to the room she had shared for most of her life with Ruby and Granny Mole. Even Granny's stertorous breathing was welcome after the deathly silence in Mum's room. Rosetta crawled into bed and pulled the covers over her head.

The doctor was more hopeful when he came to visit next morning but he stressed the fact that Sarah must have peace, quiet and rest. He promised to come back later and told Ruby firmly to go to bed and get some sleep.

Having made tea and toast for Granny Mole's breakfast and having persuaded Sarah to eat a little bread and milk, Rosetta was sitting down with a cup of tea when Jonas arrived at the front door carrying a hamper of food. He brought it into the house and laid it on the table.

'Is Ruby about?' Jonas took off his top hat, set it down on the table and began peeling off his leather gloves.

Rosetta shook her head. 'She's sleeping. She was up most of the night with Mum.'

'How is Mrs Capretti?'

Granny Mole got up from her chair by the fireplace and came over to poke her finger into the hamper. 'What have we got?'

'Just a few things to help get the invalid better,' Jonas said, winking at Rosetta.

'Grapes!' Granny seized a bunch and held it up to the light. 'I ain't tasted a grape for years.'

'Help yourself,' Jonas said, grinning. 'It will keep your strength up.'

'Are you laughing at me, young man?'

'I wouldn't dare, Mrs Mole.'

'Huh!' Granny went back to her chair clutching the grapes.

Jonas turned back to Rosetta. 'How is Ruby? I wanted to see her and put things straight.'

'She was worried about Mum. She didn't really know what she was saying.'

'She did, and I deserved it. I'd do anything for her, you know that, don't you, Rosetta?'

'Give her time,' Rosetta said, touched by the sincerity in his eyes. 'You got to give us all time to get to know the new Jonas Crowe. It's been a bit of a shock to find out we got a cousin.'

'You're all right, you are, Rosetta. I've got a lot of time for you and if there's anything I can do to help you and Billy, just tell me.'

'D'you mean that?'

'These grapes are bloody marvellous,' Granny said, smacking her lips. 'For God's sake, Rose, spit it out.'

'What?' Rosetta stared at Granny. 'I dunno what you mean, Gran.'

Spitting pips into the empty grate, Granny cast her a pitying glance. 'Bees and honey: money, you daft mare. You need money to set you and Billy up in a proper business so you can have a fresh start. With you gallivanting off and Sarah sick, how d'you think Billy's keeping the business going? Not very well, I should think. Gawd's strewth, am I the only one in this family with any brains?'

'Granny!' Rosetta's hand flew to her mouth and she looked anxiously at Jonas to see if he was annoyed.

'Granny Mole, you're right,' Jonas said, chuckling. 'Rosetta, I've done plenty of bad things in my life and I'm not proud of it, but if I can help you and Billy, just say the word.'

'You will?' Rosetta held her breath.

Jonas nodded. 'We're family and I admire Billy for what he's trying to do. He's a better man than I am, Rosetta; don't make the same mistakes as I have. I may have lost the only woman I've ever loved, but you've got another chance so don't make a hash of it.'

Flinging her arms around his neck, Rosetta hugged him until she was breathless. 'Thank you, Jonas. Thank you.'

'Save the soft stuff for your Billy,' Granny said darkly. 'You got a lot to make up for, young Rose.'

Retrieving his hat and gloves, Jonas made for

the front door. 'I'd better go. Tell Ruby I'll call again tomorrow.'

As soon as the door closed on Jonas, Rosetta grabbed her hat and went to the mirror to make sure she pinned it on at an appealing angle.

'And where would you be off to?' Granny demanded. 'As if I didn't know.'

'I got to see Billy and tell him the good news.'

'Are you off your head, girl?' Scowling, Granny pointed her stick at Rosetta.

'What d'you mean?'

'If you goes round there and throw Jonas's money in Billy's face, how d'you think that'll make him feel? He's worked his guts out to make a home for you and your kid, but that weren't good enough for you. Take my advice and keep quiet about the money until you got things sorted out with Billy.'

'But . . .'

'No buts. Go round and see him but take it slow, Rose. Get to know him again and start acting like a mum to your nipper; that's the way to get round Billy. Find out if you got any feelings for him. If you haven't, then it'll never work, not in a month of Sundays.'

'I have got feelings for him, Granny. I think, deep down, I've loved Billy all along only I was too stupid and selfish to see it.'

Spitting a grape pip out of the corner of her mouth, Granny eyed Rosetta, unsmiling. 'You

493

was crazy in love with Jonas five minutes ago.'

'I thought I was but it was just his money and power that I fell for. When he turned me down I could have killed him, but it wasn't my heart that was hurt, it was my pride. I've come to me senses, Granny. I want Billy back, and my baby. I want them both.'

Popping the last grape in her mouth, Granny wagged her finger at Rosetta. 'Then stop gassing and get on round there.'

Suddenly nervous, Rosetta frowned at her reflection in the mirror. What would she do if Billy rejected her? 'Maybe I shouldn't go until Ruby wakes up. Mum might need me for something.'

Granny Mole heaved herself out of the chair. 'I can look after Sal until Ruby wakes up. You get round to Spivey Street and pray that Billy don't slam the door in your face.'

Billy was in the shop serving a customer when Rosetta arrived, slightly out of breath, from nerves rather than from exertion. The woman paid him for the loaf and brushed past Rosetta without looking at her.

'Hello, Rose. Come to buy a loaf?' Billy's expression was not encouraging.

Rosetta hesitated, momentarily lost for something to say. 'I – er . . .'

A look of anxiety crossed Billy's face. 'It's not Ma Capretti, is it? She's . . .'

'A bit better,' Rosetta said hastily. 'I come to see you, Billy, and Martha. If that's all right.'

Lifting the counter flap, Billy stood aside, holding it open. 'I told you that you can see Martha whenever you like.'

'The shelves are empty,' Rosetta said, looking round the tiny shop.

'I've just about been managing to bake bread; cakes is things of the past. I can't do so much without Ma. Actually, I was going to bring Martha round to see her.'

They were so close together in the narrow space behind the counter that Rosetta could feel his breath warm against her cheek, smell the scent of the bakehouse on his clothes. Standing there with his shirt open at the neck and his sleeves rolled up, Rosetta was suddenly aware of the strength in his muscular forearms and the pulse beating at the base of his throat. Once, not so long ago, he would have wrapped his arms around her, held her close, taken her lips in a long and hungry kiss, but now he stood there, unmoving, unsmiling, watching her as if she were a firework that might suddenly explode.

'Perhaps we could go together,' Rosetta suggested, licking her dry lips. 'Mum would like that.'

'We'll do that.'

'Billy, I'm sorry for what I said. I didn't mean it.'

'You never do, Rose. It doesn't matter.'

'But it does matter. I want us to be friends again.'

Billy made a move towards the inner door. 'Come up and see Martha.'

Rosetta caught him by the sleeve. 'Do you hate me, Billy?'

'What do you want, Rose?'

'I want you. I've been a blooming idiot and I didn't realise what I'd got. I took you for granted and I was wrong, I admit it. I want us to be together again and I swear I'll be a good wife and mother if you'll just give me a chance.'

'How do I know you mean it, Rose? You've lied to me before. How do I know you won't get fed up again and run away?'

'Because I love you, Billy. Deep down I've always loved you but I was chasing rainbows and when I got to the end of them there was nothing there. I love you, I really do.'

'I want to believe you.'

Running her hands up his shirt front, feeling the warmth of his body and the thudding of his heart that matched the beat of her own, Rosetta pulled his head down so that their lips were touching. 'Kiss me, Billy.'

Chapter Twenty-two

Juggling work and study at the hospital with caring for her mother made life difficult for Ruby, and Rosetta's urgent desire to return home was not helping. The doctor was pleased with Sarah's progress but he was adamant that she must rest and that working again was out of the question. Without Sarah's help, Ruby knew that Billy was struggling to make the bakery pay and, as soon as she came home from the hospital, Rosetta would hurry off to Spivey Street to be with Billy and Martha.

If it had not been for Jonas's daily visits, Ruby felt that she would not have been able to cope with the extra demands heaped upon her. Without Sarah's wages they would have been hard put to buy the extras needed by a recuperating invalid, but Jonas never came empty-handed, bringing food that he said was left over from the dining room and would only go to waste if they could not eat up the pies, roast meat and cakes baked in the Raven Street kitchen.

As soon as Sarah was well enough, Jonas had

insisted on telling both her and Granny Mole that Lottie was his mother. Sarah had been stunned at first, and then delighted to have a male head of the family; no one, she had said, could take Aldo's place, but she knew he would have been proud to have Jonas for a nephew. Ruby had smiled inwardly, not daring to catch Jonas's eye, but content to let Mum think the best of him. After all, what good would it do for her to know about Jonas's murky past? Granny Mole had proved to be a bit more sceptical but Jonas had made himself popular with her by bringing daily supplies of Fry's chocolate, bottles of stout and making certain that the 'purely medicinal' brandy bottle was always refilled. He spent time at Sarah's bedside and from downstairs, Ruby could hear them chatting amicably; she often wondered what they found to talk about, but whatever it was Sarah had begun to look forward to his visits, saying that Jonas reminded her of Aldo when he was a young man. Ruby couldn't see it herself, but it was good to hear Mum laughing at something Jonas had said and gradually, a tiny fragment at a time, she found her resentment and disapproval of him being chipped away.

Sometimes she wished that he would sit and talk with her as he did with Mum, but he never stayed long, and, although he treated her like a friend, there was nothing remotely lover-like in his attitude. He seemed to have forgotten their ill-fated picnic in Epping Forest and, as time went by, Ruby began to think she might have imagined his passionate declaration of love and his proposal of marriage. Perhaps she'd been a fool to turn him down so resolutely? Maybe he was taking his new-found role as head of the family too seriously, and was content to think of her just as a cousin.

Alone at night in the bed she had always shared with Rosetta, Ruby tossed and turned, and finally, unable to get back to sleep, she would get up, go downstairs to the living room and study for her final examinations early in the New Year until her eyes were sore and her head spun with facts and figures.

The doctor only came once a week now to visit Sarah, who was allowed to get up and dress as long as she did not exert herself. Christmas was almost upon them and Ruby had neither the money nor the time to make preparations. But at least Rosetta seemed happy now that she was back with Billy and when she visited, usually bringing Martha with her, she was full of plans for the future. Ruby had fallen in love with Martha on sight, and she was delighted that Rosetta had at last come to terms with mother-hood and was happy with Billy. She prayed that the New Year would bring happiness and prosperity to the bakery on Spivey Street, but she dared not think about her own future; it seemed dull and cheerless without Jonas, but Ruby knew that she had only herself to thank for that.

Two weeks before Christmas, Rosetta came to visit, dressed in a new velvet-trimmed bonnet and mantle and with Martha wearing a miniature version of her cherry-red outfit. Ruby was touched to see her sister looking radiant, just like the Rosetta of the old days, but now she had a baby on her knee: a little dark-eyed, dark-haired edition of herself.

'Jonas has loaned us the money to expand,' Rosetta said, taking off Martha's bonnet and setting her down on the rag rug. 'We're going to buy the shop next door and enlarge the bakehouse so that Billy can take on more staff. I've had a look over the premises and the flat above the shop is much nicer than ours. Billy says I can have it done up just as I like and you can all come and visit me when it's finished.'

'That'll be nice, ducks,' Sarah said, smiling.

'Pity we got to wait till then,' Granny Mole said, dunking a biscuit in her tea, 'what with Christmas coming up and not a thing in the house, not even a pig's cheek or a pound of beef sausages.'

'Well then, I got something to tell you,' Rosetta said, obviously enjoying being the bearer of good news. 'Jonas has invited all of us to Raven Street for Christmas dinner. I'm surprised he hasn't told you himself.'

Ruby's heart gave an uncomfortable thud, just as if she'd missed a step coming downstairs. Jonas had been here only yesterday and he hadn't mentioned anything about Christmas, but somehow she managed a smile. 'I expect he forgot. He's been very busy recently.'

'Not that you'd notice anything with your head stuck in a book all the time.' Granny Mole held out her teacup for a refill. 'A body could die of thirst in this house.'

'Ma, don't nag the girls,' Sarah said mildly.

'Someone's got to keep them on their toes, what with Rose being full of big plans what won't help us a bit and Ruby with her head stuck in her books, not knowing what time of day it is.' Granny Mole glared at them over the rim of her teacup, as if daring someone to argue the point.

Billy arrived later to collect Rosetta and Martha. He came in on a burst of cold air, his clothes sparkling with hailstones. 'Cold enough for snow,' he said, grinning. 'Maybe we'll have a white Christmas.'

'Wouldn't that be lovely?' Rosetta said, lifting Martha onto her lap. 'And your first birthday just before Christmas too, darling. Won't that be exciting?'

'You look a real picture,' Sarah said, as Billy leaned down to kiss Martha on the top of her dark curls. 'You're a lovely little family and I'm so happy for you both.'

'Martha is just the first,' Billy said proudly. 'I hope we'll have half a dozen babies.'

Setting Martha on the floor, Rosetta got to her feet, pulling a face at Billy. 'Hold on there, Mr Noakes. Give us a chance.'

Granny Mole made a clicking sound with her tongue against what teeth she had left. 'Pity our Ruby's on the shelf. Men don't want a bluestocking. She'll end up an old maid at this rate. '

'Don't take no notice of her,' Rosetta said, hugging Ruby.

Billy flung his arms around both of them. 'Any man would be lucky to get one of the Capretti girls. I ought to know, didn't I?'

Rosetta flashed him a smile beneath fluttering lashes. 'I'm glad you appreciate your good luck. But just you wait until I've put all my ideas for the new shop into action. We'll be the Fortnum and Mason of Whitechapel when I've finished.'

Billy gave her a smacking kiss on the lips. 'We will that, sweetheart.' Scooping Martha up in his arms, Billy kissed Ruby on the cheek. 'You'll be round for Martha's birthday tea then, Ruby?'

'I wouldn't miss it for the world.'

Despite all Ruby's entreaties, Sarah insisted that she was well enough to walk to Spivey Street and that she was not going to miss Martha's first birthday tea even if she was to die in the attempt. Ruby worried that this might well happen but

Jonas turned up just in time to prevent a full-scale war in the small house.

'I've come to take you all in my motor car.'

'That was very thoughtful of you, Jonas,' Ruby said, with an indifferent nod of her head. She was still smarting from the fact that Jonas had seen fit to invite Rosetta and Billy to his house for Christmas and had either forgotten to mention it to her, or had thought it unimportant, and that they would be grateful to receive his charity. 'I'm sure Mum and Granny will be pleased to accept.'

Raising his eyebrows, Jonas gave her a quizzical smile. 'It's sleeting outside, but perhaps you'd rather walk?'

'Perhaps I would.'

'Don't talk soft,' Sarah said, wrapping a shawl around her head and shoulders. 'It's kind of Jonas to think about us.'

'Have we got to share the motor with that Carlottie creature?' demanded Granny Mole, rising stiffly to her feet.

Jonas shook his head. 'No, Lottie's got other things to do today but she sent a present for Martha. She said she'll look forward to seeing you all on Christmas Day.'

'We haven't been invited.' The words were out before Ruby could stop them; she bit her lip, unable to look Jonas in the eye.

'I'm sorry if I didn't think to mention it, Ruby,

but I thought it was understood that we would have a family Christmas.'

'I might be on duty at the hospital.'

'Then we'll work around your shift, or I'll go and sweet-talk Matron Luckes into letting you off.'

'You're a good man,' Sarah said, smiling. 'I don't care what anyone says, Jonas, you're a good man.'

The living room above the shop had been transformed with paper chains and brightly coloured balloons. A fire blazed up the chimney and with everyone crowded into the small room the atmosphere was warm and cheerful. Martha ripped the brown paper off her presents and hugged the rag doll that Granny Mole and Sarah had made as a joint effort. Ruby had bought her a red India-rubber ball and Elsie had spent her pocket money on two sugar mice and a bar of Fry's chocolate, which Martha stuffed in her mouth, eyeing Granny Mole as if she were afraid she might snatch it off her, and dribbling chocolate cream down the front of her new dress, a present from Billy and Rosetta.

'And what did you get her, Jonas? A rocking horse, a real pony, something that would make all our gifts seem shabby?' Still smarting, Ruby couldn't resist the temptation to goad him.

'Why are you so angry?'

'I'm not angry. I couldn't care less what you do.'

'Is that so?'

Shrugging her shoulders, Ruby turned away from him, but Jonas took her by the hand. 'My present is in the kitchen. Come with me, Ruby, and we'll fetch it together.' He dragged her out of the room, across the narrow landing and into the kitchen, closing the door behind them and leaning against it.

'How dare you manhandle me?' Ruby began, and then stopped as a puppy leapt out of a wicker basket and jumped up at her making excited whimpering sounds. 'Oh, the little darling.' Bending down, she scooped the puppy up and held it against her cheek. It licked her face, yelping ecstatically, and she rubbed her cheek against its soft fur, inhaling the warm puppy smell as if it were the most expensive French perfume.

Jonas stood watching her for a moment and then, taking the puppy gently from her hands, he set it down in its basket. Without a word, he swept her into his arms and began kissing her, softly at first, tenderly but with mounting desire. Running his hand through her hair, he held her so that she could not escape even if she had wanted to, and she didn't want to. Her lips parted and her arms slid around his neck; tongues caressing, teeth grazing, lips devouring,

Ruby felt herself swirling in a vortex of desire that sent her senses spinning out of control. When he released her to draw breath, she relaxed against him with a deep sigh, resting her forehead against his chest until the world righted itself.

Tilting her head back with his finger under her chin, Jonas's eyes bored into her soul. 'Now say you don't love me, Ruby. Say it if you can but I won't believe you.'

'Don't do this to me,' Ruby gasped, struggling to catch her breath. 'This isn't love, it's not.'

Jonas let her go and her legs refused to hold her so that she stumbled, narrowly missing treading on the puppy. 'What is love to you, then?' he demanded angrily. 'Your saintly doctor friend who lusted after you while he was promised to your best friend? That was all right, was it, because it was done in a gentlemanly fashion? Take a good look at life, Ruby; real life, I mean, not the stuff of penny romances. Would your doctor go against his family and marry you? Would you really be happy with a pale shadow of a man with milk in his veins instead of blood?'

'Leave me alone, Jonas.'

'For the moment I will, but I know you better than you know yourself, Ruby. You need me just as I need you. I'm not prepared to lose you to a romantic schoolgirl's dream.'

Before Ruby could reply, the kitchen door

opened. 'I thought you'd come to get Martha's present.' Billy's grin faded into an apologetic smile. 'Shall I go out again?'

Ruby pushed past him. 'Don't talk soft, Billy.'

Managing to avoid Jonas by working extra hours at the hospital, Ruby did not want to spend Christmas Day in Raven Street, but Mum and Granny were so looking forward to it that she hadn't the heart to disappoint them. Rosetta and Billy were going to be there with Elsie and Martha, and Granny Mole was betting that she could out-drink Lottie, given half a chance. Sarah had spent hours trimming an old dress with lace that was left over from the doll-making days and was planning to wear it on Christmas Day. Her eyes sparkled with excitement when she told Ruby that Jonas was coming over in his motor car to drive them to Raven Street and she couldn't wait to see the grand things that Jonas had done to the house since their last visit. Rose had told her all about it and said it was fine enough for the Queen to visit, should she happen to be in Shoreditch at any time. Sarah had chuckled at the idea of the old Queen dropping by for a cup of tea and a biscuit. It was so good to hear her mother laugh again that Ruby made up her mind the day would go without a hitch; nothing must happen to set back Mum's complete recovery.

Ruby had not intended to dress up for the occasion but when she came downstairs in her ordinary day clothes, the disappointment in her mum's eyes, and Granny Mole's blunt remark that she looked like a ragbag, sent her scurrying up to her room to change into the silk gown that she had worn to Rosetta's wedding. The only mirror in the house was the small one above the mantelpiece in the living room and she could only see her head and neck in that, but the appreciative expression in Jonas's eyes when he arrived to collect them made the blood rush to her face. Annoyed at herself for being pleased, Ruby greeted him coolly and concentrated her efforts on getting Mum and Granny settled on the back seat in the motor car. Having draped a fur travel rug across their knees, Jonas offered his arm to help Ruby into the front passenger seat.

'I can manage, thanks.'

'Of course you can.' Handing her a tartan rug, Jonas went to crank the starting handle.

'See the faces at the windows,' Sarah said smugly. 'I bet they'd all die for a chance to ride in a horseless carriage.'

'If he don't get a move on we'll freeze to death,' Granny grumbled, snuggling the fur rug up to her chin. 'Coney,' she said, sniffing.

'Hush, Ma. It don't matter if it is bunny fur, it's warmer than a piece of sacking.'

Ruby glanced at Jonas's profile as he leapt in

beside her; she could tell by the angle of his jaw that he had overheard the remarks from the back seat and he was grinning. As he put the engine into gear, Jonas turned his head to look at her and his eyes were brimming with laughter. Ruby found herself smiling back; maybe the day would turn out better than she had anticipated.

Tucker opened the door and Sarah, who was leaning heavily on Jonas's arm, gave a gasp of surprise and delight. Even Granny Mole made an appreciative noise at the back of her throat, a cross between a growl and an exclamation of pleasure. In the middle of the floor, reaching almost up to the high ceiling, was a Christmas tree sparkling with dozens of lighted candles and hung with glass balls, tinsel and strings of shiny beads. Dazzled, Ruby inhaled the scent of pine and warm candle wax. Piled around the tree were boxes tied with red ribbons and interestingly shaped parcels. Martha was sitting on the floor playing with a piece of tinsel and Rosetta stood by the tree arm in arm with Billy. She was smiling happily, her cheeks flushed and her eyes sparkling. Breaking free, she rushed towards them giving everyone a hug in turn.

'Isn't it wonderful? Hasn't Jonas done us proud, Mum?'

'It's all very beautiful, ducks,' Sarah said,

smiling up at Jonas. 'I never seen nothing like it in me life.'

'Nor me either,' Granny muttered. 'Must have cost a bloody fortune.'

Jonas threw back his head and laughed. 'Come upstairs to the sitting room and have a drink to keep out the cold.'

'First sensible thing I've heard today.' Granny headed for the stairs at a spanking pace, forgetting to pick up her walking stick. 'I suppose that Carlottie has been at the sherry all morning.'

'No, Granny Mole,' Jonas said, following more slowly with Sarah on his arm. 'You'll have a surprise when you see Lottie. She's given up the drink.'

'Never!' Sarah said. 'D'you hear that, girls?'

'That's not the half of it,' Rosetta said, winking at Ruby. 'Just you wait and see.'

Billy picked Martha up from the floor, giving her a smacking kiss on the cheek when she protested. 'You'll get your presents in a bit, Princess. Let's see if Uncle Jonas has got some sweeties for you.' He turned to Elsie who was hovering in the background, looking uncomfortable, and held out his hand. 'Come on, Elsie. You'd better get to the sweets quick, afore my Martha gobbles up the lot.'

Elsie giggled self-consciously and took his hand as he mounted the stairs.

'Uncle Jonas?' Ruby fell into step beside Rosetta. 'How cosy.'

'Give him a chance,' Rosetta whispered. 'Jump off that high horse of yours, Ruby. It's time you realised you can't save the world all on your own.'

'That's not fair,' Ruby protested, falling into step behind Billy, Martha and Elsie. 'I don't think anything of the sort.'

The sitting room was festooned with holly and another Christmas tree, not quite so large but equally laden with candles and decorations, stood in the corner of the room. A coal fire blazed up the chimney. Hanging from the chandelier in the centre of the room was a bunch of mistletoe; Jonas kissed Sarah on the cheek and seized Granny Mole round the waist, planting a smacker on her forehead. She protested loudly, gave him a gap-toothed grin and sat down giggling like a schoolgirl. He kissed Rosetta, who managed to move her head so that he caught her full on the lips. Handing Martha to Elsie, Billy wrapped his arms around Rosetta and kissed her until she cried out that she needed air. Jonas kissed Elsie's hand, making her blush, and then he turned to Ruby. There was a breathless pause as everyone watched and waited. Ruby's heart was hammering so loudly against her ribcage that she was sure they could all hear it. She lifted her chin and looked Jonas in the eyes as he slid his arm around her waist, drew her to him and kissed her long, slowly and sensuously until Ruby almost forgot that there were others present.

'Merry Christmas, Ruby, my love,' Jonas said, releasing her lips but still holding her close.

Granny Mole made a loud noise clearing her throat. 'A person could die of thirst.'

Smiling, Jonas kissed the tip of Ruby's nose before she had a chance to break free. 'I love you, Ruby,' he said softly.

'What's that?' demanded Granny.

With his arm around Ruby's waist, Jonas turned to Granny Mole. 'What will you have to drink?'

'I'll have a drop of gin,' Granny said. 'Can't believe that Carlottie ain't drunk the lot.'

'Ma!' Sarah nudged her in the ribs. 'Behave yourself.'

With the taste of Jonas still on her lips, Ruby went to sit in a chair by the fire. If only Poppa and Joe could have been here, she thought, watching Elsie sitting on the floor playing with Martha, Rosetta cuddled up close to Billy on the chaise longue and Mum and Granny Mole side by side on the sofa, sipping their drinks. She cast a sidelong glance at Jonas who stood with his back to the fire, an appreciative smile curving his lips. If she reached out her hand she could touch him, but she could feel his nearness like the warm glow from the burning coals. As if he sensed her looking at him, Jonas turned his head and, as he embraced her with his smile, it was as if they were the only two people in the room. But the moment was broken as the door opened and Lottie made a dramatic entrance.

'Oh my God!' Granny Mole almost choked on her gin.

Sarah stared open-mouthed and Rosetta and Billy exchanged covert grins as if they had known all along. Wearing the uniform of the Salvation Army, Lottie stood in the middle of the room obviously enjoying the sensation she had caused.

'I just come to wish you the compliments of the season,' she said graciously. 'Of course, now I'm a member of the Church Army, I don't hold with drinking and gambling and all that, but I ain't never been one to spoil other people's fun.'

'Blooming hell!' Granny Mole's jaw fell open.

'Well I never,' Sarah said, shaking her head. 'Who'd have thought it?'

Rosetta jumped to her feet and hugged Lottie. 'I knew but I didn't want to spoil the surprise. Ain't this a corker?'

Lottie shrugged her shoulders. 'A person can change, that's all I can say. Now I've got the Lord's work to do, feeding the poor.'

'We'll save you some dinner,' Jonas said, his lips twitching.

Lottie flashed him a smile. 'You a good boy, Jonas.'

It was Billy's turn to chuckle. 'I bet you never got called that before.'

'It's a bit late in the day to act like a proper mum,' Granny Mole muttered under her breath.

Hooking his arm around Lottie's uniformed shoulders, Jonas kissed her on the cheek. 'We've come to an understanding, haven't we Lottie?'

Nodding and smiling up at him, Lottie patted his hand. Ruby felt a lump in her throat, sensing that a genuine affection had sprung up between them. Her last barriers were crumbling; the hedge of thorns that she had cultivated around her heart to stop herself from loving Jonas was being scythed away as she saw more of his human side.

'I got to go,' Lottie said, straightening her bonnet.

'Well, if you ain't hungry, Carlottie,' Granny Mole said, scowling, 'I'm weak from lack of nourishment.'

'God bless you, my dear,' Lottie said, and walked out of the room, chuckling.

The spread that Jonas had laid on for them was a feast such as none of them had ever seen. There was mulligatawny soup to start with, served piping hot from a huge tureen with freshly baked bread, provided by Billy. The goose was cooked to perfection, stuffed with sage and onion, served with apple sauce and a mountain of golden roast potatoes. Granny Mole gorged herself until her eyes were popping out of her head and everyone, even Sarah whose appetite since her attack had been small, managed to enjoy a little of everything. The Christmas pudding was brought in alight with blue flames and studded with silver threepenny bits. Wine was served with every course, and to finish a huge platter of petits fours was brought with coffee and brandy.

'You done us proud, old man,' Billy said, puffing a Havana cigar. 'I ain't never seen a spread like that in me whole life.'

Jonas raised his glass. 'Here's to your new business venture, Billy and Rosetta.'

'Next Christmas we'll give you dinner,' Rosetta said, leaning tipsily against Billy. 'In our new home what I'm going to make just as grand as this one, Ruby.' She raised her glass to Ruby and winked. 'Maybe you'll have some good news for us too, eh?'

Billy laid his finger on her lips. 'Now, now, Rose. Don't go embarrassing your sister.'

Rosetta staggered to her feet, pointing at Granny Mole, whose chin had drooped onto her chest and she was snoring softly. 'She's drunk.'

'So are you, pet,' Billy said, standing up and slipping his arm around her waist. 'I suggest you, me and Elsie take Martha out for a bit of fresh air and let Ma and Granny have forty winks.'

'You want to come too, Ruby?' Rosetta swayed against Billy.

Jonas reached out and laid his hand on Ruby's arm. 'I've something I want to show Ruby. You go and enjoy your walk, Rose.'

'I can make up my own mind, thank you, Jonas,' Ruby said, getting to her feet. 'I'd like some air as it happens.'

Jonas nodded. 'That was what I intended. Better wrap up; it's cold outside.'

Instead of following Billy and Rosetta, Jonas caught Ruby by the hand and led her up the steps to Lottie's old house. Taking a key from his pocket, he unlocked the door.

'What are you doing?' Ruby hesitated as he held the door open.

'Come inside and see.'

Puzzled and more than a bit curious, Ruby stepped over the threshold. Inside, the entrance hall was unrecognisable. The drab, peeling paint had been stripped and the walls gleamed white, the woodwork glowing with warm mahogany stain. The old, cracked floor tiles had been replaced with black and white marble and the staircase curved upwards, carpeted in rich red as if royalty were expected to call. Taking Ruby by the hand, Jonas led her into room after room, all newly painted and decorated and resoundingly empty. He took her upstairs and every room was done to the same high standard, with bathrooms on each floor and separate water closets. When they reached the top floor, the attic rooms had been turned into a comfortable apartment, furnished with elegance and at a cost that Ruby could barely imagine.

'I don't understand,' Ruby said breathlessly. 'It's an amazing change, but what is it for?'

Jonas grasped both her hands in a firm hold, looking directly into her eyes. 'I've done it all for you, Ruby.'

'For me?'

'It's not finished yet, but it will be the Joseph Capretti Free Hospital. I can't bring Joe back, but at least I can see that his name is never forgotten.'

'Oh, Jonas.' Ruby blinked away tears. 'I don't know what to say.'

'You can oversee the buying and fitting out of the rooms. The treatment will be free to those who otherwise couldn't afford to pay.'

'You want me to run a hospital? But I'm not qualified yet.'

'You will be, my darling. I know how hard you've worked and I wouldn't expect you to give it up simply because you're married.'

'Jonas, I'm not getting married.'

Drawing her to him, Jonas wrapped his arms around her, teasing her lips with soft kisses until she couldn't hold out any longer and her lips parted with a sigh.

'I want you, Ruby,' Jonas said, his eyes dark with desire. 'I want you now and for ever. I'm never going to let you go again. Just admit that you love me.'

Dazed and barely able to think, Ruby struggled to control her breathing. 'I do.'

Gripping her by the shoulders, Jonas held her tight. 'Say it again. Say it, Ruby.'

'I love you, Jonas.'

'Thank God,' he breathed into her hair. 'Oh, Ruby, you don't know how long I've wanted to hear you say those words.' His mouth sought hers and his kiss was fierce with the hunger of want and need.

Twining her arms around his neck, Ruby felt the last of her doubts and fears vanish together with her inhibitions, returning his kiss until at last she drew away, breathless and trembling. 'I can't believe that you've done all this for me.'

'For us. I'm nothing without you, Ruby. I'm not a good man and I don't want you running away with the idea that I've seen the light like Lottie. Everything I've done is for you because you are the good side of me.'

'And you're a good liar too.' Smiling, Ruby brushed his lips with a kiss. 'I've seen the good side of you, Jonas, even if you do your best to hide it.'

'I'm not pretending that all my business dealings are as honourable as this one, Ruby, but I won't lie to you. I've set up a charitable trust to pay for the running of the hospital. The way things are, I'll probably make a profit somewhere along the line, but I promise you it will go back into the funds and you can look after the poor and the sick to your heart's content. Just say you'll marry me, Ruby.'

Ruby looked deep into his eyes and saw her own reflection. Reaching up, she pulled his head down so that their lips met and locked, tongue caressing tongue, heart beating against heart.

Jonas pulled away first. 'I love you, Ruby. Will you marry me?'

Knotting her fingers at the back of his head, Ruby smiled. 'Will we live here?'

'No, I thought we'd put Lottie in this apartment. She'll be able to continue her good works looking after the patients when you're off duty.'

'And we'll live – where?'

'Next door, over the club. Darling Ruby, I didn't promise to turn into a saint overnight.'

'No,' Ruby said, smiling. 'And I don't think I'd want you to.'

'Does that mean you'll marry me?'

'I think it does.'

Mermaids Singing

Dilly Court

A desperate childhood. An uncertain past. One chance at happiness . . .

Born into poverty and living under the roof of her violent and abusive brother-in-law, young Kitty Cox dreams of working in a women's dress shop in the West End – a million miles away from the reality of her life as a mudlark, scavenging on the banks of the Thames.

Fate soon intervenes and Kitty finds herself working as a skivvy for Sir Desmond and Lady Arabella Mableton in Mayfair. Bullied by the kitchen maids, Kitty is soon taken under Lady Arabella's wing and for the first time in her life she dares to hope.

But Lady 'Bella' has a secret and, unable to live with her domineering husband, she decides to leave, fighting for custody of their daughter. Kitty will do anything for her mistress, but her loyalty is severely tested as all their lives are thrown into turmoil and Kitty faces a life of poverty and hardship in the slums once more . . .

arrow books